WORLD'S END

WILL ELLIOTT

Book III of the Pendulum Trilogy

TOR

A TOM DOHERTY ASSOCIATES BOOK
NEW YORK

WORLD'S END

Copyright © 2011 by Will Elliott

Maps by Will Elliott

A Tor Book
Published by Tom Doherty Associates, LLC
175 Fifth Avenue
New York, NY 10010

www.tor-forge.com

Tor® is a registered trademark of Tom Doherty Associates, LLC.

The Library of Congress Cataloging-in-Publication Data is available upon request.

ISBN 978-0-7653-3190-8 (hardcover)
ISBN 978-1-4299-4775-6 (e-book)

Our books may be purchased in bulk for promotional, educational, or business use. Please contact your local bookseller or the Macmillan Corporate and Premium Sales Department at (800) 221-7945, extension 5442, or by e-mail at MacmillanSpecialMarkets@macmillan.com.

First published in Australia by HarperCollins

First published in Great Britain by Jo Fletcher Books, an imprint of Quercus

First U.S. Edition: March 2016

Printed in the United States of America

0 9 8 7 6 5 4 3 2 1

For the haiyens with us now,
who came from so far away

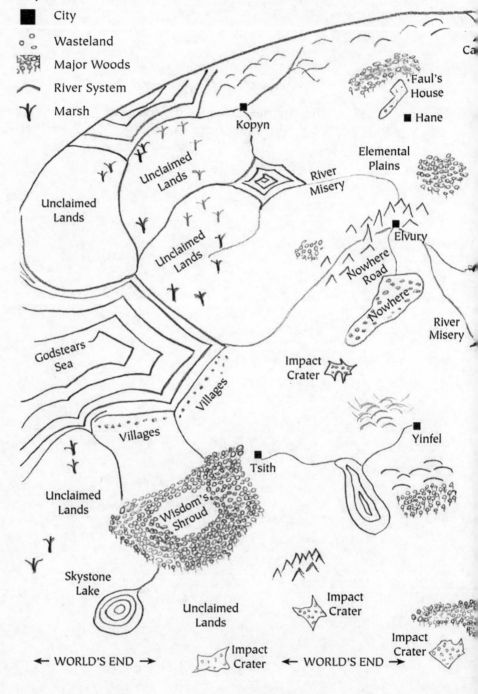

Levaal North

Key:

- ■ City
- ° ∘ Wasteland
- ▦ Major Woods
- ⌒ River System
- Ψ Marsh

Faul's House

■ Hane

Kopyn

Unclaimed Lands

Unclaimed Lands

Unclaimed Lands

River Misery

Elemental Plains

Elvury

Nowhere Road

Nowhere

River Misery

Godstears Sea

Impact Crater

Villages

Villages

Yinfel

Tsith

Unclaimed Lands

Wisdom's Shroud

Skystone Lake

Unclaimed Lands

Impact Crater

Impact Crater

← WORLD'S END →

Impact Crater

← WORLD'S END →

Impact Crater

Ca

East/West: 945 miles across World's End.
North/South: 500 miles by Great Dividing Road.

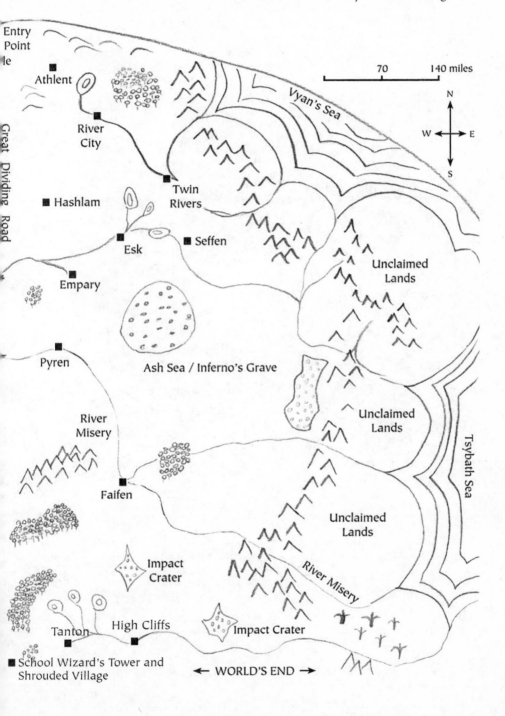

Yinfel

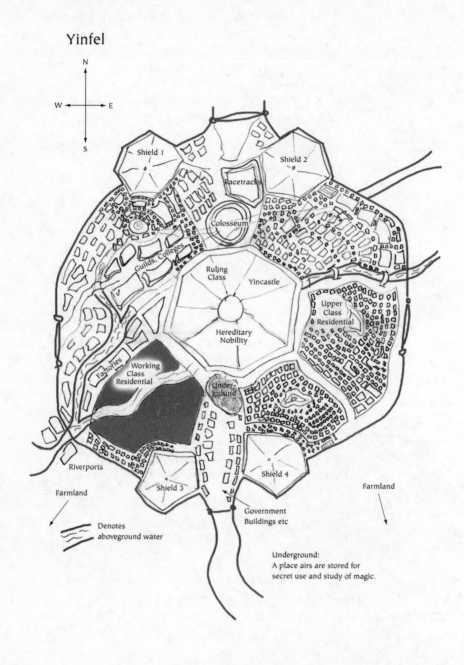

N
W ← → E
S

Shield 1

Shield 2

Racetracks

Colosseum

Guilds, Colleges

Ruling
Class

Yincastle

Upper
Class
Residential

Hereditary
Nobility

Factories

Working
Class
Residential

Under-
ground

Riverports

Shield 3

Shield 4

Farmland

Denotes
aboveground water

Government
Buildings etc

Farmland

Underground:
A place airs are stored for
secret use and study of magic.

DRAMATIS PERSONAE

Domudess: a wizard
Gorb: a half-giant
Huldeel: a villiage chief
Luhan: a traveller
Shadow: a mythical being
Stranger: a magician of some kind
Stuart Casey, aka Case: a changed man

Mayors' Command:

Anfen: former First Captain of the castle's army
Doon: Faul's nephew, killed by Kiown
Eric: a journalist (and fan of Superman comics) who went
   through the door
Far Gaze: a folk magician
Faul: a half-giant
Lalie: an Inferno cultist
Loup: a folk magician
Lut: Faul's husband
Sharfy: one of Anfen's band
Siel: a low-level happenstance mage
Tii: a groundman

Castle:

Arch Mage/Avridis: Vous's advisor, confidante, and overseer of
  'the Project'
Aziel: Vous's daughter, imprisoned in the castle; heir to rule,
  in theory
Blain: a Strategist
Envidis: a Hunter
Evelle: a Hunter
Ghost: a conglomerate of five personalities housed in Vous's
  mirror (and other glass surfaces)
Kiown: a Hunter
Tauvene: First Captain of Kopyn
Thaun: a Hunter
Vashun: a Strategist
Vous: the Aligned world's Friend and Lord

Council of Free Cities:

Erkairn: spokesman of the Scattered Peoples
Ilgresi the Blind: mayor of Elvury
Izven: mayor of Yinfel
Liha: mayor of Faifen
Ousan: mayor of High Cliffs
Tauk the Strong: mayor of Tanton
Wioutin: advisor to the mayor of Tsith

Gods/Great Spirits:

Nightmare: young god
Valour: young god

Wisdom: young god
Inferno: old god
Mountain: old god
Tempest: old god

Dragons:

Dyan: a Minor personality
Ksyn: one of the eight Major personalities
Shâ: one of the eight Major personalities
Shilen: a minor personality
Tsy: one of the eight Major personalities
Tzi-Shu: one of the eight Major personalities
Vyan: one of the eight Major personalities
Vyin: one of the eight Major personalities

1

THE CHANGE

In the doorway of Vous's throne room the Arch Mage leaned upon the forked point of his staff. The odd flash of lightning from outside sent his shadow madly dancing on the floor behind him. His thick curled horns dragged his head down.

Vous was a long way from the young aristocrat of centuries past, lusting madly and without understanding for the very power enveloping him now. A long way even from the tyrant who, with his own hands, throttled out lives rather than share that power. Losing Aziel may have been what burned out the last old shreds of himself; but he had no thought for his daughter now, no memory of both the grief and pleasure with which her sad song had filled him, as it drifted faintly up through his high window each day.

Still the Vous-things scuttled over the lawns far beneath, blood-smeared and mindless. Vous had no thought for these creations either; nor any for the drake in the sky ahead battling the winds with Aziel and the Pilgrim on its back. When she and Eric fell into the sky, when they were drawn by his power through the air towards his balcony . . . even then, Vous did not see them. The human part of his mind was gone, subsumed by something larger.

Vous's body split into several aspects. Some ran through the castle to the lower floors. Only one remained out on the balcony with its hands splayed to the sky. The Vous before the Arch Mage seemed to float just above the carpet, its thin electric form turning slowly, like a dancer making letters with his curved arms and hands. How thin and fragile the translucent body appeared. As if his skin were thin glass which one flung stone could shatter. A swishing windy sound filled the air, in conversation with itself.

'Friend and Lord?' the Arch Mage whispered through dry lips. Vous did not seem to hear, but the Arch did not dare speak louder.

The split canisters of foreign airs lay like popped-open seed pods on the ground. He'd thrown them into the chamber in a fit of emotion and did not understand why nothing had happened when they'd burst apart. He did not understand much of anything, any more. The foreign airs should have poisoned the hidden dimension where spells were made manifest, should have changed the entire world and all of history.

A part of him locked away and hidden from sight knew it had been his last desperate play in the game called power. A still deeper part of him knew that the dragons had used him from afar all along. All along, he'd had masters he never even knew he served.

As the Arch Mage watched Vous, four Strategists watched the Arch Mage. Four men ancient in years, hunched and broken by the magic their bodies had abused. They were as dead-looking as statues of burned wood and bone bent into mean shapes; each was dressed in finery but was now only distantly human. It was as though the wars they'd made and the terrible pleasures they'd indulged in had slowly twisted their very bones. Now and then their hunching shoulders twitched, or their shaking hands would convulsively strangle the staffs they held. Their wheezing breaths filled the silence like whispering snakes.

Vashun – the tallest and thinnest of the Strategists – had stowed the real canisters of foreign airs for transport to his hiding place in Yinfel City, where he had a very good use for them. Those the Arch had flung into Vous's chamber had in fact been filled with ordinary air. The Arch had thought in his arrogance he would rip holes in the past, changing all of reality like a child spilling a bowl of his most hated meal across the table. *Now* Vashun understood why Blain had left the castle while the rest of them were caught in furious squabbles with each other. Clever old Blain!

There are no friends close to a throne. Like the other Strategists, Vashun knew that today was his last within the castle. They all now knew that the Arch Mage had been the one who'd brought down the Wall at World's End. Despite this, Vashun's mood was light. And he sensed humour in the others too, as they watched Vous dance gaily beyond the Arch Mage's outline in the doorway. For power is a game, however seriously played.

So intently was Vashun watching the Arch, enjoying his confusion and suffering (with a skeletal leer uglier than death, bathed in the blooming lustful red of Vashun's Strategist robe), that he hadn't noticed the other Strategists make their discreet exit. It would soon be quite unsafe to stand this close to a god being born. Already the airs were performing in ways he'd never seen, the wild plumes seeming like life forms unto themselves, curls of misty colour flung from wall to wall. 'Arch,' Vashun said gently, placing a long thin hand on the Arch

Mage's shoulder. 'It would seem the Hall of Windows has things to show you.'

The Arch Mage slowly turned to him. On his face – one half like melted wax which had cooled again – was the look of someone lost in strange country. Ah! Vashun sipped of his pain and found it exquisite. There was more to come, much more. 'Come, Arch. There have been . . . developments. In the war. I suspect you will find events, shall we say, surprising.'

Like a servant given instruction, the Arch Mage hobbled along behind him. Vashun filled the silence with chatter of the books and accounts, and other everyday matters of the castle's running. Each word of it was a careful needle in the Arch's flesh, for it was all over and both of them knew it.

They paused before a non-magical window overlooking the Road-side lawns. Down there a large pile of bodies was heaped, the slain Vous-things which had run rampant through the crowd during the wilder moments of Vous's change. The rogue First Captain stood in their midst, small with distance but recognisable, his sword drawn. Anfen raised his head as if he somehow knew which window they had come to – and perhaps he did. Both wizards fancied he saw them there. A glint of piercing light shone up from his armour to spear into their eyes. 'Who do you suppose he is here to see, O Arch?'

'All of us.'

'Ah. I wonder, who will he visit first? O, to know the grim man's mind.' Vashun could not contain it – he wheezed with helpless laughter for a minute or more. 'But ah, your pardon. Maybe he can be stopped. There are . . . how many war mages in the new batch?'

'Many hundreds. Many hundreds more roost in the lower holds.'

'How many do you suppose we'll need? For *one* errant First Captain? He is rather, shall we say, formidable? Brazen too, mm. A little power to that sword, that armour, I'll venture. How many war mages, Arch, to kill a lone man?'

The Arch Mage shrugged and leaned more heavily upon his staff.

'Well, why don't I send them all? Just to be sure. Besides, the new ones are overdue for their first flight.' He got no argument. Vashun whistled for a servant (who was a long time coming, since most had quite wisely fled), and gave him the instructions. Vashun would *not* allow that First Captain to end the Arch Mage's torment swiftly and mercifully with a sword. The very idea was heinous.

He and the Arch Mage walked on to the Hall of Windows, Vashun's long spidery strides making no sound, the Arch's clattering hobble echoing more than usual in the empty corridors. Vashun knew what they would see in the Windows, and he believed the sights bore no deception this time.

Sure enough, across the screens were the ruined bodies of men from the force they'd sent south, sent to conquer the last few Rebel Cities. The ground was wet with blood over many miles. Supply carts and war machines of all types were ruined. Tormentors stood like peculiar tombstones over these fields of death, their dark spiked bodies bright with blood. Now and then, one or two would sway or move their arms with peculiar grace, body language the handlers had never managed to interpret or understand. 'I had no idea you created so *many* of these, Arch,' said Vashun mildly. 'My memory fools me, these days. I recall a strange dream, where we spoke of "controlled release at strategic points". And only to slay the *returning* forces. *After* their fighting was done. Yet, behold! Thousands. Loose about the realm, with not all cities yet subdued. Nearly every Window boasts of the creatures. Thousands of them. Enough to wipe out an army. As it were. You are a master of discretion, Avridis.'

'These ones aren't ours,' said the Arch Mage dismissively. As if this meant the creatures hardly existed at all.

Vashun came closer, making his customary sniffing noise, which neither of them noticed any more. He had learned to discern the scent of many kinds of fear and suffering, and longed now for this new untried flavour: Avridis Sinking in Defeat. He said, 'How do you tell, O Arch? Are "ours" given collars? Brands? Saddles, castle colours to wear? It would appear these beasts have rescued the southernmost Rebel Cities.'

'The Windows lie. Vous said so. The Windows lie.'

Vashun reflected upon this. He did find it curious that the Windows revealed these sights at this time, as though they shared his own delight in the Arch Mage's failure, and wished to rub his nose in it. There did indeed seem some *consciousness* at work in them, a thing he'd never considered before.

'So, the Windows lie. A relief to know it, O Arch. For if they were showing the truth . . . well! It would mean we have nothing left, nothing against the arms of three or four Rebel Cities. Do you suppose our position may have weakened a fraction? Or am I missing something, O Arch?'

'Here!' Avridis spun, a triumphant red gleam in his eye socket's gem. He stood before a Window which showed Tanton under siege.

'You have found an honest Window?' Vashun enquired, moving closer to look.

'As planned. The city is besieged. The war is ours, you para-noid fool.'

Vashun examined the Window's scene, shown from high

above. A good number of the castle's forces surrounded Tanton's high walls, but no siege towers or trebuchets had arrived.

'Just the vanguard. Where are the rest?'

'The vanguard will be enough, even if they are all we have. Vous is ascending. Don't you feel it? We have created a god! Vous will not forget his enemies when he steps forth from the castle. He will clear the realm of those Tormentors, whoever made them. He will bring Aziel back to me, and she shall be next to ascend.'

'An historic day, then.'

'You don't believe it?'

'I think the Windows here invite us to leave the castle, O Arch. We must find a place to hide. Just as the schools of magic were made to hide, long ago.'

'I shall not leave. Never! You truly feel we have *lost*?'

Vashun let a silence draw out, which answered the question perfectly well. The gem in the Arch Mage's eye socket gleamed red and twisted around. A tear fell from his other eye. Vashun watched it slide down the wrinkled skin with utter astonishment. It's Aziel, he marvelled. She did nothing to him, yet she has broken his mind.

Distantly there began a shrieking chorus as the war mages were roused and given their task.

'Easy, Case old man.'

Loup tried to wrench the drake's head but Case kept straining into the wind towards the castle. So much wind! So much chaos and magic and colour in the air he could barely see Eric and Aziel. They'd been pulled from Case's back towards Vous's balcony, but something else had grabbed them and now drew them skywards, to the dragons' sky caverns. They seemed to

float slowly and serenely amidst all the turbulence, as if whatever pulled them up wished to do it with the utmost care. Their
feet vanished, sucked up into a fat mass of high cloud. They
were gone. Loup was too busy trying to control the drake to be
sad about it yet, but he knew it was probably the last time he'd
see Eric in this lifetime. (And Aziel too most likely, but he'd
shed no tears for that . . .)

The drake moaned in protest and spat a gout of orange fire
with a sound more like a belch than a roar. 'I said, easy!' Loup
yelled above the wind's howl. 'Whatever's taken them up there
in the sky, *it don't want us*. You know as well's I what took em.
Dragons! Go on, keep trying. Feel that air push back at you?
You ain't invited, silly old man. Don't go whining and burping
fire at *me*. Away! Off south; I know a place to keep us a time.
She who lives there, she loves critters with wings.' Loup was
uneasy at the thought . . . Faul the half-giant also loved holding
a grudge.

Still the drake strained to follow Eric. 'Listen here!' Loup yelled,
clutching one of its ears tight in his fist. It was stiff as boot
leather. 'Let em go, you fool sky pony. There's mighty great
dragons up there! You might not be fraid of *me* when I'm mad
but what about them? Turn us around right now, old man, or
I'll rip this ear off.'

Case wheeled about, but Loup did not think it was because
of what he'd said. More likely it was due to the sight which
took his own breath away as much as it evidently frightened
the drake. The skies grew dark with moving shapes. From
hundreds of the castle's windows, war mages poured, and an
orchestra of deathly shrieks rose over the winds. The sound was
a nightmare Loup would not forget. Case may have been aided
by the wind, but Loup had never seen him fly so fast.

'See that?' Loup murmured to himself, looking back over his shoulder. 'Was like kicking a stump full of flying bugs.' He realised he was still clutching the poor drake's ear. He let it go, patted Case's leathery neck. 'Stay calm, old man, don't tire yourself. They're not following. We don't matter much, not you and me. Be glad of that. Nothing wrong with that.'

Anfen and Sharfy saw the same thing.

Far above where they stood on the castle lawns, Vous had become like a statue with arms splayed. He was naked and his body brightly glowed. His scream no longer carried above the tumult. He no longer conducted the lightning and clouds with sweeps of his thin arms – now they were open as if waiting for an embrace from something in the sky.

Beings fled around them. Some were people, the last few of those from the castle's lower floors to avoid the Vous-things' massacre. Most of the Vous-things too had fled, although now and then they came close in groups of two and three, blood and filth smeared on their clothes and faces. Their eyes burned with light.

It was up to Sharfy to brandish a weapon at them and frighten them away. Anfen, it seemed, was done with fighting. Anfen's strange blade right now appeared no more than a length of normal steel, bloodied with more deaths than Sharfy had been able to count. The sword had not a single notch down its edge. Its tip gouged the dirt by Anfen's spattered boots. Sharfy gazed with powerful longing at the sword which could cut foes from afar. How he thirsted to wield it! He'd be a king. He'd march up through the castle gates, slay the Arch, slay Vous, make the world better.

Here came two Vous-things now, threading through the

corpses, their Friend and Lord's face hungry, sneering, atop a feeble old woman's body. Sharfy waved his sword at them, but only one fled. The other ran with thrashing arms right at Anfen, who didn't bother to even look at it. Sharfy stepped towards it, blade raised, and let the horrid thing skewer itself. Only as his hand made contact with its ribcage, the blade poking clear through the back of a plain dress, did the creature seem to notice him, its baleful eyes peering into his, breathing a warm breath of rot into his face. The moment drew itself out for a long time.

Those eyes were two long tunnels of light, with a small writhing thrashing shape at their very ends. The tiny shape was Vous, he saw: Vous's body convulsing in a small bare room. It took effort for Sharfy to look away.

The Vous-thing fell from his blade and slumped to the ground. He wiped blood from his hand. Some kills in battle one kept in mind like the favoured page of a story, to retell many times. This was not one of them. The Vous-thing stared up at him, hotly, hatefully, as its last two breaths shuddered out. The light of its eyes extinguished slowly.

Serve him well, echoed the god Valour's words in Sharfy's mind. *Serve him well*. 'Just did,' he muttered to himself. 'How many times now? Saved his life. Kept him fed. All pointless.' He wiped his new sword on the grass. He'd taken it from a fallen Elite guardsman: a fine blade, well balanced, though he'd shave a fraction of the weight off if he could. He said, 'Anfen. What's Valour want us to do now?'

'Witness.'

Sharfy wanted to weep at the vagueness of it, but the single-word response was more than he usually got to his questions. He sat down on the soft lawn and gazed up high at the balcony where Vous stood with arms extended to the storming sky. Mad, he is. Everyone in this world. Me too? Must be. Look how I lived. Could've had a little farm. Tended a field, kept a herd, married. Pa wanted a fighter. Grandpa too. They got one. 'Will you kill the Arch?'

Anfen dropped his sword to the ground as though by answer.

'S'that mean you won't? Come on, bastard. Talk. They'll kill us. Right on the grass here. It's where I'll die. I can take it. You can talk to me at least. Not expecting any thanks.'

Sharfy's hands tensed on his sword as two Vous-things came near.

'Is Shadow here?' said one, then the other.

'Off south,' Sharfy answered. One of them snarled; both scurried away.

Sharfy was surprised to feel Anfen's palm on his shoulder. 'The Arch doesn't matter,' said his captain, voice hoarse from the battle cries that had torn from his throat. 'I understand now. Why speak of him? He was used. He never mattered. The spells only ever cast *him*, Sharfy. That's how it really works.'

'Not true. And you know it. We fought im. He knew what he was doing. All on purpose, all planned, everything he did. He knew what war is. Knew how to kill, make men slaves.'

Anfen sat down on the grass beside his fallen sword. 'He did not use his power, the power used him. From where did the power come? That stuff mages see in the air, what is its purpose? Does it have no life or intention of its own?' Anfen began to say more but a coughing fit cut off his words. At the end of it he spat blood.

Mad, mad, mad. Everyone. 'We can't sleep here for the night. Unless we're going in there.' He nodded at the castle steps nearest to them. 'But I know this. I might find a bed and some drink in there. Put my legs up, relax. Then some old commander will come. Make me march to World's End, probably. Without pay. He'll polish some bones. All cos a god told him to.'

At that moment the wind died down. A cry issued from Vous that was like the long note of a beautiful eerie song. All Vous-things in sight went instantly still with their heads raised.

Overhead a red drake flew, its wings labouring into the powerful wind. Two of the drake's riders fell free, but somehow didn't *fall*. Instead they floated on the air, just as debris floats on a river, their bodies drawn towards Vous. 'Looks like Eric,' Sharfy remarked. Then it occurred to him that it might actually *be* Eric, and his heart beat fast. Who the woman was, he had no idea. But when the drake's body angled forwards, he saw clearly that Loup was on its back. 'Loup!' he yelled, loud as he could. 'Down here!'

But his voice was drowned out by the high deathly shrieks of a thousand war mages. They poured from scores of the castle's windows, blackening the skies like great streaks of shadow.

'They come for us,' said Anfen mildly. 'Farewell, Sharfy. My redeemer has willed it.'

'What? No! Get us in the quiet. They can't see us there.'

'Let it end. I am tired.'

'Give *me* that armour then. Quick, before they come.'

Anfen made no move to do so. Above them Eric and the woman had got nearly halfway to the castle when they changed direction. Steadily they floated skywards, away from Vous. Two Invia flew wide circles about them as they were carried higher and higher, until lost from view in thick clouds.

The war mages were soon close enough that the yellow gleam of their slitted eyes could be seen through faces of twisted ropy beard. As one, the mass of them shifted direction and flew up, in pursuit of Eric and Aziel. From a distance it looked as though the flocking mass of them assumed a formation of an arm and fist rising from the castle to strike skywards. Vous's beautiful sung note grew mournful, as if he were sad that Eric and Aziel were no longer coming towards him.

Sharfy knew he'd live, for the moment at least. He also knew he owed Anfen no thanks for it. 'If that was really Eric,' he said, 'that's the last of him. Never seen that many war mages. We have to get under cover. They'll come back. Fuck you and your redeemer. Stay here and die.' He left him sitting there without a moment's pause, nor the faintest hint of guilt or regret.

Anfen stared up at a high castle window, and did not appear to have heard or noticed.

2

SKY PRISONS

As strong as the cold wind through Eric's hair was the sense of unreality which blasted from his mind the present moment, the past, and every experience he'd had since Vous's eye peered through the little red door's keyhole, fell upon him and named him Shadow.

None of it was real any more. The wind numbed his skin with its cold and ruffled his clothes. He was just an object being moved; that was all. The ground was lethally far beneath. The castle looked like a huge white dragon, huger than huge, tail curled round about itself, head resting on the ground, its great mouth opening out onto the Great Dividing Road. From innumerable windows came reflected glints of lightning. On the balcony with arms spread, Vous sang beautiful notes after them.

Beings on the grass, tiny with distance, stared up at Eric till the cloud concealed them. Close by the storm spat lightning at the castle or tossed it about with great flickers of white. The air held him and Aziel aloft as easily as someone's invisible palm, slowly raising them away from the castle, where Vous had attempted to draw them to himself.

Aziel's voice brought Eric back to himself. He missed what she'd said. She clutched at him in fear, fingernails digging into his skin hard enough to leave small crescent cuts. He took her hand and told her a lie – they'd be all right – and a truth – it would all be over soon.

He made himself see the air's magic and was overcome by the frantic movements of fierce colour, a many-armed wheeling star spinning slowly and enormously about the castle. One arm passed right through them, though they felt nothing more than the cold of the wind. His last sight of Vous before the clouds took them was of the man-god's eyes, two points of light, locking onto his own, seeing him but not understanding what they saw. At once Vous was fascinated by and deathly afraid of Eric. Eric had thought it a dream long ago, when he'd first heard the words *You are Shadow*. He heard the same words again now, Vous's voice carrying through the storm and the wind, spoken softly and uncertainly. 'I'm not Shadow,' Eric answered. 'I'm not Shadow. Help me. I'm not Shadow.'

Aziel's hair whipped his face. She'd covered her eyes with her hand, though there was not much more to see than the cloud's white mist. There was a sense of *falling upwards*. The two Invia – the ones who'd shadowed their flight from the wizard's tower – wheeled around them, conversing with each other in joyful, whistling calls. They were suddenly drowned out by the terrible noise of a thousand shrieking war-mage voices, growing louder, coming nearer.

They came through the upper band of clouds. As in the dragon-scale vision Eric had had at Faul's house, he saw the sky was a dome, a roof of stone spread as far as sight. It was not yet lit with the full force of daylight but was still painful to their eyes, this close to it. Great areas were cracked, broken and stained. Parts hung loose as though they might fall.

Beneath them, where there were gaps in the clouds, the world was a haze of green and blue. Distant peaks stuck their tips up like small islands in a white sea.

There behind the castle was the tall valley where the door, the Entry Point, had been. Two sheer cliffs cupped the high ridge of rich green grass, cliffs which rose till they joined the domed lightstone roof. That green valley had been filled with bodies, that first day, slain by the same creatures which pursued them now.

'They're coming,' said Aziel, still covering her eyes with her hand. A face covered by a mane of tangled ropy beard poked through the cloud, two horns exuding pencil-thin lines of smoke, black slits in its yellow eyes flickering from one of them to the other. Its mouth opened, its scream loud and high. The cry was answered a dozen times from close by. More distantly, hundreds more war mages called out.

The two Invia swooped from elsewhere in the cloud and tore the war mage to pieces with a bloody thrashing blur of motion almost too quick to see. They flung its body parts in all directions. But more war mages came, their faces surfacing through cloud soon crackling with orange fire. The unearthly cry of a dying Invia tore across the world.

Whatever force pulled Eric and Aziel through the sky wrenched them up with more urgency. Their bellies lurched. The lightstone dome rushed at them. A gap in it appeared just ahead, and then they were through it, and set down on a ledge in the upwards-leading tunnel. The ledge was only a stride deep into the dark stone, as wide as an armspan. The second Invia's dying wail soon reached them. With a rush of air, shapes shot past them from above: five, six, ten Invia or more in a blur of white wings and streaks of vividly coloured hair.

So that was why they'd been set on this ledge – to make

room for the Invia rushing down at lethal speed. Beneath them the bird-women dived into clouds and fire. Dizzy, Eric clutched Aziel and instinctively drew her back a little from the edge.

'Don't be so free with your fingers,' she snapped, slapping at his hand.

He stared at her, stunned. 'You're worried about *that*? Look down there, Aziel. Look at where we are.' Overcome with disbelief, he grabbed at her breast and squeezed it.

She shoved him off the edge without an instant's hesitation.

He fell only for a second or two – enough to register his amazement that she'd been willing to kill, to actually *kill* him for trying to prove a point – when the invisible hand caught him again on its palm and lifted him upwards, with Aziel floating just ahead of him. They were pulled urgently through the grey stone tunnel till it opened out into a vast cavernous space. Here was the place Case had been told by an Invia was the Gate of Takkish Iholme, sky prison of the dragon-youth.

It was not long before the Invias' death wails rang out: they were slain by the war mages in the clouds.

Eric's eyes soon adjusted to the vast gloomy space, unlit yet somehow still visible, as if this were a place where light had no purpose. All about them was nothing and no one, just the naked stone until the edge of their vision, where there were outlines of some type of building. Wind piped eerie music through tunnel mouths bored into the curved walls and roof. The cavern's *age* pressed down on him like heavy hands on his shoulders.

He bit into his bottom lip to keep from passing out – for some reason he'd grown dizzier. He swayed on his feet till Aziel grabbed his hand and pressed it to the metal of her necklace. At the charm's cold touch all dizziness flushed out of him. Warmth filled him.

'Do you know where we are?' she asked him.

'Where the dragons live. Only I don't see any.'

The *boom* of an enormous weight being dropped came from some way away and gave them both the odd feeling something had been listening in. This was its answer: *We are here, all right.* The stone floor gave a faint shiver. Eric stood, felt for the gun out of habit. He got the usual familiar comfort from its touch, then thought about that for a moment: How much fucking good is this likely to be against dragons? Maybe about as much good as blowing them kisses . . .

The scream of a war mage wound up the tunnel they'd been brought through. Now he was glad he had the gun – except the scream was chorused many times, so many times it seemed there must be a small army coming. Eric grabbed Aziel's wrist and they ran. Aziel was out of breath before they got very far at all and he had to drag her along at a fast walk. Back where they'd just been, the first of the war mages poked its shaggy head through the tunnel and clawed its way up. Tendrils of smoke wound from its horns, its eyes glowing yellow. Its mouth hung open in apparent surprise as it gazed around. Its scream almost seemed a question.

Eric pulled Aziel to the floor. He half expected her to reproach him again for touching her. 'Don't move, no sounds,' he whispered, taking the gun from its holster. Directly overhead came a blast of wind, a long low note. Three Invia tumbled out into the air. One turned, spied Eric and Aziel, made a shrill querying sound.

The war mage was soon joined by four more of its kind. Their screams too held questioning notes. Sudden as a bottle uncorked, there came a streaming mass of them pouring out through the tunnel and into the cavern.

'Well, nice knowing you,' Eric said. 'Some of the time, anyway.' He looked to her, hoping to at least trade a smile before their impending death. Aziel didn't speak; her skin had turned faintly blue. Coldness poured from her rather than the charm about her neck. Her eyes glowed with silver light. 'Aziel?'

'*For a brief while, I shall hide you,*' she said in a voice that was not her own. It was deeper than her real voice, and though her mouth moved in time with it, it seemed to come from far away. '*I cannot hide you for long. Keep your touch upon the charm.*'

'Who are you? Is that Vous?'

The silver eyes turned slowly to him and sent shivers down his spine. '*I'll not through human lips speak the name humans call me. You should not be seen by he who approaches. When he comes to the Gate, the intruding swarm will not have mind of you. You must run from here. Run now. Go to the nearest Invia roost. He who comes will not go there.*'

'Who comes here? And who are you? Are you a dragon?'

'*He who comes, men's mouths call Shâ. You must not be seen by him or it may begin a war among the Eight. He knows not that you are here. I must leave you for a time or he will sense my presence with you. It is not known whether you shall live beyond this day. His motions disturb the futures as would his steps throw silt clouds up in water. Flee now while I may hide you, or you shall die and I shall find others to perform your work.*'

The three Invia over their heads rushed suicidally to the horde of war mages still pouring into the cavern. The Invia moved fast through them, each leaving a trail of destroyed bodies behind them, till a storm of sparks and fire erupted. In quick time came the creatures' dying wails.

A sudden silence filled the cavern. Even the wind-music through the tunnel ceased. The war mages stopped screaming and seemed to wait, listening. A very real sense of something watching – or more than one thing – seemed to sweep over the bare rock walls, invisible but as real as any beaming searchlight.

Still the cold emanated from Aziel; still her eyes glowed silver. Hesitantly Eric said, 'Have you possessed Aziel before?'

He shrank back from her stare. *'Great risk I take to bring you here, against the man-god's will. My Parent's law forbids such deeds. I crafted this thing that she wears, this that helps protect you. A thousand eventualities I foresaw, and did prepare for each. But what has come about, I did not foresee. She shall not be slain when she wears this charm. You do not have such protection, though you may soon find gifts of your own. Her gift took a century to make.'*

'You're . . . you must be Vyin. You're our friend, aren't you? Our only friend among the dragons.'

'Name me no more, for Shâ has left his hold. Most of my siblings now agree that we need your aid at this time, Favoured one. We shall have it for you need our favour. Five of my siblings have hatred for you that is cold, patient and deadly. Shâ has hatred for you hotter than ever burned Inferno's fire. He comes now. Flee for the Invia roost. You are expected there. This girl cannot abide my thoughts much longer. She will perish if I stay with her. Ever it seems I know your kind less well than I suppose.'

The light went out of Aziel's eyes. The strength went out of her too and she lay limp, shivering with cold. Eric rubbed her arms, whispered her name. There was from different directions the heavy *thud, thud-boom* of massive weights shifting. Coldness swept through the cavern. The silence grew heavier, more watchful. The war mages seemed oppressed by it too – now and then the odd confused cry sounded among the *scrape-scratch-scrape* of their claws on the stone.

Scores of Invia suddenly poured through those openings directly overhead. None of them cried out – not even their beating wings could be heard. Yet more Invia came from elsewhere across the dome ceiling, their wings so white they seemed to glow. Among them were a rare few larger than the others, still of human shape but twice the others' size. It was one of these larger ones that first swooped at the war-mage horde like a diving bird, then all the others followed. Their dives began gracefully then became a blur of destruction, snapping war-mage bodies like pieces of brittle wood.

The war-mage screams went suddenly deafening. The air was full of fire, of glowing orbs and huge whip-crack sounds. The Invia began to fall from the sky and land in burning heaps. Some who dived down came up with their feathered wings blazing. Shrieking, they made off through the roof's tunnels, which now hummed with deep booming notes like war drums playing.

With Aziel in his arms Eric began to run. But the despair he felt at the Invias' dying wails made him stop. He watched them being slain with tears streaming down his face. Aziel moaned in his arms as though the same sadness pierced through her faint.

As the last Invia was killed, larger shapes suddenly reared up among the war mages. A black spread of pinioned wings unfolded against the backdrop of their fire. A dragon trampled them, larger – though not by much – than that one Eric had seen in the woods conversing with Stranger. Eric glimpsed fiercely burning golden eyes on a large head rearing back like a serpent's. Out from its jaws came a stream of many brilliant colours. The strange fire's light revealed a second dragon, smaller than the first, thrashing its head and tail through the crowd, trampling them, clubbing broken bodies to skitter across the bare cavern floor. One was hit so hard it slid a stone's throw from Eric and Aziel, body rolling like a tyre, its spine broken. The war mage's mouth still rasped and its yellow cat eyes fixed on Eric's as it came to rest, smoke pouring from its blackened horns. One hand extended, it said something unintelligible, then the light in its eyes went out.

Humans might have fled such a battle. But war mages did not comprehend their own mortality and knew no more fear of death than ghosts. They burned the dragons in turn with their own magic and fire, far less brilliant, but cast from hundreds of them at once.

Eric did not know whether either of these dragons was Shâ, the one Vyin had warned him about. But it was soon clear these dragons were in trouble. Hundreds of war mages were dead but there were as many still casting, hurling their fire against the dragons' hides. Holes were torn in their wings, the leathery flesh soon cut to hanging flapping threads. War mages climbed on their backs, straddled their necks, biting and clawing. Like a sinking ship the larger dragon fell, issuing a bellow of pain which dwarfed for a moment all other sound in the cavern, and left Eric's ears ringing. (He knew the sound was a cry for help; he heard also a note of reproach, like that of a loyal servant complaining he was sent needlessly to war and death.)

The remaining dragon fell in turn, rolling slowly over the ground in a way that seemed playful compared to the thrashing speed with which it had fought. Hungrily the war mages scuttled over the bodies, still casting on them and clawing at them long after their heaving and rolling went still.

Eric carried Aziel away, not bothering to run. She moaned and stirred in his arms. There was less cold about her now and her normal colour had returned. 'Aziel, come back,' he whispered, surprised at how powerful was this sense of duty to keep safe someone he didn't especially like.

Then he felt something *else*. Dread fell on him, a fear like none he'd known before.

The war mages had gone quiet after the battle, crouching to rest from their casting and let their bodies cool. But now all of them screamed at once. In Eric's arms, Aziel's eyes opened and went wide. Instinctively he put a hand over her mouth, which had opened to scream, then turned. He staggered back from what he saw, then fell, Aziel landing on top of him and winding him.

It fell from the cavern's ceiling. A rush of wind swept over them, wind cast up by wings spread wide behind the enormous dragon like vast sails. It was huger than any living thing Eric had seen. Poisonous shades were interwoven on its speckled hide from white to light brown to black, all glistening with the wet sheen of a snake with newly shed skin. Its open mouth seemed to grin. Its neck was short and bullish, its body squat, its head wider and flatter in shape than the other dragons'. Nor had it any of the others' elegance or almost feline grace. Beneath its legs hung a belly as bloated as a spider's.

Eric recoiled with as much revulsion as fear. The ground shivered and groaned as the thing landed. Those war mages nearest to it stood not much taller than the claw of its foreleg. Not sane enough to flee, they began casting on it. The dragon's eyes glittered, its mouth snapped open and a brief obscene sound came out. The twisted rising note was at once mocking, inquisitive, indulgent, and many other things besides. All the war-mage fire and magic was snuffed out. They ceased their screaming and each one went still.

In the perfect silence that followed the war mages were picked up in their hundreds. They spun through the air in a wide circle around Shâ's body. The curling wave of them went still, leaving all of them suspended motionless in the air. With each passing second they resumed motion, went still, resumed, went still.

Eric and Aziel ran. Both were all but mindless for that sprint while the great unclean beast loomed mountainous behind them, distracted by its new playthings. And yet only naked air was between it and them – it had only to turn its head and notice two small shapes fleeing across the bare stone floor. The distant collection of buildings they headed for seemed to get no closer. Neither of them paused to look back, but they heard the dragon's thumping footsteps, felt the stone shivering, and they could not tell whether it merely moved among its captured things or whether it pursued them. Eric was a child again, caught in a nightmare free of reason's limits, unable to wake. They both wept in helplessness as they ran. Now and then came more exclamations in Shâ's terrible voice. Eric caught only portions of each outburst's mocking meaning, but what little he understood was far too much.

It was surely just minutes but it seemed far longer, the time of running until the first of the structures they'd seen from afar came within reach. It had appeared they got no closer up until the moment their breath ran out and their run became an exhausted stagger. Then they were cowering behind a column made of the same stone as the cavern floor, shoulder to shoulder, their hands pressed against its wide cool surface, coughing as they tried to catch their breath. Fine dust coated the cold stone floor they pressed their bellies upon. The stone still shivered from Shâ's footsteps.

3

THE MAYOR OF YINFEL

Like storms which had skirted its land to strike elsewhere, Yinfel City was untroubled by the latest outbreaks of war. Its people had spent the days since Elvury's fall, and since the Wall's destruction, as if nothing much had happened at all, besides a dramatic rise and fall on the markets of various metals, crops, cloth, enchanted goods, potions, and so on. In fact, times were good. The city was flushed with Elvury's cash. Many merchants – some who'd prepared for Elvury's fall with uncanny anticipation – grew rich enough to begin eyeing off not just the nicer homes in the Third Section, but the smaller dwellings within Yincastle itself.

Refugees from Elvury kept trickling in steadily from the north. Most were allowed within Yinfel's gates to resettle, and charged a hefty one-off tax to pay for extra slum housing in the ghetto near Shield One. Failing the tax – and many did fail, having abandoned their wealth in the rush to flee – they were turned away, sent to fend for themselves in the outskirt farming villages. Once-wealthy hands were now required to dig through dirt for their keep.

The city itself was larger and grander to behold than Elvury

City; without the natural defence of mountains, its walls were by necessity very tall, made from slabs of enchanted black stone, guarded over by four enormous Shield Towers, two per gate. Yincastle, the massive crown in the city's middle, was inaccessible to all but the wealthiest, and money alone was not enough to live there. One had to have an insider's mind and morals too, and the ability to keep one's mouth shut on seeing something that would disturb the citizens below, should rumour escape. A few bloodline families – and those they now and then plucked from the civilian areas of the city – had kept the place to themselves for millennia, throughout all the wars no matter who won or lost. They'd held Yincastle for themselves long before Vous was conceived.

The city's two worlds were shut off from one another. The inner world was safe, if the outer world was fed and comfortable. If the outer world was fed, if there was enough amusement and gossip to sate their curiosities, why would they care how Yincastle was run? Why would they care who ran it?

Yincastle itself had many layers. The outer folk – newcomers grown excessively rich and therefore allowed in – were almost as ignorant of the place's inner workings as were those in the civilian realms. One learned to close one's ears and eyes to strange comings and goings through the high arched doorways. And to ignore the distant sounds heard from the high windows which glowed orange late at night. One learned to ignore rumours of underground chambers far beneath Yincastle, tunnelled so deep below that magic air existed there, and where improbable things were said to be done by the city's elite. It was true that every now and then, people vanished as if plucked off the prosperous streets. But the same, surely, happened in every city.

It was in Yincastle's highest tower that the orange windows glowed at night, a place from which one could survey the entire city below, active as an insect hive in daylight, a sparkling nest of lights by night. Here, out of reach of any war machine, the smooth silvery bricks still bore drake-claw marks from a long past war, the same war which had made room for Yincastle's current elites.

Izven peered out through one of those very high windows now. The pulsing orange light behind him bathed the chamber in glowing warmth. Naked, his body looked soft and vulnerable as he surveyed the city's night lights, spread beyond him like a web full of struggling morsels he was in no hurry to bring closer and consume. The visitor he expected was late.

Behind him there was a clink of chains as Lalie shifted on the huge bed. She was not concerned about the chains clamping her wrists, the belt about her waist, nor indeed her own near nakedness. She had leeway enough to crawl about on the bed a good distance. She was released whenever she wished to relieve herself. She was fed luscious, beautiful meals – the best food she'd ever eaten in fact. Hot baths were insisted upon twice daily.

There were others here of course who did not enjoy the facilities as much as she did. They too were chained up throughout the chamber, to beds and couches, always frightened and wanting to return to their homes and families, not yet understanding there was simply no way that could happen after all they'd been through and witnessed here. Lalie was quickly tiring of their complaints.

This chamber – though it didn't bother her – had seemed quite peculiar at first. She had thought mayors were like stern parents: boring, straight in their ways, pushing papers around, blathering about taxes and grain supplies, now and then parading in front of people like roosters proud of their feathers.

She was no stranger to some of the games men enjoyed, either. The high priest had used her for many peculiar sexual rituals, involving other women, involving Offerings. The trick was to understand your flesh was just a plaything of the spirit inside, the spirit already pledged and therefore owned by sleeping Inferno, who would one day waken and claim it. What happened to the flesh didn't matter, as long as the mind was undamaged. As long as the spirit stayed keen, pure and hot as a candle flame. Pure enough to be brought within Inferno's divine fire.

The sexual games played in this chamber had therefore been no shock to her, but she was surprised to find a mayor, along with his high officials and friends, so very preoccupied with them. All day, in this large, circular chamber, and in the other rooms adjoining it, the games went on and on. She had begun to wonder: did they even *bother* with taxes, laws, wars and all the rest? Was all that just a clever disguise?

The others held here were mostly women and girls, with just a few men for those with different tastes. A high official – some friend of Izven, some important guest of the city – would walk in and gaze about with the air of a person quite familiar with this fondly remembered place. They would sometimes disrobe, do whatever they wanted to any of the sexual servants on display. Or they'd ask for one – there were dozens in this chamber, many ages and sizes, mostly young and sleek, like Lalie – to come with them, somewhere private. The chosen ones would usually return, but sometimes they didn't. Those who came back often wore welts, bruises, cuts. Perhaps they'd be vomiting, pale, shaken, needing tending by the nurses.

Of course Lalie had known the minute Izven guided her out

of the Mayors' Command meeting at Elvury, reserving for her a place in his personal caravan, that his charity was not pure kindness. He made a good show of it, the half-bald, pot-bellied man parading her before as many of the other cities' officials as he could, practically spoon-feeding her like an underfed lamb he was caring for. No fool, she'd played along, peering up at him with eyes large and adoring. She'd expected to pay for the meals and shelter on her back or knees, to either Izven or one of his men. Such a prospect had mattered little to her, mere motions of the pretty suit her spirit wore, garments briefly crumpling here and there, at times even enjoyably.

At any hour of the day – mostly at night – the mayor would appear, would guide people in, some times whole groups of them. Izven had kept many guests from choosing her for their pleasure, all bar one or two whom he instructed to use her with care. This made her suspect he had something else in mind for her. She had remained here, after all, while many others had departed to make way for fresh arrivals. And he spent time speaking with her, but never with the others.

It was an honour, the mayor had explained, for her and these others to be chosen and brought here, even if they died in their duties – some of the mayor's friends had such tastes, that was all. He spoke to her of many things, seeming to enjoy his own voice. Of history he spoke, and of Otherworld, of magic.

He left the window and came to her bed now, and began to speak of such things. She mostly blanked out his voice, pretending to listen, until he said, 'I even dabble in a little spell craft myself.'

'There's no magic in cities,' said Lalie.

The mayor toyed with a curling strand of her hair. It was growing long and thick again, already responding to the good food she received here, the lotions and oils brought in on trays. 'Usually not,' said Izven in his scholarly voice. His voice never changed, however excited he became. His eyes lingered on the man – perhaps a relative – mechanically fucking someone at the other end of the chamber, to the sound of whimpering and rattling chains.

Lalie knew a little of spells, especially slow-cast ones, which one did not need to be a mage to cast. She repeated, 'There's no magic in cities.'

Izven kneaded her breast, his stubby fingers digging in to the point of pain. She squirmed since that was what he wanted, but if he *really* hurt her she'd bite and claw him, and he knew it. He said, 'There is a space below, Lalie. Below Yincastle. Deep below. I go there now and then. With certain friends. Are you thirsty?'

'No.'

'Call me "Mayor", Lalie. Titles are important.'

'I'll give you a title of my own,' she said, smiling with bared teeth.

He looked at her with no change of expression. 'You delight me. Do you know, Lalie, that genuine, committed followers of Inferno are quite rare? I mean those who practise the hidden rites, as you did.'

Izven gestured at a servant to bring a drink. 'O, we have *some* Inferno people here in Yinfel,' he went on, 'but they're not committed. They've not taken the vow of property. They think they have, but most don't know the true words of that vow. Do you remember telling me those words when I asked you what they were, on our trip here from Elvury? That was when I knew you were genuine. A noble and misunderstood Spirit is Inferno, Lalie. I do not swear to him myself, understand. But I *appreciate* him, and his followers. Do you feel he will awaken in our life-times?'

She shrugged, the chains clinking. Whether or not he did, her flame would join his fire.

'I feel he may,' said Izven, fondling her more gently now. 'I expect a visitor tonight. A very important visitor. Can you guess where he's from? The castle. *The* castle. Where Vous lives.' He examined her surprised look. 'Yes, it is a well-kept secret. We are Aligned with the castle now, here in my city. But really, we always were Aligned. Soon the people will learn of it, and there shall be changes they will not like very much at all. It won't matter. A lot of them will die.'

She thought of Anfen, and all the other men like him, how fanatical they were in their fight against the castle. What Izven said was impossible. She scoffed.

Seeming to gauge her thoughts, he said, 'It is all a game, Lalie. There is a lot of pretending. There must be, or people would not play it as we wish them to. And only a couple of hundred people truly understand that it is a game, and under-stand how we play it. It grew much easier when the schools of magic and half-giants were gone, you see. But even when they were here, our game was played the same way. The Mayors' Command did their work against the castle in earnest. But they were only generals, Lalie. Generals whom we selected, trained, whose very minds we created. They know warfare well, such men, but that is all they know. They used the men and tools we gave them. They reported all they did to us and they answered to us. But we do not share our private designs with them. All this time, there were only one or two cities left who weren't secretly Aligned.'

She couldn't understand it. 'But, all the wars . . .'

'Never mind those! People must be managed; herds must sometimes be culled. The world had to be kept busy while the Arch Mage did his work and created a new Spirit. His own armies and ours, for what if they turned their attention inwards instead of at some outside threat? Men feel they need to fight. So we let them, as long as they do not fight us. That's all, Lalie.'

How could the whole war have been orchestrated? It was impossible. Such a thing was too big and chaotic to truly control. She refused to believe it. 'Do you mean that your city . . . and all the cities who fight with each other . . . are really friends?'

'Friends,' he said contemplatively, settling back on the bed beside her. He ran a finger over the chains holding her wrists as though they were a sensual part of her. Over in the corner, the other man's mechanical fucking went on and on, his body like a machine someone had forgotten to switch off. 'Think of it, Lalie, as a game we mayors and lords all play. It is a *serious* game, of course. When the army of my city battles another, I wish earnestly for victory. I am proud when we win; I am upset when we lose. But ever I remain here, in Yincastle, safe and comfortable, managing Yinfel's people. We Free Cities were earnest in our game against the castle for a long while. But all along we understood it was indeed a game. Fighting men do not see it that way. We cannot let them. If they did, they would not fight and die as they do, all to be just minor pieces on a board.

'Avridis – the Arch Mage – is someone I partly admire. He has always played the game differently. He was just an apprentice wizard, not born into any of the ruling families, and so not invited to play our game at all. But through his talents in magic he fought his way to a place at the table with the rest of us.

For a long while, he played as a winner – a better player in fact than many of us. His part may be over now, but he has surprised us before. We shall see.

'Lalie, the only *real* rule of the game is that we, the game's players, are to remain high-placed no matter what else happens. At the very least kept in honour and comfort, away from the toiling rabble. It is a rule usually adhered to, but not always. Some mayors are foolish. Now and then – even for a decade or two – fools of one city or other get a place of power, fools who don't understand the game. They would, if they could, change the rules altogether. Tauk the Strong of Tanton is one such fool. Liha of Faifen is another of them. She is probably dead now, when she could be enjoying life as I do. Earnest people, admirable in their way, but limited by silly ideas. Foolish.' He sighed.

Lalie curled up beside him, no longer sure what to believe. 'Ilgresi? His city fell. Did you . . .'

Izven laughed, each *ha* so controlled it was practically spoken. 'Ilgresi the Blind is no fool. We are distant cousins, he and I. He is now in Tsith. He knew very well Elvury would fall. He helped. He made a deal with Avridis. Do you really think, Lalie, that such a wealthy city's inner workings could have been so rotted through without its ruler knowing? He was surprised only by the timing of it – we all were. It happened a few days early. Those horrid creatures are as difficult to control in large numbers as they are to kill. Few things go to plan perfectly. It did not matter, our "dramatic escape" looked good for the generals.'

'You knew Elvury would fall?'

'All of us knew but Tauk and Liha. We lingered in that city only because of this unexpected business with the Pilgrims.'

Lalie nodded. The mayor had quizzed her repeatedly about

Eric and Case, not seeming to mind that he got the same answers each time.

Izven's drink arrived in a small glass, and he gulped it down in one swallow. It made his face flush and pupils dilate. He dismissed the servant with a gesture like flicking away an insect. 'You have more questions. Ask, Lalie.'

'Are you friends with the Arch?'

'*Friends* is a peculiar word. It is all a dance, Lalie, every action, every word. Some of the dance's moves are courteous and graceful, even seductive. Other moves are swift and brutal as a cudgel's blow. We dance about each other all the while, Lalie.' To her astonishment, a tear came to Izven's eye. It slid down his cheek. She understood a moment later it was just an effect of the drink he'd consumed. He said, 'If I told you the Arch Mage would come to visit us, would you be surprised, Lalie?' Verily, she was speechless. 'Ah, but not quite him,' said the mayor. 'A Strategist comes, Lalie. Vashun is his name. I have expected him a while, but he is late. It does not matter, does it? For we may find ways to pass the time as we wait.'

He surprised her with the suddenness with which he pinned her body beneath his, his hands about her throat, squeezing air out of her while his pale soft body pressed down, entering her with violence he'd not before given a hint of. Lalie gasped for air as his hands now and then eased to let her draw a partial breath. A distant part of her rebelled against being used this way: I am one of Inferno's chosen, she thought; I am she He spared from the hall of death! I am for *Him*, not you!

Then as if in response, Izven's words echoed again: *A noble, misunderstood Spirit, Lalie. Do you feel he will awaken in our lifetimes? I feel he may . . .*

A smile spread across her face in spite of her lack of breathing air. She could not be certain, but she believed she understood what the mayor had meant.

There was no knowing how much time had passed since she'd blacked out. A group of men surrounded Lalie's bed in quiet conversation. One of them was far taller and thinner than the others. His clothes glowed with shifting colours. His voice was a rasp filled with ugly humour: 'We have learned that even entities as great as dragons can and do . . . miscalculate, shall we say.' There was wheezing laughter. 'So this is the girl, yes, yes. How much is it that she knows of their practices?'

Izven said, 'Much, Strategist. All the common rituals, all the waking ones. Many Offerings too, though of course . . .'

'We need not trouble with that.' The tall thin one dismissed the others with a nod. They went and browsed like folk at market through the other chained women and girls. The Strategist reached out a long finger, so white and thin Lalie thought it was bone. It touched her belly, sending a ripple of cold through her. 'The waking rites may be useful. There is less to it all than one might think, Izven. Especially in this case. The Spirit's personality already lives. It is only diminished. It is difficult to explain the science.'

Stiff and wooden, the Strategist leaned over Lalie's body. His rustling voice seemed to savour itself, broken here and there with wheezing gasps. 'Being human at first, Vous was . . . difficult. A fire is a misleading but . . . sufficient analogy. With Inferno we need but pour fuel upon it to *reawaken* it. There is no need for the long process we had. To attract and build that initial . . . spark.' Vashun touched Lalie again, though no cold ran through her this time.

She swatted feebly at his hand.

Surprised to find her awake, Vashun wheezed laughter. He said, 'Rest, little one. A long trip is before us, but I am sure you will . . . enjoy . . . its destination. Think of it as the final stretch of a journey you long ago set out upon.' He twisted a long thin hand, questing for words. 'The less pleasant scenery is behind you now. Ah, but all our journeys have such, for a stretch. A little trial is needed, here and there. To sort the . . . devoted, from those who merely . . . posture.'

Not knowing what he meant, Lalie bared her teeth. Vashun stepped back a pace, smiling as if pushed by a blast of pleasant warmth. He breathed deeply. 'Ah, mm! You would ask, had you speech, where it is that we go? To the Ash Sea, little one, to the Ash Sea. There is someone there we must, ahh . . . awaken.'

Lalie gasped. A wave of chills rippled through her as understanding struck. She clung tightly to this part of the dream, cherishing its warmth, hoping more than anything else that she would awaken to find it real. By night, to the clopping hooves of the steeds that drew the wagon, she did so.

IN THE SKIES

What Eric had taken to be a city was no more than a cluster of stone monoliths, menhirs and upright slabs fashioned not unlike large gravestones, all made of the same basalt grey skystone of the cavern's walls, roof and floor. Although Vyin had called it an Invia roost, no Invia were about. Some white feathers littered the floor between the thirty or so stone pieces, some of which – like the bulbous trunk they presently hid behind – had been made in imitation of trees, with delicate stone lattice leaves fanning from trunks either squat and round, or tall and lordly. Many pieces were broken, smashed upon the ground, partly dissolved by time to dust. There seemed little order to the roost . . . it was as if the structures were placed with the randomness of tossed stones, or pieces left upon the board of an unfinished game.

They were too far now from Shâ to see whether or not any war mages still lived for the dragon to torment. They could faintly make out the dragon's huge silhouette, with just glimpses of its poison colours. It remained perfectly still for stretches of time, then trampled into motion. It was unreal to see something so huge move with such nimbleness.

Eric had never been so winded and exhausted as when they finally came to rest after their sprint to the roost, nor had he ever known such terror. Nor had Aziel, judging by her shivering and quiet weeping. He tried to understand the fear the great dragon had given him, but he could not. His death had seemed just as likely, or more so, when he'd gone through the door and lay clutching his briefcase in the corpse-strewn field while a war mage murdered nearby. And death had seemed just as likely before he and Case had been rescued from a Tormentor in the woods, or when they'd stumbled into groundman traps, and several other times besides. This time, though, the fear had gone beyond such a trivial concern as whether he lived or died. He did not know how that could be so.

'Aziel,' he whispered. 'That . . . thing. It wants to be free from here, do you understand? It wants to live among us, among people. I don't know what role we play in all this, or why we've been brought up here. But we can't let that happen.'

She didn't answer but he'd come to read the looks of her face. It was still his fault, he knew, that they were here at all. Well, maybe she was right – he'd wagered his life in the tower, when the tall, bald-headed wizard he'd never met before had advised him to fly to the castle. Now he almost heard Aziel thinking: Arch would know what to do. He'd know far better than you would.

Then Loup's voice was loud in his mind: *Shut your flapping gums, you stew-brained bastard. Think them dragons don't have ears? Don't go speaking your mind aloud! One of the great beasts possessed Aziel not long back. It may be in her right now, for all you and I know, listening to your every word . . .*

They watched the dragon's huge silhouette a while longer, the air still heavy with its presence even at this distance. They began to wonder if it would ever leave. At last its wings spread, beat the air and with apparent difficulty bore it aloft. For a horrible moment it wheeled in their direction, but instead turned a full circle on its way to a gap in the ceiling. At last it was gone from sight.

They looked at each other to confirm it had really gone. Then they laughed with relief. Joy and a sense of renewed freedom flushed wildly through them both. Aziel clutched him and drenched his shirt in tears. He stroked her hair till they both slept in the soft dust.

When his eyes opened the Invia roost was bathed in softly flickering white light.

There was peculiar quiet in the vast cavern, with no notes being played by wind through the roof tunnels. Instead there was the occasional sound from far away of stone creaking like the timbers of a boat at sea. The lone voice of an Invia called out softly somewhere in the gloom, as if not wishing to wake the dragon prison's two human guests. Eric coughed from breathing the cavern floor's dust, the sound an echo of Ventolin inhalers and doctor visits a world and a lifetime ago. That old plain world was now too alien to have ever been real.

The flickering light about the Invia roost seemed to have shut the rest of the cavern off in darkness, as if a kind of night had come to its vastness. His sight did not reach beyond the roost perimeter. Far afield, the other Invia roost was a small glowing thing on the horizon.

Aziel lay on her back in the soft dust, her lips parted and brow furrowed, one arm flung off to the side with its palm up, the other on her chest. Her breath disturbed the dust near her mouth. He smoothed away a strand of hair which had fallen across her face. Her necklace seemed for now little more than

a piece of plain metal, but when he ran a finger on it coldness
pulsed from it like turgid heartbeats. It appeared to hang loose
on her, giving the false impression that it could be removed.
He swept the dust away from her mouth with both palms so
she would not breathe it in, his hands making a faint *sssss* sound
across the stone.

In the gloom outside their roost it seemed the sound was
echoed, magnified: *sssss*. Something quite large slid over the
floor out there, moving closer. Eric took the gun from its
shoulder holster with one hand, keeping the other on Aziel's
necklace. The gloom beyond the roost hid perfectly whatever
was out there.

The sound of beating wings above made him jump. A lone
Invia took her place upon the thin stone ledge stretched between
two nearby pillars. She had scarlet hair and did not look at him
beyond one indifferent glance. Nor did the two other Invia who
fluttered down from the dark overhead and joined her. They
sat further afield on the stone branches of something tall and
tree-shaped. All three closed their jewel-bright eyes.

The sound outside came again, closer: *sssss*, without doubt
something sliding across the stone. He thought he saw a patch
of rippling darkness move sideways. There was the faint glint
of a single gem briefly unclasped in the dark. Something's eye.
He pointed the gun at it. A voice gave a faint exclamation.
Amusement? Then silence.

When he looked about again there were two more Invia in
the roost. They'd come silently. Both now looked beyond him
into the dark, at whatever crept around out there. 'Who's there?'
Eric asked quietly, taking a step beyond the pillar. He felt no
fear. After seeing Shâ, he doubted much else in the world could
scare him.

It was half a minute's silence before something quietly answered: 'Do you invite me nearer, Favoured one?'

'I am in your home,' he said. He was sure that he spoke now with a dragon, for its voice was nothing like the speech of Invia. 'Is it my right to invite you nearer, if I am in your home?'

'This is not my home.'

'Aren't you a dragon?'

'A home is a place one chooses. Is it not? Otherwise it must be called a prison.'

'To me, your whole world is a prison. I can't go back where I came from.'

'Did you choose to come to this world?'

Again the familiar memory replayed: Eric jumping head-first through the door. 'I don't know any more if I chose to. There are illusions and there's magic, things which can force a person to choose the wrong thing. All I know is I can't leave.'

'My home is where light glints off melting glaciers, where the great ones beat shapes in the land and tossed their thoughts into the air as threads of wild colour. All for men to toy with ages after, it would seem. May I come near? I wish to see the sleeping one from closer. I shan't wake her. She is beautiful, in her way.'

'I can't stop you.'

'You can with but a word.'

'In that case, no. You may not come closer.'

'Why?'

'I don't know who or what you are.'

'I shall reveal it.' There were sounds in the gloom he could not decipher. It was like something made of cloth and metal being folded, flesh rubbing against flesh. A faint waft of heat came and went, and stepping into the roost's flickering light he saw a woman with long curled hair like a black vine down her shoulders. She wore leather garb reminding him vaguely of Siel's clothes, though this version was what the queen of a forest tribe might wear, leaving bare her arms, flat navel and much of her thighs. 'Have you a name, Favoured one?' she said.

'Eric. Do you?'

'Shilen, call me that.'

'Are you an Invia?'

'Do I seem to be one?'

'No.'

'What do I seem?'

'Well, you *seem* to be a woman. I thought you were a dragon. If you're a woman, why are you here? I've heard no people ever come here.'

'Some do, but not many.'

'Are you a "Favoured one" too?'

'I dwell here. For I am not of the lands beneath, and I have my own arrangements with the brood. At times I speak for them. You are known, Pilgrim. You are now deemed the foremost, the firstborn among the Favoured, just as Vyin is said to be firstborn of the brood. A spell shall be laid upon you while you are here. It will be for you to choose the others of your kind, those who are Favoured. There shall not be a great many chosen. A hundred, or a thousand. Maybe more. Maybe fewer.'

'Let me get this straight. The dragons will be free. And I decide which people are Favoured.'

'Yes.'

He became aware the gun was still in his hand. He put it back in its holster. 'I won't ask why this duty falls on me, because I've learned that asking why is never, ever helpful. What happens to those I don't choose?'

Her laugh shook and sprung the glossy curls about her shoulders. 'What concerns you about them? They will go as their choices take them. They may hide in their grooves and ruts. Let them cross World's End and live among those who dwell there. Or make more war among themselves, as they seem to prefer. May I see your friend? She who lies sleeping nearby?'

Eric turned to Aziel and saw yet more Invia had come in silence to perch upon the tops of pillars and stone trees. Shilen strode between the pillars and crouched by Aziel, the leather skirt falling back from one thigh. Her smile bloomed as if she saw a fine joke hidden in Aziel's sleeping face. Shilen's eyes gleamed up at him and he saw that her eyes were slitted. Or perhaps it had been a trick of the light, for now they were normal again. She said, 'Do you like her hair better than mine?'

He didn't answer. Colour rippled through Shilen's curls till her black hair became the same flaxen colour as Aziel's. One long finger traced the line of Aziel's forehead, cheek and chin. Aziel didn't stir. 'Do you desire me?'

The answer seemed pulled out of him. 'Yes, I do.'

'Do you desire her?'

He looked at Aziel for a little while. 'Yes.'

'Tell me of this desire.'

'What should I tell you?'

'Tell me what you wish to do to her.'

'No. I want nothing.'

She laughed softly. 'You are afraid even to speak of it. Why? You have surely had such fear today as to make mere speech a trifle.'

'I don't know why.'

'It is a private matter, of your kind, such business as this?'

Eric shifted on his feet, not wanting Shilen's gaze on him,

nor this talk. At the same time he wanted both those things equally strongly. 'I want to protect her.'

'That is not all you desire to do, Favoured one. Why do you not give in to this unspoken desire? If you are hungry and presented food, surely you eat? Say it, at least. Say what you wish to do to her. I shan't hold your words as an oath to act.'

His face felt hot and fevered. He stepped closer to them both, tried to swallow, his mouth dry.

'Show me what you wish to do,' said Shilen. 'I shall give you something else you desire, in exchange.' She reached into a pocket in one of her skirt's leather folds, then was holding in long slender fingers a black key. She studied his face as he stared, puzzled.

'What would I want with that?' he said.

'A home is somewhere you choose. Did we not agree?'

He extended his hand. With warm fingers she pressed the key onto his palm, closed his fist around it. Her touch was as cold as its metal. 'Tell me what you wish to do to her,' Shilen whispered, running a hand through Aziel's hair. 'We have an agreement now. And tell me truly. I can see lies.'

His throat seemed to close up, but the words were drawn out of him. 'I want to rip her clothes off.'

Shilen looked deep inside him and seemed to approve of what she saw there. 'Then why not do it, Favoured one? You are the foremost of the Favoured. It is your right. Do it.'

Eric's hands trembled as he kneeled by Aziel's body. If a spell influenced him or not, he could not tell – but Shilen seemed at once a teacher to impress and a student to win over with daring deeds. He clutched Aziel's dress about the neck, pulled it till the fabric ripped, revealing cream-white skin beneath, breasts that were larger now they were freed than they'd seemed when clothed. Aziel sighed but did not open her eyes. Shilen nodded, and his hands seemed to move on their own a long distance away: they tore the dress past her navel, ran a hand over her soft goose-pimpled skin, a fingertip nestling in her belly button. 'Good,' Shilen said, her own fingers still playing through Aziel's hair. 'Is that all you want with her?'

It was not all, but now he knew he was dreaming, and no harm could come from dreams. He took his own clothes off. His blood felt like a fevered liquid fire all through him as he ripped the dress away from her legs. He did not know at what point Aziel's eyes opened but found them fixed on him, as full of fear as of desire. She did not seem to notice Shilen, still stroking her hair.

Just for a moment Aziel struggled to get up, said, 'Am I dreaming?'

'Of course you dream,' Shilen told her. 'You both dream.'

Eric hardly seemed in control of himself any more. It was a dream as he lowered himself onto her and pushed himself inside her. Aziel's legs closed round behind his back and held him there.

'It's safe,' said Shilen softly. 'You dream, man-god's daughter. Favoured one, this is yours to take.'

Aziel moaned, pushed herself up against him, grabbed his arms. Eric felt drunk, his arms full of powerful strength, his fists clenched upon the dusty stone to either side of her, sweat dripping from his face onto hers.

Sssss: more things moved outside their Invia roost, more ripples of deeper darkness shifted around in the gloom. Invia wings beat the air as the creatures, curious, flew down from their perch and came closer, forming a ring about them.

The darkness fell away and Shilen no longer crouched there. Dragons had come. Claws scraped and clicked on the bone-hard floor, disturbing the dust. Lengths of glimmering, rippling scaled skin slid past them and seemed to house them in a moving nest. Fierce ancient eyes, beautiful as gems and filled with savage wisdom, watched the Otherworlder fuck the man-god's daughter.

Many dragons were about them now, some small, some large, scales of many gleaming colours. Eric felt as though he were one of them himself. For a brief time he saw himself through dragon eyes, and his limbs were dragon limbs, Aziel beneath him likewise a length of rippling scaled flesh, as joined to him (and as dear to him) as a limb he could control.

How long all this went on, Eric could never have known. Sometimes it was Aziel's face below him, sometimes Siel's, sometimes Shilen's, but always it returned to Aziel. Sometimes she cried out and fought against him, pushing at his chest as someone struggling free of a nightmare. But more often she pulled him nearer, sucked at his neck, cried and moaned his name, said crude things he'd not have dreamed she could say.

When he came, stars burst behind his eyes. He seemed in that instant transformed into a blinding, separating burst of white light, to float above the whole scene, blasted into the air by pleasure and now glimpsing his own naked body still on top of hers, glistening with sweat and bright Invia blood he did not remember being spilled on him. He saw the dragons leaning their heads over to lick the blood off Eric's and Aziel's bodies, then watched them run back into the gloom as if they'd now learned all they needed to learn of humankind. Shilen was not there.

From high above, he looked down upon himself, pulling his clothes back on, running, weeping with shame for what he'd done. For it had been no dream and a part of him at least had known it all the while, and that part of him had not cared. He ran alone through the vast dark space, crying out in anguish now and then and not caring who or what things heard him. Then the storm of emotion passed and he was back within himself again, lost, with only faintly glowing Invia roosts in the distance, but without knowing which of them he'd come from.

There came into view a shape of bolder dark than the surrounding gloom, as dark as black on grey, a tall twisted ziggurat with many tiers, the black metal moving as if it were liquid. With jarring suddenness as he went near its motion ceased and did not resume. He came to a flat bed of grey stone laid in solid waves the shape of sand dunes. His hand felt for something in his pocket, and closed on the black key Shilen had given him. At the moment his fingers touched its cold metal, there appeared before him a little red wooden door.

He stared at it for a very long time, his eyes locked hard on the keyhole. There was no light gleaming through, as for instance from a sky on the other side. But it was the exact size and shape of the old door he remembered under the train bridge.

That door had been set in a graffiti-clad wall, next to a concrete bike path which ran past an unkempt urban park, home only to litter and the odd passed-out drunk or drug addict, resting like discarded syringes in the grass. Here, the door was set on the sheer side of a slab of stone twice a man's height, with nothing else around it. Eric's mouth was dry. Could this be real? Was it truly what it appeared? He took out the black key, but for some reason his hand refused to put it in the keyhole.

Shilen's voice from close by made him jump. 'For what do you wait, Favoured one?' She stepped into view, crouched down beside the door and studied him. 'The charm the man-god's daughter wears, Vyin made for you. She stole it. Are you angry about that?'

'No.'

'It would have given you great power.'

'I never asked for power. If the dragons gave me power, it wouldn't really be mine. It would still be theirs.'

Her gaze upon him changed subtly, became more wary. 'If not power, what then do you wish, Favoured one?'

He pointed at the little red door. 'This. If it will take me home.' Still he did not trust the sight of it. He wanted too much for it to be real, had seen too many magic tricks to be certain the door *was* real.

Shilen said, 'If I were to freely offer you great power, Favoured one, yours to use with no conditions, for whatever you desired . . . would you accept the gift?'

'No.'

'Only because you don't believe the power I speak of shall truly be yours. Favoured one, do you realise I could compel you to do what I wished, had I the desire to control you?'

'Then do it. Compel me.'

She sighed. 'I won't. As you wish then. Use the key, Favoured one.' She rose and moved away from the door.

He fell to his knees before it, looked through the keyhole. The other side was dark. A patch of white light fell upon a wedge of the concrete bike path. *It was real.* His hands trembled as he stuffed in the key. Suddenly there were tears streaming down his face as he turned his wrist and pushed the door open. A burst of wind rushed at his back, skittering dust and litter from the path. He clawed at the dirt, pushed himself through on hands and knees.

'Farewell,' said Shilen, but he didn't hear her.

5

OTHERWORLD AGAIN

Still on his knees he patted the ground around him, hardly daring to believe it was real. Yet here it was, the place memory had cast him back to too many times to count: the concrete bike path, an old liquor bottle half buried in the hard dirt next to it, which Case himself might well have drained of its contents and left there, neglected and forgotten by all the world. The door shut quietly behind him. He still had the black key, still had the choice to go back.

It was night. He may have sat on that very spot for a long time if it hadn't occurred to him that the light he saw was *moon*light. That in itself was miraculous: there was a proper sky above him again. He scrambled to his feet, ran past the graffiti-clad wall, over towards the newsagency side of the tunnel.

What he beheld seemed more magical than anything he'd seen in Levaal. The beautiful clouds were fat grey brush strokes over a bright gibbous moon, beaming its white light proudly down. Tears streamed down his face; his whole body shook. He didn't know at all what the tears came from: grief, joy, gratitude? Also a peculiar anger directed he knew not where (at Shilen? Himself?). He sat in the moonlit gutter, staring up at the sky for a long while, the moon and the stars beyond it a sight too beautiful to look away from.

He barely noticed in all that time how quiet it was, how not a single car horn sounded. He did not reflect that no trains passed on the tracks just above him. And he barely thought about whatever it might be sending little shivers through the ground he sat on.

When the night's chill broke through and the moment finally passed, he noticed the streetlights weren't on. The moonlight was all. And now he heard the silence – the absence of background traffic.

The newsagency windows were broken. It had been before him the whole time, but only now he saw it. Part of its side wall had caved in. He took a few steps out onto the road, saw nothing in either direction except a piece of litter scraping across the bitumen, pushed by wind that quickly ceased. The silence, now that he'd heard it, pressed down on him and was total. He took a breath to call out but intuition was like a hand clasping over his mouth: *shh* . . .

Now in the distance, there was noise he could not identify. Two heavy thudding sounds, each sending a shiver through the ground he stood upon.

He went back through the train bridge, past the shut door. How loud it seemed, his shoes scuffing over the dirt. He paused, examined a patch of moonlit ground out the tunnel's further side. Yes, he saw it now: there were familiar holes punched into the hard dirt.

He crouched, touching them. A dozen such holes, give or take, identical to Tormentor tracks. A strange coincidence? Surely none of those beasts could have possibly *made* these holes.

'Let's walk home from work,' he murmured. Along the once-familiar street by the rail tracks, the houses and apartments had no lights on at all. There were broken windows and caved-in walls, just like the newsagency's. There was a wide split in the bitumen road, which was so filled with potholes it could hardly be called a road any more. Eric was filled with an irrational sense that if he could just make it home to his apartment, everything would be OK. All this evidence of something horribly wrong would erase itself.

Dodging wide cracks he walked up the rise in the ground, and turned about at the top to look back at the city, but there were no lights at all. He heard a sound of something very large moving. Glass broke, metal squealed: he got the impression of a tank rolling over ruined streets, crushing cars as it went. The noise abruptly ceased. Wind rustled the overgrown grass of Case's old park at the bottom of the street and swept through the shoulder-high weeds all along the path.

Eric turned again to head for home, but stopped dead, seeing further up the rise a shape looming in wait for him. It stood jagged against the moonlit sky, the spikes and points along its flanks curling like fingers beckoning. Its arms were long, each with five jagged finger-blades stretching down so they almost touched the ground. The Tormentor's face was like features gouged and chipped out of glistening obsidian, tilted sideways on its neck and gazing, it seemed, right at him.

The backwards step Eric took was purely from surprise to find he was observed. What at another time might have been fear was instead cold anger at the violation this creature represented, imposing itself like this upon his homecoming. He took the gun from its holster, held it aloft, stepped towards the Tormentor. Slowly one of its hands rose; it seemed to be asking him not to shoot. A greater shock came when its mouth opened and a voice issued from it: '*Waste*,' it said.

Eric was so amazed to hear it speak he laughed. 'What? What did you say?' Its flat stony eyes looked down from a metre above. 'You said "waste",' Eric said. He was near enough now to reach out and touch it. 'Do you mean I'd waste a bullet, if I shot you? What the fuck . . . why do you *care* if I waste my bullets? How do you even know what a bullet is, what a gun is? What the fuck are you even *doing* here?'

Its voice was like feet scraping on dirt. '*Here you . . . will find . . . what kills . . . dragons.*'

Eric pointed the gun at its face. He wanted to shoot but his hand seemed to lock. 'What kills dragons?' he said.

Its mouth did not move to shape the words which scraped out. '*The haiyens have . . . no name for them . . . in your speech. The haiyens . . . must teach you . . . to live in a world . . . which they come to. Your flesh is . . . their clay. Your flesh is . . . their home. Your flesh . . . is them. They . . . collect . . . clay. Until the time they . . . as your kind . . . has now learned to do . . . become gods.*'

'I don't understand you,' Eric said. His hand holding the gun shook. 'I miss my apartment. I just want to see my apartment.'

Distantly there came more sounds not unlike those he'd heard before: squealing metal as something was crushed. Something crumbling and falling with booming thuds to the ground, then quiet. The Tormentor tilted its head away from him, seeming to look into the distance behind him.

'Why don't you kill me?' Eric asked it.

It did not move or answer. He stepped yet closer to it. A rage brewed deep and hot within him, one he didn't understand at all. He held the gun to its head. 'Why don't you try to kill me? I'm right here. Do it.'

It didn't move. Its wavering spikes all went still. '*A high place . . . will give you . . . sight of them.*'

He fired the gun. Its *boom* was unbelievably loud. Part of the Tormentor's face flew off. A larger part slipped more slowly to the ground, carrying with it one of the creature's eyes. Its body did not fall, still did not move. 'What did you do to this world?' Eric said.

Its voice still came: '*This work, my kind . . . did not wreak. Nor man . . . nor dragon.*' One of its arms – shaking – slowly lifted, pointed to the top of the rise. '*Go there. See. Learn why you must . . . set the dragons . . . free.*'

Eric went to where it pointed. He turned back twice to see if the Tormentor had toppled over yet, but it had not. Further along towards his apartment, along the same footpaths and roads he'd taken to walk home from the office – with a mind for microwave dinners, failed novels in progress, comic books newly purchased – buildings were mounds of detritus, piled like the rocks he and Case had walked through in the rubble plains. Cars were crushed flat, streetlight poles were knocked over, power lines a messy tangle. Slabs of road were tilted up. A dog appeared among the wreckage of a corner shop. It sniffed the air as if it had forgotten people altogether and could hardly believe its eyes now to see one. When Eric called to it, it ran away.

The path ahead was blocked by a pile of debris. He climbed it, slipping on loose slabs and boards, ignoring the now-familiar smell of death worming up from the pile's depths. At that moment he gave up any hope of finding his apartment still standing – or perhaps he understood how pointless the quest was in the first place. Instead he headed up a hilly side-street not even vaguely resembling the road it had been in his memories. The homes to either side were destroyed; the corner street sign was unbelievably one of the few things undamaged. Pitt Street. The pizza place's green and red sign poked out beneath wreckage. (A girl wearing glasses had asked him out, here on this spot. His mouth full of pizza, he'd stammered in his amazement by way of reply, which she took as rejection and fled, her face pointed down with embarrassment. He'd never seen her again.)

A gust of wind came to break the silence with its howl, the smell of smoke on its breath. From here he saw the city's silhouetted skyline. The buildings' lights were all out.

Something scuttled in the rubbish, too big to be a rat. It was the dog from before, hobbling along now with a strange limp. But then he saw it *wasn't* the dog. Its head and forelegs moved on their own, being dragged along as if blown by bursts of wind. Eric had taken a few steps towards it but now he recoiled, the gun in his hand again. Something he could not see dragged the dog's body through a gap in the rubble.

He grew aware, as the wind's howl died away, that there were now many little sounds all through the ruin about him. Little taps, scrapes, creaks. His hair stood on end, despite how silly it seemed to be afraid – how could any unseen thing here be worse than the huge beast Shâ? The Tormentor's voice echoed to him as if to contradict: *You will find . . . what kills dragons . . .*

He took what he meant to be one last sweeping look around at the place which had once been home, where life had been so simple and safe. It was then a shape moved through the city between the buildings. He rubbed his eyes, thinking because of its size alone that surely his eyes had been deceived: it was taller than some of the buildings it stalked between, and lit by its own light. Its shape defied his belief further yet, for it was like nothing he'd seen, stranger even than seeing Nightmare in the sky. Its three-pointed head was made of teardrop-shaped parts. Inside each, glassy reflective points – eyes, surely – quivered like jelly. Two arms, if arms they were, held aloft enormous orbs, one pitch black, the other white and glowing brighter than the moon overhead, the beams pouring out from between the buildings like searchlights. One shone through to where he stood. There was something insect-like about the huge thing, its arms and legs thin as vines in proportion to the thickness of its head. It was a god, surely . . . though a god no one in Levaal had ever mentioned to Eric.

It was in view only for a few seconds between two buildings, just long enough to assure him he'd actually seen it. Distantly he heard things being crushed and metal squealing as its feet pressed down.

Something moved in the piles of brick, concrete, wood and aluminium sheets he stood upon. Little piles of debris were disturbed and fell pattering down the heap's sides. As though many things had come awake, all about him now was the rattling shuffle of moving things. Small shapes began to creep out from between the disturbed rubble. They were hidden enough and small enough that he saw no more than moving shadows.

He jumped down and ran back the way he'd come. There at the top of the rise the Tormentor had not moved, though now it had picked up one of the blasted-off pieces of its face. It balanced the piece of itself on one hand, trying with little success to place it back on its face, since its blade-fingers did not bend.

Eric hesitated and then approached it again. 'What was that thing I saw?' he said, pointing off towards the city.

The Tormentor seemed to know what he meant. Its voice

grated out: 'Haiyens call it . . . That Which . . . Governs Cycles of Events.'

'And what are haiyens?'

The Tormentor didn't answer.

'That huge thing – is that what did all this, all this destruction? Is that what kills dragons?'

'No. It comes . . . later. After the rest . . . is settled. To change . . . time. When it comes, all is . . . already over. So do not . . . fear it. Those small things . . . which you fled from . . . are what you should fear.'

'Tell me one more thing. Why are you here to help and guide me?'

He waited but it did not answer. He left it there trying to reassemble its face. Something did not sit right with him about the Tormentor being here at all.

The park near the train bridge was alive with rustling grass, although now no wind blew. He slowed to a walk, dug around his pocket for Shilen's key, and went to the door, which he knew would open for him the second he chose to go back. Sure enough it did, as soon as his hand twisted in the lock: it opened with no more ceremony than a puff of wind. When it closed behind him he was crouched on the stone floor of the dragons' sky prison once more.

Shilen stood waiting for him. 'You don't seem surprised to see that I've returned,' Eric said.

'Are you home now, Favoured one?'

And then he understood he'd been deceived. The destroyed world he'd walked through had been no more than an illusion. Probably the kind created from his mind and memories, filling in the details of a world the illusion's caster had never been to (whoever that caster was – Shilen, or another dragon?). The door he'd gone through had *not* taken him back to Otherworld at all. The Entry Point was not here, or the dragons would have escaped through it, long ago. The Entry Point was behind the castle, where the dragons could not get to it. His home then was not all in ruins.

While he would later be glad it had been an illusion, in that moment he was seized by incredible anger. Without hesitation he took the gun from its holster, pointed it at her and pulled the trigger. Shilen yelped in surprise, her body flung back.

He was perhaps more shocked than she was. From the second her spinning body fell to the ground he went numb. He dropped the gun, utterly sickened, and made a noise in his throat.

Shilen's voice seemed to come from elsewhere in the dark. She groaned.

'I'm sorry,' he said, as if that could be any use.

Her shoulders shook as she pushed herself upright again. She turned her face to him. Blood so dark it was black seeped from her forehead, past her nose and mouth. She smiled through its sheen, her teeth white for a moment till they were drenched. 'You have hurt me,' she said, 'but not too much. No one promised my duties would come without pain.'

He went to her. Misunderstanding his intent, she said, 'Stop. Don't be foolish. You cannot kill me.' She palmed the blood from her eyes.

'You aren't human, are you, Shilen? A human could not survive this kind of injury. But I'm sorry I hurt you. Very sorry.' Clumsily she stood up, swaying on her feet. 'What are you?' he said.

'I'll not answer.'

'Are you a dragon in disguise?'

'I speak for them. That is all you need to know. Since your

answers come with a price, so now do mine. Do you understand what you just saw?' She pointed at the door.

'An illusion.'

'No. You saw a future. When seers see futures they see only probabilities . . . *usually*. But what you just saw is what comes. Unless you help us.'

'Why should I believe you, Shilen? You've just shown you are perfectly happy to lie to me.'

She seemed angrier at this remark than at his having shot her. 'You tell tales to children to impart lessons. That is no worse than what we have done. The future you just saw is what awaits. Did you enjoy it? That is your home, all dead and gone, if you choose. Choose now, Pilgrim! The dragons are useful allies. Help them while your help still matters to them.'

He picked up the gun he'd tossed away. She flinched back from him. 'I'm just putting it back in the holster. I'm sorry I shot you.' Why am I the one in this position? he thought for the thousandth time. Predictably there was no answer. Shilen crouched down, shivering. 'Is there anything I can do to help you?' he said.

'Be grateful. I choose not to return the pain you just gave to me. Will you help the dragons or not?'

'Wait, I want to understand things properly. You are speaking for the dragons, and I'm speaking for the human race. Is that right? I'm first among the Favoured, you say.'

'The lord of your kind, if that term better suits.'

'No one else seems to know that.'

'The dragons shall make sure they do.'

'And in exchange for that, they want me to help them get free. And they will save my world, Otherworld, Earth? They will prevent what I just saw, at the cost of killing most people here in Levaal. Is that right?'

'Killing your kind is not the reason the dragons desire to be free.' She made it to her feet again. 'Are we to bargain now, Favoured one? If so, name your price for this arrangement, if being lord of your kind is not already enough.'

He had no idea what to say to her. Again he seemed to hear Loup's voice: *Tell em whatever they want to hear, lad. Tell em you're a dragon yourself, if it please em.* 'All right, here are my terms. People in Levaal are to remain free.'

She scoffed. 'Are they free now?'

'They're free from dragons, even if they imprison each other. If I'm lord, I'll put a stop to that. But when the dragons are freed, our cities will be left alone. *We* are to be left alone.'

Again she swayed on her feet, then crouched down in apparent pain, and he got the impression she wasn't badly hurt at all, that she was just exaggerating. He could not be sure.

She said, 'That is not a price, Favoured one. You have simply described what will already be. Dragons do not wish to dwell in the cities of men; their homes are mostly found in what you call unclaimed lands. Why not name a price? Do you wish for protection from other men? You shall have it. You wish for magic power? A life many centuries long? You shall have them. Treasures the envy of your kind, and even the envy of some dragons? You shall have them. If you wish.'

'That beast I saw before, the one named Shâ . . .' he began.

'*He* will remain here,' she said in a quieter voice, as if that dragon were lurking in the dark nearby.

Eric crouched down too, as if pushed by the weight of all humanity. That was how it felt. 'What is it the dragons want of me, Shilen? Not of my species, but of me. Why am I here speaking with you now, out of all the people they could have picked?'

'I cannot answer, for I did not make the choice, Favoured one.' Light faintly gleamed in her eyes, as if the human mask she wore had slightly cracked, as if something else peered through her face. A hard edge came to her voice. 'Speak your wishes now, clearly. The dragons will accept them as law, provided you keep me as an advisor in your affairs. It does not mean you must do as I ask, but you must speak with me whenever I wish it. That is all they ask. The dragons do not break agreements. Nor should you. You and your mate shall have the throne between you.'

She stepped in his direction and seemed to grow in stature till she towered above him, her eyes blazing. 'And this too is now law. You shall not ever again, under any circumstance, play with those mechanics which elevate a man to the stature of a god. That beyond all else is forbidden. Too little is known of those sciences, even to the dragons.'

'Don't the dragons like what became of Vous?' Eric said. He'd had no idea the question was a dangerous one, but anger seemed like a burst of heat pouring from her, so hot he stepped back in surprise. That was answer enough for him: whether or not the dragons had somehow had anything to do with creating Vous, the result had not met their expectations.

Shilen said, 'All knowledge of those arts will be destroyed and never sought again. If you, as lord and firstborn of your kind, ever work with the gods *against* the dragons, know that this is a violation of the laws of their Parent. If you do service to the gods against us, the Eight will ride across World's End to swing the Pendulum high on purpose, and so waken their Parent. All humanity, even the Favoured among you, will be destroyed. You are warned.'

These words shook the cavern and sent him staggering backwards. He closed his eyes, but when they opened she was a woman again, with flaxen hair stained by a wound he had caused.

She said, 'Gifts you shall have, if you will take them. Blessings of protection and luck you shall have also. Together the dragons and your people shall preserve this world, and Otherworld, from the danger in Levaal South.

'And hear this: it is rumoured some of your kind seek to awaken Inferno. Do not let them! Levaal has gods enough. If Otherworld would be defended, Levaal must set its dragons free. For the dragons and Otherworld share certain enemies, and we will fight those enemies with fury.' She said all this softly, conjuring pictures in his mind of humans riding dragons across fields of battle, enormous wingspans casting shadows on hordes of armies, fire pouring from the dragons' mouths to glint on thousands of spear tips below. And Eric rode the dragon leading their march.

Shilen said quietly, 'Accept the gifts you are now offered, Favoured one, firstborn, lord of men. Accept the dragons' blessing. You do not yet know your privilege. You among all of your kind who ever walked, breathed, or toyed with fire and magic. Go, be with your mate. When you both wish to, you may leave this place and claim your throne. You are invited to return here as you wish, and bring with you whoever among your kind you choose.'

She stepped out into the dark and was gone. The door had vanished, leaving only the slab of stone it had been set into. Eric stared about, not knowing which way to go to find Aziel, when the faint glimmering light of an Invia roost in the distance glinted as if switched on to guide him back. Further away, high above, so far he could only faintly hear it, was the ominous noise of heavy weight shifting. With the sound the very slightest shiver ran through the stone where he stood. Eric hurried his steps.

6

HAUF

Long before he reached the Invia roost he heard laughter, so high and sweet it seemed some enchantment was in play. He ran the rest of the way back. As before, the roost seemed to get no closer till he was upon it.

He had expected to find Aziel still asleep, or perhaps shivering in the dark. She'd be clutching her ripped dress to cover her nakedness as best as she could, maybe weeping, wondering if what had happened to her had been a horrible dream. He felt *he* was the one dreaming when he came into the roost and found her sitting high on a ledge between two pillars, with Invia on either side of her, looking as if she had become one of them herself. The laughter was hers. Threads of her dress hung freely from her shoulders and waist. Her necklace poured forth gleaming radiance, making solid the otherwise flickering dreamy light of the roost.

Invia on nearby structures – he counted them: eight – watched her with cocked heads, big eyes and what seemed to be amusement. He had never seen such looks on their faces before. They did not turn to him when Aziel finally noticed his arrival. She made not the least motion to cover her breasts; in fact she stood up proudly, naked as all the Invia were. Her smile beamed down at him.

This was so contrary to what he'd envisioned – tears, anger, accusations – that all he could say was, 'Aziel . . . be careful up there.'

'They won't let me fall. Watch!' She jumped into the air, her ripped clothes and hair trailing gracefully behind her, face filled with light and joy. As she began to arc down from her leap, all the Invia rose from their perches, the two nearest reaching her in a blink, taking her by an arm each and setting her gently down. They flew straight back to their perches, watching her.

'I have learned so much,' she said. A touch of sadness came to her smiling eyes. 'We have to leave soon and take the castle. The ones there now aren't allowed there any more. It's ours. I suppose you're nobility now. They said you're coming with me.'

'I'm sorry about your dress, Aziel. And . . . the rest of it.'

'Don't be a fool! We have a world to govern, Eric, and you bother yourself over a ripped dress?'

'It wasn't just the dress.'

'I'm aware of what happened,' she said, and he was glad to see a touch of her familiar regal annoyance. 'It was a dream we both had, did you not know it? A dream, and real, all at once. As is life itself. Come. We should leave soon.'

'Won't your father still be at the castle? Won't the Arch?' She shrugged as if neither was of great import. 'Aziel, they might have other ideas about us claiming their home.'

'They're entitled to whatever ideas they like in the privacy of their own minds.' She sounded solemn and – he could not deny it – powerful. Then her voice and manner changed to those of a delighted girl: 'You must meet Hauf! He's nearby; he's been waiting for you. Hauf! Come. He has a gift for you, Eric.'

A shape loomed in from beyond the perimeter. It was a dragon, but one smaller even than Case the drake. Its skin was dark as the cavern floor and walls, cracking as the dragon moved with apparent difficulty towards him. If not for Aziel's light manner, he'd have run from it, for its face was vicious. Its body was lean but heavy muscles rippled about its shoulders and legs. It came slowly, straight for Eric, dark eyes glittering.

'This is Hauf. Don't be afraid of him. He's the smallest dragon here, I think. But he's very strong. He's made of stone, on the outside at least. The Invia say he doesn't use magic. He can fight, though. He survived a fight with one of the Majors, long ago. He didn't win of course, but he survived. That's what they say, at least. It made him famous among the lesser dragons. Hauf doesn't fear magic at all.'

The dragon paused with its head lowered at Eric's feet, eyes glaring up as if it meant for all the world to rip his throat out. Instead it set down a small, plain-looking amulet. From deep in Hauf's throat came a growl like angry stone. Words were faintly discernible in the sound: 'You may call me three times. Then I am free.'

'Oh!' said Aziel. She clasped her hands together. Eric reached for the amulet, only because he feared Hauf would bite him if he did not. 'He won't hurt you,' Aziel assured him.

The dragon watched him pick it up, grinding its teeth with the sound of rocks being chewed to powder. Slowly Hauf turned to limp into the dark beyond the roost.

'He's nicer than he looks,' Aziel confided. 'Most dragons are, I think.'

He looked at her, wondering who had convinced her of this, and how. 'I can think of an exception. I'm sure you can too.'

She would not meet his eye. 'Why must you bring that up again? Most of the others don't like *him* either. You needn't worry. He'll never be free. They won't let him out.'

'So I'm told. Listen, Aziel. You may not care about this, but I do. What I did to you earlier . . . it wasn't a dream, do you understand? I never meant to touch you in that way. It's not something I'd have done to you at all, if I'd been able to think straight or control myself. I think there was some kind of magic at work. That sounds like an excuse I know. But I want you to know, I'm sorry.'

She interrupted him with laughter. 'Not some thing you'd have done at all? Let's see about that. There's no magic here now, Eric. Unless *I* have powers. Do I?' She stepped closer to him, pushed her body into his, her lips onto his, not concerned at all for the Invia who still watched them.

After a minute or two, neither was he.

As they made to leave the roost one of the Invia drew their attention to a little chest made of something like ivory, half buried in a mound of dust. Inside it were gowns, several of them. One fit Aziel perfectly, though the rest were far too large. While she examined these Eric ignored her commentary and stared at the amulet Hauf had given him. It was cool on his palm, light in weight, and the colour of dull steel; entirely unremarkable to look at. Part of it depicted what was perhaps an eye. If it were magical, he felt none of its effects and his mage eyes saw nothing unusual.

Aziel dug around in the chest. 'Look! There's even more in here. Here! Something for you, I think. It's a shirt. O, it's armour. See? There're three of them. This one might fit you.'

She held up a sparkling chain-mail shirt. He ran a hand down it, imagining Loup's voice issuing words of caution about taking gifts from strangers, especially strange dragons. 'Aziel, what have we learned about taking objects we find lying about? Beautiful objects or not.'

'*We* have learned more than we ever dared dream we would know,' she snapped. 'Here we are, in a place where no one else dared to come. And we are made rulers of everything! We wouldn't be here at all if I hadn't taken the necklace. So there's your answer. *We* have learned some gifts are too perfect to refuse.'

She tossed the chain-mail shirt at him. He caught it. 'I have a hunch I know what kind of queen you're going to make,' he said.

'I'm trying to be practical. You'll need protection. We may be about to do something very dangerous.'

He held aloft Hauf's amulet. 'What about this? Is it good for anything?'

'Weren't you listening? Hauf will come if you call him. Maybe he can hear you through the amulet. Though he won't be able to help us within the castle.'

'Why not?'

'Spirits and dragons can't go there. I don't know why, but everyone knows it to be true.'

For a while longer he watched her rummage through the chest as though she'd owned it for years. 'Aziel, these gifts . . . Look, help isn't usually given freely. As a queen or empress or whatever you are, you ought to know that.'

But he slipped the chain-mail shirt on nonetheless, and took the other odds and ends Aziel dug out of the chest: pieces of seemingly plain jewellery, things like coins, coloured gems, some which gleamed bright, others which were dull. There were half a dozen dragon scales of various colours, big enough to be scales from the brood's Parent. Including – he almost heard Kiown's jealous, anguished scream – a black scale.

Aziel waved goodbye to the Invia. They did not respond at all. The chain-mail shirt clinked faintly for a few steps then seemed to settle itself on Eric's body. They heard beating wings behind them as one or two of the Invia left the roost and flew into the gloom above.

Aziel showed no sign of trepidation as they got nearer to where they'd entered the dragons' sky prison, easily found by following the trail of dead war mages. The place Shâ had revealed himself for the first time to human eyes, unless others like Shilen dwelled here. (Did Shâ know that we watched him? Eric wondered. Was that display of cruel power somehow part of the dragons' plan, a message to the new human lords? Emphasising, perhaps, what Shilen had told him: *The dragons do not break agreements. Nor should you.*)

War-mage bodies grew more common the closer they got to the tunnel leading down: war mages broken and twisted into odd shapes, unclosed eyes here and there still glowing catlike and yellow, though most had faded out. Overhead, the cavern ceiling began again its song, with new wind blowing through the tunnels. Aziel looked up and waved, as if the eerie notes had bid them a personal farewell.

When they neared the downwards-curving tunnel, Eric gazed at the two dragons lying dead among the piles of slain war mages. The larger one's body was of golden shades, in places coppery red, or edged with silvery white, now vandalised all over with whiplash burns, punctures and tears. Still it was breathtaking, like something beautiful dropped senselessly from a great height and broken. A lump came to Eric's throat, hot tears welled in his eyes as he recalled the cry it gave while it died.

It need not have died like that. Shâ could have come down right away, ended the battle with ease, and spared this magnificent thing its life.

'Eric, we have to go,' Aziel said, pulling at his arm.

He began to turn away when one of the dragon's eyes peeled open. A faint, pleading groan sounded from its lips, barely audible. Eric recoiled in horror – not horror of the beast, but horror *for* it. He hadn't the power to help speed up its death; he could not bring himself to try shooting it. He wept. 'I can't help you. I'm sorry, I can't help you.'

Its one open eye looked into his, saw so deep within him he felt naked to his very innermost layer. He did not know if it had understood him or not, only that it suffered and could not be helped. Aziel, weeping also, pulled him away from its gaze and towards the tunnel.

7

GOD OF BEAUTY

'Don't pant like that, old man,' Loup said, thumping his heel into Case's side. The castle was well behind them now. The weather had calmed and the airs were weak of magic, the way Loup much preferred them.

Loup's foot had hit Case more softly than Aziel's many slaps during their flight north from the tower, but the drake was worse tempered now. A growl sounded in his throat: as impressive a growl as Loup had heard him make. He said, 'Whoa now! Well, you almost convinced me: you're a mighty ferocious beast. Ease up. Faul's place is up ahead, just out of these woods. Full of food and ale for you, if she'll let us back in. Your wings might be tired, but your back's not much chop to sit on, let me tell you. These scales of yours, the war drakes used to have em smoothed, back in the war days. That blood you smell's *mine* – you chopped my legs up real good. You don't hear me complaining and wheezing like my lung's full of wet cloud.'

Case wheezed loud in argument. Before Loup could berate him further, a sight in the woods below caught him off guard. For a fleeting moment, someone stood visible in a clearing where the trees gave way to a little stream, trickling down layers of stone like steps. It was a small figure in a white gown, either a woman or a very effeminate man. The figure's head was raised to the sky, and one of its flanks was half exposed in similar fashion to the world's Friend and Lord himself.

Loup thought, Long flight. Funny airs at the castle. Seeing nonsense now. Poor young Eric, wonder how he did up there. Aziel I've no grudge with, but can't say I miss the silly thing and her whines.

The woods came to their abrupt end, giving way to the stony plains about Faul's home, hard turf she somehow convinced to sprout enough food for her enormous appetite. Beyond her land spread out the blasted plains, which almost made Faul's hard acres seem a fertile pretty place. Loup shuddered at the thought of the two lone Pilgrims, lost and stumbling across it as they had, totally unmindful of the huge magic cast in that place so long ago, echoes of it still rumbling uneasily across the rocks and brittle weeds. You could hear it from Faul's porch, up late on certain nights.

'Down now, Case,' said Loup, patting the drake's neck. 'Rest time soon. First, we show Faul we're sorry. Don't matter whether we *should* be sorry or not, that's half-giants for you. Look there! You can see the spot she buried that Invia, even from here.'

Case set down a short walk from Faul's house. Loup slipped off his back, then murmured and grumbled as he roamed the edge of the forest. Now and then he ducked down to the dirt, picking up small weeds and pebbles, sometimes flicking them away with an impatient noise in his throat. He found the occasional crystal among the stones, good healthy power in them for common household magic, the type the fancy old schools would've scoffed at. 'Folk mages, they call us,' he grumbled, adjusting the grudge like a favoured old garment pulled about him. 'Cos we knew magic was to help *folks*! That's us, no point, horde it all away in high towers like a stoneflesh gathering stones about him. Pat ourselves on the back for how much we know, how clever we are to keep things secret. Pah!'

There ahead in the trees, that was where Far Gaze had fought the dragon, though no sign of their spell work remained as far as Loup could see. The woods seemed quiet and watchful while his gnarled hands dug through grass and dirt. Tree spirits were awake today, no doubt of it.

With no warning at all there began a sudden riot of birdsong. Beginning in the trees some way off to his left, the sound spread all through the woods, loud enough even to wake up old Case and get him up on his feet, staring about in alarm. Loup had never heard birds sing that way in his life. He looked up through the treetops, trying to catch sight of them. They were hidden, if they were really there at all. Magic? The air bore no obvious signs of casting, just the usual faint unease that had been around since the Wall fell. In spite of his wariness, the birdsong began to fill Loup's heart with cheer, just like downing a cup of strong wine. He had half a mind to kick his boots off and dance.

And he may have, had not all the song ceased as abruptly as it began. One or two birds took flight further back in the woods, wheeling in the sky over the treetops. Maybe it had been natural, after all. All was still again.

Loup hoped the gathered things would be sufficient for what he needed – he didn't fancy being near these woods longer than he had to after that. He jogged back to Case, who was already asleep again, bless him. 'Wake up, old man. You hear all that? What ye make of it, eh? What're those birds up to?' One amber eye opened, gleamed like a polished gem and peered into his own. *Not the faintest idea*, it said with total indifference.

Loup set his findings down on a patch of dirt he cleared away with his foot. His weathered hands twisted roots, stems, branches. Case's amber eye serenely followed his movements. Loup muttered, 'Half-giants, when they get a small grudge, well you can win em back only if you done em some good turns, back before they got mad at you. That's for a *small* grudge. Long memories they have, but that works to the good too. Old Faul, I blessed a load of her crops, back in that year when Tempest got mad, made them floods at Tsith, then went off west and the rains never come back awhile. O aye, Case old man, we'd visit her now and then, gave her news of the times, what the cities were up to. No safe journey to get out here, either. She'll remember that.'

He cursed and muttered, twisted the stem of a flower about a dark brown pebble he'd spit-polished, given over entirely to intuition: even the speech burbling from his mouth had no more thought or deliberation than a stream's water. His gnarled fingers twisted, snapped off, tied together. 'Aye, old man drake . . . not much magic t'this, just a little kick, we'll give it . . . more time'd be better, but we'd best hurry . . . them songs in the woods – something's afoot . . . not much magic to this . . . but she'll remember, old Faul will remember . . . good friends we was to her, back awhiles . . .'

Soon taking shape in his hands was a spindly wheel of vine, flower stem, grass. Here and there shiny pebbles hung from it like berries, each polished to gleaming. Loup fixed his eye upon it from many angles, detecting at last a thin thread of magic playing about from pebble to pebble. Anyone could make something like this, no need to be a mage at all. 'Curious, she'll be, old Faul,' said Loup to the sleeping drake. 'What's this old thing on my doorstep? she'll say. Who did that knocking? We'll see what happens then, Case old man. We'll see.'

There was no sign of Faul as Loup neared the house with the large wreath carried before him. Now and then a wooden *thock, thock, thock* came from Lut at work at the further end of the rear yard. Loup laid the wreath on Faul's front doorstep, tapped the door twice, then ran. From where he crouched behind spiny bushes he heard the merciless *thump* of her boots clomping through the house. Slow strides – good sign!

The large door creaked open. There she stood, hands on hips, staring down at the gift he'd crafted. Come now, Loup thought, his heart speeding up. Pick it up, lass. It'll tell you who made it. Let's let it all be: forget that pretty dead Invia. Me and old man Case had naught to do with killing her anyway . . .

Slowly, slowly, Faul's body leaned forwards. Down on one knee she crouched, delicately picking up the wreath in thumbs and forefingers. She stared at it for many long minutes. Slowly, slowly, she slipped it over her thick bull-like neck. (He'd allowed room for that neck of hers, but even so only just room enough.) Faul's fists went back on her hips. Passing through her mind now – if Loup's hands had done their job right – would be memories of old times, good deeds done to her and by her, an appeal to her good side. It was an old and obscure art, the forgiveness wreath, but there was no other way to deal with a half-giant someone had stirred up.

Loup's gut whined in hunger. As she heard it, Faul's voice boomed: 'RIGHT THEN. COME ON, OUT IN THE OPEN WITH YOU. I THINK I KNOW WHO IT IS.'

Loup stood, gums grinning, hands fidgeting. *Clomp, clomp,* down the steps she came, huge wooden boots pounding, scattering pebbles. 'ALONE?' she roared. 'I SMELL . . .' she sniffed. 'IT'S NOT DRAKE, BUT SIMILAR.'

'It's drake, aye, lass,' said Loup.

'DON'T LASS ME. AND DON'T COWER LIKE THAT. AS FOR THE WREATH, IT WORKED. WELL-MADE ENOUGH, WITH NICE STONES IN IT, THOUGH THE VINES COULD BE THICKER. YOU'RE FORGIVEN. BUT IT'S NO DRAKE I SNIFF. IT'S SOMETHING ELSE, LOUP.' Without warning she stomped off to where he'd left Case sleeping. The drake stirred and woke well before she reached him, eyeing her nervously. No doubt Loup's promise of food and ale was the only thing keeping him from flying away. 'AHA! SO HERE HE IS. FAMILIAR, SOMEHOW. HIS NAME?'

'Old Case.'

'CASE? HM. LET'S SEE THEN.' Case flapped his wings frantically as she scooped him in her arms to test his weight. He was longer than she was tall, but somehow she made him seem quite small. 'SETTLE!' she boomed. 'DON'T BREATHE YOUR FIRE ON ME, IF FIRE YOU HAVE. I'LL BLOODY SCORCH YOU BACK IF YOU DO. LOUP, SOMETHING IS WRONG WITH THIS DRAKE.'

'Long flights, he's had.'

'NO! NOT SICK, NOT ILL, NOT ALLERGIC. I'M TELLING YOU, IT'S NOT A DRAKE AT ALL. THIS IS A MAN.'

Loup had no response to this absurd statement but to shrug and smile. His belly rumbled again. 'Eats like a drake, Faul,' he ventured.

'HM. YOU'D DO LIKEWISE, EH? COME THEN, BE FED. BUT WHATEVER THE MISCHIEF IS HERE WITH YOUR "DRAKE", I'VE NOT SEEN ITS KIND BEFORE! YOU'LL TELL ME ALL YOU KNOW OF THIS STRANGE CREATURE WHILE WE EAT.'

Loup scratched his head, wondering what he could possibly

tell her of this drake-shaped, drakecoloured, drake-sized and rather drakish critter, who sounded, acted and otherwise *seemed* – to him at least – very much like a drake.

It was then the bird chorus began again, an explosive riot of beautiful cries in harmony, clicking percussion made by beaks snapping against tree trunks. Faul leaped, and dropped Case thumping into the bracken underfoot. She glared at Loup, suspecting some trick. He shrugged, his poor empty belly moaning. Faul glared at the trees. The birdsong died down. In its place came the faint voice of someone, or something, singing a wordless song. The voice was high, thin, at times fading to little more than the sound of wind. Loup shivered. Without a word Faul scooped the drake in her arms again, her big red glaring face full of disquiet. 'SOMETHING'S IN THOSE TREES,' she said. 'SOMETHING THAT'S NEVER BEEN HERE BEFORE. GOOD OR ILL, LOUP? I'VE NO NOTION.'

'Me neither, Faul. But if I knew I promise I'd tell you.'

Faul's human husband, Lut, was tall, bearded, well-muscled from yard work and handy with most weapons, yet seemed a midget next to his wife. He set across the huge table mounds of bread; butter and honey in pots; meat of many kinds, dried, raw, baked and roasted; ever-cold skins of milk; mineral-blessed water in fat stone jugs; bowls of dark berries; fat cream-filled pastries; and more besides. After the road and the flight, the spread brought tears of joy prickling Loup's eyes. He pecked at the edges of the feast, more mindful of half-giant etiquette than normal. (Rules: display obvious hesitation whenever reaching for food, even from his own plate. Each morsel was to be held up for Faul to claim, if she wished it, before he'd bite into it.

She never claimed, and even if she did not visibly acknowledge the courtesy, the gestures mattered.)

Between mouthfuls she questioned him about the drake and where he'd come from. The answers never seemed enough. Faul insisted old Case wasn't simply a drake.

'WEIGHT'S ALL WRONG! HIS MANNER TOO. JUST FAINT, BUT I SPOT IT. I KEPT DRAKES LONG AGO. ALL MANNER OF EM, ALL AGES AND COLOURS. HE AIN'T ONE!'

Loup told her of the Wall's destruction, of the tower in the far south, and its odd wizard. The rest of his tale he left alone, meaning to save some of it for breakfast . . . indeed to mete it out over as many meals as Faul would allow.

'MUCH EXPLAINED, THEN,' she said when he'd finished. The day had begun to darken. She pulled from her mouth the bones of a rabbit she'd sucked the baked flesh from, leaving its skeleton almost intact. She patted her cheek with a towel. 'THE SKIES ARE RESTLESS, LOUP. MORE THAN THEY HAVE EVER BEEN.'

'Aye, them airs got stirred up. Since the Wall it's been bad enough. Then this Vous business? O aye, gave it all a mighty shake.'

'NOT YOUR SILLY MAGIC-AIRS! TO THE ASH SEA WITH THAT NONSENSE. I MEAN THE *SKIES THEMSELVES* ARE RESTLESS, LOUP. THE DRAGONS STIR, TURN OVER, AWAKEN, STRETCH THEIR LONG, SCALED LEGS.'

'Aye, they do.' Loup soaked some bread in a water bowl so it could be chewed with just his gums; the dried meats gave him a pang for his teeth, most of them pulled out for use in rituals which had seemed important at the time. 'Do ye love em like your birds, Faul? They've wings too.'

Her fist thumped down. 'NEVER MET EM! THAT A DRAGON

CAME SO CLOSE TO MY HOME AND LEFT ME BE, STANDS THE REST IN GOOD STEAD, BY MY JUDGEMENT. NOT THAT THEY CARE! I'M AN INSECT TO THEM LIKE ALL THE REST OF US. CAN NAUGHT BUT NIP THEIR SKIN, GIVE EM A WELT OR SCRATCH OR TWO, FOR THE PRICE OF SQUASHING ME. I ACCEPT IT! CAN'T CHANGE THE NATURAL RANK OF POWERS, HOWEVER MUCH VAIN MEN WISH TO TRY. MY PEOPLE AND DRAGONS NEVER MIXED. THEY NEVER HUNTED US, NEVER HELPED US, NOR WE THEM. UNLESS IT'S TRUE THAT THEY MEDDLE WITH THINGS FROM OUT OF SIGHT, AS SOME CLAIM. THEIR CLAWS SWIRLING THE AIRS OF EVERY SPELL HUMAN MAGES CAST, THAT'S WHAT SOME RECKON!' Her fist thumped down again, rattling the table and flattening the last pyramid of bread rolls (whose sturdiness Loup had been admiring). Lut broke out of what had seemed a trance of fondness, gazing at his wife. He gathered the rolls as they pattered to the floor.

'BUT WHEN THEY'RE *HERE*, THOSE DRAGONS?' said Faul. 'BAH! NO TELLING WHAT WILL HAPPEN. WILL THEY EVEN BOTHER WITH US? I WOULDN'T IF I WERE THEM, LEST IT WERE SERVED FOR MY DINNER! BUT MARK THIS: THEY'VE A MIND TO COME DOWN VERY SOON, AND THEY SHALL. ANOTHER YEAR? OR MERE DAYS? SOON! BELIEVE IT, LOUP. I HEAR THE BIRDS WHEN THEY SPEAK TO EACH OTHER. SILLY BIRDS THINKING LIKE GROUNDMEN THAT OTHERS CAN'T FATHOM THEIR CHAT. THE DRAGONS COME! AND YOUR SILLY HUMAN WIZARDRY SHAN'T ACCOUNT FOR MUCH THEN.'

Loup smiled – she meant human wizardry in general, he supposed, rather than his own humble craft. *He'd* never had ambition to 'change the natural rank of powers', whatever she'd meant by that. He held aloft a little red berry whose kind he'd not before seen. Faul indicated with her posture that the courtesies were no longer needed. He popped it in his mouth and massaged it with his gums till it spat juice over them.

He didn't know whether Faul was right or not. Levaal's guardian, the Dragon-god asleep far beneath the castle, supposedly had laws against the brood returning to the world below. No wonder Dyan had slunk about like that, mostly hiding himself within a woman whom he'd convinced he loved her. Loup pondered all this, unaware he was murmuring wordless sounds through his gums.

'I'VE EATEN ENOUGH,' Faul told Lut. 'PACK IT UP. SOME OF THIS WILL GET US STARTED FOR BREAKFAST.' She belched loud and long, rattling the windows. It was then – as though in response – that the birdsong came a third time. This time it seemed to surround the house.

Lut, ever calm, went about clearing up the plates and cups with the merest glance out the window. Faul stomped out to the porch, seeming at once wonderstruck and nervous. Visible now, some of the singing birds flew in a circle, others sat facing the house. 'STRANGE BEAUTY,' said Faul, listening awhile. 'IT GLADDENS ME. THOSE *BIRDS* ARE GLAD. THERE'S LITTLE MEANING TO IT OTHER THAN: GLADNESS! THOSE ARE THEIR TRUE VOICES, LOUP, BUT THEY NEVER SING THIS WAY. THE SONG IS PRETTY, SO I'LL ABIDE IT, IF WHATEVER CAUSES THIS MINDS ITS OWN—'

Then the song played within the house. The caged birds – dozens of them, in the adjoining room – took up the same voice, adding their own spirals of harmonious notes and clicking percussion. 'NO MORE OF IT!' Faul boomed, no longer glad at all. 'NOT UNDER MY ROOF. NO MAGIC COMES HERE WITHOUT MY KNOWING WHO MAKES IT. I DON'T CARE IF IT'S A DRAGON THE CAUSE OF IT! A PINCH AND STING HE'LL GET, SQUASH ME

OR NOT.' She yanked on the same wooden boots Loup recalled
her wearing when she'd chased Anfen's group from her yard.
In one hand she grabbed a mallet no man would've been able
to lift with two. 'COME!' she boomed, setting off towards the
trees.

'Easy, Faul,' said Loup, hurrying after her with Case in tow.
'None of us knows what done all that. Could be things we never
heard of. Or you may be right and it's a dragon. Best leave it.'
He and Lut hurried in pursuit of her across the brittle yard.
The birds near the house scattered and went back to the trees.
More of their song came from there, the same place Loup had
heard it earlier. Faul headed that way, but before leaving her
yard she came over a rise in the ground and paused. The other
two caught her up. All three of them stared at some kind of
mirage which had sprung up between where they stood and
the trees.

There was a fountain, fashioned like a bird with a long neck,
made of polished white stuff which gently glowed. Water
trickled from its beak to a bowl at its base. Lut went closer to
run his hand down its curved neck. He dipped one hand in the
pool of liquid, flung water from it off to the side. Where each
drop landed, things sprang into being as if the drops had given
them life: a winding bunch of flowers, growing from an
upwards-thrusting ivy-green vine, its stem catching light as
would stained glass. Where another flung drop fell, there
appeared part of a garden. A footpath made of polished gold
wound through a riot of colours and shades. The way these
things appeared was as if shreds of a veil had been pulled from
the rough, stony yard to reveal the true beauty hidden beneath
it all the while.

More such sights sprang wherever the drops landed. Lut,

wonderingly, dipped his hand back into the bird-fountain's liquid, and splashed the waters in the other direction. More wondrous beautiful things came into being: flowers whose long petals were like carved amethyst curls; leaves and vines which glimmered into a vast new set of shades when viewed from the slightest change of angle. Each colourful thing was spellbinding in its own right. As a chorus, it was irresistible, a riot of beauty. Into the air trickled the sound of a brook – though they could not see it – splashing its gentle waters over stones. The bird-song came again, more quiet and soothing this time, gentle lullabies promising dreams, promising all would be well.

'NO MORE!' Faul boomed as Lut's hand reached to dip back into the fountain's waters. She gazed suspiciously around at it all. 'PRETTY, I'LL GRANT IT,' she said. 'BUT I NEVER MINDED THE OLD YARD, COARSE AND HONEST AS SHE IS. HERE ARE GIFTS GIVEN BY ONE WE CANNOT SEE. WHAT DO YOU MAKE OF IT?' She looked at Loup for explanation.

He shrugged, flashed his gums, longing for a chance to fling some of the bird-fountain's water on the brittle turf and see what it might create. Loup's only thought was that a Spirit must be behind it, but which? Deeds like this were in no tales of the gods he'd heard before.

A human voice gently worked its way in among the chorus of birdsong. Faul shook herself, grunted, as if to resist being calmed. Then they saw him, dancing through the garden, bare-foot, one flank exposed, a slender white hand flinging drops from a bowl held under the other arm. It was Vous. Loup recalled in a flash the glimpse, as he'd flown over the woods, of this very figure standing by a stream.

Vous appeared then vanished with progressive steps of his dance, in and out of the garden of which they could see only part. Loup found his movements hypnotic, simply because of how much pleasure they gave to behold: he was sure the human form had never held itself nor moved with such grace as this. The furious look all of them knew from books and artworks that filled Aligned country was not only absent, the familiar glare seemed quite impossible on this being's face.

Where the drops he gaily flung fell, more of the half-hidden garden sprang into being. The trickling brook at last appeared, spilling thin threads into a small pool which Loup wanted more than anything else to dive into, whatever may result from it.

Vous hadn't seemed aware of them until he twirled quite close, his glance sweeping like a light over them all. A soft rustle of echoing laughter played about them, perfectly in place with the gentle birdsong. With a playful sweep of his arm, he invited them to join him, to take up some water from the little fountain, fling it where they would. Loup rushed forwards, but Faul's fist closed around his arm and yanked him back. It was like being dragged from pleasant sleep. Her other hand, Loup saw, had done the same with Lut.

Vous saw this too, and laughed, joyous bells pealing. His dance grew faster, faster, a few more drops flung here or there, while he himself flashed in and out of visibility. Then with no warning the birdsong ceased, Vous disappeared altogether and did not return. The partly revealed garden remained, with streaks of normalcy left through it: streaks of brittle scrub, rocks and weeds, splashed over a beautiful painting only partly completed. The stream's trickle was the only sound in the sudden quiet.

Loup, Lut and Faul looked at each other. The air whooshed behind them, something heavy landed, and all three turned, startled, to find Case the drake gazing serenely at what Vous had left here. 'HE'S GONE!' said Faul. Then she began striding purposefully into the woods.

'If he's gone, what's the rush?' Loup called after her. 'Where you headed?'

'THE CASTLE,' she replied. 'HE'S GONE FROM THE CASTLE, THAT'S WHAT I MEANT. THE CASTLE IS SITTING THERE, LOUP, RIPE NOW FOR THE TAKING. IT'S A MATTER OF TIME TILL SOME FOOL MAYOR LEARNS OF IT, CLAIMS IT, THEN WE'VE A NEW WAR-LOVING LORD TO CONTEND WITH. NOT WHILE I'VE GOT STRENGTH IN ME TO WRING A NECK OR TWO. IF THAT FOOL ARCH MAGE IS ABOUT, HIS IS FIRST FOR WRINGING, AND WITH ALL HE'S DONE TO DESERVE FAR WORSE, CALL HIM LUCKY IF I SHOULD FIND HIM. HE'S GONE AND MADE HIS GOD, LOUP! I NEVER THOUGHT HE'D DO IT. HOW LONG DO YOU THINK TILL HE BEGINS HIS NEXT? AND THE NEXT WILL BE HIMSELF, IF HE'S NOT STOPPED.'

Lut crouched by the pool of water. Gold light radiated around it. He stuck a finger in just as Faul turned to tell him not to. 'Warm,' he called. He cupped a palmful of it to his lips, sipped it. 'Only water,' he said, shrugging. 'Tastes clean. Real clean.'

'BE WARY!' Faul cried.

Loup pondered that, but he was suddenly tired of being wary. How many more years of life did he really need? He dived head-first into the golden pool. 'Water's warm,' he called when his head emerged, gums bared in a wide grin. 'Ease up, Faul. I'll be out soon, then I'll come along with you. Back to the castle, fine. But what's the point in anything, if you can't stop and admire something pretty, now and then?' He splashed water at old Case, who'd lowered himself by the stream to cautiously lap at it with his tongue.

'OH, GO ON THEN,' Faul boomed at Lut, who looked at her plaintively. 'TEN MINUTES.'

He smiled through his beard, ran to the pool and jumped in.

8

THE HAIYENS

Siel dreamed. It was a sleep sliding her gently and patiently into death. The deep dreaming part of her which knew of her coming death went along gladly with the slide's easy, gentle momentum. It put up no fight, for now she did not have to deal with the pain of the wounds Shadow had inflicted when he'd bounced her off the stone. Nor had she to bother with the trouble of long slow healing, all to go back to a thankless world which would only open its arms to her again like a cruel mother.

About her limp body in the glen was the hissing slide of swords from their sheaths. There were panicked shouts of the mayor's men, a fight beginning. But those sounds were just jarring notes against a song which had begun around her. Strange music reached to Siel in her dream. It sought her out from the place she was sliding to; assured her she need not leave this body yet, that her healing need not be painful. There was more to learn here, the music said, more to experience. Worthwhile things – that was a promise. The music played about her as would a stream of warm water; it poured over her as if gushing from the holes of a flute, fat raindrops beating down on drum skins, interspersed with cries like bird calls, full of joy.

She did not hear the fight breaking out, the men shouting,

a body falling into the soft undergrowth nearby. She knew only the music a friend played for her, only the strange and powerful music which coaxed her tenderly back from the brink of death, knitting together where the skin had split and where the bone had cracked.

Far Gaze had heard Siel crack against the slab of rock, and he'd thought right away that was that. No stranger to violence in a vast number of forms (victim, witness and inflictor), he was nonetheless ill to see her slender body bounce on impact, to actually *bounce*. He knew at once her back was probably broken, maybe her neck too by the way she landed and the tilt of her head.

Nor was Far Gaze especially prone to sentiment – those who were had picked the wrong world to try and survive in. But as companions went, Siel had not once pestered him to frivolously cast magic, and one could be fairly sure she'd not be the first to flee if a fight went bad. The sight of her lying limp, dead soon if not already, did not please him at all.

A blur tore across the ground away from her. The trail of heat left behind it was intense enough to be felt for a second or two even from where he stood, at the mouth of the cave. A flash of fire shot up along the trail but on the mossy damp turf it did not last long.

Far Gaze knew immediately it was Shadow. Shadow too had made those screaming sounds which had brought him and Gorb to the cave mouth in the first place, and had brought the mayor and his men running up the tunnel back towards them (their scuffing feet echoing on the cave walls so it sounded like a hundred or more of them came, rather than a half-dozen).

Far Gaze ran the short distance down to Siel's body and saw

his concerns were founded. He contemplated finishing her off in mercy, but true warriors never wanted to die that way – true warriors viewed their whole lives as preparation for their death, and would sometimes curse those who ruined the moment. But he could certainly not heal her. Very few natural illnesses could outwit him, especially in the young and strong, but he knew not enough of healing to instantly mend someone's spine in two places and patch together a skull. He doubted any mages did. He called to Gorb, 'Can you heal, giant?'

Gorb came over, crouched down and ran a thick thumb across her arm. Tears crept down his cheeks' fat slabs. 'I'm no wizard. Couldn't heal my dogs; can't heal this.'

'What have you done?' came the Tantonese mayor's accusing voice from the cave mouth. Tauk the Strong strode over with his six men in tow, two unsheathing their swords, boots slamming down through knee-high ferns.

Far Gaze shivered with sour distaste. Mayor of the entire world, he thought. Now was not the time to approach a half-giant with weapons drawn. Quietly he said, 'Gorb, remain calm, whatever they say or do. These men have been through a lot and are not thinking properly. That mayor owes me massive debts and I mean to claim them. You'll have a share. He's worth little to us dead.'

Gorb did not seem to have even noticed the men. He still traced a finger gently over Siel's arm and spilled tears on the mossy stones he kneeled on. Siel's eyelids fluttered, her face at peace and looking younger than it had before.

'Answer the mayor,' demanded one of Tauk's men.

'What for? Don't you trust your eyes?' said Far Gaze. 'Clearly the giant and I have committed murder.'

The mayor raised an arm to calm and restrain his men but

anger blazed in his own eyes too. 'We have suffered enough fear and loss on this journey, and I have had enough cheek from you, mage.'

There was not time to shape-shift into his wolf form, which would make either fight or flight an easy enough business. But even in human form there were things Far Gaze could do. He breathed deep through his nose the green glen's troubled airs. The glen's magic sat within his body and spirit as a fluttering moth would sit in his cupped hands. The little glen itself seemed to flow into him, all its long lazy days. He knew it intimately, as if he'd spent a hundred or more years among its mossy stones and burbling water. He knew now its morning bird calls, and what things prowled through it at night. He knew which ways he could run, ways where the men – if they chased – would fall, twist their ankles. He knew where to lead them into creatures that would prey on them, if they pursued far enough, knew a dozen nearby places where he could hide himself completely. His normally grey eyes and greying hair tinged with the green of its ferns.

Gorb seemed to notice the approaching men for the first time. He slowly turned, stood, frowned at their drawn weapons. Immediately a small black shape flew at him, stuck on the hand he used to bat it away. A dart. There was time only for the half-giant's face to cloud with anger before he slumped forwards to his knees and joined Siel in unconsciousness.

Far Gaze's mouth hung open in disbelief. 'And what was gained by this?' he said.

'A precaution,' explained the man who'd blown the dart, putting the flute-like instrument away. The man's eyes were lowered with shame.

'You had better not be here when he wakes,' said Far Gaze.

'He's right. You will go back to our city,' said Tauk quietly to the man. 'Above ground, by road. Say nothing of us, nor where you have been.'

The man looked stricken. 'He won't go,' said Far Gaze matter-of-factly. 'He'll abandon you, sell information about you and live as a free man.' He did not know whether or not this prediction was accurate – it was a guess, no more. The trust people put in magicians' predictions, promises and threats was a constant source of amusement, and some compensation for being pestered to cast. Far Gaze watched the ensuing argument among the men with pleasure.

Although it was now clear Tauk's men would not fight him, the spell of kinship was still active in him. The glen whispered something to him he did not understand. His confusion must have shown. One of the men paused his shouting to look at Far Gaze and say, 'Now what stirs you, mage?'

'Something else is here,' he replied, turning full circle and staring about the glen's walls of trees and vines. The glen itself seemed watchful, anxious; it seemed to flex and brace itself in resistance to something unknown, as it would to a sudden shift in weather, an unexpected storm. 'What is it?' demanded the mayor, sensing more games. 'You said the Tormentors had all fled north!'

'It is not those creatures. It is something unknown. The glen itself is nervous . . .' But then there they were, as suddenly as if having sprung from the ground. Not Tormentors – they were five, then six beings of slender build. People, it seemed at first glance, each wearing full-length hooded robes of varying green and brown shades. Two of them pulled back their hoods. Their heads and faces bore no hair at all. Their eyes were oval-shaped and larger than human eyes, their ears flat to their heads, their mouths almost lipless. They looked frail, neither feminine nor masculine. They gazed up at the mayor's men, something discernible only by the backwards tilt of their heads, for those oval-shaped eyes – from a distance, at least – looked blank, the same colour as their skin.

The men stared down at them in turn. Everything was very still. The spell within Far Gaze commanded him to flee, for nature seldom trusts what it doesn't know, and these things had never in history set foot in these woods, nor (Far Gaze assumed) had they set foot beyond World's End at all.

Far Gaze did not run. He knew, long before Tauk's men would consider it, that these beings had not shown themselves for a battle. But he also knew the men's mood and was not at all surprised, looking back later, that a battle unfolded.

Two of the newcomers reached inside pockets of their gowns, producing instruments. One was a spherical black ball; the other appeared to be a baton, long as a man's forearm, with twisted knots on its ends. When those two beings crouched beside Siel's body, the mayor's men screamed and charged. They were led by the one the mayor had banished and whom Far Gaze had lied about, for that man was now all too eager to prove his loyalty by spilling enemy blood.

The beings did not move until Tauk's men had almost charged upon them. The one with the baton stood up, away from Siel's body, and swung his instrument quickly, making it a wheel-shaped blur. This was the point, looking back, that Far Gaze's memory went from a clear chronology to a jumbled mess of images and sounds, as if the events were all a deck of picture cards spilled across a table then scooped up again. He remembered the newcomers standing motionless right up until the swords swung down on them; recalled them cringing away, crying out with high voices, perhaps not comprehending until that very moment that they were under attack. He recalled one of them falling back, surely dead with a slashed wound from shoulder to hip, two shades of blood gushing out, one much lighter than human, the other almost black. And the men lunging furiously at the others, till they were repelled by something invisible that seemed to shove them hard every time they came near, till they were all pulled around like boats in a whirlpool, unable to break out of it. One man gored another by accident in the confusion.

Far Gaze recalled music of a kind he'd never heard, a fast little crescendo which only hurt his ears, but killed the man nearest to the newcomers. Killed him neatly, without mess or fuss: just like that, he dropped down, dead.

The remaining men fled while the mayor himself stood grimly watching it all. One of the fleeing men brayed that Tauk had not fought, that he'd mistaken him for a warrior, once. Tauk yelled back he'd given *them* no order to fight and could not govern the wits of a determined fool.

Far Gaze fled the glen. The mayor's men found him later, the group of them panting, wounded and frightened, almost having forgotten the possibility of Tormentors in the area.

All these things happened in a different order each time Far Gaze (and the other men) tried to remember them. Chronology resumed again from that point on: the mayor and the man who'd yelled at him, off having quiet words away from the group. Which was to say the mayor himself doing the talking, and offering the man the chance to reappraise whether Tauk was a warrior or not, with sword in hand, right now, one of Tauk's arms injured or not. The chastised man hung his head, bent to one knee, offered his neck, a gesture Far Gaze had not witnessed before but which made sense to him, with what else he knew of Tanton's warrior culture. After that, it appeared all was forgiven between them.

The group of them went back to the glen, having vowed to slay the strange people, despite whatever magic they wielded. 'Are you with us?' Tauk demanded of Far Gaze, his remaining men pressing in around him with weapons at hand.

Far Gaze met the mayor's eye, solemnly agreed he was with them, meaning only to follow at a safe distance then take the valuables from their foolish corpses. Perhaps he'd take Tauk's head too, with spells of preservation upon it in the same way one preserved meat on journeys. He envisioned going to High Cliffs or maybe Yinfel, burying the head nearby, asking a price for the mayor of Tanton's head, receiving scoffs and astronomical offers. Then after a day or two's rest, he'd return with the head and collect. A debt was a debt.

But in the glen there was no second battle, for there was no sign of the other peoples. Except for the one slain, who lay with arms arranged in a way clearly deliberate: one flat by his side, palm down, the other across his chest. Five strangely coloured flowers had grown about his head of a kind Far Gaze had not before seen.

More surprisingly, Siel lay nearby, but not as she'd lain before. Her hair was dirty with dried blood, but she was quite alive. She peered groggily at the men as would a drunkard. She tried to speak but, like a drunkard, threw up instead down the front of her shirt then fell back again, sleeping. Gorb had not yet woken from his poisoned slumber and lay exactly as everyone had left him, none the wiser.

Upon seeing Siel, Far Gaze was surprised by the quick bloom of joy that went through him – surprised, that is, by its intensity, which easily countered the disappointment he'd felt to learn that there'd be no trip north or east with the head of Tauk the Strong. (At least not without bringing the rest of him too, alive and well.)

9

TO THE TOWER

The poor tired mayor was faced with yet more decisions as the men ate from their provisions. 'Your counsel, mage?' Tauk said at last, turning to Far Gaze his bloodshot eyes.

Far Gaze spoke in the quiet, ominous and indifferent tones an advisor would use, careful now not to needle the mayor's pride. 'Your city's fate is now beyond what you do. If you return there, you will find citizens being butchered by the last men ever to fight in castle colours. Or perhaps you'll find the city held its own, without you there to guide it. That brings political consequences you don't need me to spell out.'

'Say them anyway.'

'As you like. You'll have missed your city's direst hour in generations. Many will say you are no longer needed. Worse, some will claim you fled in fear, anticipating the city's loss . . . that you returned only when it was safe. You had best return there in secret, if at all, and then keep a close eye on your generals. If it turns out your city has won, that you return and are by some miracle still accepted as mayor, your next threat is High Cliffs.'

'Why them?'

'Simply because they are closest. Then you must worry about

the other cities. When they learn what has become of the castle's armies, I think you may guess what will occur to all the mayors. There is a power vacuum to be filled. You know history well, Tauk the Strong. It's unlucky your city had to bear the final wound of *this* war, right before another begins, without time to rest and feed your weary, wounded men. And without time to replenish your city's food stocks.'

Tauk, if it were possible, looked yet more sober and exhausted. 'I know you have no need to lie or mislead me.'

'Indeed not. You owe me your life, and the lives of six trusted men. Expensive lives, all of them. I want you safely in charge of a rich, prosperous city.'

'Yet it would seem I cannot return there.'

'Not openly, Tauk. And if possible it must not be known you ever left. And that's *if* Tanton survives the battle it fights while we speak here. The next battles are soon to come, if today's allies become opportunists.'

'Where go you, mage?' asked one of Tauk's men.

'To the tower I came from, before I met you all. To speak with the wizard I have heard lives there.'

'To ask him of the new people?' said another of the men, when the mayor didn't respond.

'Among much else, yes.'

'What's to ask?' said Tauk. 'It's plain we have a new enemy.'

'Enemies do not heal each other.' Far Gaze looked pointedly at Siel, sleeping under a blanket.

'Indeed. We do not know what they did to the girl,' said Tauk thoughtfully. 'Did they enchant her? Possess her? Infect her with something that will spread among all our people? Do you know any more than I do of their magic? If you do, you've not said so.'

'I know not *whether* they use magic, not as we know it. When it was cast, the airs were not affected.'

'And that is all you know? Very well. We shall take the girl with us till she is recovered, and observe her. We'll take that body too,' he said, pointing at the corpse of the slain one. 'And we will depart this hour, before the giant awakens to discover he was poisoned.'

Far Gaze supposed that at least the mayor had not suggested killing Gorb where he lay. And unlike some mayors, he at least seemed willing to digest an unpalatable truth or two. Yet a look had come into Tauk's eyes Far Gaze did not like at all. He'd seen it before: the very moment a man of power has discovered the way a situation may be used, and all else be fed to Inferno. Whether the new people brought immense gifts, or whether they were as the mayor feared a grave threat, from now on any argument would be moot until Tauk had what he wanted.

Far Gaze could quite easily have predicted Tauk's next remarks before they came: 'The castle threat may have weakened, or gone away altogether. But a new one rises from the South world. The cities need each other, mage. Now more than ever. This is no time to attack Tanton! The other cities will be told of this new threat.'

Far Gaze inclined his head as would an advisor at court. 'And should we come upon more of the new people, whatever and whoever they truly are?'

'That is easily answered,' said the mayor, steel in his eyes. He turned to his men, pointed at one of them. 'Go at once to our city. Take the secret routes. You have the pass tokens? Good. Tell the generals of this new threat.'

'And if the city is lost?' the man said.

'Then all is done and nothing more matters.' To another of

his men he said, 'Go to High Cliffs. Tell Ousan the same, that the new people prepare for war, that we must stand together, or surely we shall fall. Do not tell him where I have been nor who goes with me. Take this, so he knows your words come from my mouth.' Tauk rummaged in one pocket for a specially marked coin. 'Do this, and you will be a wealthy man for your remaining years. Your grandsons too.'

'I need no more incentive than love for my city,' the man replied, a catch in his voice.

'Does he speak truth?' Tauk asked Far Gaze.

Far Gaze rubbed his chin, pretended to appraise the man. 'He does. Mayor, a word?'

Tauk dismissed the men with a wave. One went to retrieve the dart still stuck in Gorb's hand. Far Gaze said, 'There is a law, Mayor, penned by no man, woman, wizard, or Spirit. It is called the law of unintended consequences.'

'The law of survival overrules it,' said Tauk, steel in his eyes again.

'Verily. You may be breaching *that* law too, if you attack the new peoples, and if you encourage other cities to attack them. You may create an enemy where there was not one before.'

'Exactly,' said Tauk with a smile.

'It seems . . . extravagant, Tauk the Strong, for a hedge against fights with a neighbour, to begin a war between worlds. One's city is an important consideration; surely one's world is a higher one yet. We do not yet know the new people. It may be they are great friends to us, if we allow them to be. You and your city may be the first to welcome them and gain their favour.'

Tauk put a hand on Far Gaze's shoulder, the weight of his arm's muscle heavy. 'Mage, they have come to *our* world, *our* home. It is not for us to prove them friends.'

'Perhaps in healing Siel they already have.'

Tauk scoffed. 'No! They must declare themselves in our tongue. And then prove it! And pay whatever homage we deem they owe for their trespass. You have seen all else that has come from that place, mage! All else brings death, terror and poison.' Tauk's tone said the matter was settled. 'Whatever way history turns on my decisions, you as a witness may have a hand in its telling, mage. You will speak in truth of what I have done.'

Far Gaze quelled the anger building in him. Men like Tauk, all of them, thought in such terms: as if 'history' were a living judge ever witnessing their deeds, a damsel to impress, a class-room filled with tomorrow's great rulers, eagerly studying their every word and deed.

'You will accompany me to the wizard's tower,' said Tauk, squaring his shoulders to show it was an order, not an invitation.

'Certainly,' said Far Gaze with his advisor's head-tilt again. 'Although I know nothing of the wizard there. I shall shift form, Mayor. You may tie the girl to my back.'

'So you may run off with her? No,' said Tauk. Far Gaze had indeed considered doing just that – again he had to hide his flaring rage. 'I will carry her on my steed, if the beast can be found. And you will remain a man, not a wolf, so that I may speak with you if I need to. We leave at once.'

'And the half-giant?'

'He will wake in an hour or two. I wish to be nowhere near him when that happens.'

'Very wise,' said Far Gaze, bowing low, privately seething.

While the steeds were brought round (a difficult job, finding a safe path for them through the soft and often slippery damp ground), they examined the newcomer's slain body. The throat had a windpipe for speech, ears for hearing, a nose. Two small neat holes were beneath the ears at the jaw's edge, whose purpose Far Gaze couldn't guess. (Breathing under water? Something else?) The eyes were not blank as they seemed from a distance; they were a slightly lighter shade than the skin, with a dark point in the middle. This one's skin had gone greyish and chalky in death. In life it had been a creamier tone, in places the very lightest shade of brown. It did not seem to possess a sex. Opening the sword wound that had killed it, he saw what must be the heart in the dead centre of its chest. It appeared better protected by a plate of either bone or hard cartilage than was the human heart protected by its sternum.

'Shall you cast to preserve it, mage?'

'No. Let's see how it decays, compared to the flesh of Tormentors. Mayor, I suspect they left the body here as a gift for us.'

'Why would they do such a thing?'

'For us to do what we are doing now. Examine it and understand them.'

Tauk spat in irritation. 'They left bodies of my men here too. A generous people. Just how do you know their intent? It may be for religious reasons, to leave one of their slain where he was killed. Some who swear to Valour and Nightmare do similar things. It may be they were simply burdened already, and could not carry more.'

When the horses arrived the men quickly packed, eager to be away from Gorb before he woke. The half-giant hadn't moved at all. Far Gaze itched to leave him a written note but had no materials for it, and the mayor's men were watching him . . . subtly enough, but they wanted him to know it.

Siel hadn't woken. Far Gaze removed her soiled shirt, dressed her in a fresher one from her pack and insisted upon riding a steed with her until Tauk consented. From then on Tauk's men watched Far Gaze's every move with suspicion. Wise, he reflected.

10

THE HALF-GIANT RISES

Half an hour later Gorb woke, stretched, scratched his head and looked about in confusion. An insect had bitten his hand and left a nasty mark. He peered at the wound, trying to judge what had bitten him – an odd-looking bite! Powerful poison. He didn't remember much at all.

Bald's weeping burbled from the cave mouth, the way he cried when he'd had nightmares. It wasn't how he cried when in danger, so Gorb relaxed.

How strange the men had all left without him, and that – as he saw when going back to the cave – they'd neglected to take with them the guns Bald had made. The temptation to take the guns while Gorb slept must have been enormous.

Maybe he'd misjudged the mayor after all, and misjudged his men. Maybe they *were* good people, men of honour. Guilt flushed through him as fast and profound as any rage he'd ever felt. Guess I owe the man a favour, he thought with a sigh. 'Come on, Bald, it's a long way to Tanton. We'd best head off,' he said. And they did just that.

11

WESTWARDS

The stoneflesh giants over each horizon stood motionless, so tall they hardly seemed real. Most faced south, clearly still roused, but they gazed into that foreign land with the same infinite patience they'd had when the Wall stood.

The countryside was a strewn mess of broken wagons, dropped belongings, corpses of humans, horses and Tormentors. The piles of their remains here and there were like funeral displays made from glossy polished black stone. It appeared the bodies had been shattered by tremendous blows.

At a gentle pace for their overworked horses, they went by a trading route which was part paved stone, part beaten-dirt track. To their left, the red veil at World's End had almost entirely cleared, showing a sky the same colour as their own. Beneath that sky were plains of smooth glassy rock, eventually rising up to wall-like hillsides, alive all over with twisting tendrils of fog. Occasional rock structures jutted through the flats, some human-sized, some much larger, all of which seemed to have been sculpted by something's hands rather than by time and nature.

Tauk rode with his face almost completely covered in a hood, lest he be seen by men of other cities and discovered so far from his home. Only two of Tauk's men remained with them, and both were showing signs of madness, the kind felt by hunted creatures. Their eyes seldom left the new southern land being revealed, as if they expected an army of terrors to charge through the long gaps between stoneflesh giants. Now and then both men furtively glanced at the foreign being's corpse slung on the mayor's horse and covered with blankets. They looked just as anxiously at Siel, who rode with Far Gaze's arms about her, the reins in his hands, her head flopping forwards on her chest.

Further west, Levaal South showed a clutch of sheer hills that leaned towards one another like a conspiring group. A river trickled between them then curled towards the boundary before it turned abruptly away, not wishing to share its water with strangers from the north. Far Gaze did not himself feel the men's fear, but he too felt a certain strange stillness in the south. It was not watchful, not brooding, just stillness itself: the land like an ocean turned to ice or stone, motionless when the eye expected to see motion.

Far Gaze waited for Siel to come fully awake. The new people's healing had kept her asleep, he was sure, for there'd been noise and motion enough to wake her many times. When at last she stirred he whispered in her ear: 'Maintain the look of someone drugged and dazed. Feign sleep. The mayor and his men are going insane. They watch us closely. They will question you. Now is not the time to speak with them of the unknown. Do not argue with what I'm telling you now, or I won't defend you. Speak with me later. We may need to flee them. But first I need rest as much as they do.'

She gave no indication of having heard. He knew that she had.

*

When the day's ride finally ended it was a mercy. Another full day at that pace would bring them to Gorb's village and the tower. 'Is this spot safe?' said Tauk of the incline upon which they made camp.

'Yes,' said Far Gaze solemnly, not knowing whether or not it was, and hardly caring. The night was cold enough to frost their breaths – indeed the weather had got cooler since the Wall fell. The men spoke little, ate from provisions and of foraged roots, their eyes ever suspicious over the embers of a small fire. Far Gaze laid his blanket over Siel. 'Where does the girl lie tonight?' asked one of the men, his question not as casual as it sounded.

Far Gaze met his eyes. 'Pass me your food. I'll bless it for taste.'

The man drew back, shielding his bowl. Tauk smiled at Far Gaze and laid a hand on the man's arm. 'You need not fear my men. These are hard times; the road's been cruel to us. But we'll not forget our honour.'

Far Gaze sipped from his bowl. 'I never doubted it.'

They put out the fire and soon the men snored. Far Gaze went under Siel's blanket and shook her gently awake. Their heads close together, they spoke in hardly more than breaths. He studied her closer than she probably knew, seeking any sign of change in her. 'How were you healed?' he whispered.

'Do you expect me to explain their arts?'

'I see they have not changed you overmuch. Tell me all that you remember.'

She paused. 'After I fell . . . I was dreaming of strange realms. I don't remember much of it now.'

'Lands in the south?'

He felt her shrug. 'Then there was something rushing around

me like water from a flood. It was sound, but I could feel it as if it was water.'

'Was it music?'

'Yes. It carried me from one dream to another, as if each place we stopped bore a signpost on the way back to here, to being awake and alive. I can explain it no better. The music seemed to promise I would return to those places. It was strange, but it made me happy. Then I woke in pain.'

He hadn't told her the extent of her injuries, but maybe she'd guessed. 'What was the music like?'

She struggled for words. 'Different from music we know. Maybe the Pilgrim has heard its like, I don't know. If I concentrate I can still hear parts of it, faintly. It makes me think of lush places where things grow.'

'And when you woke, what did you see?'

'There were two of the new people near me. One had a little reed, or something like it. He blew into it. My eyes opened as the last notes came. It did not sound in waking like it had in sleep. It was thin and high, not very pleasant. Seeming to press into my head almost like someone's hands. In sleep it was all around me, sounded very different. The other one, he had something in his hands he wished to hide from me. I didn't see what it was.'

He thought of the little black sphere he'd seen in one of the new people's hands. 'You are well, now?'

'Aches, dizziness. I feel strange. Not sick, not well. I hope it passes.'

'Your thinking? It's as normal?'

'I don't know.'

'How do you feel about the new people?'

She didn't answer for a moment or two – fine instincts for

a trap, had Siel. 'I know nothing of them,' she said. 'No more than you.'

'That's not what I asked you.'

'That's the answer you're getting.'

'Why did Shadow attack you?'

He felt her shudder. 'Don't speak of him.'

'You have seen worse terrors than him, I am sure. Why such fear of Shadow?'

'He can travel across the world in moments! He's got some sort of . . . attachment to me. He may come here, tonight. His powers are greater than yours, far greater. You could not stop him if he came here. We must go back to the tower. Now. He cannot reach me within it.'

'No.'

'Why not?'

'Lower your voice! If I sneak away, these men will take it as an act of war. Did you not see their mood today? The mayor's city is in dire peril. More accurately, his power is. They say he is a good man, as mayors go. Invite them to leave their high seat, you see a certain . . . kinship.'

'I know your opinions of our leaders well enough. Stay if you wish. I'm going.'

'If they find I've let you leave, they'll cut my throat.' He pondered. 'Attempt to, anyway.'

'You fought a dragon. I think you can handle three men.'

A dragon who did not truly wish to kill me, he thought. 'No mage is immune to an arrow or sword edge when he sleeps. I do not wish to travel in constant alertness! I must be free to meditate.'

'They'll not hold you accountable for my fleeing. I will take a steed and be four hours ahead of you before they wake,' she said. He knew there was no point arguing with her. He considered casting to make Siel sleep. 'What will you do?' she said, already eager to leave.

'These men are half mad. It would please me to be free of them. But with each day I keep them alive the mayor's debt grows greater. He will remember it when times are less perilous and sanity returns. He will owe me much of his city by the time he returns there. Far more than he can pay.'

'Do you really feel such a debt is apt to be honoured?'

'I do indeed. Or he will never have peace for the rest of his days, wondering in what shape and form the oath-breaker's curse will come. Whatever things he treasures most, he will fear most for and never love those things again. Be it his offspring, his wealth, his fate after death, or all of these together. Should he honour a tenth of what I claim, I will be content.' He contemplated the off-chance of Siel meeting up with Gorb again. 'And of course, I owe the giant a share, which I'll pay. Leave, if you must. Take the grey stallion; they use the other as a pack horse. Go now. And silently!'

'They go where we go. Why should it matter so much that I leave? Am I free or a prisoner?'

'Until they know what the new peoples did to you, you are neither. You are regarded as property.'

'The "new peoples" healed me from death,' she said with feeling.

And made a friend of you, I see, he thought. Aloud he said, 'Tell the wizard to prepare for guests who are going mad. *If* indeed he allows us back in his home. Take care when you return there. Remember, the waters about the tower can boil.'

12

WHERE DID SHE GO?

Far Gaze had assumed the night's rest would do at least something to cure the men's anxieties, even when they rose to find Siel had fled. But rough hands lifted him to his feet and out of sleep, the blanket still wrapped about him. The circle of protection he'd cast about where he slept had evidently failed to take hold thanks to the polluted airs. A blade was at his throat, the point of another between his shoulders.

Sour morning breath poured over him. 'Where is she?' someone demanded.

It was not yet light. 'Who?' he said, yawning.

The hands gripping him clenched harder. 'What do you mean *who*? How many women did we camp with? She's gone. A stallion with her.'

'I see. Take me to the place the horse was tied. I may tell you more.' The hands released him.

Tauk was still a sleeping bundle near the dead campfire. His two men – Vade and Fithlim, if Far Gaze remembered their names right – put their weapons away but watched him closely while he crouched near the spot, closed his eyes, hummed and murmured, waved his hands in imitation of magic gestures. 'Ah,' he said at last.

'What have you learned?'

'The winds, the very grass blades, tell me she has gone to the same place we go.'

One of the men, Vade, detected the faint sarcasm in his tone. He reached again for his weapon. 'Why does she go there?'

'I don't know.'

'This wizard you claim is there. What does he look like? From where does he come?'

'I don't know.'

'But you are certain he exists?'

'I am not certain I exist, let alone him.'

This brought weapons out of their sheaths again. But the mayor had woken and was now on his feet. The other two rushed over to tell him what had happened. All three looked at Far Gaze with renewed suspicion, but at least they put their swords away.

'We depart,' Tauk called over. He said it like an edict from the gods, as if all Levaal depended on them packing their blankets and leaving this patch of grass now rather than in an hour's time. Far Gaze's lip curled, but he bowed low.

They'd put a mile behind them before day had whitened the sky, hooves thumping the road with a beat more urgent than yesterday's. Huge on the horizon loomed a stoneflesh giant, its torso twisting just slightly, perhaps to follow their passage. They were now near to those fields where a Tormentor had taken them by surprise in the night, and nearly killed Siel. The ruins of wagons and bodies both human and Tormentor littered the fields to both sides. What had happened to the humans was clear enough, but there was no indication at all of what had slain the Tormentors.

As if he could see Far Gaze's memory of Gorb blowing a

Tormentor apart with one of his guns, Tauk sat upright in his horse and cried in dismay: 'The weapons! The giant's weapons! Inferno eat us all! We forgot to bring them!'

There was no going back, of course. The three men stayed quiet, allowing Far Gaze some welcome time for reflection. To his eye, heavy blows had slain the Tormentors along the road. The stoneflesh giants couldn't have done it – they moved too slowly and the racket would have been heard halfway across the world. There was no obvious sign on the ground of any struggle, nor had the airs any lingering effects from spell casting . . .

The strange southern land continued to reveal itself through coils of white mist. Here and there on its flat expanse were what may have been homes constructed within crescent shells of stone, their insides made of vines, ferns, flowers and hanging teardrop-shaped leaves, with ponds of clear water in the middle of their floors. If they were homes, there was no sight of who or what lived in them. The stone ocean they sat upon stretched as far as sight.

One of the men – Vade – cried out and drew his weapon. He pointed to the south, where in the mist they could make out people standing in a line of five, upon a wave-like rise in the stone desert's floor. 'Them!' Vade screamed. He turned his horse, sword raised, and looked ready to charge over till Tauk snatched the reins from his hand.

'Be still,' the mayor commanded.

All four of them stared at the new people. The new people stared back. They wore the same kind of brown-green robes as the earlier group, if indeed these weren't the same ones. Far Gaze raised an arm in greeting but got no response. A coil of mist rose about them, veiling them from view. When it settled the new people could not be seen.

Fithlim waved his sword, stared about them, screamed, 'They're here!'

Tauk drew his own blade, swung it in a figure eight.

Vade rounded on Far Gaze. 'You waved to them,' he said. 'You told them to come here! Where are they, mage? How long have you been in league with them?'

Far Gaze groaned. 'Tauk! Your men become a burden to us. Reel in their passions or I shall have to.'

'The mage betrays us!' cried Fithlim, charging. Far Gaze lurched back from the swipe of his blade but only just. Anger filled him fast and dangerous. He was not even aware of what he cast – he knew only of a flare of red briefly consuming his vision. Afterwards Fithlim – whose sword had drawn back for another slash – fell onto the ground and writhed, clutching his ribs.

Instantly the burn flushed through Far Gaze, with a feeling like fists pressing his temples almost hard enough to bend his skull. For a brief time he was in more pain than the man he'd cast upon. Its intensity eased but spread through the rest of him. The seconds crawled slowly as it passed. The spell would not have taxed him this badly in wolf-form; human bodies were just not made for such magic.

Fithlim's and Vade's horses both cantered away, spooked by the hot wind which had accompanied the spell. A second rush of wind passed through them, but it had nothing to do with Far Gaze. With it was the cry of a playful whinny, musical to hear. An explosion of colour rippled across a length of scaly flesh, there among them only for an instant. The horses bolted, tipping off their riders.

Far Gaze alone saw clearly who, and what, had swooped down on them: Dyan the dragon, with Stranger and a second woman upon his back. Dyan flew up into the clouds in a fast smooth arc. Far Gaze understood the meaning of the playful whinnying cry: *'Hello, wolf!'*

The burn faded out of him at last. He ignored the hysterical questions of the men, and Fithlim's cries for healing. He went instead to find and calm his horse, in the process pondering whether the mayor and his debt were worth the trouble. I will make sure they are, he thought, licking his teeth.

13

BLAIN AND HIS UNDERLING

In a clearing in the woods by the wizard's tower, Strategist Blain tugged his beard, glancing from the Invia to Kiown and thinking fast. His life had become a cascade of bad luck: outwitted by Domudess without a spell needed; thousands of troops vanished, his best Hunter now dragon meat, his remaining Hunter stupid enough to attack and steal from Invia! Now they had to flee before the damned thing woke up, or it would tear them both to shreds.

A glance at the object Kiown had snatched from the Invia's body showed at once the thing was crafted by one of Levaal's great powers, almost certainly a dragon. It looked plain enough to normal eyes, as the great charms often did; in the Hunter's hand a pendant of thin black metal hung on a loop of chain, with a rectangular stone set in its middle. The stone was blue, but the colour changed in similar fashion to the way colours shifted on Blain's own Strategist robe.

Kiown stared down at the pendant, mouth hanging open. His eyes were wide. There was no doubt he was in love with the thing already.

Easy does it, Blain thought, though he'd begun to sweat. Don't panic. It will change him, whatever it is. But not all at once.

Blain tugged at his beard and murmured a quick incantation to master himself. The light that began to flash in Kiown's eyes disturbed him. It went from white to violet then went out altogether.

Blain stepped towards him, walking stick raised as though to punish an underling; in truth he needed to see if Kiown still *was* an underling. 'Idiot!' he said. 'Do you know what you've just picked up?'

Kiown did not seem to hear. He stared at the pendant's stone.

'That thing is of dragon-make!' Blain cried. His robe flashed fiery crimson. 'Nor was it made by any Minor dragon. Humans should not reach out and snatch such things like biscuits from mother's pantry.' His staff shook in his hand; his knuckles were white.

Kiown looked at him. That hint of violet was in his eyes again, there then gone. He stood up. The amulet's chain clutched his wrist like a closed trap. Carefully – lovingly, Blain thought – he peeled the thin black chain away and swung the amulet on his finger. Round and round it went, the stone flashing. 'Would you like to hold the amulet, Strategist?' Kiown asked politely, an air of innocence about him. He extended the amulet on his palm.

O marvellous, Blain thought, wiping his brow. I thought I was the tyrant here. He looked towards the tower, just visible over the treetops. Domudess's window was not in view. Blain cleared his throat, stalling. 'What about that?' he said, pointing down at the unmoving Invia Kiown's poisoned knife had felled from the tree. 'You think it might not wake and claim back its trinket?'

Kiown mock-bowed, produced a knife from his boot. He pulled the Invia's head back by its hair and swiftly cut its throat. Unconscious at the point of death, it did not cry out.

'Have you a death wish?' Blain yelled, forgetting caution. 'We don't know how many more of them are about. Not just them – a dragon's nearby too!'

'O. A dragon.' For some reason the taller young man smiled.

'At least get the pretty thing's blood, now it's dead,' said Blain, crouching to catch the blood in his hands. Tiny glimmering things like crushed diamond dust flowed in the dark fluid. 'Useful stuff,' Blain murmured. 'Good for potions. Your pack? A container?'

Kiown ignored him, giving the corpse a shove with his boot. He paced back and forth, deep in thought, leaves and sticks crunching under his boots. Now and then the violet-white light flicked on in his eyes. Blain watched him, letting the Invia's blood spill on his robe to soak in. He'd be able to suck it out of the fabric, still potent even when it became days old. The rare liquid was good for far more than just potions, of course, but there was a reason he'd kept that fact hidden.

'Interesting!' said Kiown in conversation with himself.

'What's interesting? Death by dragon rage, does that interest you? Did you see Thaun's body? I should say *bodies*, plural. That's what dragons do when men displease them.'

'Mind-control,' Kiown said, tapping himself on the forehead. He turned back to Blain with a smile. 'I didn't know that you'd set mind-control in place on me.'

'That was years ago!' Blain spluttered.

'I'd taken my fierce loyalty to Vous to be a virtue. You must use mind-control with all Hunters. Yes?'

'Your loyalty *is* a virtue,' said Blain in hurt tones. 'A grand virtue. He is our Friend and Lord.'

Kiown chuckled as if to say *touché*, then resumed pacing, the cone of his hair flopping behind him like a strangely made crown. He said, 'What's interesting is, I am *aware* now of the mind-control. But that does not cancel the loyalty the mind-control causes in me. I still love him.' He stroked the amulet's stone. It responded to his touch with faint pulses of colour. 'And now I am conflicted, Strategist. I am fiercely loyal to Vous, and must remain so. Your mind-control, I now see, will kill me the instant something tries to remove it.'

'It was Avridis's work, not mine,' said Blain. A lie of course – Blain and the other Strategists had developed this magic, the utterly inescapable death-trap designed to keep valuable Hunters from ending up in service to Rebel Cities. He said, 'But that aside, you're right. Tamper with that mind-control and it will kick your brain to slop.' The Invia's gashed throat had eased its flow down to a trickle. The front of Blain's robe was soaked. A clay bowl would be his pick of the world's treasures right now. What a waste, spilling through the leaves and roots!

When Kiown had turned his back, quick as he could Blain drank and licked the Invia blood from his palms, careful to keep it from staining his beard and showing what he'd done. He'd tried this stuff once before, and remembered the feeling: a century of age falling away at once, flushed out by the blasting heat of artificial youth. That other time the blood had been nowhere near as fresh and pure as this. With great effort he kept the buzzing power from showing in his robe colours. Ah, better than any magic air, he thought, his eyes on Kiown's bracelet. Could take the trinket off the little bastard right now, except I don't know whether the thing is safe to possess. Let's test his strength at least . . .

'Loyal to our Friend and Lord,' said Kiown ruminatively, still pacing. 'Yet I have just received a gift from the dragons. A great gift.'

'So your loyalties are now divided.' Blain made a show of struggling to his feet, though he felt like leaping over the tree-tops. 'I see. Most awkward for you.'

Kiown nodded. 'The puzzle is: why do the *dragons* wish to elevate a man in this way, when that man must be loyal to one of the Spirits? The Spirits are the dragons' enemies.'

'O come back to your senses, sapling. You weren't chosen! The dragons *may* have had a person in mind for this grand treasure. But . . . *you*?' He said it with enough scorn to make the tree leaves shrivel. 'You think they regard us little humans highly enough in the first place, that they'd pick a human *slave* to do their high work? A mind-controlled slave at that. The Invia you just killed, she didn't leap down to bestow the gift upon you, did she? She was surely waiting for someone else. It was random chance, your snatching it up, and nothing more. The dragons' cosmic bad luck continues.'

Kiown's eyes narrowed. Blain peered into him and shuddered with disgust. 'Ugh! You're right to worry. You've now meddled with designs of the great powers. You see why mind-control was needed? At least we made something half useful out of you. You'd not know how to void your bowels without instructions.' Blain spat in Kiown's face and laughed at him.

The way Kiown's lips pulled back in a snarl reminded Blain of Vous during his famous rages. Out came the sword, and he charged. He was fast of course, but no faster than a pissed-off Hunter should be. The Blain Kiown hacked into – with impressive fury, Blain judged from the other side of the clearing – was obviously not real, though it threw its arms up in feeble defence, splashed realistic blood around and wailed peevishly. The sword nicked off fingers, an ear, a hand and other parts, each of which quickly grew into a new Blain the second they'd thumped down on the floor of fallen leaves. Each of these new Blains threw its arms up in feeble defence, wailing peevishly.

With growing fury – *now* he moved a touch more quickly, perhaps, than a Hunter should – Kiown rushed through the clearing, decapitating each illusion as it manifested, searching for the real Blain. There we are, Blain thought. The amulet has power, naturally, but it can't make an instant wizard-lord out of him. Well, let's put him back in his box.

The real Blain stepped forwards, growing in size till he was half as tall as the nearest tree. He grew taller still, his legs becoming thick as pillars. With Invia blood coursing in him there was almost no burn to the spell at all. He gave himself the illusion of a cloak of fire, made his beard flaming, created a trident and turned his face into something bestial and terrible.

The giant-looking Blain – giant only in Kiown's mind and Blain's; no one else would see the illusion – strode forwards, making the ground in Kiown's mind tremble. 'I care not for your new trinket,' his terrible voice roared. 'But cast off any notions of being chosen for great things! There's such a thing as fortuity. It gets the better of kings, gods and dragons all. You're still my puppet and always shall be. Behave well or you're done with. In the name of our Friend and Lord.' Blain brought his foot down, making the ground seem to shake so much that Kiown lost all balance and fell.

Kiown stood again and dropped his sword. Not in fear, but as a chess player might knock his king from the board. The illusory Blains he'd cut down melted to liquid and sank into the undergrowth.

Blain's tribute to Vous of course was not sincere – Blain had helped to create Vous, knew him as a young man well before the Project, and knew very well there was nothing at all to swear fealty to, let alone worship. But he would not have Invia blood within him for long – the charade of loyalty would have to be kept up, since Kiown's mind-control was still in place. Blain would in fact have killed Kiown the moment he dropped his sword, if it weren't that he had no wish to touch the dragon-made amulet himself. Nor could it be left lying here abandoned. It was best observed.

Kiown stared up into the giant Blain's eyes. There was no fear in him. 'In the name of our Friend and Lord,' he repeated. *Let's not forget it* went unsaid, but unsaid rather loudly.

That episode of antler-butting settled, Blain pondered the dead Invia. He wished to preserve as much of her body as he could without annoying any dragons or other nearby Invia. The thing's flesh could be eaten and magic benefits gained, just as with the consumption of its blood. Blain knew precious little of the paltry arts of preserving meat or flesh; that was magic for slaves and nobodies. But he supposed Invia flesh would decay slower than most kinds. For the moment, it could be buried.

Kiown obeyed instructions to dig a hole in the clearing. Blain hectored, lectured and insulted the young man as much as usual. But he knew something had changed, and suspected the other knew it too. Kiown made no smart replies; indeed he hardly spoke. 'You realise you can't go north again,' said Blain, 'even if your duties require it? Not with that Invia's Mark upon you.'

'I'm not Marked,' said Kiown.

'O you're not? What relief. I dreamed you slew an Invia.'

'I'm not Marked,' Kiown repeated.

So certain of it! On reflection, Blain believed him. 'The trinket's work?'

'I suppose so, Strategist.'

'Ahh. What else does it do?'

'We shall see.'

'In time, eh? May it make you somehow useful.' Soon the Invia was buried, and the patch of ground looked almost as it had before. Blain marked the spot by counting paces to a nearby tree and notching its trunk. He went closer to the woods' edge and gazed at Domudess's tower. Calm ripples of silver flowed through the moat's waters. 'What do we do about that wizard then, eh?' he muttered into his beard.

Kiown shrugged, yawned. 'Kill him, if you want.'

'How?'

'I'll do it.'

'That easy? You couldn't best me just now. He bested me once already – didn't even cast a spell to do it. He's got tricks of his own. You believe it, up in that tower of his.'

For an hour or more he watched the tower with a huntsman's patience. Domudess did not appear at the window again, though surely he knew they were still nearby. 'I suppose we do no more than this,' said Blain. 'We watch him. Day and night. Let's see if the dragon returns here. Perhaps they're old friends.'

So they waited. Blain had little trouble passing the time, with centuries of memory to paw through. He also watched Kiown. Now and then Kiown took the amulet out, peering into the faintly glowing stone as if to read things written inside it. Thoughtful, thoughtful, he'd become. What's going on in that tiny brain? Blain wondered, vaguely troubled.

Blain had seen and held great artefacts too, many of which the castle had robbed from the magic colleges when war mages flew forth to destroy them. None of those artefacts, so far as he knew, had been made by a Major dragon. One charm he'd handled had been crafted by a Great Spirit, if their guesses were right. When the Arch Mage learned of it, he'd seized it. Then Vous had seized it from him and somehow destroyed it during one of his more recent rages. What would they say, the countless slaves and victims of the castle's rule, to see the men behind it all squabbling over morsels of power like children over stolen chocolates?

This thing Kiown now possessed would not reveal its secrets in any hurry. The greater the artefact, the longer it usually took to solve the puzzle of its power. Kiown's hand was in his pocket yet again, stroking the thing. Already dearer to him than his own cock. I have a feeling this one *was* intended as a gift, whatever I said to him, Blain thought, fingering his beard irritably. Could he possibly have been chosen to keep the thing? Could the Invia have indeed been sent for him? No! Surely not . . .

He paused his reflections. That Minor dragon was nearby again. He could feel it as clearly as if feeling heat from breathed fire. Nearer the dragon came, then it shot away again. He quickly lost all sense of it.

Kiown, he noticed, stirred and looked off to the east. Interesting, Blain thought. He knew the dragon was nearby too.

14

A REUNION

The stallion put uneventful miles behind Siel through the night. A brief rain shower washed the last of her own blood from her hair. There was just enough light to show the road before them, but her head was turned constantly to the south, eager for a glimpse of the beings who'd healed her. The night showed little of Levaal South save the odd hint of luminous fog. Not even a sound seemed to come from that place, which poured its stillness and silence across World's End and into the north, just as it had poured its poisoned airs. Nonetheless, the temptation to turn her mount south and ride into that strange land began to grow in her.

There had been no sight of either Tormentors or Shadow across a landscape like a dark sea beyond the path. How slowly the hours crept by till at last the sky turned white again. About her here and there were ruins from wagons. It looked as if a marauding army had come through this place. But none of the spiked tracks in the ground looked fresh, and the only Tormentors she saw were dead ones.

With no warning the stallion reared up, whinnied in panic, and very nearly threw her off. She held on for life. Trained for battle, the stallion recovered quickly from what had shocked it and veered off the road. She did not at first see what had bothered the horse, but now there stood a man on horseback. Except he was too large to be a man – his horse too was enormous. They blocked off the road, standing motionless and facing the southern world. His plate armour shone with its own light.

Siel was reminded of stories of the god Valour, who so many said did not exist at all. Indeed she had doubted it. Yet what else could this be? Drawing level as she passed him, and meeting his eyes, he spoke one word: 'Caution.'

Once past him she looked back over her shoulder. Valour's steed – if Valour it was – stepped off the road gracefully, slowly, proudly. She knew it had been no happenstance vision – her horse had seen it too.

Caution. Of what? She was indeed newly alert for the next mile or two, but the road was again hers alone. She began to doubt her own memories, until a high whinnying sound came from directly overhead; it was not unlike laughter. A shape ducked through the clouds' lowest layer, long and dark, seeming to ripple as it moved. Wings spread wide to either side of its long body. Siel's heart sank. Now she understood the reason for the warning.

Dyan the dragon descended, landing off the road some way ahead of her, feet pressing heavily down in knee-high grass. Siel's horse pulled to an uneasy halt despite her urging it on faster. The dragon's scales were a range of colours from creamy white to glittering blue. Upon its back were Stranger and a woman Siel did not at first recognise. Now she remembered – it was the Hunter who'd accosted her in the woods near the tower.

Dyan's eyes peered into Siel's, sparkling with light, his mouth curved up at the sides in its permanent grin. The two women climbed down from him. Stranger's face wore clearly her profound misery. The Hunter stretched like a cat, pushing out her huge bust as if it were a weapon aimed at Siel. 'Good morning,' she said, smiling. 'Care for a ride?'

'Valour is near,' Siel said, ignoring the women and looking into Dyan's eyes.

'That cannot be, for I would sense him,' the dragon answered, belatedly adding, 'Great Beauty.' This drew a laugh from Evelle. Stranger buried her face in her hands. 'It is no less true to say to her, than to you both,' said the dragon. 'You are *all* beautiful. Why must one be the greatest?'

'Exactly,' said Evelle. 'Why can't he love us all? Don't be greedy.'

'Dragons' hearts are larger than those of men,' said Dyan. 'There is more in them to share.' He shook himself like a dog, leathery ridges slapping against his hide, tail lashing around then settling in the grass.

'What do you want with me?' said Siel, hoping she sounded bolder than she felt.

'Many things, Great Beauty,' said Dyan.

'Then why not take *her* with us too?' Stranger said bitterly.

'No room.' Evelle smiled. 'Unless we cast off some luggage. The luggage that always complains. Dyan, let's fly again. Show me these haiyens you speak of. I must see them! They sound interesting.'

'They are not as special as you might think,' the dragon said ponderously, his tail lashing around the grass. 'Their arts were taught them by a god who is not native to this plane at all, not native even to the South world. When you marvel at them, remember that. They are really not so different from you.' He nodded his head at Siel. 'Ask her. She has seen them. I see signs of their arts upon her.'

'O!' Evelle came nearer to Siel, peering at her with renewed curiosity. 'Where are they? Where can we find them? What did they do to you?'

Siel put a hand on the curved blade in her waistband. Dyan said, 'Go no closer to her, Evelle. She may hurt you.'

Evelle scoffed, then went on. 'Where are the haiyens? Tell me. Then we'll leave you alone. Speak up. I like to cut people. Mostly men but sometimes women too.'

'You will find them across the World's End boundary, I'm sure,' said Siel.

'Aw. Dyan won't take us over there.'

'Not yet,' said Dyan. His mouth opened, shockingly wide and red as he yawned, teeth brilliant white. 'A time comes when I may cross, if I wish. I am undecided. It depends on whether the other dragons descend.'

Siel supposed the dragon would spot lies, if she told any; but the new people were probably no longer where she'd last seen them. So she pointed back the way she'd come and described the glen. Evelle smiled sweetly. 'Good girl! No cutting for you. Come, Dyan. It sounds a quick flight.'

'Do you wish to join me?' said Siel to Stranger.

Stranger looked at her sadly. 'I accept that I must be tormented for a time. The novelty of his new interest will wear off. Soon, I believe.'

Evelle rolled her eyes. 'O hush. Dyan saved your life.'

'He saved me from *your* employer!'

Dyan's voice came louder and silenced them both. He spoke to Siel: 'You and I shall meet again. If you go to the tower, beware the human casters there. Two or three, there are. For humans, they are strong. I shall hide myself from them next time – they will not sense my approach. Tell those who matter enough to hear it that your land has a new lord and lady, king and queen, first among the Favoured peoples. Whatever titles you wish to give them. Their names are Aziel, daughter of the man-god Vous. And Eric, the Pilgrim of Otherworld. Soon they shall claim the castle from the mage who dwells there. A new Spirit has joined the others. Vous, humans have called him. Of Vous, we know little. Shall he be loyal to the power which made him possible? It was we, the dragons. But he is not what we envisioned. As a god, he has nothing like the personality he displayed as a human.'

Siel felt suddenly dizzy, as sick as she had after this creature had lured her to the woods. Dyan's wings fanned wide behind him. 'Spread this news,' he said. 'The cities shall do the new rulers' bidding, or they shall fall. The dragons shall be with the first Favoured peoples, in spirit and thought for a time, and in flesh soon enough. Blades raised against the Firstborn Favoured shall be deflected by hides of scale. Our eyes miss nothing. Be well, girl. It is a time of joy for my kind, and yours. Fear not.'

'Ohh, interesting!' said Evelle, clapping her hands. She and Stranger climbed back onto Dyan's withers. The dragon launched itself again among the clouds.

Siel had lost track of time during the exchange. Head spinning, she urged the horse onwards.

Eric is lord? The idea was absurd! Dragons were capable of lies, jokes and errors, surely just as people were. But the words kept bounding through her mind: *Otherworld prince. Otherworld prince.*

15

STRANGE HANDS

As the lightstone went dark Kiown stirred, jolting Blain out of a journey through his memories. 'What is it, sapling?' he said. Kiown didn't answer, but for the first time in many hours put the dragon-made amulet back in his pocket and clutched his sword hilt.

Blain followed his gaze. There were people at the water's edge. Four of them. Women, Blain thought at first – slight of build, wearing hoods. Blain got up more nimbly than usual, the effects of the Invia blood he'd drunk not quite out of him yet.

One of the newcomers crouched at the tower moat's waves, tentatively poking a finger into the water. Another of them paused by Thaun's body and did something with her hands. Blain did not understand the gesture – some kind of spell? Why bother? Men did not get more convincingly dead than Thaun. Blain squinted for evidence of casting in the airs and saw none. The being removed from her clothing what was apparently a musical instrument, for she blew into it and there came a high reedy sound. For a good while the others watched her blow a few long notes. Nothing else happened. She put the instrument away and all of them stepped into the water.

'Madness,' said Blain. 'Nightmare cultists, must be.'

'Their hands,' said Kiown. 'Look at their hands.'

'You tell *me* about their hands, shithead. You've got the pretty night-vision charm we gave you, not me.'

'Two fingers, a thumb. Larger fingers than they should be. The fingers also seem to be double jointed.'

'Eh? Spell it out for me, turd. And speak sense!'

Kiown turned to him, a flicker of violet-white in his eyes, lip curled. 'They aren't human, Strategist.'

Domudess's bald head was at the window again. The wizard called something down. The four in the water were halfway across. The hems of their gowns floated to the water's surface. The fish – darting light flashes – seemed drawn to them from elsewhere in the water. Domudess watched them come, then his head withdrew from the window. Withdrew with – Blain suspected, though he could not be sure – a glance directly at him and Kiown. 'Not human,' Blain mused. 'Then what do you suppose they were?'

If Kiown knew, he kept the answer to himself. Blain fingered the crusty dried Invia blood on his robe-front. Maybe it's time he parted with that dragon charm, he thought. Far too silent and brooding, he's become. Not sharing his thoughts. Two more days watching him. Then I'll slay him and take it, while there's still some pop in this dried Invia blood. Bury that charm with the Invia body, perhaps. Ugh! If the others could see me now. Me, Strategist Blain, digging holes in the woods and plotting against shithead. Ah, how I miss my chamber in the castle . . . The people with strange hands disappeared under the arch below the tower. 'Were you jesting, whelp? They looked human enough to me.' He turned, but Kiown was no longer beside him.

*

Blain waited the night out, tugging anxiously at his beard. His eyes never for a moment left the tower windows, each aglow with soft amber light. The wizard's head did not reappear. Blain sensed him moving about in there, though just barely. The tower did much to hide him.

It was not until the first of the morning's light that Blain discovered the wizard's visitors had come down from the tower. To his immense shock he saw they'd been silently building something on the grass beyond the water. They had stepped away from it to appraise it: some sort of pole, with a bulbous head that might have been a glass orb. It stood easily twice a tall man's height. A faint light glowed within the orb.

Domudess came to the window again. He called out words in a tongue Blain had never heard – troubling, for he'd heard them all, even many varieties of groundman babble. The visitors went back through the tower's waters and under its archway.

Blain tugged his beard until a good chunk had come away in his hand. When full daylight came his mage eyes saw what the thing they'd built was for: threads of reddish darkness from the airs were pulled down into the orb. In fact, it appeared the thing was drawing out the foreign airs, such as those Avridis had caught in his airships when the Wall fell. In a thin steady stream, the foreign magic was pulled into the glass and did not flow out again. The orb did not disturb the winding ribbon of power which threaded as always through the tower's upper window and out through the one on its further side.

'Little shit,' Blain grumbled, meaning Kiown. Had the Hunter stayed, he'd have seen with his night vision how the device had been built.

The little shit himself dropped to the ground behind him

from a tree branch. Blain wheeled about, immediately splitting into a copy of himself, flinging his real self out of sword range.

'Morning, Strategist,' said Kiown with a most respectful bow. Blain knew full well the 'joke' had been a test of his defences and reflexes – killing him just now would have been perfectly easy. He kept his anger within, also his deep disquiet.

'Where've you been?' he said peevishly. 'I've had need of your eyes.'

'The mayor of Tanton comes.'

'Good! From where? How far?'

'He's an hour or two away.'

'You spotted them? If they're an hour or two away, how'd you get back here before them? Eh?'

Kiown shrugged. 'I'm more useful than you supposed, Strategist Blain.' He looked over at the visitors' construction, rubbed his chin. One hand went to his pocket where presumably the amulet sat. 'Do you mean to persuade the mayor to join your cause?'

'*Our* cause, I hope you mean. If he's still a mayor, why not?' Blain eased himself to the ground. 'His city was meant to be attacked. Could have lost the battle by now. Could be why he's fled. Why'd he come here? Is our friend Domudess in league with him too? Curse this all! I'm like a household pet trying to fathom its masters' sport.'

Kiown did not answer, for he was again no longer there. Little bastard! Blain thought, lashing the ground with his stick. Biding his time. An attack's coming, I know it, and he'll have me. Ah, but I've played more games than he ever will, the turd. I said two days till his heart stops; let's make it one. Nervously he fingered the dried Invia blood on his robe and looked back to the spot where its shedder was buried.

16

THE SILVER SCALE

Vous's storm passed at about the same time as a chorus of dying Invias' cries began to rain down from directly overhead.

When that began, Sharfy had at last given up on coaxing Anfen to a safer place for the rest they both sorely needed. Anfen sat on the lawns surrounded by bodies of Vous-things. Now and then his gaze roamed to the castle's high windows, as if he could see directly into the eyes of whoever was on the other side of the glass.

Sharfy never claimed (aloud) to be Levaal's brightest mind, but he knew a lost cause when he saw one. So it was that when the Invia wails grew more numerous and filled him with a terrible dreamlike grief, he abandoned Anfen at last and ran blindly away.

He woke now to a cold morning and could not remember having lain down to sleep, or even having sought a place safe enough to rest. Hungry and thirsty, he rose, stretched, explored – and found he was still close to the castle, though a few foothills blocked him from it. The roads were unfamiliar but a sign pointed the way to what must have been a military village. This then was the country where favoured Loyalists had dwelled, rich country the envy of the entire world. Now no one was here at all.

At a guardhouse by the road there were indications people had left in a hurry. Sharfy plundered its cupboards of gourmet meats and breads, all preserved by someone's spell work, good as fresh from the ovens. He stuffed himself without shame, belched in utter contentment and thought that only a drop of ale could make things more perfect. Then he found the barrel he'd parked his rump on was filled with that very stuff. Even though it was warm, the ale was so good he'd have been glad to drown in it. Instead he got cheerfully drunk and sang songs to himself all afternoon.

How strange that the finest hours he'd known in years – let alone the finest since being dragged from an inn on this pointless quest to keep a madman alive – should happen here, deep in enemy heartland. To Anfen, he thought meanly, downing yet another cup. He envisioned with pleasure Anfen stuffing dry grass into his starving mouth.

Valour's voice sounded sternly in his memory: *Serve him well.*

And what's that job pay? Sharfy thought with sudden rage. Anfen gets a fucking sword at least. Charmed armour! Never seen armour like that. Feels sorry for himself, wants to die. What do I get? What's the stupid god do if I disobey? Kill me? Go ahead. In any event, was Valour here? So Sharfy poured another, then jumped and screamed at the sound of flapping wings as a bird swooped past the guardhouse window. For an instant he imagined he'd heard the Spirit's hooves. 'Bastard Spirit,' he spat, shoving the chair into the guardhouse wall, then for good measure kicking it to pieces.

'Anfen?' he called later, staggering still drunk from the guardhouse with a filled pack of supplies. His beer-soaked vision was blurry. For an hour or two he strolled through the eerily silent countryside. No one about, friend, foe or stranger. The castle loomed over all, seeming closer than it actually was. The clouds swirled uneasily, gathered from east and west and pushed in a straight line south.

As Sharfy sobered up he knew there was no way around it: he must return to where he'd left Anfen or his own guilty conscience would kill him. 'Anfen?' he called over and over. But no one heard him. Wagons, homes and stores were all abandoned. He paused when it pleased him to eat or drink fine food intended for castle Loyalists. Those Loyalists had been Vous-things all along, he reflected – willing to kill, and to share their Friend and Lord's madness. Only at the end had they looked the part.

A night and day passed in similar fashion, then another. Only twice did he come across living people, castle men returned from duty elsewhere, wandering dazed through their now-abandoned homeland, unable to comprehend what could have happened here. They looked right through Sharfy as if he were an unconvincing illusion, and they left him alone.

Having seen those strangers, it was not with total surprise that Sharfy came upon a lone woman in the square of a village township. The pointed wooden signs named the place Loheem. The woman sat upon the stone edge of the water fountain, evidently in deep meditation. It was a particularly pleasant village, if one forgave it the many statues of Vous splayed in various poses (the eyes were all too alive, made of glittering gems none would ever have dared carve out to steal).

Sharfy had been seriously contemplating retirement here. Apartments and homes had beds which seemed to warm themselves when nights were cold. They had running water –

streams which sometimes ran through living rooms of houses, warm enough for bathing on cold days, with fat fish swimming through. There were all manner of little domestic wonders Sharfy had not dreamed of, and which the Mayors' Command had never provided its most loyal soldiers. Several shops were abandoned with doors open; there was plenty of plunder left to take. There would be more to steal once he figured out how to break into the locked iron boxes, fat and heavy with treasure.

As he explored his new home, it very much seemed that he was the last person alive, aside from a handful of stragglers whose confused calling voices could now and then be heard, far away. It began to occur to him that all this *was* his reward for aiding Valour. He had inherited his own perfect village. In fact he began to recall tales of the Spirits granting the noblest warriors a place in some kind of eternal paradise, if their service in life had been worthy.

And more than that. It now seemed Valour had provided him with company! An ideal companion. The woman sitting on the edge of the water fountain was quite beautiful, in a dark and savage-seeming way. She wore leather of a fashion he'd not before seen, garb the colours of no city. She turned as he emerged through a doorway. Her face showed no fright, but it was clear she'd not expected to see him. Curls of flaxen hair bounced about her shoulders as she quickly stood up.

Sharfy could not help but be aware of his sword, the fact they were alone, and that should he want her, there was no man close enough to stop him. But that was the kind of thing Kiown would do. That thought was enough to put an end to it.

He knew better than to smile at her and add to his already convincing ugliness the spectre of stained and broken teeth. He nodded instead, crouched down. 'Sharfy,' he said, thumbing his chest. 'S'not my name, but's what they call me.'

She nodded, watching him.

'Been in many battles,' he said, unsure as always where to begin. He thumbed a scar. 'See this? Tell you where I got it.'

'I already know,' she replied.

'Eh?'

'Word of your swordplay reached the dragons themselves.'

Although pleased, he pondered this. 'Why talk of dragons?'

'Why indeed. Warrior, was it your voice I heard yesterday, calling someone's name?'

'Aye.'

'Would you mind repeating the name for me? I too search for someone.'

'Won't be the same name, whoever you're looking for,' said Sharfy, vaguely annoyed and wanting to get back to tales about Sharfy. 'Anfen, his name. Won Valour's Helm. I fought with him. Many times.'

'Where was he, when last you saw him?'

'Why you want to know? Who you looking for?'

'Would it disturb you if I said I seek he whom you named?'

'Yes! He's my friend. And aren't you . . . I thought—'

'I can pay for the information,' she said. Fingers with long nails dug into a small leather pouch.

He scoffed. 'Got money enough. No stores left to sell. Don't need gold or coin.'

'Of course. Something better.' From the pouch she produced an object that glowed with silvery light. He had to blink to make sure his eyes really saw it: a large dragon scale. Silver? He'd never heard of a silver scale. He swallowed, mouth suddenly dry. 'Can't crush it,' he said, bargaining feebly.

'This is not an organic scale,' she said, holding it before her solemn face. 'It is rather a kind of charm. It is, however, of dragon-make, and it holds the powers of all the scales' colours within. It does not need to be crushed, warrior. Simply press it to your forehead, concentrate on its touch, and you would be able to use it over and over. That is, if you *wish* to use it. I do not advise it. I only tell you what the scale does.'

Sharfy swallowed. 'Why not use it?'

'It will show you things forbidden to men's eyes and minds. Perhaps you are strong enough to see? I cannot say; you alone can. It will show the ancient past, before humans ever came here from Otherworld. Those are times the dragons remember, times the dragons still dream of. Times they walk through, in their memories. Or so it is said.'

She held it aloft, side on, gleaming like a slit larger than her eye. She said, 'Whether you use this gift or not must remain your choice. If you choose to use it, heed my warning: do so no more than once per day. Too much knowledge is perilous. The hidden times and places have a certain . . . allure. But I see you know this already.' His face of course betrayed him. 'I see we have an agreement,' she said.

He swallowed. 'Maybe. Yes. Sure. But I mean, he might be dead. Anfen. They might've got him. The castle.'

'Such is our agreement. I accept my risk, if you accept yours.' She came nearer and dropped the scale in his lap. 'Now, brave warrior. Where is he?'

So he told her where he'd last seen Anfen, and answered several other questions about him, which he'd not later remember. Then she was gone.

With trembling hands he took the scale, pouring silver light out through his fingers. He took it to the small but luxurious apartment he'd chosen for a home.

Days passed. With the silver scale pressed upon his forehead he forgot the apartment's other, plainer treasures. His mind was filled with scale visions, or something very like them. He never went out of his body (as had happened with his black scale vision at Faul's house, when he'd been taken to see horrors he had not the faintest ability to comprehend); instead he seemed to see back in time, just as the woman had intimated, to a Levaal where humans had not yet set foot.

His gaze swept fast along on the winds, sometimes high as the lightstone ceiling. Great dragons roamed free, their enormous bodies pounding into mountainsides to reshape the spilled rubble as they wished. Their claws rent out gouged paths for glittering rivers to run, eating the stone they misplaced as if it were great mounds of chocolate or meat. Like delighted children painting, they flung magic through the air, adding colours and energies of their own to those their Parent had already set in swirling motion.

He saw in his visions that the gods Mountain, Tempest and Inferno wandered the realm in those days too, lived *with* the dragons. They were not of the same kind at all, but of similar stature; the old Spirits were here observing, not yet given Nightmare, Valour or Wisdom as younger siblings. Observing, watching to see that the dragons did not alter the very rules of the Spirits' governed elements: ensuring they did not invent a kind of water which did not flow, nor an ice that could not melt, nor fire that could not be extinguished.

And Sharfy understood in the vision that indeed the great dragons did not do such things, but that this was not for *fear* of the Great Spirits, whom the twelve great dragons, being greater in number, could band up against and destroy. The rules were followed, rather, as a courtesy. The Spirits were advisors and guides to them, playmates, even allies, ready to fight alongside the dragons, should anything cross over World's End from the South.

Sharfy saw that out in some of the unclaimed lands, magic of such potency had been cast that humans could never dwell there. Nor would they ever try, besides a few wandering lost or seeking obscure treasures here and there, things hidden beneath thick layers of ice, stone, and buried in silt on the floors of Vyan's Sea.

The great dragons, the brood – Sharfy saw them all. Out in the great frozen wastes they occasionally squabbled over matters Sharfy could not understand. The squabbles were ferocious, but more akin to sport and game-playing than the dead serious warfare of men. Here they were, all Major personalities in glory terrible and wondrous: Vyin and Tzi-Shu, not yet enemies, their heavy bodies prowling, wings only just powerful enough to lift their huge bulk skywards, riots of colour glinting off their scales. He saw Shâ, before that dragon's being became poisoned with envy of humanity and hatred of imprisonment. And the Minor dragons Sharfy saw swarming through the skies in all the vast array of shapes and forms dragons assumed. The dragons of this age could not know or predict the rage their imprisonment would, so very far into the future, create in their hearts, minds and magic.

Sharfy learned – deeper than his mind, deep as his bones – knowledge which astounded him; they showed him that the unlikely histories murmured in taverns, read from ancient stone tablets, were *real*, not mere myth. The wildest myths were real!

The madmen who swore by them had been right all along. It was strange how glad this made him . . .

But each time Sharfy woke from these visions, all the knowledge fell from him. Fell like small dead bones from his hands when he thought he'd held something living and warm; fell and clattered among the litter of the apartment, crushed to dust, scattered. The moment he emerged from these visions he'd thrust the scale immediately back to his forehead.

In those brief returns to himself – sprawled across the bed, open mouth too dry now to spill drool down his face as it had done at first – he understood he would soon forget who he was, just as he was forgetting to eat, to drink, to care that he'd soiled himself. He had forgotten completely she who'd given this wonderful gift to him. Of Anfen and Valour he thought hardly a thing.

The room stank of his sweat and the waste that had spilled out of him. His chest rose and fell slowly, his heart sluggish, now and then picking up when his mind's eye beheld another miracle of knowledge.

It was in this state of filth and weakness that Shadow found him.

Sharfy's eyes peeled open, sore in the weak daylight spilling limp through a high window. His head spun, the feeling so much like being hungover he assumed briefly that he was. He had no idea what he'd seen or learned in the last vision, only that it had been mind-blowing. It always was.

The stink of his own excrement was an assault. His empty stomach roiled.

The pretty silver scale gleamed on the floor at the end of the bed. He felt dizzy with pleasure at the sight of it, and felt an emotion the reverse of envy, just as negative, directed at Anfen. Anfen with his miraculous sword and armour. Who needed such things when you could peer behind the world's curtain and see what no one else had ever seen?

As usual, Sharfy did not reach for the scale but lunged for it. He was mid-lunge when a familiar voice said, 'It's killing you.' The voice spoke observantly, devoid of feeling. He had not expected to see Eric standing at the foot of his bed, but there he was. Sharfy's lunge for the scale veered wildly off target and he landed hard on the cold tile floor.

'It's *mine*,' Sharfy said. Rather tried to say – his throat was so parched the words hardly came out.

Eric made no move to take the scale. Sharfy crawled along the floor and snatched it. His legs barely moved, stuck all over with severe pins and needles. It *was* truly Eric, wasn't it? Yes, though his eyes had gone peculiar. They were big and black. They just stared down and seemed to move around at their edges, too large for his face.

'I'm trying to work something out,' said Shadow. 'But I don't know much about how it all works. I'm learning. You might help me. I did a bad thing. To Siel.'

'Eh?'

'I did something wrong. Didn't know what that meant, before. "Wrong".'

Sharfy edged away, shielding the silver scale. 'Eh? What'd you do?'

'Killed her. She's dead.'

'Huh. Why? Why do that?'

'She hurt me. So I hurt her back. Thought it would make me feel good. It didn't. It hurt me much worse. It hurts different from how the man's sword hurt.'

Sharfy shook his head to try and clear his vision. This wasn't Eric, he decided. Eric died, up there in the skies somewhere. That many war mages? He'd never make it through, not tough enough. This was his ghost, talking lies. 'Go away. Busy.' Sharfy clawed his way back to the bed.

How strange and large were the eyes of Eric's ghost. It said, 'I'll leave. Just want to find something out first.'

'What?'

'Killing Siel was bad. So if I make sure someone else *doesn't* die . . . would that be doing something good?'

Sharfy shrugged. 'Who cares?'

'Would it make the dead person come back?'

'No! Don't be stupid. Only gods can do that.' He fondled the scale like a lover's breast. 'Dragons too. Maybe.'

'If I did something good . . . would it make the bad thing I did *less* bad?'

Anything to get rid of the ghost. 'Yeah. Sure it would.'

Shadow reached down and plucked the silver scale from Sharfy's hand with a movement too quick for him to follow. Sharfy's impression was that the scale had simply disappeared and he was deeply confused, blinking at his empty hand.

Eric's ghost said, 'You'll die soon. You need to drink. And eat. And wash.'

Sharfy saw Eric's ghost now held its hands behind its back. 'You took it?' He looked around for his sword. 'Think you know so fucking much?'

'I shadowed you. Saw what happened. She wants you to kill yourself. Could have done it herself – she's strong. She didn't want to do it herself. She thought it would be dangerous for her, to kill you herself. Because for her, there are rules. She's not allowed to be here with people at all. Not allowed to interfere. So she wanted to make you choose to do it yourself. That's still not allowed . . . but it's not *as* not-allowed.' He paused. 'I don't know what all those things mean. Do we have rules, like they do? Am I allowed to be here?'

Sharfy grabbed the elite guardsman's sword from the floor. It was far heavier than he remembered it. He snarled, vision blurring so that he saw three Erics standing there. He raised the blade overhead and missed all three. The sword vanished in his hand just as the scale had. He toppled forwards, hit his head, and was at best half-conscious from then on as someone gently tipped water in his mouth, carefully put food in there too, poured water over him, changed his clothes. 'You think I'm Eric,' said Shadow, and told Sharfy his real name.

'Shadow? Nah.' Sharfy peered up with narrow eyes. 'Just stories,' he murmured. Although in truth he'd begun to wonder.

17

A BETTER PLACE

It seemed to Anfen he felt Shilen's approach long before he saw her slow dance-like strides through the flotsam of human wreckage which lay before the castle. She walked proudly, as if she had caused it all herself, these scattered bodies murdered by Vous's great change. Or as if she were the crowning piece in a sprawling work of grim art, its lone jewel. So seemed her approach to him: both dream and real at once, life moving through death, graceful, without fear and inevitable.

Anfen's eyes had remained mostly on the window, where he sensed rather than saw the Arch Mage gazing out. The Arch Mage, whose fall from power had happened with such impossible speed he could not yet even see the reality of it before him. Perhaps recognition would occur soon. Perhaps he expected Anfen to charge up through the castle and make the final ending easy.

Anfen would not do that. Mercy indeed awaited with a very sharp edge, but the Arch would not be forced to take it; that was far too easy. He must choose it. He must admit his loss, come down and bare his throat. Only then.

If Valour had wanted Anfen to witness the final stage of Vous's great change, he had fulfilled his purpose. Vous had flown into convulsions of energy, taking lightning in all his splayed fingers. His shrieking voice spewed mindless sounds. Or perhaps it was a language, the language of the Spirits. Was he greeting the other gods? Announcing his place among them? Were they pleas, cries of fear? Perhaps all of these. Waves of energy had pulsed out from the castle, invisible to Anfen's eyes. But he had felt them: like a new warm element, between wind and water, flowing over him. Valour's breastplate had grown warm, near unbearably hot for just a brief while as it shielded him from the magic.

The instant Vous became a Great Spirit was too brief for human perception. In that instant, a ripped hole in Levaal's reality opened up like shreds of torn canvas flapping in wind bursts. The argument with reality – slow by mortal standards, urgent as it had ever been by other measures – was in an instant of action decided. Vous the man was now Vous the Great Spirit, youngest of the gods.

Silence and eerie peace fell after that instant. A breeze breathed through the castle lawn grass, gently rustling the clothes of the dead as if in consolation, or in thanks. The image of Vous upon the balcony remained, motionless and lifeless as paint flung upon a wall long ago.

The hours and days drew out; he didn't count them. If he died before the Arch came down it hardly mattered. He supposed that Valour, his redeemer, must be far away, for suddenly the Spirit didn't much cross his mind. He didn't think of much at all – he was glad and relieved to be dying. Perhaps dead already, he didn't know.

He knew when Shilen came that he was not dead – not dead at all. He watched her come without moving, without thinking, until she'd eased herself down in the grass beside him. The sweet but strange smell of her just faintly trickled into the background reek, as if to make him aware of the reek for the first time. And he smelled its foulness now in full, and wondered why he was here.

She followed his gaze. 'There he is,' she said at last. She raised a hand, waved *hello* at one of the high castle windows. How light and easy was her voice, rich with humour.

For the first time he could remember, deep within him, something heavy seemed to shift. He knew not what shifted; only that it was something which had held down all chance of joy or laughter. He laughed now. Then his laugh became a hacking cough, his head spun dizzily, and he collapsed.

It was the smell of food – again, accentuating the reek behind it – that drew him back to wakefulness. A bowl was before Shilen, holding meat with golden skin gently steaming, vegetables too. Every part of Anfen commanded him to eat, but for the first time he seemed to see the woman properly, when before she had seemed part of a fevered dream. He drew his sword out, held its point two hand spans from her, off to the side. She pulled back, fearful. Good. 'Name yourself,' he rasped.

'Shilen.'

For some reason his mind flashed back to that night in the woods, when he had gone down suicidally to meet Stranger, leaving the group he led at the mercy of whatever might find them.

He put the sword away, sat, took the bowl she offered and devoured everything in it. The meat was some kind of poultry with soft bones – he ate those too.

'Water?' she said, offering a cup.

He snatched it, drank, spilling much down his chin. Drops

splashed onto Valour's breastplate. 'What do you want?' he said.

She struggled to find words. 'I would be . . . honoured, if you told me . . . something of your redeemer.' He looked up at her sharply, reached for his sword again. 'Don't hurt me,' she said.

'I'll tell you nothing of him.'

'As you wish, warrior.'

'Don't ask me that again, ever.'

'Yes, warrior. Shall I leave?'

He spat.

She sighed, stood up, gazed around and said, 'When I was young, my mother told a tale of a brave young man. Would you like to hear it? She asked him one day why he had chosen to be born to her. The young man said he had come into life to prove himself to her with sword in hand – he just needed an enemy to kill. His mother said, "I have known you in other lives, and have already seen that you are strong with a blade, and unafraid of death. There is nothing more for you to prove with a sword. There are other things you must prove to me." She took the sword from him – reluctantly, he released it – and she took him across the realm to an island where no one had lived before.

'It was bare, just grass, rocks and turf. She told him to make it into a garden. It would grow all he needed to eat. Its living things would become his friends, if he cared for them. And one day, others would come to live there with him, and share in its splendour, if it grew beautifully enough. This was how he must prove himself. He must guide a barren place to growth and beauty.

'She left him there and he did as said. He wrenched out the rocks and weeds with his bleeding hands, swam to the mainland when he needed to, wandering far to find seeds to plant and young animals to raise. With time, lovely things indeed grew all over his island. He learned that plants and trees speak a certain quiet rustling language. He could hear it, but could not speak it. He was lonely, but did not wish to leave.

'As he grew older, he discovered he was in love with the flowers and vines and trees. He thought of what his mother had said, about others coming to share this beauty with him, which he had worked so hard to bring to life. Lonely though he was, the thought of sharing it made him jealous and angry. So he let the island's edges go bare and foul, and stacked there piles of animal bones and skulls, so that from afar, it seemed a deathly place. He kept for himself the inner, beautiful part of the island's middle.

'In the end . . .' She shook her head, tsked. 'Well, it is just a foolish story.' She gazed around. 'But this place, with all its bodies in the grass. A strange and awful place to choose as one's home. Your friend had better taste, I must grant him that.'

When she said 'friend' Anfen heard redeemer. He stood up, sword drawn back. 'Speak no words against him.'

'I have spoken no word against your friend, Anfen,' she said, fingering a flaxen curl nervously. 'Nor against Valour. I have never seen him. I wish I had.' She looked at him sidelong. 'Many say he does not exist.'

'He does.' Anfen slammed a fist into his breastplate. 'I am his witness.'

'What did you witness?'

'The change. A new Spirit has come.' He put his sword away, hesitated to speak. 'How does your tale end?'

She shrugged. 'That? Well. The man grew old, savouring his solitude, his secret knowledge of growing things. When he felt lonely, he imagined that those who would have come to his island would have been revolting, angry people, and in this way he comforted himself. He felt he had passed the test his mother set for him for this lifetime, and wondered what the next would bring.

'Then, one day, he heard footsteps, the sound of claws scraping the island's dead stony edges. He heard harsh voices speaking. He was no longer alone. On that day, he learned that some beings find bareness, rot and piles of bone as beautiful as others find flowers and vines. He learned that some find screams of pain as lovely as others find the sweetest music or birdsong; and that some would sooner drink blood than wine or a brook's water.

'It was with such folk he ended up sharing his island garden, for they were drawn to the bareness of its edges which they saw from afar. They decided they would stay there. They corrected the beauty in the middle by stamping it out, tearing down its trees, burning it all down.'

'And of the man?' said Anfen.

'Him they held in high regard. They sang his praises, for crafting such a place for them. They forgave him the small blemish of green and growing things in the island's middle – *that* was easily fixed, after all. He was kept with them, given a longer than normal life, but forbidden ever to leave. Though he was chained there, they revered him, held feasts for him, and pleasured him.

'As their idea of beauty was different, so too was their idea of pleasure different. What they ate at their feasts was different from what others ate. Slowly and bitterly, the man learned their ways, acquired their tastes, changed himself. Never again was he as happy as he'd been before they came.'

Shilen gazed about the field and its bodies again. 'A silly tale, of needless suffering. Warrior, is your work for Valour now done?'

Anfen slumped down and thought of his redeemer, Valour, as he'd appeared that day of his resurrection, giving him life again from death at Kiown's blade. A gift, that renewed life had seemed at the time. But it had brought him here to this land of enemies and bodies in the grass.

'I have places I wish to see,' said Shilen after a while. She said it sadly, he thought, as if she knew it was pointless to invite him to come with her, much as she'd like to. 'Places where there is much more beauty than here.'

He considered the breastplate Valour had given him. How plain it suddenly seemed. Shilen looked up at one of the castle windows. She laughed. The curls bounced about her shoulders, seeming to laugh along with her. 'Is that why you linger? To slay that foolish mage? You need not trouble yourself. Others come to deal with him. It's said there shall be a new lord and lady, a new king and queen, whatever you wish to call them. Have you not yet carried your share of Levaal's burdens?'

He owed her no answer to the question, he knew. But was *he* not owed an answer to it? Had he not dragged himself across the world, forsaking every comfort? Troubled, he watched her walk away, her steps not part of any ritual dance beyond the swaying hips of a beautiful woman.

Slowly he rose to his feet and followed her.

And so Anfen was not there to witness Aziel's return to the castle, when she was carried from the heights of the sky prison's Gate in the arms of an Invia with violet hair. Aziel's feet pressed down on the lawn not far from where he'd sat. She smoothed the dress she'd found in the sky prison, which the wind had badly ruffled. Eric's feet were set down on the grass beside her seconds later. Both of them laughed, surprised to have made it back alive again to this world below.

18

FIRSTBORN OF THE FAVOURED

Once they'd set Eric and Aziel down, the Invia immediately took to the sky again. Wind from their beating wings ruffled Eric's and Aziel's clothes. During the long descent, the castle's shape had been so clearly that of a huge dragon that Eric imagined once or twice he'd seen its white marble bulk faintly rise and fall, as if with breath.

Something had changed since they were gone – both of them felt it. Things were quiet and still. Staring up at the enormous structure from ground level, the chain-mail shirt seemed to clench in on Eric's body like a flexing muscle. Aziel's hand found his, swung in his palm, her smile so easy his own nerves calmed. Her beauty at that moment surprised him.

'Can you feel it?' she said, beaming. 'Father's not here any more. He's gone.'

'Good.'

She laughed. 'No, it's bad. Very bad. Arch is very afraid of Father. He has to watch Father all the time, like a man trying to control a fire. But not any more. Arch will be free to fight us, if he wants to.'

'You've said many times that he loves you.'

She shrugged, again laughing. 'Monsters love things in a

different way from people, Eric. If they love people, they love them like pets or possessions. Anyway, I never knew much about Arch, how he really was inside. Or Father for that matter. They all lied to me a lot. I learned things, up there.' She glanced skywards. 'All this knowledge just poured into my mind while you were gone. It was amazing. Even if Arch *did* love me, that will change very fast when we tell him to leave. It might be dangerous for us. The dragons can't help us in there. I had thought those two Invia would stay around to help.'

'Did they ever tell you why dragons can't go inside the castle?'

'No.'

'But the dragons gave me an amulet that can summon Hauf as our only defence? Hauf is a dragon. No help! I don't get it, Aziel. Why can't the Invia come in to help us, if the dragons really want you and me to kick the Arch out? I seem to remember Case saying Invia could go inside there no problem.'

'Maybe they can. Maybe they will. The dragons chose us to lead, that's what's important. Arch is a powerful man, but he is only a man. If he defies the dragons, one way or another he will regret it. Whether we punish him or someone else does. But you can't rule if you don't have at least a little courage, Eric.'

She took a distasteful look around at the bodies strewn on the lawns and bounded up the white steps. Eric followed her inside after one last look at the lawns Case had slept on after his first night in Levaal. The old wino seemed to have spilled a nightmare across the grass which no one had troubled to clean up.

Inside, stairways and halls twisted through great domed rooms in all directions like veins through a body. It was now empty of the bustle of staff, but for a few lone tapping echoes from deeper in the maze of hallways, their makers ever out of sight. All was lit by a white glow which seemed to come from the walls and floors, not unlike the sheen of lightstone. Even at these lower levels the air was thicker with colour to Eric's mage eyes than nearly any other place he'd seen. Vous's likeness adorned each wall in carvings, statues and paintings. Here and there were holograms of flickering light depicting him in motion. It was reminiscent of groundman light art, though far less beautiful.

It looked as though hordes of busy workers had quickly fled. One or two confused people roamed on the far side of vast warehouses. They wore castle grey but there was no one left to steer their controlled minds. Filling those warehouses were heaped mounds of grain, meat on hooks and racks, and stacked crates of produce. 'Won't this food rot here?' Eric said.

She shrugged. 'Most of it gets preserved. It will be looted soon unless we find someone to protect it.'

'Preserved, how?'

'Spells, of course. Usually the stoneshaper mages do it. People can be taught how to do it too but only the ones who can see magic. We will have to find or teach new people, right after we find guards and an army. The early part of our reign will be filled with quite dull matters, Eric.'

'Christ, *look* at all this food. I heard there are cities starving.'

She shrugged. 'There are.'

'Then why is all this food kept here?'

She lectured as if to a simpleton who should already know these things. 'The best stuff is for the troops and Loyalist villages. If you don't keep them well fed they turn on you, or try to. There are lots of Loyalist villages nearby; everyone wants to live in them. You have to reward the loyal ones, or at least make a promise that you will. The cities were mostly conquered, so their people aren't very loyal. That's a difficulty. Sometimes they rebel and riot. You have to control their food supply until they behave. Sometimes their water too. Hungry people make poor rebel armies, Eric. So of course they are kept a little hungry. Some places, like Hane and Kopyn, they simply never behave no matter what their mayor does. So they don't get to eat much. And sometimes the Strategists send diseases through their populations so they have more to worry about than rebelling.'

'Well, that's all changing, Aziel. If I'm in charge here—'

'You and me both, don't forget. There's no point being angry with *me*. I didn't arrange this.' She gestured at the stacked warehouse they walked past. He recognised the huge iron containers he'd seen back in the underground highways, which had been bound for the castle. This shipment had been half unloaded before the workers had fled. Barrows lay strewn, spilling grain across the floor. Following his gaze, Aziel said, 'I only explained how Arch and the Strategists do it. They devise a system for each city, with little changes here or there to suit its people. Then it all takes care of itself. Every now and then, they experiment with one city or another to see what happens. It's rather like a game to them, managing it all. They once kept Seffen's food almost completely cut off for a year, just to see what would happen. The people survived, somehow. Most joined the military just so they could eat. But they weren't very loyal, so they were sent to die in campaigns. If you wish to run things differently, I don't mind.'

'Isn't that what you want too, Aziel?'

'I don't see the need to be as cruel as the Strategists were. But we are ahead of ourselves. First, we have to tell the Arch that he's leaving. Let's start finding a way up. Some stairways are hidden from the lower staff. Where the walls have a streak of lighter colour, there's usually a hidden stairway. Ah, at last! Here.'

She pointed to a patch of bare wall. Sure enough, after a moment a winding stairway appeared as if his gaze had conjured it. They made their long ascent up many turns of the steps till both of them were panting. Aziel grew more familiar with the surrounds the higher they went. She also grew more excited as they neared the high halls where her throne awaited her. Eric trailed behind her, confused by a dozen different fears and doubts. A wave of unreality had struck him: how could *he* of all people have ended up any kind of lord?

But then, had he not played computer games where one built and maintained an empire? Would the reality of it be so very different?

When at last they came to the uppermost level, the Arch waited for them at the end of a hallway, leaning heavily on the forked staff he clutched. 'Aziel, it is wonderful to see you.' He bowed low, horns scraping the floor.

19

INVITATION TO DEPART

The Arch Mage turned to Eric. 'Anfen is gone.' He said it like the statement held some meaning Eric would take straight away – as if it decided something final. Perhaps, *you have come for me, but it is futile.*

The Arch surely could no longer be called human. Eric looked at the creature's half-melted face, his head burdened by thick horns. It was hard to believe, though he saw it plainly: here was an architect of pain and misery on a worldly scale. A starver of cities, creator of wars, enslaver and torturer of innumerable people, and all of it no more to him than moves in a game.

Beside the Arch, seven grey-robed servants waited. About them was the faintest hint of sullenness, even nervousness. The Arch said, 'Do you hear me, Pilgrim? Anfen your warrior is gone. Someone led him away. I know not who she was, but I doubt he will return alive. I trust your plans did not require him? I thank you for returning Aziel to me unharmed. It has been a troubling time for me, waiting. A test I have passed.' He turned to Aziel. 'Much has happened, many profound things. Aziel, would you leave the Pilgrim and me alone for a moment, to discuss these events?'

'No, Arch,' said Aziel.

He looked surprised. 'Are you sure, Aziel? By what means did he sway your mind? Is it the charm he possesses? Perhaps it is the charm *you* wear. It appears to be very powerful. Why not set it briefly aside, Aziel, and see if your thoughts become clearer?'

'The dragons sent us, Arch.'

He hobbled a few steps closer. 'It's clear to me you sincerely believe that. Which dragons?'

'Which dragons do you think?' said Aziel, laughing. 'The ones in the sky.'

'Those are not the only dragons in existence. But you should know that's not possible, Aziel. As I told you long ago, the dragons do not deal with us. They accept that this world is ours. It is as their Parent decreed, in what we call the "natural laws". The dragons are not permitted to interfere in matters of men.'

She laughed again, her voice so queenly that Eric was taken aback. 'It's all changed, Arch. I won't tell you all the things I learned. You do not need to know. The castle is ours now. Eric's and mine. You have to leave. You may have an hour to collect your things.'

Confusion was plain on the Arch Mage's ruined face as he peered at each of them in turn. He said, 'I will humour you for a moment. There are just two of you here, with no army, no guardians at all and no weaponry. Only those charms, which seem too complex for you to wield on your own. And you are ready to take the controls of the world in your hands at this most dire time, without any guidance?

'My life has been very long, Aziel. I have much yet to teach you. About power. Magical power, political power. There is a great deal to learn. Here, for instance, is a useful way to deal with rebellious underlings, and enemies.' He raised the forked staff, pointing it at one of the grey robes behind him. The elderly man's face contorted. His body trembled then collapsed into a liquid pile, the colours of his flesh and garments swimming through the puddle like reflections on silvery water. A flush of blood-red oozed in. The man's face stretched out, mouthing silent cries.

The other grey robes stirred, uncomfortable, but held their positions. 'He is quite conscious,' the Arch said, leaning back to touch the puddle's edge with his staff. 'Feeling every moment of it. I doubt a man has ever been in more pain. I could draw it out longer than any Tormentor's kill. Place him in a room somewhere, forget about him for a hundred years. Make it known you do this sort of deed and what enemy would raise his blade to you?'

'Stop it now,' said Aziel.

'I show you this to prove my worth,' said Avridis. He lowered his forked staff to the floor. The puddle exploded into red water, splashing either side of the hallway's walls, over the other grey robes' clothes. With revulsion Eric wiped off the drops that hit his shins and shoes.

Avridis said, 'I have much more knowledge you may find useful. Are you truly determined, Aziel, that this squeamish man,' he gestured with the staff at Eric, 'is he who shall sit beside you? One never wants a surgeon afraid of blood. Nor rulers, I assure you. He is of no great importance back in his own world. Nor truly in this one.'

Eric drew the Glock. The gem in the Arch's eye socket twisted about and gleamed red. 'That weapon can't harm me,' he said. 'You have little ammunition left. Spare your shots. Better yet, keep *me* as your weapon. I am far more dangerous, and the world already knows it. Aziel, why not set aside that charm for just a moment? Let me examine it, to ensure it is safe for you to wear. They often have many more effects than one notices at first.'

'Did you know, Arch, that the Invia could sometimes hear me crying out from the skies?' said Aziel. Eric glanced at her sidelong, saw she was shivering with anger.

'You are the daughter of a god, Aziel. Not merely a lord's daughter. Your upbringing could never have been conventional.'

'All those years, you kept me here. All my life, you tried to change me, change what I am inside. Sending people to be killed next to my room, so I would hear it, so I'd think I'd *caused* it. So I wouldn't care about people dying any more.'

'Be calm, Aziel. That was your father's doing. Yes, I let it happen. I could not have stopped it. But there was purpose in it. To create a gemstone there must be pressure. To create magic, one must burn oneself.'

'I never had a say in that purpose.'

'How many people do, Aziel?' He took a hobbling step towards the window, to the spread of green land divided by the Road. 'They are but slaves and subjects out there. How many decided to be? Even the dragons do not choose their fate, or they would not be imprisoned. And yet now you *do* decide, Aziel. Here in the castle you were prepared for the unpleasant business of ruling. Have you truly thought it through? Every decision you make shall result in someone's death, directly or otherwise.

'Rule is far from easy, Aziel. Those of the realm shall see only your power, luxuries and faults. You will be insulted, resented, stolen from, threatened. Some shall raise armies of the disaffected to march against you. You shall be called a monster when you suppress them – indeed you must briefly become a monster to suppress them. These things will happen no matter how well you rule. There will be so very few you can trust. There are people for whom to slay a lord means far more than the most comfortable ordinary life.' He gestured out the window. 'All that shall be yours, yes. But you may not roam freely through it. You will be the most comfortable prisoner in all the land, but indeed a prisoner you shall be, and the most confined one of all. A prisoner in a dungeon has but an armspan for his flesh, but his mind is free. Never *your* mind: ever burdened, it will be, by the troubles of the realm. To empathise, to feel those troubles as your subjects do, is impossible. It is too much weight to carry. A day of it would make any lord insane. It is why your father wished to relieve you of your care – for your own sanity.

'And that is not all. Like Vous, ever will you wonder who among your servants lurks the halls, a knife hidden in his clothes. Some shall hide the knife for years, edging ever closer to your back with the most loyal deeds and words until you trust them completely. When you first discover such a traitor, how will you trust anyone else afterwards? That fear alone helped destroy Vous's once brilliant mind.

'Brilliant he was, Aziel, long before you knew him. In his rule I shielded him from many perils. I kept the cities from stealing his place – yes, you would be shocked to know how badly the mayors lusted to be made into gods! They *shall* march against you, especially now that Vous's change succeeded. I kept the magic schools from interfering. I suppressed the half-giants, the folk magicians, the cultists. I conquered every threat. I brought down the Wall, unveiled a new land of treasures and powers for us to claim, if we are bold enough. And I gave Vous godhood, eternal life, unimagined power. I still have this knowledge. I can make you both gods. No one has been offered greater gifts than this. Offered now, freely.

'Much was learned about god-making. The process will be faster this time. Certain of the rituals we used aren't needed at all. Sacrifice speeds things along. It is best not to be . . . squeamish. Worship by the citizens made no difference, to my surprise – we spent much time and effort on that. It is politically useful, but not needed for ascension. We should construct your godhoods in secret.'

'I don't want to be a god,' Eric said wearily.

'Nor I,' said Aziel.

Avridis looked from one to the other. He seemed too surprised by their reactions to speak.

Eric said, 'I have just one question for you. I want you to explain something to me, something about power.'

'Of course.'

'Why is it there are men who cannot enjoy a feast on their own table without hungry people outside their window, to make their food taste better?'

'None of the Strategists ever asked that question.' The Arch Mage pondered. 'I suppose power must be exercised to be felt. You will discover this, no matter how sentimental you feel now. Without now and then lifting a weight, how would one know one's arm had strength?'

A wave of shame and depression washed over Eric. He did not know what he'd expected; perhaps that his question would have put the Arch in such a bind he'd physically collapse. He'd not expected a calm, unhesitating answer. Much less an honest one. 'You're leaving the castle,' Eric told him. 'Go now.'

'I did not answer to your satisfaction? Aziel, have you nothing to say?'

'Leave, Arch.' She touched the necklace – how plain its

metal looked. 'Don't try to hurt us. The charm will kill you if you try.'

The Arch looked from one to the other, genuinely surprised. He said, 'I doubt the charm protects you both.'

The moment the Arch began to raise his forked staff, Eric fired the gun. Aziel jumped and cried out at the noise. It was not clear whether his shot had missed – surely it hadn't, but the Arch did not react. The grey robes moved forwards, suddenly joined by half a dozen pouring into the hall from adjoining rooms. They flocked about Eric and Aziel, blocking their view of the Arch, shuffling an advance that pushed them both back into the wall. The first one of them to touch Aziel reeled back, hands blackened, withered, the flesh melting away. The man's face expressed little, his mouth opening to emit a flat sound: '*Ahh, ahh-ahh-ahhh . . .*'

Eric shoved another of them away, jumping up to aim for a clean shot at the Arch. There were too many bodies between them. Passively the grey robes pressed in, mindless people of all ages, their eyes imploring. Behind them the Arch spoke in the same reasonable-sounding voice, as if Eric's shot at him had been mere quibbling over a detail in his employment.

'Get out of the way or I'll shoot,' Eric told the grey robes bearing in.

'They're mind-controlled,' said Aziel. Two more had touched her. Their arms had been partly burned away by Vyin's charm but still they pressed in. 'They're not really alive. Kill them.'

'I'm not going to kill them. Move. All of you, out of the way. I'm trying to free you.'

The Arch's voice droned calmly on. 'Aziel, you must reconsider your choice of partner. He is unable even to stomach the death of those already dead. Meek lords slay more innocents than any tyrant. A meek lord fills his realm with tyrants, Aziel.' Hands closed on Eric's wrists, pinned his arms. The gun clattered to the ground.

'Aziel, take a true look at him,' said the Arch. 'Is this a lord of men? I have not even cast upon him. Shall I, Aziel? Shall I slay him, so you may choose another? I shall do it quickly, if you wish it.'

Fingers pressed into Eric's throat, cutting off his air. He thrashed around, kicked, freed himself for a moment, then screamed: '*Hauf! Help me!*'

20

HAUF

As his air was cut off, Eric couldn't help agreeing with the Arch's assessment: he was definitely no lord, and this was a pathetic way to die. He freed his hand and struck as hard as he could at the grey robes pressing in. It made no difference to them.

Then the whole castle seemed to shiver. There was a crunching, splitting noise. The floor near Eric's feet erupted into pieces of tile, marble and plaster. The gripping hands released him. Suddenly he could breathe again. Scattering grey robes fell and rolled across the floor, their faces vacant even as Hauf barrelled among them, tearing them apart in just a few seconds.

The castle trembled again, seemed to heave and convulse with sickness. The Arch Mage fell into a wall, his shocked voice crying: 'A dragon? You brought a dragon *here*? Aziel, make him dismiss it . . . you've no idea the danger . . .'

The castle floor tilted, knocking him into the wall. It tilted until the floor became the ceiling. All of them fell heavily, all but Hauf, whose claws dug in and held him secure above them. His growl was louder than the quake's rumble. He took slow deliberate steps across the ceiling until he was directly over the Arch's head.

The Arch Mage struggled to his feet, clutched the staff, pulled a deep breath inside himself. Great winding spires of magic drew into him. They puffed up his body, made it bloated, his skin stretched. His head and face grew large, his lips hung open. With a great huffing noise, *hoom*, his mouth poured many-coloured fire at the ceiling above. Waves of violent colour splashed all through the hall.

Eric dived at Aziel entirely from instinct, without time to think that Vyin's charm might protect them both. It seemed a shell of clear air formed about them, deflecting the Arch Mage's colourful fire. The grey robes' bodies were blasted from existence.

On and on the Arch's desperate fire went, his body now a conduit converting the raw airs into refined destructive power. There may have been better things to cast, had he the time to think. Had he known a dragon would come, he'd have used magic to escape, just as he'd escaped Vous so many times. He'd not have tried to fight it. In that moment, however, he was shocked: the two young ones had spoken truly. The dragons *had* sent them. For an instant, all became clear to him: I did their work all along. The dragons used me. Now they discard me, as I discarded so many generals and mayors. As I tried to discard Vous . . .

Hauf, part dragon, part golem with skin of stone, did not care for spell craft, least of all the spells of men. The colours of the Arch's fire poured into Hauf like water down a black ditch. The Arch, spent and almost burned out by his own casting, dropped his staff and fell on the shaking floor. Foul smoke poured out of him. Heavy as a mountain Hauf dropped down upon him, bones breaking with his weight. The Arch Mage cried out, joyously welcoming his death.

But again he'd misjudged. Hauf took one of the Arch's horns in his mouth. Slowly he twisted his head sideways, pulled until the horn broke off and came loose with a thread of brackish fluid. The Arch's body twisted, thrashed. Hauf set a paw down to still him, took the other horn in his mouth, pulled it free and spat it away. Still the castle roiled and shook itself. 'Aziel,' gasped the Arch Mage.

'Do I slay him, Firstborn?' said Hauf in his voice of stone.

'He may stay,' she said, struggling to stand on the shaking floor. Her necklace glowed with silver light. 'Shift your form now, Avridis.'

'Obey the firstborn,' Hauf commanded.

Black smoke poured into the hall as the Arch Mage shifted to his animal form. The silver light of Aziel's necklace beamed through the smoke to show a bird, black like a crow but larger. It writhed and thrashed, one broken wing under Hauf's front paw.

'In this form, you will stay,' said Aziel in a voice that was not entirely her own. Purple light flickered in her eyes. 'I shall find a cage for you. You will be fed and given water. And you will know what it means to be caged, as I was caged, under your care. Caged, like those who sent us here to rule, and whose wishes you defied. Word of what befell you shall be spread so others know we truly are firstborn of the Favoured peoples, Favoured by the dragons, Lord and Lady of Levaal North.'

The castle shook harder yet. Eric slid into the wall.

'Call off the dragon,' Aziel yelled to him.

'How? Hauf! Leave us. Your work's done here.'

Eric could not hear his own voice above the castle's rattling; but Hauf turned to him and lowered his head. He said, 'You may call on me twice more. Then I am free.' Hauf collapsed into a pile of black stones. Within a minute, the castle ceased its convulsions and went still. The black bird hobbled and squawked, mournful sounds. It stumbled towards the window but could not hop up to the sill. It held aloft broken, mangled wings. Its one eye gleamed red, sad and angry. At last it was clear Avridis understood.

21

THE NEW ARCH MAGE

Eric ran from that hall, not knowing where he went, or even why he ran. The light that had shone in Aziel's eyes and the cold power in her voice went through his mind. Suddenly he felt like an animal whose foot had come down very close to a trap, one that would have closed if he were arrogant enough to accept the dragons' offer and declare himself lord. His encounter with Shilen loomed in his mind too: the visions of Earth destroyed, his familiar streets buried in ruin.

He went down flights of steps to the lower levels, still full of adrenaline. It did not make sense that the castle seemed to be in order; furniture, objects and the rare servant should have been a wreck, if indeed the castle had physically turned itself on its head at Hauf's appearance. Was it possible the quake had been limited to that single hallway?

He paused for breath before a window looking out onto the Great Dividing Road. Without much thought he took Hauf's amulet and drew his hand back to fling it out into the air. At that moment he noticed four unusual figures moving about among the dead Vous-things strewn on the lawns: a drake, a half-giant and two men.

Faul and Case he recognised at once. 'Loup, is that you?' he called.

It was indeed Loup with them. The folk magician climbed aboard the red drake. Its wings thumped the air and brought it skywards. Eric called to Loup again until he'd located the right window. Case's growl was happy as he hovered in the air outside it. Eric reached out, stroked his nose, got his hand licked and a whiff of breath he could have done without.

Case thrust his head through the window. Loup climbed off his back onto the sill, while with many grunts and growls Case pushed himself through the space slightly too small for him. Part of the window frame broke away. Below, Faul and Lut marched up the same steps through which Eric and Aziel had come.

'That Arch still here?' said Loup. 'Give you trouble? I ain't got a mind to fight him, but Faul does. Grumbled about what she'd do to him all the way here.'

'He's dead now, Loup.'

'Dead?'

'Well, incapacitated at least.'

'Vous killed him, eh? I knew that'd happen.'

Wearily Eric recounted the tale, showed Loup the amulet. Loup murmured to himself, worried, as he examined it. 'Dragon-make, this. But then you knew that already. Far too interested in our petty doings, are those great beasts. Whatever they told you, Eric, it comes back to them getting out of their cages and *that*'s all. When they're out, none but them know what comes next.'

'Loup, they say Aziel and I own the castle now. That we rule it.'

Surprising him, Loup grabbed him by the shoulders, his

gnarled hands gripping hard. 'Listen to this. We may love our dogs and goats. We tie em in the yard for their own good, or we kill em when it suits. Maybe we improve their lot on the whole, or maybe we don't. But I'll tell you this just once. I think you're a twit half the time . . . you should've never flown north like you done, nor gone through the door at all, but I respect you. *You* choose. Choose for others or for yourself, but either way, *you* choose. And not cos the dragons wish it upon you. I can see in your eyes you only half believe all this is real. But real it is, and this choice matters. I'll be right here advising ye, if ye wish it, whatever Queen Aziel has to say.'

Aziel's voice called from the floor above theirs, seeking him. 'And there's your queen now,' muttered Loup. 'Listen. You know her heritage, lad. You know she was born with lordship in her veins. I'll not tell ye what to do, but you could be of service to the rest of us. All of us. You could keep her restrained! Dull her fangs, cos she'll grow long ones when she's on that throne, and use em too, you mark me saying it. Power may not do her well at all, lad. Does most men ill who wield it, even ones who don't assume they got a right to it. Keep an eye on her. That's the best thing you could do, *if* you decide you'll take this job.'

Loup grabbed Eric's wrist, the one which held the amulet. He peered at it suspiciously. The metal was still warm – it had grown warm when Eric summoned then banished Hauf. 'Can't fathom this,' Loup murmured. 'It does more'n just summon that dragon you speak of. Casting something about you now, but I can't see it nor fathom what it does. It's not too distant from what Aziel wears, but hers is mightier. Heed this: don't keep calling that dragon to help you. Not unless it's that, or death. No dragon's made to be a man's pet and helper. They even begrudge our use of drakes, it's said. I'd wager Hauf broke some law among his kind, and was bound this way in punishment. To be a man's pet, that's worse than death to that prideful kind! When Hauf gets free of you, he'll bite out your throat.'

'Loup, I don't want to be any king or lord. I don't know what I want. I was going to toss the amulet away.'

'No! No, no! Powerful thing like this left to chance will seek out those wanting power. Remember: wizards cast spells, aye, but spells cast wizards too! Not always, but often. This thing isn't casting you, but it might cast the next who has it. You already took it as your own. That's like taking an oath. Ill comes, great ill, if you break it.'

'YOU, PILGRIM!' Faul's voice boomed, making Loup and Eric jump, and Case's head rear back so fast it hit the wall. Faul strode in, boots thumping on the castle floor as if it were her own front porch. Lut scrambled in behind her, a short-sword in hand.

'Hi,' said Eric.

'Afternoon,' said Lut, nodding.

'THAT FOOL AVRIDIS. I'LL KICK HIS HEAD ACROSS THE REALM, WHATEVER TRICKERY HE TRIES TO WEAVE. BRING HIM HERE!' She smashed one great fist into the other.

Loup explained what had happened.

'THEN LISTEN, MAN-KING. READ THE SIGNS ABOUT THE LAND! YOU'VE NO ARMY. THE CITIES DO! AND MEN LOVE WAR. THE NEAREST CITIES MAY BE DEAD, ALL STARVED OUT, PLAGUED WITH TORMENTORS, I'VE NO NOTION. BUT HIGH CLIFFS, TANTON, YINFEL AND OTHERS: THEY'VE MEANS TO SEIZE THIS PLACE, AND YOU NO MEANS TO HALT THEM! THEY'LL COME, WHATEVER YOU CLAIM THE DRAGONS DECREE. BE GLAD THE MAYORS ARE DISTRACTED WITH THEIR OWN STRIFE, AND BY

BUSINESS AT WORLD'S END. DISTRACTED . . . FOR NOW! THE
DAY THEY LEARN THE CASTLE IS RIPE TO TAKE IS THE DAY
THEY RIDE HERE, THINKING THIS PLACE HOLDS THE SECRET
TO POWER, RULE, GODHOOD AND MORE NONSENSE BESIDES.
YOU NEED HELP. I CAN GIVE IT, BUT NOT FOR FREE.'

'I'm listening, Faul.' Indeed his ears rang.

'THERE ARE A THOUSAND OF MY PEOPLE IN THE UNCLAIMED
LANDS. I'LL NOT SAY WHERE LEST WE ONE DAY NEED TO HIDE
AGAIN. BUT IT IS CLOSE ENOUGH TO BEAT THE CITIES HERE.'

Loup spluttered, lost for words.

'SURPRISED? OF COURSE IT'S TRUE. EVEN STRAGGLERS OF
MY KIND THINK THEMSELVES THE LAST ONES LEFT! NOT SO. A
THOUSAND AND TWELVE ELDERS, MORE IF THEY'VE BRED.
KNOWING THAT LOT, THEY WILL HAVE DONE! THEY DEPARTED
TO THE UNCLAIMED LANDS THE SAME DAY THE BOUNTIES
BEGAN. I'VE A MOUNTAIN'S SOUL, NOT TO BE SHOVED, SO I
STAYED PUT, TO BE EYES AND EARS FOR THE REST. AWAITING
THE DAY AVRIDIS OR VOUS FELL. THE DAY HAS COME. I'LL SEND
WORD. LUT KNOWS WHERE THEY HIDE. GO, LUT! GET A STEED
FROM BELOW AND RIDE.'

Lut nodded, turned to leave, but Faul – with as much speed
as Eric had seen in any half-giant – rushed to block his path.
She picked him up over her head and planted a long noisy kiss
on his face. A big red welt had already risen from forehead to
cheek by the time she set him down. 'WATCH FOR ELEMEN-
TALS. BIRDS SAY THE FIRE ONES ARE ACTIVE OF LATE.'

'Shall do. G'bye,' said Lut. Down the steps he went, not wiping
her spit from his face.

'A WEEK OR TWO, MAN-KING. LUT RIDES FAST AND MY FOLK
CAN MARCH FAST. SURVIVE THAT LONG AND YOU'LL HAVE YOUR
ARMY. NOT GREAT IN NUMBER, BUT A FAIR BEGINNING. NO

CITY WILL TROUBLE YOU WHILE WE SAY SO. I'LL NAME OUR
TERMS FOR THIS BEFORE YOU AND THE QUEEN.'

'Whatever terms you want are fine with me,' said Eric. 'Aziel's
upstairs, looking for a cage for her new pet bird.' He climbed
aboard Case and whispered in the drake's ear. Case clambered
up on the window sill then out into the air outside.

'Where to now, lad?' said Loup nervously.

'Anywhere. I'm going for a ride. By the way, Loup, how'd you
like to be the new Arch Mage?'

Loup sputtered. 'What?'

'I know you're not the most powerful wizard. But I don't
know much about magic. You can at least teach me about it.
Job's yours, if you want it. See you later. Go, Case.'

'O no, you don't.' Loup ran for the window, jumped out into
the air and clutched onto Case's tail just as the drake began to
fly away. In surprise, Case burped fire. Exasperated, Eric reached
out a hand to help Loup onto the drake's back.

22

WORLD'S END

Of all the things Far Gaze despised – and the list grew daily – having to use any kind of combat magic in human form was foremost. The airs' lingering foreign pollution had filled his body with a queasy, lasting sickness. If the mayor's men came at him again, he thought he would prefer to wear a few sword wounds than cast to fight them.

The man with broken ribs coughed, then shrieked in pain. It was some compensation. Far Gaze rode behind them like a herdsman. The men sensed his mood well enough and they hardly dared speak. City men like these who didn't study magic closely had little idea of its limits – they probably assumed he could set them all aflame with just a thought or two. He would let them think so at least until they reached the tower. When things calmed, he would try to re-establish some trust, for Tauk would honour no debt to someone who'd become an enemy.

The tower was not far when a sight halted the horses in their tracks well before the men saw it. A man on horseback was facing towards World's End. A large man, too large in fact to *be* a man. There was a golden haze about him, rippling the air like the lapping of disturbed pond water. One of the men gasped, whispered something, kissed the chain about his neck.

Tauk drew his blade and raised it. His nervous horse pawed the ground. 'Say your name,' Tauk cried.

The stranger turned his head their way. 'Do you not recognise him, Mayor?' said Vade breathlessly. 'Here is my patron Spirit.'

'Valour!' the other men exclaimed together.

The Spirit's words fell heavy about them: 'Is Nightmare close?'

'We saw him far to the east, Valour,' said Tauk, quickly sheathing his sword.

Valour said, 'A dragon is close. I claim this foe. He is not yours. Have you seen him?'

'We have, Valour. He flew past here.'

The light of Valour's eyes was piercing and cold. It fell upon Far Gaze. 'Have you seen the dragon?'

'I battled the dragon you speak of,' said Far Gaze, desperately trying to recall what lore he knew of this Spirit. 'For many days, I battled it. That was long before you named it as your foe.'

Valour's gaze stayed upon him a while longer. 'That is well. You are to remain here. It is to war I ride.'

Far Gaze remembered what Blain had said of the Pendulum's swing, of the dangers of great powers crossing World's End. If Valour crossed, something mighty would come into the north. Was it up to him, then, to argue with a god? To tell a god not to do what it wished to do? He wiped sweat from his brow, took a deep breath. 'Valour. What of the Pendulum swing? If you cross World's End, will not things of your great stature cross back?'

Valour said, 'Things transpire beyond ken of Spirit, of dragon, of man.' Slowly his head turned back towards the south. 'War strikes hot blades to their new shape.'

'We shall join you!' Tauk cried. Tears of joy were in his eyes, the other men's too.

'I know that you shall,' said Valour. 'Weapons, you shall have.' The men's swords sparkled and grew hot. Frantically they drew them, tossed them away. The blades fell on the grass, dissolved into sparkling misty light which quickly vanished. New blades were in their holsters. 'Armour, you shall have,' said Valour. There was the rattle and chime of chain mail as new armour wrapped around the men's bodies. It gleamed with bright silver light.

Joyous, they whooped, spurred their mounts to him. 'Your arm is well,' said Valour to Tauk. 'Your body is healed,' he said to the man with broken ribs. 'Your steeds are refreshed, and ready. You men are fed, and well, and ready to ride with me to war.'

Far Gaze saw the debt he'd endured so much for slipping away. 'Heal me also, I ask you,' he said. 'Heal me of the sickness these foolish men caused me, and give me your blessing, Spirit. I battled your foe, a dragon. It was a foe beyond me, but I fought with courage. You know I speak the truth.'

Tauk glared at him, but Valour did not react. Across the boundary of World's End, a group of the new peoples – the haiyens – stood among curls of mist, watching them. The Spirit's steed took two strides towards them before it halted.

Valour turned his head, looking back behind as if he'd heard something in the distance.

'Does something trouble you, Spirit?' said one of Tauk's men.

'For what do we wait?' cried Tauk, eyes gleaming with battle lust. 'Lead us on!'

'My witness,' said Valour. His great steed took a few slow wheeling steps then dashed north with great speed, kicking up a huge plume of dust behind it.

The mayor's men tried to follow. Their steeds ran faster than horses naturally run, but not fast enough to keep the god in sight. Far Gaze went on his way to the tower, bitter to have lost his indebted mayor – for now at least – but glad to be alone. He felt too sick right now to shift into wolf form, but suspected that the next time he did, he might just stay that way.

So, that was Valour. Sword drawn, eager for war. Meting out blessings just for men who craved battle. How much easier would life have been for Far Gaze if he had been a man like them? He felt like weeping. A mage's true place was to guide others past dangers they scarce understood. Men such as those, demanding and bellowing, blades drawn to swing at any moment. He saw it now: the schools of magic were right to withdraw their services from humankind, to live aloof and away from them. They'd been *right*!

Alas for him, it wasn't long before Tauk and his men returned. Their weapons were drawn again and the light of battle was still in their eyes. 'You are our captive,' Tauk announced. 'Will you fight us now, brave mage? Now that the blessing of our patron Spirit is in our blood?'

'I never wished to fight you.'

'I dismiss your claim of debt,' said Tauk.

Far Gaze sucked his teeth. 'That choice will end poorly. Are you sure that is your wish?'

'Ha! Bind his hands. None of your cheek now, mage. I'll not gag you, but I'll cut your wolf tongue out. Bind him! We ride. The tower is close.'

23

UNDRESSED

While Anfen and Shilen walked through the quiet countryside she told him more tales; rather, she seemed to speak them to the air, and he heard them as he heard the bird calls and peaceful wind. The country was familiar to him. With Loyalist pride he'd led men through these lands, all of them young and stupid, their heads full of lies about those evil Rebel Cities. Lies which made them willing to march, proudly notching kills on their belts or kit bags.

Anfen remembered how he'd lined up those men and women before a ditch he'd made them dig, his belly roiling, sick, hands trembling. Not with fear, but doubt. He had carefully thought through his loyalty – it wasn't blind at all. Yet here was a trembling family, young and old all together before the ditch they'd dug. Accused of practising rites the castle forbade. He'd seen the totems and stones with his own eyes, objects of the most forbidden and dangerous kind. He had his orders. He thought of the castle, of honour, of being the leader of men they'd made him. Then he'd cut their heads off with his own sword when all of his men had refused to.

A leader no more, he followed Shilen through fields battered by castle-army boots. He thought he saw a Vous-thing in the distance – or perhaps it was Vous himself – in a gaily moving dance of sweeping arms, spilling white and gold light into the air. He was there and gone in a second. Anfen rubbed his eyes – surely just more tricks of his mind.

Shilen's latest story had finished. He'd missed how it ended. 'Is it really true, there is a new lord coming?' he said.

She smiled, radiant. 'It is true. He knows and loves you, warrior. It is the Pilgrim.'

Anfen laughed. 'The Otherworld prince. His lie came true.'

'Yes, and Aziel shall be with him. She is nothing like those who raised her. A ruler from each world. The worlds are joined, after all, warrior. I think all worlds are joined.'

'All worlds? How many worlds are there?'

She smiled but did not answer. She ran ahead, her hair flying behind her. He followed, sword inhibiting his run. He unstrapped it, let it fall to the ground. She'd passed from sight down an incline by the time he looked up – how fast she moved! A lake came into view, ringed on its far side by rocky hills touched with snow. Light steam rose from the water. Shilen's clothes fell about her feet. She turned to him, her tall full body the finest he'd ever seen. Her laugh was bells pealing. She dived into the water.

Anfen unstrapped the breastplate and let it fall to the ground. He stripped off his clothes and dived in after her. Despite the white snowy caps on the far shore's hills the water was warm, it was perfect. *She* was perfect. Her free, clear laugh joyously declared them the owners of the lake, and for all he cared they were the only people still alive in the entire world. Anfen had never been so free, so happy as he was in this moment.

'Come to me,' she said. He swam out after her, the water's warmth pouring life into his blood. She floated on her back, seeming to glide on the water's surface. Her arms opened wide to embrace him, wider yet . . . then they seemed, impossibly, to stretch till they surrounded him in the water. 'Don't fear me,' she whispered.

He didn't fear, for suddenly there was no will to live left in him. He went cold.

Her skin changed from its healthy glow till it was white as the clouds. Scales poked through it until they covered her. Her neck stretched and arched above him. Her head lengthened, sleek and long. Eyes brilliant as jewels, slitted like a serpent's, looked down at him and deep inside him, further than he could look inside himself.

'Kill me,' Anfen said. 'Give me peace.'

'I don't wish to kill you,' she said in a voice gone deeper but still musical. 'I wish to swim with you.' Her body pushed through the water, pulling him along in the current it created. One long white wing stretched tall and fanned like the mast of a sail, catching wind. 'This is a better place to call home,' she said. 'Isn't it, warrior?'

24

LESSONS

'No,' said Shadow.

Sharfy turned to him. 'What?'

'The answer is no. I don't.'

It was Shadow's third or fourth completely random outburst. The ghost had taken to following Sharfy around as he skirted the land a ways south of the castle, now and then calling Anfen's name.

Sharfy also sought to find the woman who'd deceived and bewitched him (as he saw it). In truth he hoped he wouldn't find her. Honour required that he slay her, but he'd never slain a woman before, let alone a beautiful one. Doing it would not be easy.

Shadow's large eyes peered into his. They were curious pits waiting like hungry mouths to have something put in them. Sharfy said, 'Go away. What? What do you mean, "no" what? What answer? Huh?'

'You said, do I think I know so much. No, I don't. You can teach me.'

'Know. Teach. Eh!' Sharfy rubbed his temples. 'Worse than Anfen, for travel talk, you are. Never said that.'

'Back at the bed. When I made sure you wouldn't die.'

'Answer me *then*. Answer questions *when someone speaks em*. Not days later. Stupid.' Shadow's head cocked sideways, the way it did when he seemed to have understood something new. 'Not like that, either,' said Sharfy. 'Nod your head if you agree on something. Like this, see? Got it?'

Shadow's head became a blur of motion, so fast it was just a streak of colour.

'Funny,' said Sharfy. He resumed walking. 'What are you, anyway? Ghost?'

'I don't know.'

'Tell me. Don't hold back. Reckon you know stuff about other people. Why not you?'

'I can't shadow myself.'

'Why'd you kill Siel?'

'That hurts. Don't talk about it.'

'Pah! You killed her. You deserve it to hurt, if you killed her. I killed people too. Never a woman. What's it like? Bad huh? Knew it. I only killed people who tried to kill me first. Got it? That should be a rule for you. Kill people who try to kill you first.' Sharfy reflected. 'Or one time when I robbed someone . . . but that's bad too. Long time ago. Don't rob no one less you have to. Got it?'

Shadow nodded.

'Why'd you kill Siel? She was all right. Pretty good bow-shot. Saw her miss a few times. Not much, though. I think it was that touch of magic she had, made her a good bow-shot. Skinny girl like her shouldn't be able to pull the string back all the way like she could. I could shoot better. But bow's a coward stick. For men with no sword play. Or women I guess. But you need a few bows. That's a shame. Should all be swords. All those wars. Just a few swords should do it. Like in Valour's Helm. Your ten best, our ten best. Fight! Winner wins. No more armies marching, killing everyone who don't deserve it. That'd be better.'

Shadow nodded.

'Anfen!' Sharfy yelled. Shadow dashed off ahead of him. 'Good,' Sharfy called. 'Stay away.'

But Shadow returned. 'Wrong way,' he said.

'What?'

'He's not the way you're walking.'

'How you know?'

Shadow's body orbited his in ten or more fast blurs. 'There was something over there made of air.'

'Elemental? Don't go near em. Dangerous. They kill people without meaning to.'

'I shadowed it. It didn't like to be shadowed. But I said I'd leave it alone if it answered a question. So it did.'

'See? That's what I mean. You know how to do that. But need me to tell you how to answer a question proper?' Shadow looked at him, waiting. 'All right,' said Sharfy. 'Which way? Point the way. That way? That way's a lake. Why'd Anfen go to a lake for?'

Shadow said nothing.

'Don't answer the question later. Answer now. See?'

'There's no answer.'

'Huh. Then you say, I don't know. You already knew that! Don't joke around. So we'll go to that lake. If you lied, I'll cut you. I don't care about your fancy tricks. I don't back down. There's one for you. Don't ever back down.'

Shadow nodded.

They went beside a thin winding river in a glacier-carved groove, feeding out into what locals called Crown Lake. Sharfy had been here twice before, in his late teens, fishing. Near the shore he'd learned the value of facial scars with women who liked their men bruised and battered. He'd gone and overdone it, of course. Never handsome, but he'd had fewer scars and dents back then. 'Listen. You know anything about Valour?' said Sharfy.

'There,' said Shadow, pointing at the lake.

'Valour! Where? I don't see him. What's . . .?' Sharfy cut his words off. He'd taken the sight at first for a strange boat with a white sail. Bigger than a canoe, a bit smaller than those fishing boats over at the Godstears. But the sail flexed and moved like an arm would move. It dipped down into the water and the whole thing capsized. Its neck arched over the water, gazing down at its own back, or so it seemed. 'Dragon?' Sharfy said, hardly trusting his eyes. He rubbed them. 'You see it?'

'That's her,' said Shadow.

'Huh? What?'

'The one who gave you the silver scale.'

'Don't be stupid. A woman gave me that. Not a dragon.' He saw something by the water's edge, possibly clothes. Possibly a dress. 'Maybe it ate her. Good! I don't have to kill her now. Never wanted to. Only thought she was pretty.' It was then he saw Valour's breastplate. 'It ate Anfen too!'

'No. He's swimming with it.'

Sharfy saw him then, a limp shape seemingly being pushed about on the water's surface by the dragon's wings. Shadow vanished from Sharfy's side and quickly returned. 'She didn't see me. I know things about her now. I'll forget a lot of it soon.'

'Know things? Like what?'

'She's going to kill him. But she also likes him. It's strange.'

'Huh? Makes no sense.'

'She's like men are when they have meat set before them. They like it. But they eat it.'

Sharfy drew his sword.

'You can't hurt her,' said Shadow.

'Shut up.'

'That sword won't cut her. She's strong.'

'Anfen's sword! That'll cut her, that'll cut anything. If he left the breastplate, the sword's there too somewhere. Get it. Go get it. Quick.'

'You can't kill her with any sword.'

'Get the sword!'

Shadow whizzed to the water's edge, then away into the fields adjacent. 'It's there,' he said upon returning, pointing to where Anfen had dropped it.

'Get it,' said Sharfy.

'No.'

'Get it!'

'I won't touch it. It hurt me badly.'

'Get the armour then.'

'No. It might hurt me too.'

Sharfy swung his blade at Shadow, just a warning. Shadow's mouth opened wide for an instant, eyes too, all of them wide enough to swallow him. Sharfy cringed back, recovered, lunged again. Shadow dodged. 'Your sword can't hurt me. The other sword can. But we shouldn't fight.'

'What's that dragon want with my friend?' Sharfy said, as if Shadow had had some part in it.

'She'll kill him. And take that armour away.'

'Dragons don't wear armour. They got scales. Make some sense, stupid ghost.'

'She wants the armour. There's magic in it, she wants its magic. She's going to kill him then take it.'

'Can *you* kill her?'

Sharfy had meant it as a taunt, an insult. He hadn't expected Shadow to say, 'Maybe.'

'But she's a dragon! How?'

'I scared a dragon away, once. From Siel, in the woods. It liked her. It didn't know I was there. When I shadowed it, it thought I was another dragon which crept up on it. It was very scared.'

'Do it now! Go, do it now!'

A winged shape flew over their heads. Sharfy ducked down, covering his head. He heard something heavy drop in the grass, not far away. When he looked up, Eric and Loup were climbing off the back of a red drake. Loup did a double take upon seeing Sharfy.

Shadow was no longer beside him.

25

SHADOWTRAP

Case's behaviour had become strange when the lake's blue-white hills appeared on the horizon. As though he'd caught a scent, his wings beat harder, faster in fact than Eric or Loup could recall him moving. The drake responded to none of their words, to no yelled threats. His breath came in big huffs. From his nostrils flared a glow like red coals. Soon Eric and Loup both just had to hold on.

On the lake's waters something came into view which both men at first thought was a white boat with one sail raised. Case landed heavily in the grass and shook himself until his passengers climbed off.

Eric had barely set his feet down when a wave of heat hit him and knocked him on his back. A streak of colour tore across the ground from where Sharfy lay. It blurred in a fast orbit around him, its human features growing long and distorted. Eric knew it was Shadow. Little threads of colour were sucked from the blurring streak and into the amulet he wore, the same amulet which had summoned Hauf. After his brief resistance Shadow was caught inside it, drawn in just as he'd been caught in Aziel's necklace. The force of it pushed Eric tumbling across the ground. Where Shadow had circled him was a blackened burned ring, puffing up smoke.

Loup would have been flabbergasted enough by the drake's behaviour, more so by the sight of Sharfy lying there in the grass (Sharfy, who he'd assumed was by now beheaded from boasting too much in a tavern somewhere). The sight of what he now recognised as a dragon playfully swimming out in the water stunned Loup to silence. Then he saw Anfen was out there with it . . . then he saw Vous, the god of beauty, dancing without a care further around the shore. And then Shadow was sucked into Eric's dragon-made charm.

So Loup collapsed on the grass, mouth open, staring at nothing, unable to speak, think or move. His overtaxed mind gave no warning about the brief holiday it would now take. It embarked. He did nothing more for a little while.

Eric climbed painfully back to his feet. The amulet was so hot he hurled it away. Like an insect it scuttled back to him, crawled up his pant leg, put itself in his pocket.

'Eric!' Sharfy hissed, angry. 'Why'd you do that? He's going to fight the dragon. Let him out of there.'

'I don't know how.'

'Get down out of sight. That's a dragon, in the water. You're dumber than the ghost. Get down before it sees you.'

The drake bounded towards the shore. He growled loud, apparently eager to get the dragon's attention.

Sharfy cocked his head – he thought for a moment he'd heard the sound of hooves approaching. It couldn't be hooves – the sound was too similar to distant thunder. He went quite pale. 'What's the matter?' Eric asked him.

'Valour's coming.'

*

Out on the water, Anfen had not seen the drake and its passengers arrive. If Shilen had seen them, she gave no indication. 'Why did you fight for your masters?' she said. Her eyes peering down seemed to shine with love. Her voice was deep and gentle. 'It's so silly, so easily answered. Yet you've made such a puzzle of it, it has destroyed you. I could tell you why you fought. Shall I? Do you fear the truth more than you fear death, warrior?'

Shilen pushed herself further out towards the blue-white icy hills. Anfen's body rolled like a log but she would not let him sink. As the world spun overhead, water, skies and the lake's bank, he thought he saw Vous again, dancing gaily on the shore, flinging flower petals into the air. Anfen envied him. 'Kill me,' he said.

'I shall. First I will tell you why you fought for them. You fought because you believed yourself weaker than them. You were free all along to leave them to fight their own wars, with you no part of it. If every man did that one simple thing, there would be no masters of men, at least no masters as cruel as yours are. That freedom is a gift you never knew you had: that choice. Dragons do not have that choice. Dragons envy it.' She pointed her head skywards, bright yellow eyes gleaming as if they pierced all the skies to meet the gaze of listening dragons above.

He wept. 'They raised us to know only that path. From birth, they taught it to me. How was I to know different, until I walked the path I walked, and learned the truth? How does a child with a wooden sword know better, with smiling adults all about him?'

'But still you haven't learned the truth, even in this moment when your life is about to end. Those human masters you obeyed never loved you. Those who respect them the most, who obey them swiftest, are the ones the human masters hate the most.'

'I fought against the bastards too.'

Her gleaming eyes poured love over him. 'No. Two kings who mean to play at war need the other side as badly as their own, warrior. You ever followed other men's will. Because you suffered, you thought your service to them had value. It did not. Not one drop of blood spilled truly mattered to them. Now your torment ends. Now I shall make you free.'

Her jaws descended on him at last. The two parts of his body floated gently to the surface as she pushed herself through the water away from him, swimming as she had dreamed of doing for a long time. Each movement and ripple of water was a joy to her. Dragons knew patience, and knew to savour things; for they now knew times could come unbidden when memories grow more precious than any material treasure. Precious were these collected journeys to take with them into cages, then to stroll through at leisure when stone walls shut them in, crushing and cold.

While Shilen loved and savoured the water, with no more thought for Anfen's corpse than she had for the other floating bits and pieces, Vous danced gaily on as if he shared the joy of her freedom and wished for her nothing less. She did not see him. The wind carried his flower petals far. A gust took a clutch of them further and higher, as if a grateful spirit had caught a handful of it on its journey away from that place.

'It got him,' said Sharfy. He blinked, rubbed his eyes. The two parts of Anfen floated only briefly before they sank under the surface.

Loup recovered from his shock at all he'd recently seen.

He crouched down beside Sharfy. 'Who got what? What got who?'

Sharfy did not answer – he just stared at where Anfen's body had been.

'It's Vous,' said Eric in amazement, pointing at the grassy field where the Spirit danced in and out of their sight. Flower gardens had sprung up about him. Like Vous, they too faded in and out of sight.

'Don't fear that nutty Spirit,' said Loup. 'We've other troubles. Old Case is going to bring the dragon over. Look! He's burping flame now to get its attention. All of you sit still, don't move. No sounds.'

'Let the ghost out of that charm,' said Sharfy.

Eric took the amulet from his pocket. It was cool to touch again, but holding it felt like holding a spider he wasn't sure was dead or not. Uselessly, he shook it. 'I don't know how to let him out, Sharfy. I didn't know it was going to trap him like that.'

'You didn't know, neither did Shadow,' said Loup. He said it as if this were important. 'Surprised him good, and he didn't feel it coming.'

'Too late now,' said Sharfy. 'Anfen's dead. You helped kill him.' He raised his sword in two hands, surprising Eric and Loup so much they almost allowed him to plunge it into Eric's chest. Loup got his wits back, grabbed Sharfy's arm by the bicep. There was a snapping noise. Sharfy dropped the sword, clutching his hand. He threw a punch at Loup, connected, sent him sprawling away.

'Stop it,' Eric said in a voice hardly his own. His charm gave a burst of heat. Sharfy not only stopped – he went completely still. Eric understood he'd just cast his first spell, without meaning to or knowing how. The charm quickly cooled again.

Loup rose from the grass, rubbed his cheek. 'Leave Sharfy be,' he said. 'A dragon just killed his friend. My friend too.' A tear was in his eye. 'Let Sharfy out of that spell, lad. Amulet was what cast it? Through your voice, aye?'

Eric gawked at the amulet quite helplessly. 'Free yourself,' he ventured. Nothing happened. The muscles of Sharfy's face twitched. 'Move again. Step forth. Be freed.' Nothing.

'Look with your mage eyes, lad. Airs are a little kicked up, but not much. It's naught too serious, he's alive. We'll figure it out. Sharf, if you hear me, hold tight and we'll fix you. But I got to shut that drake up before he brings the murdering dragon on us.'

Loup ran over to Case, tried grabbing hold of one of his ears. The drake's head thrashed around, butting him down. 'One more bruise,' Loup said from the ground. 'What's the difference? But I won't be dragon food today, you stupid mule. It'll eat you too, believe me. *Hush it now!* No more of that fire.'

Shilen's body turned with slow grace, her face now pointing towards their shore. Briefly it seemed she went still, and then her wings fanned wide. In no hurry, she angled them so the wind took her sailing to the shore.

Loup sighed. 'So it ends. Why not here? It's a pretty enough spot. Say your last words, lad. We'll catch up with Anfen's spirit on our way out, if we're quick enough.'

When she was closer, Shilen unexpectedly dived till she was out of sight beneath a rippling spread of bubbles. Loup dashed back to Eric. 'Hear me, lad? We're done. Drake's called her over. I should've seen it coming. The birds bring him eggs to eat, he brings dragons *people* to eat. All that flying; it must've been what he was doing all along. Wasn't ferrying us around for free. He was looking for a dragon to offer us to. Don't run when it gets here, don't fight it. Might be that we can talk our way out, but that's all. The dragon Far Gaze battled didn't slay him when it might've done. They must like some sport.'

'She won't eat us, Loup,' said Eric.

From the water emerged not a dragon but a naked woman. Eric knew her face at once. She slipped her dress over her head, and glanced at a gleam of light where Vous had vanished from sight. The dress clung to her wet body. She crouched by a discarded breastplate for a minute or more before she picked it up and carried it with her. Valour's hoofbeats were still distant but growing ever louder.

Shilen jogged towards them, wet hair flopping and spraying water in the air. Case ran to meet her, joyful as a hound. She held up a hand in warning and he went no closer. 'Well met, man-lord,' said Shilen. She looked at Sharfy, still frozen.

'Leave him be,' said Loup.

'He is your business,' she said.

'Aye, lass, he is. You leave him alone. Which of the great beasts are you?'

'Beasts? That is a matter of perspective,' she said gently. 'Do you mean, which of the Eight am I? None. The sky has not yet weakened far enough for them to come. It shall do. Fear not. My name is one you've never heard. Call me Shilen. Few know me. You are privileged.' She turned back to Eric. 'Manlord, I gave you a task.'

'To take back the castle?' said Eric. 'We did it.'

'How did you two slay the mage there?'

'I summoned Hauf.'

She smiled. 'You did that while inside the castle? Tell me what happened.'

Eric nodded. 'Ahh. Now I understand why you didn't send any Invia to help us. That was what you wanted all along, wasn't it? For me to call Hauf, while we were in the castle. To see what would happen. That's why you sent us to do it alone.'

'Our deeds have many purposes, man-lord. A throne should not be freely given. To fight for it ensures you know its value. You earned the throne, be proud upon it.'

'You used us.'

'Summoning Hauf within the castle was a great risk. You slew the most cunning human wizard of these times, using a tool we gave you. You may have used any other tool you liked. This is the freedom you asked for. What happened when Hauf came? Tell me. You have been given much, with little asked of you.'

Eric laughed. 'Where are my manners? The castle shook, that's what happened. Now tell me why you killed Anfen.'

'It shook? Tell me more of that.'

'No more to tell. Use your imagination.'

She carefully set the breastplate down and squeezed water from handfuls of her hair. 'To answer you, I slew Anfen because he asked, in fact he begged, to be slain. And not because I hurt him. I wished to swim with him, that was all. Death was all he spoke of. He was slain quickly, with mercy. He knew no pain. That is the truth. Your children, I hear, slowly pull the wings off insects. Such things are not to our taste.'

'Nice of you to do a man's bidding,' said Loup, wiping a tear from his eye.

'I regret to have pained you,' she said, inclining her head. 'One must care for those dear to him.' To Eric, 'Taking the castle is not the only task I gave you. I have heard that Inferno may soon awaken. He will swallow the cities with his fire. Have you no wish to stop this?'

'I'm human. You're a dragon. Who is better placed between the two of us to stop him?'

Shilen laughed. 'Who is better placed to avoid his shambling steps, once he is awoken? I tell you this, man-lord, in trust that you reveal it to none but your mate, Aziel. A dragon was sent before I came, to prevent Inferno's waking. He has chosen not to, seeking instead a life of play. He gambles on the great ones not gaining freedom, and he has made a terrible decision. Trust him not.'

'Dyan?' said Eric.

'You know him? That is well. Do not speak to him of this! He feels that by some late token gestures, he may regain favour; that his crime will be forgotten. But he is doomed. Inferno is a minor concern of ours, to have sent one so wicked and neglectful as Dyan to deal with it.'

'So minor that you'd break the law of your Parent?' said Loup.

When Shilen gazed at him her eyes seemed briefly like her dragon eyes, yellow and slitted for just an instant. Her words were to Eric. 'You made clear your wish for freedom, man-lord. Do you now wish for us to manage your business? Shall we handle the burning god? We can do. But such a service brings costs you may not like.'

'I never wanted to be a king of anything. Do what you want.'

Shilen stepped towards him. 'Take care, man-lord. You speak now for your people. Your words matter. I give advice as parent to hatchling. Heed me! Something dangerous stirs in the Ash Sea. It may be they cannot awaken him. Men have not yet learned it is unwise to play with things beyond their measure. This business occurs in your realm, is done by your subjects. It is your business more than mine.'

'She's lying,' said Loup wearily. He still wiped tears from his cheeks, one of which was bruised from Sharfy's punch. 'No way would the great beasts let old Inferno wake up, if they could stop it. Not old Inferno. No one wants him wakened. Man nor dragon nor Spirit.'

'I answer you only if the man-lord asks,' said Shilen. 'I am his link between humanity and dragonkind. Direct your questions through him.'

Eric held aloft the amulet. 'What happened to Shadow?'

'Ah, you have him,' she said. 'Good! Be careful, he is dangerous. Even dragons cannot sense him, when he comes near. Your charm is a shadowtrap. Other shadowtraps have been made. They are few, and distributed with great care. They won't hold him long. Nothing can.'

'How do I free him?'

'Don't!' Again, just for an instant her eyes flashed yellow and were slitted. 'As much as may be, he must be controlled. He has a purpose. Do not ask me! I do not know it. I will speak one final warning to you, man-lord. Another man-lord rises in the south. It is deemed he will be your foe.'

Eric laughed. 'Deemed by whom?'

'Of that I speak no more.' The thudding sounds had grown steadily louder. All turned their eyes south-east. 'Whose hoofbeats are they? Someone comes.' She reached a hand to Sharfy, touched his face. His body flopped down. He went on all fours, coughing. 'Who comes here?' she said.

'Valour,' he said, then looked up at who spoke. Recognising Shilen he lunged for his sword. With a flick of her fingers his sword skittered away from him.

'You'd better run,' said Loup. 'Gods don't like dragons.'

Indeed when he turned back to her she had already gone.

*

The breastplate was the reason Shilen had drawn Anfen to swim at this lake, for she had perceived something of the power within it, and did not dare take it from him while he lived. He had freely chosen to discard it in the grass; he had asked to be slain. That made things much safer; no natural laws of the Parent had been broken. Loup was relieved, though Shilen's masters among the Eight would now extract the artefact's strange power, and undoubtedly shape that power into a key to unlock a way into the other realm, the adjacent realm which Anfen had called the quiet. The dragons had little knowledge of that place, which their Parent in its wisdom had hidden from them.

Terrible light gleamed from the slit of Valour's helm as his steed thundered into view and came to a halt by the lake's edge. He dismounted, the ground shivering where his boots fell upon it. His anger darkened the sky. 'Where is my witness?' his voice boomed.

Eric found the words pulled from him: 'Dead now, Valour. Slain by a dragon.'

'What of the protection I gave him? What of the armour and sword? With those, nothing beneath the skies could do him harm.'

'Stolen by the same dragon that killed him,' said Eric and Sharfy together, neither of them in control of their speech.

'Where then is his body?' said Valour.

'It sank in the water.'

Valour drew his sword. 'You have failed and defied me, all of you here. You will join him. Step into the water, where you will sink in death beside him.'

It was as they took their first few involuntary steps that Vous's laughter burbled and fell about the fields like rain, dispelling

Valour's darkness. Valour mounted his steed and rode it to where Vous danced and sang through gardens he'd made there which were only half revealed. Quick and graceful he danced around the slashes of Valour's sword, did not seem to care that Valour's steed kicked and trampled fountains and flowers. Vous blew kisses in the air which burst into exploding sparks of gold. He turned Valour's parries and thrusts, and his steed's kicking legs, all into an unwitting dance. Ever came his laughter, more joyful as Valour's rage grew and grew, his battle cries becoming deafening. Off into the distance Vous led him until they were gone from sight and Valour's screams were no more than faint distant thunder.

Loup stared, mouth open, long after the two gods had gone, so gobsmacked he didn't see Eric climb aboard the drake again without him. Case took to the sky, leaving the others behind.

26

BY GORB'S OLD VILLAGE

With Far Gaze captive, the mayor and his men arrived at the village where Gorb had dwelled. It was abandoned, with many of its homes smashed, parts of walls and roofs lying about like broken eggshells. Tormentor tracks here and there punched the ground. The broken body of one lay piled by the well.

The men paused to roast a goat they'd found tied in a yard. Tauk kept flexing with wonder his newly healed arm.

'Where did the Spirit go to?' said Vade, examining the blessed armour he'd been given. It was between white and silver. Where firelight fell on it there sparkled patches of ruby light.

'He went to fight the dragon he'd named his foe,' said Fithlim.

'Nay! Not the one who flew over us: he went to fight one of the greats.'

'You believe the mighty beasts are free now?'

'Nay. I believe our patron rode to the very skies. He wished us to follow him, but we could not.'

'Nay! He wished us to remain here and guard World's End from other perils. A fight more to our degree. If we do this duty well, he will return for us, take us with him to help him slay the sky dragons.'

'Greetings!' called another voice, causing all three men to

draw their blades and stand. Blain hobbled towards their fire with the help of his walking stick. Kiown followed him.

Quickly the mayor moved the haiyen's body away from the fire to where long grass concealed it. Blain raised his left arm, forearm to his forehead: *No weapon here, we wish to speak.* Vade and Fithlim kept their blades out nonetheless, pointed to the ground. 'Hail,' they said.

'Hail and be seated,' said Tauk. 'Share the fire. But you both look fed enough and not in need of our meat.'

'Your tied-up companion looks hungry,' Blain grunted, nodding at Far Gaze. He lowered himself slowly to the ground.

'Never mind him, old man. He is a criminal by my city's rule.'

'If the city no longer exists, does the rule?' said Far Gaze.

'Shut up! I'll have that tongue of yours cut out.'

'I know this "criminal",' said Blain.

'Is that so?' Tauk eyed Kiown. 'A fighting man, I see. Your grandson? You little resemble each other.'

'Well, that's high praise!' Blain laughed so hard he nearly fell in the fire. 'No! No relation to this filth.' He shuddered in disgust, made perfectly sincere gagging and choking noises. The men looked at each other uneasily. All the while Kiown examined his amulet as if he were the only one here, dangling it by its chain like a pendulum. 'Well, let's get this over with,' said Blain. He cast off the tattered cloak he wore. His robe's colours bled out into the night. Tauk's two men rushed to their feet. Tauk held out a hand to calm them. He said, 'That is a Strategist robe?'

'It is. Rather, it used to be, for I have fled the castle. I am Blain.'

'So, you know a Strategist, wolf? We learn more of you yet.'

'Come now, Mayor: he and I weren't friends,' said Blain,

laughing. 'Don't worry about that! I tried to befriend him, but we battled. In the tower yonder, as it happens.'

'You said nothing of him being a Strategist when he approached us?' Fithlim yelled at Far Gaze.

'I forgot,' he replied.

'Easy, Fithlim,' said Tauk. 'For our part we forgot to feed him. He owes us no loyalty. Leave him be.' He tossed Far Gaze a shank of meat.

'Yes, I was a Strategist,' said Blain. 'But our world is changed now. Dwell in the past if you must. But know this: I was first to leave the castle, first to abandon Avridis to his doom. Betrayal can be a virtuous act. The soup-blesser disagrees, hence our quarrel, some days ago. It's good we meet, Mayor. I had hoped you would come. You are wise to return here. The tower has become a nest for the new folk! The new people, who call themselves haiyens. They build strange contraptions about it, and maybe elsewhere through the land too. Do you know anything of the haiyens?'

The mayor and Blain exchanged carefully worded stories, both omitting more than they told. Blain turned his attention to Far Gaze. 'Must he remain bound up? A more sincere enemy of Avridis you shan't find. Has your city Aligned to the castle?'

'Valour bade we tie him,' said Vade.

'Pff,' said Far Gaze.

'You cannot bind him, he is a dragon fighter!' said Blain, and snorted. 'Did he tell you that tale too? I don't believe it. That same dragon bit my best Hunter in two.'

'Of that, he spoke truly,' said Tauk uneasily. 'Valour heard the claim too, and did not dispute it.'

Blain's ensuing bark of laughter stunned the mayor and his men to silence. 'Do Spirits never lie, make mistakes? But forget that. Perhaps we've a future, eh? An empire to build. We'll see. Keep the Spirit's gifts. Ignore his words and actions! You heard me, ignore them. I know a thing or two of Spirits. They are not men. They don't move, think or speak as we do. A Spirit's truth is several truths at once, some which make lies of the others! And a man – even a great man, Mayor – becomes someone else if brought into a Spirit's service. I studied many cases. We had to know Spirits well, for we meant to create one. Fallible as men? *More* so. More profound beings make more profound mistakes. Don't be angry! You need me. My knowledge is far more useful than your sword. Better than an army of dimwits willing to die at your word.'

'I do not see my soldiers that way,' said Tauk, barely containing his fury.

Blain hardly noticed. 'We shall have alliance. I offer it, here and now. If the Spirit returns, we'll see. Until then, be Tauk the Strong once more, strong as your own will ever has been. Ah, yes! I have been an enemy to you. I and the other Strategists: your enemies. But you alone of the mayors we respected, Tauk. We knew you for a renegade among that stupid bunch. It was no game for you. War with your city was something we feared.'

'There is a tongue to cut out,' said Far Gaze. 'I cast upon you when I was attacked, but never stooped so low as flattery.' One of the men kicked him.

'None of that, you fool,' said Blain. 'His speech can't hurt you. Restrict him, yes, till he shows willingness to work with us. Do not strike him! Our resources are few. Mayor, we five are alone. Six, if the mage will join us. Ah, but empires have started with less than what we have between us, and from beginnings less auspicious than these. The game's not done yet.'

'Has Vous made the change?' said Far Gaze.

'By now, he must have,' Blain grunted. 'Who knows what he's become? To guess . . . beauty, vanity, something of the sort. It was his preoccupation, when human. Gazing at himself in mirrors. Collecting pretty things, and pretty people. Some of them he froze alive in ice or resin, kept in a hall like museum pieces. Destroyed anything that displeased his taste, with fury Inferno could never have matched. Ah, he was indeed a vile man to know!' Blain sighed, fondly reminiscing.

'As It wills,' one of Tauk's men ventured. The other offered Blain and Kiown some meat. Both refused it.

Blain laughed. 'As It wills? So, they still use that empty phrase. The giant slumbering thing has naught to do with anything. It wills nothing! Not till the Pendulum swings high indeed, and let's hope that's far from now. Tales speak grimly of times when it prowls the land, changing its world. As for Valour, you say he wished to ride across the boundary and fight? Then I'll wager another Spirit pulled him away before he could. That's why he fled north. The young Spirits are new to such times as this, you see. They were never here without the Wall. Nervous and skittish, all of them, I'll warrant. My guess? An old Spirit sensed Valour's intention, drew him away before he could cross. Perhaps Mountain. And away they'll keep him, if they can. Don't anger, Mayor. It's just a guess. The old gods have seen times like this before. They're older, wiser. They keep the young Spirits in check.'

'He went to fight a dragon,' said Vade. The look in his eye demanded Blain agree.

'As you like,' said Blain, shrugging. 'Guessing the purpose of Spirits is an old and futile sport. I've played it longer than you know.'

'Where is Siel?' said Far Gaze.

'Yes, where's the girl?' said Tauk.

'What girl?' said Blain.

'She was healed by the haiyens,' said Tauk, a part of the tale he'd not told Blain. 'We know not what traps or trickery went with their healing.'

Kiown had been twirling the charm on his finger, admiring the stone. 'Siel did not come here,' he said.

'Did you slay her?' said Far Gaze.

'If I had, you'd do what?' said Kiown.

'Shut your mouth, sapling!' Blain roared, his robe pulsing crimson. 'Respect! Fighting *you* was like squashing a wet turd, only far less pleasant. This soup-blesser showed more fight than you by far. Now, Mayor, never mind the Spirits. What of us? I have troubled to find those who know opportunity. Want your city back? I'll give it. And more! Vanquish all your foes. Eh? It's likely the other Strategists will be among your new foes. I know em all, better than they think. I'll outwit the lot of em. If you reject my allegiance, you'll be no enemy of mine, just a lone wanderer in dark times. Magic armour and sword or not. Ever waiting for the return of the Spirit who barely noticed you in the first place. Who has now forgotten you. Bah! Whether it angers you or not, it's the truth. If you wish no alliance with me, say so now and I'll search for wiser men.'

'I choose between my options, wizard,' said Tauk.

'Bravo,' said Blain.

'You say the new people are still nearby? The haiyens, as you call them.'

Blain pointed back at the tower. 'Domudess is with them. Colluding. He speaks their tongue.'

'Then we capture him. And them. And we take what knowledge they have, by force if they do not give it freely. What you say of Valour may be true. We care not. We were given his gifts and blessing and we know honour. We will do what duty he has given us: protect this land from these unwelcome visitors.'

Blain tugged his beard thoughtfully. 'Attack the haiyens? You have good faith in Valour's gifts, Mayor. I respect that wizard Domudess! He bested me once already. It cost me a Hunter, a good one. Are you sure this is a fight you wish to have?'

'The haiyens beat these same men once already, with ease,' said Far Gaze, yawning. 'They did not tell you that part of the tale.'

'We lost a man, they lost one of theirs,' said Tauk, his voice edged. 'But we are now refreshed and healed. Whatever you say of Valour, Blain, his blessing is upon us. We are not afraid to fight those beings again. Stay here if *you* are afraid, and mind the wolf-mage doesn't shift form.'

'Pah! Let him shift.'

'No! Strategist, I want no alliance. This is my offer: to employ you as an advisor. Get me my city back. I know not how or why, but these haiyens are key to that task, else Valour would not have blessed us and tasked us to guard against them. I need no "empire", just my beloved city. You will have a place of privilege there, though it shall not be known who you are and where you come from. But you advise, you do not lead. *I* decide, you advise. Agreed? My offer to you is generous. I have not forgotten history.'

Kiown scoffed.

'Manners, sapling!' Blain screamed, aiming a swat at him with his walking stick, which missed. 'Fine, fine. Terms accepted. I'll serve you well, O Tauk the Strong.' Blain's bow – made with uncharacteristic physical grace – was somehow sarcastic and sincere at once. He hawked, spat and said, 'Now. Let's devise a plan, and capture our prey.'

27

CONTACT

The men crouched and murmured around a diagram of the tower Blain scratched into the ground. When something moved in the long grass of the paddock directly across from Far Gaze, he knew at once it was Siel. 'Where do you go?' Fithlim demanded when he stood.

'The grass,' said Far Gaze. 'If that does not displease our new Friend and Lord.'

'Mind your cheek,' said Tauk distractedly. 'Go watch him shit, Fithlim, if it eases your mind.'

Far Gaze crouched alone in the grass, facing away from the men.

'I can put arrows in three of them before they see me,' Siel whispered from nearby.

'Don't. They wear armour given by Valour. Anything could happen.'

'Just the traitor, then.'

'Kiown? Leave him. The group forms a new alliance. Why remove a traitor from their group? It would be a service to them. Blain thinks he may earn my loyalty with kind deeds and words. They speak of forming an empire. With Tauk it's not impossible and Blain knows it. They're best watched – I'll watch them. And pretend to join their cause, perhaps.'

'What is the charm Kiown has? He won't stop staring at it.'

'Dragon-make. Powerful.'

'Another!'

'They come, Siel. It can't be long now. They involve themselves more and more openly and their Parent does not seem to stir. Sooner or later a Spirit will cross the boundary. Probably Valour. He is roused. The other Spirits may hold him back awhile, but not forever. Then something big will come *here*. The worlds themselves are at war, whether we befriend the new people or not.'

'The haiyens want no war.'

'They must teach us of Levaal South's gods. Ask them to do this. And to teach us of its dragons, if dragons are there.'

'What do these men plan to do now?'

Far Gaze scoffed. 'To attack the haiyens, of course. When all you possess is a hammer, everything seems a nail. All these men know are swords and spilled blood and comparing their cocks in taverns. Are you among the new people?'

'Yes. But I've not spoken to them. They're very nervous of us.'

'Why?'

'Because they see how we treat each other. I think they watched me in secret, to judge my character. Domudess kept me on the tower's middle floor. The haiyens are on the upper level. I don't know if they're the same ones who healed me. Four remain up there. Others go about the land, doing work. Lots of them move about the lands in secret.'

'What work?'

'Making things which purify the airs. Cleaning away foreign magic which spilled into ours. They don't use that kind of magic, the kind mages see in the air. They know other arts. They would teach us, if we could be trusted.' She laughed quietly and bitterly. 'Domudess tells me little of them. But the haiyens are not here for war, he says.'

'Does the wizard know this group is here?'

'Yes. Blain and Kiown have been here for days. Domudess sent me to learn what they intend.'

One of Tauk's men called over: 'Hurry, soup-blesser.'

'I broke that one's ribs,' said Far Gaze. 'Valour healed him. See Tauk's arm? Healed. It doesn't mean the Spirit is on their side. The men think so. The haiyens had best be cautious. Go, tell them. I hope the water boils when these men cross it. The mayor reneged on his debt to me. I'll eat his soul. I'll slay his offspring, and *their* offspring. I mean it. All of them, if it takes all my remaining days.' He stood, adjusted his pants and went back to the men. He was careful not to look, but he heard the whisper of grass moving and knew she'd gone back to the tower.

Some minutes later, she returned, this time walking in plain sight. Beside her was Domudess, oddly tall, his poised gait like that of a lord. Blain wheezed in shock to see him, glanced about like a cornered animal. Several paces behind the tall wizard, four of the haiyens came.

'We have learned you wish to fight,' said Domudess as he neared the fire. Indeed the men had drawn their swords and stood. 'We came to speak, so there need be no bloodshed. You are not permitted in the tower. The balance of energies there is presently delicate. You would upset it.'

'Be seated then,' said Blain.

Tauk snapped, 'Quiet, *advisor*. Don't forget your place. Hail, wizard. We wished not to fight, but to talk. We prepared for a fight in case one was needed. Do your companions speak our tongue?'

'Of course they do,' said Domudess. 'But I shall speak for them. They wish to cause no accidental offence with clumsy words. Swords come so easily to hand in this place. They have taught me some of their arts, and revealed some of the events soon to happen. Challenge or disbelieve their claims as you like; it hardly matters. They have done us much service already.'

The haiyens stood motionless behind the wizard, careful it seemed not to look at anyone directly. All were of slender build, all the same height but for a taller one, who had a coin-sized hole or indentation like a smudge of shadow between his eyes. They wore cloaks of dusty brown. Domudess turned to them. 'Before you, before the mayor. Are not the words I'll now speak sufficient to be your own words?'

'They are,' said one. Its voice was like a loud breath.

'Have I learned enough of your ways and history to speak on your behalf, in these past months? Have I proven my intent is the same as yours?'

'Yes,' said the same haiyen.

'Are you content with this?' said Domudess to the mayor.

Tauk looked suspiciously around the abandoned village as if for ambushers. 'Are they too busy, or perhaps too regal, to speak with a mere mayor of these northern lands?' he said.

'Too busy,' said Domudess. 'They must depart. The existence of both our peoples depends on their work. There is much to be done.'

'What is wrong with their voices? They sound weak and sick.'

'They long ago ceased using verbal speech among their own kind. They speak with their thoughts. They sound as they do because they are unused to speech.'

One of the haiyens uncurled his long two-fingered hand, pointed at Far Gaze. A shiver went down his spine to be acknowledged directly. 'Shall you come to learn of the way dragons may be slain?' said the haiyen. 'Your friend has accepted the invitation. You will return and tell this realm's lords what you have learned. To inform their course, for choices they must soon make.'

'What choices?' Tauk demanded.

'Not all haiyens are of the same purpose,' it said, still addressing Far Gaze. 'Our history is long and complex, like yours. Our history may be longer, for now haiyens are divided in only two ways, while your divisions are many, and harder to understand. Those of us who have come to visit your realm are all of one purpose. But the lost haiyens have other designs. Your survival does not interest them. They are far to the south in our realm – none of them shall come here. They have scattered us far and wide, and we hide from them. They shall make your lords promises pertaining to the dragons who shall soon be here, among you. They shall offer to slay them. This they can do. But they will reveal only part of what else they intend. Will you come with us? Your friend will come.'

'Do you mean Siel?' said Far Gaze.

Domudess nodded. 'I learned much of you both, when you stayed in my home. I recommended you both to the haiyens.'

Far Gaze stood, his heart beating fast. He felt an intense sense of honour, as if he'd at last been thanked for a lifetime of difficult service. He shook the feeling off, in case it was the effect of some enchantment. He doubted it was. He said, 'I'll go with you,' and bowed low. The haiyen who'd spoken mirrored the bow slowly, as if he feared the slightest mistake in the gesture would cause the swordsmen to charge at them.

'One of them stays here,' Tauk said. 'I wish to hear whatever is said from your own mouths, foreigners, not from a wizard's. I represent not just my city, but now my people.'

The haiyens stared at him without answering. Their silence was confused rather than angry, Far Gaze judged. But he felt a flare of anger at the mayor, made worse when Tauk unsheathed his sword. 'One of you will stay and speak with me or I will deem it the act of an enemy. And deem your presence here an invasion.'

One of the haiyens said, 'Think of raindrops sliding across a slab of stone. The drops merge, join a stream. A few drops sit alone until the stone is dry again, and then they are gone. Some drops are flung in the dust beyond the stone floor, and immediately lost.' Awkwardly the haiyen bowed.

Tauk and his men looked at each other, baffled.

Domudess said, 'What you just heard was an agreement: one of them will remain here, although this saddens them. Do you see now why it is better that I speak for them in this business? They do not know you, Mayor. So their words are extremely cautious. Already you have reached for your weapon after mere speech.'

'We encountered these people before,' said Vade testily. 'We have seen how easily they can kill. One of them produced "mere" sounds, and one of our friends fell dead as stone.'

'It would take but your arm and blade moving sideways through the air for the same result,' said Domudess.

'Are these before us the men of their kind?' said Fithlim.

'They have neither men nor women.'

The men were taken aback. 'Elementals adopt the form of male or female, but they are neither,' Tauk ventured as if offering a fig leaf of understanding. 'I thank this – has he a name? – I thank him – I say *him* for convenience – I thank him for staying.'

Domudess nodded. 'It is well that you thank him. Being here makes them ill. There is something about our time which is harmful to them. Harmful to us too, but we are accustomed to it. They come to do us a great service, Tauk. The bad airs are going to be cleansed. And we will learn much.'

'Do they slay the Tormentors too? We have seen many dead ones.'

Domudess looked at the haiyens. Silent communication passed between them. 'They do not come here to do that work,' he said.

'That does not answer it. Did not the beasts come from their lands?' Tauk pressed.

'The beasts did not. They resulted from a mingling of poisoned airs. The Tormentors are our own people, Tauk. Our own people, warped horribly by poison, fusing them in several realities at once. Do not blame the haiyens. Those who ruled our lands created an army of the creatures quite deliberately.' For the first time Domudess looked at Blain. 'Is that not so?'

Blain shrugged, winced. 'We made some mistakes, I admit it.'

Domudess's stare lingered on him for a while, more damning than any retort. 'It is time for you to leave,' he said, turning to Far Gaze.

The haiyen with the mark on his forehead gestured for Siel and Far Gaze to stand together. A pulse of cold came from the mark in the haiyen's forehead, sweeping over all three. A tunnel which seemed made of wind and light opened before them. The mayor's men cringed back from it. Siel stepped into it. Her body became a speeding, twirling blur of itself unwinding into a spiral of colour, then was gone. Two haiyens went in after her. Their bodies vanished almost instantly.

Far Gaze hesitated. This was nothing he'd seen or heard of before.

'Go now,' said Domudess sharply.

Far Gaze stepped in, felt himself unmade like a garment pulled by a loose string in its sleeve. It was painless but unpleasant. All was cold. He forgot who he was, what he was – he was aware only of fast swirling motion. Consciousness slowly returned with the sound of running water.

28

HOW TO DEAL WITH DRAGONS

Said Tauk the Strong, 'You say the dragons will be free, that they will make war upon us. You say those haiyens you call "the lost ones" will offer to slay the dragons for us. Tell us why we shouldn't accept their offer.'

'There is a better way to deal with dragons than fighting them at all,' said Domudess. 'It will require new thinking from you. The good news is that if you can accept this new way of thinking, the solutions are easy. Persuading you – and others – shall be the most difficult part.'

'I am listening, wizard. Speak.'

Without interrupting, Tauk and Blain listened to what Domudess said. Tauk's men fidgeted, now and then grumbled under their breaths, shaking their heads in disbelief at what they heard. It was clear that only their mayor's silence kept them from walking away in disgust, or perhaps even drawing their weapons. The haiyen met eyes with no one and kept his gaze carefully on the ground, not even looking at the fire.

When Domudess had finished, Tauk sat dumbstruck. At last he said, 'You are surely joking.'

'It is the best way to deal with them,' said Domudess. 'As I said, convincing you that this is so will be the hardest task.'

'And how do *you* know, wizard?' Tauk roared. The haiyen flinched. 'It seems you take many things on faith. Have you tried this practice upon the dragons yourself? Suppose I accepted what you say. How do we spread your message to the cities? How do I explain this to my generals and my fighting men?'

'The cities should all be evacuated,' said Domudess. 'As for the rest, we can discuss how after we are agreed this is what must be done.'

'Evacuated?' Tauk laughed, shook his head. 'You mean *surrendered*! Let me make sure my ears don't deceive me. You say that by being good, gentle people who lay down their arms . . .'

'Don't make it so simple,' said Domudess, the first hint of anger showing in his voice. 'It is not about being "good". We are all made of energy, not unlike the energies in the airs. What appears solid is in fact energy condensed, all vibrating at a slow rate. The more positive we are, the faster our energy vibrates. It begins with good thoughts and deeds, with positive emotion behind all we do, instead of fear, anger, hate. To banish all negativity from one's mind and actions moves one to a different energy vibration, where the dragons cannot perceive us. In a way, it is a kind of magic, Tauk. And one need not be a magician to use it. This world is designed so that many things block our moving to a higher state. Once we step back from trying to change the external world and clear the blockages within ourselves, this particular magic becomes effortless.'

'We know how to banish our fear. We destroy that which causes it.'

'This change is a hard one to make. I am a master of the old magic ways, but a mere student in these new ways. The journey is one we could share. To hear the lesson is easy, to practise it is less easy. Could you watch a beast eat your children before your eyes and still love it? Could you?'

'Of course not.'

'Now you begin to see how much work is ahead of you. Take the vilest poison-spitting monster that ever was. Could you look at it and, say, admire the cleverness of its design? Could you understand that it is simply doing what it was created to do, the same way a fire burns whatever wood it touches, with neither innocence nor guilt? And could you honour its rightful place in creation? Could you watch the monster belch flame over your city, Mayor, over all you've held dear, then approach it with no hate, no envy of its power, no desire for revenge for what it did?'

'This is madness.'

'If you could, the dragons would literally not see you. You would occupy a different state of being, as one looking down upon the dragons from a high place they are unaware of. If all of us could do this, the great dragons would see none of us. We would no longer exist in their perceptions. We would know them, but they would not know us. Do you ever wonder where the dark-skinned peoples went? Why there are nowadays so few of them? It is because they know a version of these same arts. They can come back and forth into our perception as they wish. When the dragons come, they shall not see them.

'I share your doubts – it will not be easy to teach masses of people this knowledge, people who for generations have known only war. Perhaps it is impossible to teach them. But those who learn shall survive the times when dragons are again free. It is unknown how much time we have.'

Tauk and his men were laughing now. 'I see,' said the mayor, wiping at a tear of mirth. 'So, we shall lay down all our weapons, abandon our cities, love our foes and let come what may.'

'You do not understand,' said Domudess.

Blain had watched and listened in silence. Now he said, 'I heard what happened, off east. A fight, with the mayor's men and the new peoples. Eh? You know of it? One of the mayor's men died, slain by a haiyen. Was it love that killed him?'

'I never said the haiyens knew no ways of combat,' said Domudess. 'Nor did I say that positive force could not be dangerous, if it were attacked. But we are discussing a way to deal with dragons. Not with angry men.'

'Who will teach us in these ways?' said Blain, plucking at his beard.

'You shall never learn,' said Domudess. 'Not you, Blain. I know your mind. Even if we wished desperately to teach you – and we do not – even then, you could not learn.'

Blain scoffed. 'These sword-molesting imbeciles could learn a new science, but not I? I who helped create a god?'

'Your mind is a container of the wrong shape for the knowledge, that is all. If the dragons come, you will have to hide.'

'If all you say is true,' said Tauk, 'could dragons not still see our cities? The buildings we use for homes? Answer that! Could they not burn those buildings with their breath? And burn all those inside the buildings, whether those people "love" the dragons or not?'

'As you were told. The cities must be evacuated. All of them. New cities can be built later. But they must be built with love in the hearts and understanding in the minds of those who build them. Such cities will be safe from the dragons.'

'What is wrong with our cities now?' demanded one of Tauk's men.

'They are places of war. They are prizes men warred over. They were built to farm wealth and breed soldiers, so that men could play as lords, and wage wars as if playing games upon a board.'

'So all our history is without any honour to you, wizard? Each time our city repelled attack, we were committing a crime. This is the most absurd thing I have ever heard.' Tauk rubbed his eyes and looked around as though to ensure he wasn't dreaming. He pointed at the haiyen. 'These people have advanced magic arts. If they aren't willing to share them, why are they here? They came to our lands uninvited. Lay down your arms, they tell us. Cease using the magic you know. Leave your cities free for anyone to take. If I had the ear of an enemy, and I thought him stupid enough to do those things, I'd say the same. At best, it's madness.'

'They do not tell you what to do,' said Domudess quietly. 'They present a choice for you to consider.'

'How soon till the dragons come?' said Blain. He caught the mayor's eye with a look which seemed to say: *Give them a little more rope.*

'It may be another year, or it may be days. Fearing them is the worst thing you can do. Be aware of them, but do not fear. The next worst things are to worship them, and to fight them. It is not a fight you can win. You may slay a few Minor dragons – at great cost – but all men in the world together could not slay one of the Eight. No matter what the dragons do, you must understand and love them.'

'Have you wasted my time for your amusement? My city is under siege. It could fall at any—'

'Your city won its battle,' said the haiyen. It was the first time it had spoken since the others had departed. The haiyen's oval-shaped eyes were on the mayor, its hands folded before its chest. Tauk froze, his eyes wide. His two men leaned forwards eagerly. 'If that gives you peace, know it to be true.' The haiyen said no more.

Domudess smiled. 'I shall explain. In the tower I have ways of observing some faraway events. I took it upon myself to examine your city, when we learned you had come here. It seems a half-giant – you may know him, his name is Gorb – visited Tanton, Mayor, with the guidance of a groundman. He arrived a little after the castle army arrived. The siege began and unfolded as you would expect. Gorb brought with him a strange kind of Otherworld weapon, along with one of Tanton's own Engineers, who knew how to make them.

'It seems Gorb told your generals that you are a man of the highest honour, that you had ridden through many perils and battles to fetch the aid your city needed. He showed the generals the weapons. With great haste they summoned the other Engineers, who built many more. Some of the weapons worked. Most did not, but there were enough. Gorb taught a group of your soldiers how to use them. The siege force scattered rather quickly when their officers were picked off and slain from a long distance away by something able to punch through armour. Your city is safe, and so is your place there. A hero's welcome awaits you – the half-giant has seen to that. Something you did must have impressed him.'

Tauk and his men were lost for words, unsure whether to believe or not. Blain said, 'If that pretty tale's true, it won't be worth a cup of drake piss when the dragons come. Otherworld weapons, are they enough to deal with dragons? I'll venture not. So tell us how the beasts can be slain.'

'No! Enough of their comedy,' said Tauk. 'Whether they speak truly of my city or not, my decision is made. I make it on behalf of all peoples of this realm. We will not lay down our arms and bare our throats. We will not abandon the cities we have shed so much blood to defend. There is one reason you would school us to do things leading to certain defeat: you are our enemy, not those "lost" haiyens you speak of. You, wizard, are a traitor to Levaal North, and to its people. You are now our prisoner, along with this invader.'

A look passed back and forth between Domudess and the haiyen. There was something sad in it, also something which said: *As we expected.* Then the pair of them vanished before Tauk's men had risen to their feet to detain them.

Blain noticed for the first time that Kiown was no longer with them. He had no idea when the Hunter had slipped away.

'To the tower!' Tauk said. He and the men ran there fast; Valour's armour gave them no need to pause for breath. From the tower came loud breaking noises. A crack appeared up one side and spread like a hatching egg. There were sounds like thick stone slabs being crushed. The top parts of the tower broke away and fell into the waters and onto the small platform beneath. Domudess stood motionless at its base as slabs of wood, brick, and a rain of dirt fell all about him.

It took only a minute or two for the whole tower to become a mound of rubble, shrinking in on itself, dissolving. The moat's waters retracted. Soon there was just a mound of sand in the structure's place, no more than two cupped hands could hold. Domudess crouched, scooped it all into a small leather bag, careful to get every grain, before tying the bag's string, putting it in his pocket, and vanishing again from their sight.

'Where's the haiyen?' said Blain, hobbling fast to catch up with the others.

At that instant something swooped over their heads, causing a rush of wind which knocked all four of them to the ground. A heavy *thud* sounded on the grass close by.

Blain was the last of them to get back to his feet. He rubbed his eyes, hardly believing what he saw. A dragon was before them, its long tail lashing the ground. Light glittered from its eyes and many colours flashed over its long slender body.

Kiown was sitting aboard its back with two women. 'Get off,' he told them. Evelle leaped to the ground, a sad pout on her face.

Stranger begged: 'Don't take him away from me, don't take him—'

Kiown pushed on her chest with one boot and she fell back onto the grass. To Evelle he said, 'You know what to tell them. I'll return later. Up, Dyan. Fly.' To Blain's utter astonishment, the dragon obeyed him. The Strategist lowered himself back to the ground and tried to steady his hands.

Evelle crouched beside him. 'Kiown spoiled our fun,' she said. 'Anyway. He said to say, this is one of the things his charm does, in case you were wondering.'

Tauk and his men just stared as Dyan became a dot on the horizon's sky. Blain swallowed. 'He . . . he can command dragons?'

'Only Dyan,' said Evelle. 'It's Dyan's punishment for being a bad dragon and playing around with women, instead of doing what he was sent down here to do. They made him a slave to humans. Kiown said a white dragon told him about it.'

'There's a second dragon free . . . ?'

'Yes, a girl dragon. She looks different from Dyan. When we came near, she turned herself into a woman. So, Dyan has to obey whoever has the charm. O, Blain, another thing. Kiown also said to say that you're *his* advisor now, not the mayor's.

And that the mayor's not a mayor any more, he's the general of a new army. But he can call himself Mayor for a while. We'll be using the men of his city as our army until we recruit more, if the mayor's willing. If he's not, we'll use them anyway. It will be easier if he goes along with it. If he doesn't . . .' She laughed. 'Well, guess.'

'Where'd he go?' said Blain weakly. It was just beginning to make him numb, it had not even begun to hurt yet: that he'd had the opportunity to take that amulet and out of caution he'd chosen not to. Command of that dragon could have been his. He thought, I'll have it yet! That fucker knew all along, he was waiting for the dragon to come near enough for him to bring it under the amulet's spell. Maybe back when we fought, he could've slain me with ease, but instead he kept me around for my usefulness! I'll play along for now, but when he drops his guard, the charm's mine . . .

Blain was so lost in thought he didn't hear Evelle's answer. 'Kiown's off to Levaal South. He said there's someone there he's got to speak with. It's all very exciting, Blain. Isn't it?'

29

CITY OF THE LOST HAIYENS

Dyan shot through the sky like an arrow fired, now and then dipping or swerving to catch gusts of wind for a boost to their speed. Sitting aboard him was so natural that Kiown felt like a limb moulded to his back. It was still hard to believe that this mighty creature actually obeyed him; it could turn and slay him with ease at any second. Shilen had explained the amulet would not allow it.

She had also told him what was expected of him. As long as he played his role – to be a lord of men, in opposition to the Pilgrim and Aziel – he was free to act as he would, or so she'd claimed.

Well, he would see if she truly meant it . . .

They'd crossed World's End many hours back, with no ceremony and no noticeable effect. Nightmare was still patrolling the skies near the boundary, although he'd clearly failed in his attempt to stop the stoneflesh giants from crossing. Near the boundary Kiown had seen two, both standing motionless in the southern realm. Other than the haiyens themselves, there was no indication yet that anything had crossed back in response.

As they flew he tried to compare the worlds of North and South. From the skies, Levaal North seemed like a sculpture assembled by whimsical forces not concerned with cohesion or beauty. The South was a more finely made sculpture, formed by an artist . . . but over time set upon and trampled by something huge, mindless and destructive. The range of mountains they'd just flown over had shapes too deliberate not to have been *crafted* by something quite conscious of its work; but a mountain-sized pile of loose shattered stone through the middle of the range ruined the picture. Blankets of sparkling green forest laid out in twisting patterns had vast crushed swathes through them, leaving blackened indentations where nothing had grown back.

The strangest thing to Kiown was the sense that this had all happened long ago, this damage to the South world. And yet natural processes had not covered the tracks of whatever had done it. Was time different here? Indeed there seemed no darkening of day and night by which to keep track of his journey. So it was he could not have said how many hours or days they'd flown.

Still, all this was not as strange as Kiown's brief glimpse of Otherworld, with its peculiar points of light in the night sky. Could it really be true, he wondered yet again, that a world existed with no magic in it? 'Is there magic here?' Kiown asked Dyan.

The dragon's voice seemed to rumble from its gut, carrying despite the buffeting air: 'There is magic, as we know it. But it comes from the North, has been trapped here since the Wall was built. That kind of magic is no longer used here for spell craft. The beings here know that my elders can sometimes perceive what gets cast, and by whom, when the airs cycle back through them. That's how dragons manipulate humankind from afar. The fuel your mages use passes through the dragons' minds.

And dragons can fuse their intentions into those very airs, well before your mages use them for spells.'

Kiown knew Dyan was now effectively human in the eyes of his own kind, regarded as lower than a drake. He'd been banished, cut off for good. Still Kiown had not expected Dyan to reveal such things openly.

'As water cycles from the sky to the ground and back, so do the airs cycle all through the realms,' said Dyan. 'It was how my elders caused war among the gods, and provoked Inferno's madness.'

'Shilen didn't say a thing about that.'

'Indeed not. It is a well-kept secret, that dragons do much to change the world beneath. Such manipulations are difficult – we lesser dragons can hardly participate. Even among the Eight, far more of their designs fail to manifest than succeed. It is one reason they find it necessary to distribute charms among humans.'

'Have you been to this country before, Dyan?'

'Long ago.' But Dyan would answer no more questions about the place, as if the subject were traumatic.

Kiown ordered him to find a safe place to land. He descended to a high bare plateau with a good view of the plains beneath. Nothing living could be seen and there were great rends and cracks in the ground, very much like the results of enormous hammer blows.

Kiown held aloft the amulet. The desire to fondle it in peace was one reason he'd wished for a break from flight. 'You are unable to lie to me, when I possess this,' he said. 'Is that so?'

'There are some secrets I may not tell you. In all other matters, the choice to betray you is one I cannot make.'

'You may not tell? Why not? The other dragons have exiled you. You're no longer one of them.'

'The words would not pass my lips, if I attempted to tell you.'

'The charm does that?'

'Yes.'

'Then tell me this. I am going to meet the haiyens of the South. I may say things to them the other dragons won't like. I may *do* things the dragons won't like. Will this—' he shook the amulet by its chain '—inhibit me? Will it betray me to them?'

Dyan peered closely at the charm. It was some time before he answered – Kiown was getting used to the idea that dragons were seldom in the hurry that humans were. 'There are natural laws,' he said at last, as if this answered the question.

'Which means what?'

'Your choice shall remain yours. Dragons may inhibit your freedoms, they may kill you. But such actions count against them. If our Parent wakes, those dragons who have offended against the laws to a high degree may be punished. They may be slain, or worse. We may be punished collectively or as individuals. We shall not know until it happens. This gift of yours was given freely, and does not restrict your freedom. If Shilen learns of your plans – whatever those plans are – she may decide to take action. But it will have nothing to do with your charm.'

'So I can do what I want. This charm will aid me in whatever I do. Even if the "brood" won't at all like the actions I choose. Is that right?'

Dyan's head lowered: *Yes.*

Kiown paced for a while, thinking of the conversation with Domudess. There was something in this realm that had slain some of the dragons, back in ancient times. But other than the damage to the land itself, he'd seen no sign of it. Was Dyan telling the truth now? He could not tell. But if Kiown was truly to be a lord among men, he refused to rule at the behest of the dragons.

(Vous, my love – I am yours, yours for all time, whatever it is you have become, he thought. His throat burned up. Quickly he snuffed out such thoughts and emotions, or tried to. Dyan could sense moods, and at times it almost seemed he could hear certain of Kiown's thoughts.) Kiown said, 'How far to fly now? How long till we reach the lost haiyens?'

'I have not been in this country since the split formed among the haiyen people. But we have come a long way south. There are powers in this region I do not understand. They are becoming aware of us as we linger here. We should fly.'

'Are they things you could not handle, if it should come to a battle?'

'Should not a warrior take care with his finest weapon?'

Kiown laughed. He moved to get back on Dyan but suddenly someone was standing between them. A haiyen. Kiown's sword was in hand in a heartbeat.

The haiyen spread his hands, showing them as empty. 'I bring a warning,' it said.

'I'm listening.'

'What you intend to do is known.'

'Prove it. Say what it is I intend to do.'

'You mean to fly to a city of the lost ones. You mean to bargain with them, for their help. If you do this, they will deceive you.'

Kiown moved two paces closer to the haiyen so that he was within striking distance. 'Go on. Deceived in what way?'

'They claim they have control of the entities they brought to this land, the entities which slew dragons here, long ago. The truth is they are under control of those entities.'

Kiown watched the haiyen silently for a moment. He could

not tell whether it spoke truly or not. 'Dyan. Leave us be for a moment. Go for a brief flight, but be ready to return quickly.'

'Are you sure?' said the dragon.

'Is this haiyen the only one here?'

'He is all that I perceive close to us. But I did not perceive him until he revealed himself. Those things further away show no sign of approaching yet.'

'Then go.' Dyan spread his wings and launched from the platform. When he'd flown out of hearing range, Kiown said, 'The lost ones, as you name them. Did they or did they not defeat the dragons who came to your realm, long ago?'

'At too high a cost.'

Kiown laughed. 'Do you know the land we live in? Do you know the way we have lived? There is little to risk for us. It is already war-ravaged.'

'Your actions affect more worlds and planes than just your own.'

Kiown laughed again. 'Then those other worlds should have done more to aid us in our plight.'

'Others cannot make your choices for you.'

'Your "lost ones" must have been desperate, to do what they did. How exactly did they slay the dragons?'

'They brought beings into the world, beings who should not exist here. Those beings are worse than dragons.'

'How so?'

'They have no consciousness. They cannot be communicated with. They simply *are*. And they destroy.'

'Have you a better way to deal with dragons?'

'Yes. Some of my people have ventured into your lands to teach these ways.'

'Thanks. You've told me all I need to know.' Kiown's arm

whiplashed through the air; his blade cut through the haiyen's neck with such liquid ease he didn't feel its swing impeded at all. He kicked the fallen head over the ledge then rifled through the pockets of its gown. There was nothing worth keeping. He waved his arms to get the dragon's attention as it circled above the platform. 'Dyan! Let's go.'

It was not much further before the city of the lost haiyens came into view. Dyan slowed his flight as they took the sight in. Great climbing spires rose like a huge crown on the landscape, high as mountains, made of something like polished black glass. All the country beneath, far out of reach of the city, was trampled and cracked. Something unthinkably huge – something to make stoneflesh giants seem insects, by the look of things – had come trampling through here many, many times. The tall city seemed the only thing not cracked and broken.

Kiown breathed deep, and felt the kind of pleasure one feels coming home after a long voyage. Those towers! Nothing had been built like them in all the North. He thirsted for such a tower to call his own, marvelled at the high platforms and bridges stretching from peak to peak. He saw haiyens strolling on those platforms as Dyan flew nearer, saw them pause and turn their faces up, frozen in their steps, likely amazed to see a dragon in their sky.

Kiown sensed Dyan's nervousness. He understood it: a human gambling his life was gambling but a few decades. A dragon was gambling far, far more. He patted Dyan's neck and said, 'Trust me.'

30

THROUGH THE REALM

As all this occurred Eric wandered, not happy but at peace, and glad to be free of other people. Now and then in the clouds above him – grey slabs moving over their background white – were fleeting forms of Invia dancing and diving between clouds, following his movements but never coming close enough to speak.

Whether word had spread or not that a new power had assumed control of the castle, people began to return to the northern lands. None knew who now ruled, nor which cities it was safe to return to, for tales of genocide in Aligned cities had spread far, tales so brutal and senseless few truly believed them until they saw the ditches and piles of bones with their own eyes.

Eric camped one night beside a road leading to Athlent, one place where such massacres had occurred. Soon two men approached his fire, wearing the white of the castle's army. 'You ride a drake,' said one of them. 'Like he from the fables, named Shadow. But surely you are not he?'

Eric held aloft the amulet, not knowing what would happen, and said: 'Both of you are Favoured.'

The two looked at each other for a moment, then one of them

cried out: 'A lord has come, a lord has come! We will tell the citizens of your realm, Lord, we will tell them! What is your name, Lord?'

'Batman,' Eric said, and he laughed.

'We will tell them your name, Lord! Have you a lady?'

'I do. Alas, it is Aziel. But I suppose it could be worse.'

'We will tell them you have come, Lord!' the men said. They departed, their lord helpless with laughter for a good while after they'd gone.

From then on, whenever he encountered people on the roads or in small towns, he said those same words – *You are Favoured* – and got similar reactions. None asked what it meant to be 'Favoured' and in truth he didn't truly know either . . . but all who heard those words were similarly affected. Many would pack their things and head straight for the castle as if he'd set important tasks before them.

He had no wish to return there. Days of freedom stretched out behind and before him. He lived from the land, catching the wild but docile poultry with his hands, roasting them over fires, sharing food freely on the edge of the woods with a man who had at first tried to rob him. He told the man he was Favoured. The man tearfully swore he would find and slay all of Eric's enemies. 'All of them, Shadow, my master, every one.'

'Get to it. Leave none of them alive, my son.'

Eric set traps here and there using sticks and rocks the way Siel had taught him. He threw the amulet off into the woods, amused by the way it scuttled back every time through the leaves and twigs, always returning no matter how far he threw it. Once he put it in a makeshift boat of sticks and bark, and set it adrift in a fast-gushing stream. For most of a day it was gone and he'd begun to wonder if he'd perhaps done a grievously stupid thing. When at last the charm returned, he knew that Shadow was no longer imprisoned within it. He didn't know how he knew, but he did.

One night when he'd made his fire and was singing songs to his sleeping drake, Shilen returned to him in human form. Case did not stir. To look at her, it seemed impossible she had ever been other than this tall Amazonian woman, leather clinging to her full body. There was no hint now of the white shape so graceful on the water, one wing raised to catch the air and a head snapping down to end Anfen's life.

Eric poked the fire with a stick, stirring a small red storm of embers. 'I thought you dragons needed a human to hide inside. That's how it was with Dyan.'

She sat down across from him. Her large eyes shone with fire-light through a veil of flaxen curls. 'It has been considered safer to travel disguised within a human. Things change. The natural laws are more relaxed than they once were. We test the laws, little by little. When Dyan was partially hidden within a human, he went near the castle. To go there is forbidden to dragon and Spirit both. And yet nothing untoward happened.'

'Why is it forbidden?'

'Because the castle is the place where human rulers dwell. As our Parent designed. We are not to go near, and never to go inside it. Dyan was told to go close, hidden inside a human body. Our Parent did not stir. I went near the castle in a thinner disguise, hiding in no human body, instead merely changing my shape. Again, our Parent did not stir. You helped us test the laws further, by summoning Hauf inside the castle. And then our Parent *did* stir.'

'I see. So that was as far as you could go.'

'It was much further than we dared expect,' she said, a gleam in her eyes as if they were both in on the scheme from the beginning. 'I do not know the next test the great ones plan.'

'They'll come themselves, won't they? But that's not a test, is it? That's the real thing – what you've all been waiting for.'

'Yes. It may be soon, or it may not. Life in your realm must continue as if it is a century away, though it may be only days. You have chosen some Favoured ones?'

He lay back with one leg crossed over the other and smiled. 'Sure have.'

She leaned towards him, hair almost hanging in the fire. 'Why the amusement?'

'I'm smiling at my selection criteria. Everyone I've seen I've declared Favoured. Drunks, wanderers, this old crippled woman. One guy I think was dying. They're all in the club now.'

He saw in her anger a faint hint of slitted eyes. Just for an instant. 'I advise you to think through your choices,' she said. 'Those selected are going to aid your realm, when aid is needed. You are not permitted infinite numbers. Those you choose will be protected from the dragons, and they gain a small measure of power.'

'What sort of power? They become wizards?'

'No! Their strengths are accentuated, that is all. Only slightly. They keep their vices and flaws. If you Favour all thieves, your realm will be filled with very skilled thieves. It is unwise to be careless.'

He dropped the stick in the fire, puffing up another burst of sparks. 'These aren't my rules.'

'This is your realm now, Eric. Who else makes the rules?'

'You do. You gave me a limited range of choices and claimed

it was freedom. Now I act within the limits you imposed, and you don't like that either.'

'So you do this just to test the value of my promise that you are free.'

'Guess so. There's one thing I can't get past. You and all your kind are infinitely greater than us. I might not like it, but I admit it. The lowest dragon does things no human can. Why then are you so concerned with us? Why do we matter to you at all?'

She hissed an angry breath. 'Imagine for a moment that animals could understand your speech, and see as you can see. If you approached animals with a show of your power and knowledge, they would be greatly impressed. Would they not? You would be like gods to them. Would it then be true for those animals to assume that you are perfect beings, with no problems of your own to solve?'

He laughed, surprised and delighted by the truth in it. She went on, 'And that these gods before them had surely moved on beyond war and division among themselves?'

'Definitely not.'

'So, do dragons know no division and conflict? The Eight are truly united only in their desire to be free of the cage. More goes on here, man-lord. Ever more than you are allowed to perceive. And you have a role in it. I dare not tell you everything here and now, however much it would make things easier for us both. Concern yourself with your realm, and heed my advice only, never another dragon's. And never *any* Spirit's. Business occurs that affects your realm, Eric. I was sent to return and tell you of it.'

'Sent by whom?'

She hesitated. 'Vyin sends me. Among that which I may not

tell you are ill tidings.' She put her forehead in her hands, the distress convincing enough to make him believe it was genuine. 'The slain warrior's breastplate is important,' she said. 'I intended Vyin to have it. It contains magic which allows entrance into a plane we had not been able to get to before. Now we can enter that hidden place. We had once thought it to be just a myth of men. The hidden realm is real! The slain warrior Anfen called it "the quiet". Valour can go there as he wishes. That place, Eric, may hold the answer to unlocking our prison. When we first spoke in the skies, it seemed at least a human lifetime before our likely freedom. Now it is imminent.'

'So why do you look so upset?'

'I am powerful in your eyes. Dyan is also. Yet he and I are not of the Eight. In Takkish Iholme I was waylaid. In the Gate. If they are watching it, going unnoticed is . . . difficult. The wrong dragons took the breastplate from me. One of the brood consumed it, and now digests the knowledge.'

'You mean swallowed it?'

'Yes. Soon he will send forth a key he shall create, and it will be for me to go to the hidden realm and do their work. My task is to destroy their cage. I can do so.'

'There is, I would suggest, extremely little I can do about all this, Shilen. I am but the head bird in your human poultry pen.'

'As you say it, it shall be,' she spat.

He sat up, surprised by her anger. He had supposed she was here once more to steer him to a destiny laid out already, moving with the volition of a pinball bouncing. Had she come to him for *advice*? 'What do you want from me, Shilen?'

'You govern the affairs of men. For that, gifts were given to you. A god of flame, diminished but restless, shall have his embers warmed by foolish men who wish to play with power.

You will say we dragons could stop it. You can stop them waking Inferno but I cannot. Hauf's test showed our Parent's sleep grows shallower. The castle rumbled? Then you felt it stirring. We dragons dare not break more rules of interference at this time, not until all have descended.

'And your realm has other business. A rival lord for you rises in the south. He too has been granted gifts, of a kind I know not. He will take your throne, if he proves worthier of it than you. You will not love his rule, if you did not love how Avridis ruled. This new lord will be a tyrant of great cruelty. You asked for freedom. I shall not interfere. If you are defeated, it will be so. And your early actions indicate your defeat is likely enough.'

She leaned forwards, the crackling fire shining in her eyes. The woods behind them seemed to listen to her words. 'You appear to treat all this as a game. Think of this: two great wrestling beasts push up against each other. Their strength is equal. Ah, but if one only had an insect's strength more, he would win, his foe collapsed at last. If you are but an insect, Eric – or as you put it, poultry in a pen – you have now entered the grand ancient battle. And your tiny serve of strength may make a great beast collapse.'

Eric sat up, began to ask a question, but she was gone. If she'd meant to kill his light mood, she'd succeeded. The night's quiet was watchful. Something shifted in the woods behind him, fleeing with quick steps when he turned.

That night he dreamed of a thousand war mages being eaten by Shâ, dreamed of the whole land filled with them falling dead and thick as raindrops. Dreamed of a dragon's jaws opening bigger than the sky to devour the world, which tilted like a table, sliding everything down into the closing maw.

*

Come morning, there was a distant rumbling he thought was thunder. The ground shivered.

Something struck the dirt nearby. Another object fell, and another. Hailstones the size of coins landed all about him.

He got to his feet, inspecting a small chunk of quartz-coloured lightstone. It faintly shone, growing slightly brighter in the gloom of early morning, just as the vast acres of the same stone across the sky too began to lighten. Another broken piece fell into the grass some distance away.

31

THE LORD RETURNS

Case's lazy flight returned Eric to the castle. By its front gate a ring of half-giants stood guard. Many of them were bigger even than Faul, although some – perhaps juveniles – were small enough to pass as large humans. Crowds of gawkers came to stare, many never having seen a single half-giant, let alone a small army of them. This was the desired reaction. Word would gradually filter back to the most distant cities, likely with great exaggeration of the half-giants' numbers. Avridis was gone, but the cities would know the castle had been claimed, and taking it over would require a bruising fight indeed.

And wonder of wonders, here rode 'Shadow' on his drake. He had stepped from the story books and become real, to bring a prosperous age with him from Otherworld. Surely he would, no matter that the world seemed to shake now and then, no matter that little pieces of lightstone here and there rained down . . .

Entering through the window of Aziel's former bedroom, Eric found food for Case and for himself, rested up in her bed, then explored at his leisure the countless luxurious suites of those upper floors. A few possessions and trinkets left behind showed that high-ranking military folk had dwelled here. It was all abandoned now. There weren't even any grey-robe servants left.

When finally he found the place Aziel had commandeered as her new throne room, he saw she'd gotten on with business quite comfortably. She was a sight to behold, regal and calm while activity flurried around her. Advisors had come from the cities, their best and brightest eager for work. They rattled off figures from sheaves of paper, standing in patient lines outside the chamber, filling it with their quietly excited whispers. A new start. A new age. Here they were, part of its machinery. Proud as parents of the growing new empire. They hardly had a glance to spare for Eric, or for the red drake smelling of beer hobbling along behind him.

'You'll be pleased to know the food has been distributed,' Aziel snapped at him by way of greeting. 'The cities will eat. That's what you wanted?'

He couldn't help laughing at her accusing tone. 'Yes, Aziel. I think people should generally be allowed to eat.'

'Fine. Now *you* work out how to make the cities behave themselves.'

'What precisely do you mean by that?'

'Think of yourself as their father,' said one of the advisors, a hunched older man smiling through yellow teeth. 'He provides for his children. But he must now and then be stern. A mild, staged uprising with very swift suppression shall do the trick. In two weeks the thing can be done. No youngster will touch the hot stove after the first one has a severe burn or two.'

O Christ, Eric thought. So this is what it means to be Sauron. This is what it means, when Frodo keeps the ring. You get to hear bureaucrat types making it sound pragmatic to fill ditches with bodies. He said, 'All of you in this room, listen up. I deem you are all Favoured.'

Sudden silence fell, broken by a breeze of excited chatter passing through the chamber. Aziel gaped at him, shocked and angry. The advisors babbled fervently or fell to their knees declaring loyalty. Most needed no further instruction. They ran from the room, filled with new zest and power, certain of their tasks. 'Why did you do that?' Aziel yelled. 'We have to know what they're up to. You can't give them run of the realm!' Eric laughed and climbed aboard Case. 'Where are you going now?' she said.

'I might go watch them wake Inferno. Should be quite a show.'

'Didn't Shilen tell you to stop them?'

'I think it was more of a suggestion. She also said we're free, not her servants or pets. Let's find out if that's true.'

'Eric, don't you dare leave. I need you here. There is much about rule you need to learn. I'll find a new lord to replace you, if I have to.'

'You'll have to make sure he's from story books, as I am,' said Eric, smiling. 'The fable about Shadow is the one reason people will tolerate Vous's daughter being in power. Without me, they'd throw you out of here in five minutes.'

He saw the truth sink in. Her eyes frosted. The gears of her mind clicked over almost audibly: *They never lay eyes on this chamber, young sieur. You could be killed, your death kept secret for decades. For decades, they could think you're still here, alive. I might even find a lookalike to appear on the balcony and wave now and then . . .*

She said, 'This is no game.'

'Actually, Aziel, yes it is. That's just what it is.'

As if to state agreement Case leaped out the window and into the sky.

It *was* a game. About his realm he flew. He gladly lost track of the days. When he landed to eat in villages and towns, the people called him Shadow and honoured him. When the mood struck he declared them Favoured by the dragons. None ever asked what this meant, and indeed he hardly knew himself. Case lapped up buckets of ale people set before him and belched fire. People clapped, delighted. They asked Eric if the times of turmoil were over; he said that was up to them. They said Shadow had stepped from the story books to bring them an age of light. He repeated Shilen's words: 'As you say it, it shall be.' They nodded as if this were great wisdom. Perhaps it was.

In Aligned cities like Hane, people were being fed again with stores from the castle. Lands about these cities were newly planted with seeds. People were dealing with the gift of freedom with suspicion and great difficulty. Few could truly accept that there was now no tyrant to rule and starve them. But the food deliveries kept coming. Little by little, like lone candles lit in vast dark rooms, a degree of liberty slowly came to the hell holes Vous and the Arch Mage had created in the cities.

The Tormentors were mostly gone from the fields and roads. Now they were as rare a sight as elementals, leaving behind only the grief they'd caused, holes punched into the ground and their broken forms here and there, minus a part or two taken to be studied for its magic, or finger-blades taken to smiths for forging into swords. Who had slain the things or driven them out, none knew. People said Shadow had done it, and by Shadow they meant Eric. Some claimed the last ones had been seen stalking among the cliffs and hills to Elvury City to take refuge there. Indeed many tracks led to that place.

Now and then the sky rumbled – but not with thunder. Chunks of broken-off lightstone fell, sometimes marble-sized, sometimes bigger.

32

IN THE QUIET

In the place Anfen had called the quiet, where time did not exist, there was a twilit landscape whose purple darkness was broken here or there by frozen explosions of light: magic as crystal forms suspended in the air, expressions of power like the letters of a divine language, written instructions waiting to be hammered into reality's tapestry. They were spells, alive and yet not alive. When the shadowy creatures called Shapers drifted along to read them, Levaal's reality changed – changed as the spell caster intended, and to the spell caster's eye, the change was immediate. Almost no mages knew that when their spells were cast, here in the quiet their casting waited silently outside of time, until the Shapers did their work.

There were woods and fields in that place, hills and mountains too . . . but in all, they were vague mirrors of what lay in the familiar world where mages played with magic. The Great Dividing Road was here too, like a long solid tattoo binding this place, which might have been the land's soul, to its body, in the day-world. Sometimes people came to this place in their dreams, not knowing where they were and not remembering it at all, come morning. They could be seen like fleeting shadows, hardly more discernible than wind bursts.

Valour guarded this place. When Vous had enraged him, distracted him, and steered him so far across the world he had forgotten the original reason for his rage, Valour had come here to vent his anger.

For the first time, a dragon had come into the quiet.

Shilen had spoken mostly the truth to the man-lord. Mostly, though not always. She found conversation with him distasteful, but managing the kingdoms of men was now her duty.

She had a new task before her. She prowled now in the quiet, her long white body less physical here than it was in the day-world. There was no magic here of the usual kind – the airs held no power, so she could not cast if Valour should happen to find her here. Now and then Shapers could be seen, moving silently and seeming to consume the hung crystal-things. They did not stir when she came near.

It was Tzi-Shu who had swallowed the warrior's breastplate, fused with Valour's magic. His eyes had shone with new knowl-edge and he had praised her for bringing the object to him, even though she'd meant it for Vyin (which surely he had known). The great and terrible one had warned her to beware of Valour when he'd given her his fashioned key. Tzi-Shu would one day make a meal of Valour, he had said. It was he, after all, who had left a scar upon Mountain, the Spirit the brood most feared.

Shilen knew that discovery of this place had disturbed the mighty Eight. How many other strange hidden realms were there, realms they could not go to? She had sensed their disquiet.

Now and then she saw the last of the Tormentor beings. They hovered like strange puppets made of paper, being blown about by wind. Many had been smashed to pieces. Valour had slain them in huge numbers, coming to this place to vent his fury. He had already tried to cross World's End and set the Pendulum swinging high. The other Spirits had cooperated to keep him back.

Ah, how much misplaced faith humans put in gods! They would think Valour had slain Tormentors to save their lives, when he was just venting fury like a child throwing tantrums. A mountain of Tormentor corpses was scattered by the Entry Point to Otherworld. The stupid human mage had planned on using them to invade that place. Their Parent would never have allowed *that*. Their Parent may indeed have directed the angry god to slay them.

Shilen paused her prowling steps. In the distance now, there he was: Valour, the angry young god. His steed reared up its kicking legs, bellowed, its voice like thunder, back at the sky. The force of the sound made shimmering waves on that horizon. The Spirit's aura was red with battle lust. Luckily he did not sense Shilen prowling here – but she was nervous.

Valour called a war cry to match his steed's. They turned southwards – luckily – and rode with speed. Shilen watched him slam his great sword into pillars of rock, shattering them. At last he rode further than her sight could follow.

Shilen searched the twilit woods and fields, avoiding the strange life forms when she saw them, never touching the diamond-shaped gleaming things, the magic waiting for the Shapers to make spells become real. At last she found what she had come for. There it was, in the north-west corner, a huge pillar thicker than any tree, stretching up till it touched the sky.

There was a pillar to correspond with each god. Inferno's was mostly crumbled pieces strewn over the ground, broken long ago when the other gods fought him. Mountain's she had seen when she first came here. She had attacked it with all her might but left hardly a mark upon the hard icy white surface.

This pillar, Shilen felt, was Nightmare's. It was less solid, of different make. She may be able to harm this one, perhaps. She opened wide her jaws, bit in and wrenched with all her strength. A cold piece of it broke away.

She was surprised that it came free with such relative ease (however much her jaws now ached). Would not their Parent who designed this place have made the defences of the brood's prison stronger? But then, she supposed this strange realm had not been expecting the company of any dragons. With great effort she tore away another piece, and then another, each piece removed weakening the cage.

33

LEVAAL SOUTH

In Levaal South where the haiyens dwelled, time and age were not the same. Time in the North and in Otherworld ran like a stream in one direction; in the South, time was a turgid icy whirlpool in a revolving cycle. Siel and Far Gaze learned much and were changed much in that unknown, uncounted stretch of time, under the guidance of the haiyen traveller.

They stepped out of the tunnel of wind and light onto a high platform ridge, which circled a vast flat plane beneath. Archways and pillars all across the ridge crumbled slowly to ruin. Out on the flats was a lake, perhaps in truth an inland sea, its cloudy water as blue as lapis lazuli. Floating above the water was a giant round crystal, held in the air by nothing they could see, its light beaming down in great shafts to the waters, making white smoke waft up where the light beams touched. Here was more beauty than Vous ever dreamed of creating and it made both Siel and Far Gaze want to weep in joy, even though they had no idea what it was they beheld. The lake's far shore was too distant to see.

Their guide – the haiyen with the mark in its forehead – spoke to them with only its thoughts. 'You have been deceived about the nature of your world, and told nothing of the nature of ours. Many visitors come to these waters, from other worlds and planes of being across the universe. But visitors no longer come from Levaal North, nor from the world your Pilgrim knows, which you call Otherworld. In *that* world, people are trapped. Even death sometimes fails to free them.'

'The Pilgrims Eric and Case spoke nothing of this,' said Far Gaze.

'They knew no more of it than you. Their world and yours are not protected by the Dragon-god, as all your wise men have long believed. Those worlds are held captive by it. The Dragon-god did not create your world; it only changed that world better to suit itself.'

'Is this world free?' said Far Gaze.

'No longer.' Their guide's sadness blew over them like a breeze. 'No longer, but for a few rare parts of it. This is one such free place. Do you see the visitors below, from other planes and worlds?'

As their guide said it, they indeed saw beings moving across the flat plain towards the water. A multitude of them came into sight, now and then materialising below with small light-ning-like flickers to join the slow march to the shore. Great numbers milled all along the water's edge, some standing knee-deep, some wading out further into the still blue where the water reached their necks, some swimming or floating languidly out across the surface to the distant shore. The huge round crystal's pulsing light bathed them from above.

It was not only humans wandering across the flats to the shore. Some beings they saw were smaller than groundmen, others large as half-giants, with a few bigger yet. Some things moved on four legs, others were shifting wispy shapes which coiled and twisted through the air. A sense of peace washed over them from their guide. 'Guests from many worlds you see below,' it said.

'For what purpose do they come here?' said Far Gaze.

'The waters rejuvenate the soul.'

'Only humans have souls, I was taught,' said Siel.

'You have been told your soul is a small part of the Dragon-god's thought,' said their guide. 'And told that when you die, you enter his dreams and are eventually reborn. It is not so. Your soul is even older than that creature. Only your body is young. I brought you here because you have wounds and scars from your prison world. You are invited here to heal them, if that is your wish. Be warned, only once in a lifetime may one enter the crystal lake. Many times you have been here before, though your mind does not permit the memory. A deep part of you knows. It is that deep part which makes you wish to weep at the beauty of it. It is that deep part which recognises this place.'

Their guide did not seem to need his answer straight away. So Siel and Far Gaze watched the display beneath: all manner of forms, all manner of shapes. Some looked like statues made of metal. Others walked like human beings, but were covered in scales and plates. Some wore bodies partly animal: bird people, feline ones, heads with antlers, horns and more. Some seemed kin to trees. Some seemed hardly physical at all; there were orbs of light, clouds like light brush strokes of dark shimmering paint which barely had physical form.

'Those haiyens who have chosen to part ways with us, whom we call the lost ones, do not see this place any longer,' said their guide. 'They closed it off from their awareness, long ago. When they did that, it meant these visitors could no longer venture through our realm. Now visitors may only come to places like this, which the lost ones have forgotten. Long ago, all could come here, and freely travel as they would. Our world was a great exchange of knowledge and information until the Dragon-god came. When it seized the North, Levaal became divided. Still we haiyens waited near the place you call World's End, before the Wall was built. Waited there as guides, to help those who could survive the journey through the Dragon's world of the North.

'Those brave and strong enough to survive the North's perils would cross World's End. Our kind waited to heal them and guide them through this realm to *our* adjoined world, our Otherworld. Levaal South too has an Entry Point, at its most southern part. Like yours, it too is usually closed off.' A burst of immense sadness came from their guide. 'We are prevented now from going back to our Otherworld. The lost haiyens guard the Entry Point. Once, we passed back and forth freely. You have questions. Ask them.'

Siel said, 'Were they human, those you speak of, who survived the journey through the Dragon's world, and came to yours?'

'Yes,' said their guide. 'And other races too, many others. These worlds are older than you know. Once, people of the Pilgrim's world knew of Levaal. Some found ways to escape there through a door. Often, they did not know that our world here, a place of healing and purity, waited for them at the end of their journey. They only knew they must escape their prison world, whatever else they found. Those souls who came through were made strong by their journey. We valued and honoured them here.'

'Did not the Pendulum swing when people crossed?' said Far Gaze.

'That began only when dragons from the North ventured into

our realm to steal back those who had escaped here. In that time, powerful Spirits – those beings which men call gods – came to protect Levaal South. We do not know where they came from, nor who called them, but they are here still. They are not gentle protectors. They are powerful and dangerous, even to us.'

'And you have dragons here?'

'Some dragons came to us from your realm,' said their guide. 'Before your realm, they came from other places – they have not always been in Levaal.

'The dragons who crossed World's End first came here to hunt those who'd escaped the North world, just as they hunted in Levaal North for those who escaped from Otherworld. Those dragons learned that visitors from other worlds came here, to the lake's waters and to many temples and other places to learn and exchange knowledge. Those dragons grew wise and were content merely to exist here. They learned much from the visitors; and they taught much. Vyin was one such dragon. Their minds began to roam independently of the limits their Parent had set for them. It was the first time they broke the natural laws.

'This angered their Parent, who called them back. Their Parent imprisoned them after a battle which destroyed lots of Minor dragons, and killed four of the brood. The destruction of those four meant, in essence, the dispersal of their power. Young gods formed from this loose energy. Perhaps the old gods of the North – Mountain, Tempest and Inferno – helped to create them. In its anger the Dragon-god gave its world over to humankind, creating new natural laws to govern the dragons' imprisonment. It built the Wall, and made sentries to guard it. All this occurred the last time it was roused from slumber. Since that time, it has slept.'

Far Gaze said, 'Who really destroyed the Wall? And why? The Arch Mage was surely no more than an instrument in that task.'

'We do not know what being's willpower was truly behind that deed. If it was the Dragon-god, it was done because it feels its opposite power, slumbering in our lands, can at last be defeated. If it was the Eight who had this deed done, it was done only so they could be free of their prison.'

'Is it true then what Blain says, that there is a Dragon-god in the South?' said Far Gaze.

'There is a force here of equal power to the Dragon-god of the North. It too shall sleep until the Pendulum swings high, and its opposite awakens. It came here soon after the Dragon-god arrived, to balance that being's power. But it is not a dragon. It is a force of creation, not destruction. We know it to exist, though we have never seen it.

'Go now, and bathe in the crystal's waters. Those others who have come can see each other, but because of where you come from, they shall not see you. These visitors do not see us, the haiyens, any longer, either. No longer can we speak with them. Go down to the waters. Nourish yourselves. We've more travel ahead of us.'

Siel and Far Gaze climbed down one of many sets of stairs indented on the sheer stone wall. The flat plain they crossed gave a little underfoot, as though it were the skin of something living. The sky was a haze of deepest purple, penetrated by only a few upwards-reaching white beams from the huge suspended crystal. For a time they seemed alone on the plains. About them they gradually sensed, then saw, the others who'd come, and heard whispers of their voices. There were human beings among them with skin of many colours, people green, blue and gold, some larger than half-giants, others wearing wings. Beings like lizards walked upright, their tongues flickering out of their mouths almost too quickly to see. There were tiny people with silvery skin and black almond-shaped eyes. There was something huge on four legs with a face like an insect's; something dragging itself along with tentacles, its large face almost human atop a long curved body. All moved in a serene, slow walk towards the water.

A being made of what looked like snow faded into view directly ahead of them, its skin or perhaps clothing appearing as patches of white and grey. It moved like liquid. Two small ones just like it moved ahead of it. Siel reached out to touch it, but her hand passed through as it would pass through smoke; the being didn't notice her. A sound she'd thought was gentle flute music turned out to be their voices in conversation.

Siel wept. Far Gaze kept his eyes straight ahead. Part of him recoiled from this strangeness and demanded he flee. He did not know any more whether to believe the haiyen's tales and stories – there seemed no longer any way of knowing the truth. He looked back where they'd climbed down from. Their guide waited and watched on the ridge, just a small black shape against the purple sky. 'Why do you weep?' he whispered to Siel.

'All of them, so peaceful,' she said. He looked at her in surprise – he assumed she wept from some kind of fear or disquiet, not this mix of joy and grief. 'Look how different they all are,' she said. 'And they're at peace with each other. No fighting. All of them here for the same thing. Allowing each other just to *be*.'

'Why should it make you sad?'

'We are the *same* as one another. War, war and death. We punish each other just for being born in a different city. Why aren't we like this instead?'

Pointless question, he thought. One with no answer.

They came at last to the water, forgot each other and bathed in it. Each of them now felt as if he or she was the only one here, that they'd come to a private reality in which the lake was his or hers alone. Perhaps all who came here felt the same thing. Now and then were glimpses of the others about them like glimpses of ghosts, and brief whispers of conversation. Crystal light beamed into their bodies; it filled them till it poured out and surrounded them in a protective shell of healing light.

There was the sound of rain sweeping over the water, the beautiful sound of a sea's waves lapping, the sound of life itself drawing and releasing breath. They breathed with it, became one with it. There was no need for fearing or even thinking. All would be well; all things were connected to one source of being, like droplets from the same lake flung away only briefly. Come whatever chaos and death to temporarily trouble long, ancient dreams, all would be well for all was eternal, and fleeting troubles were but flavours of experience. The huge round crystal beamed down its shafts in the water to depths beyond sight.

They both found the haiyen's words had been true: a part of them remembered these waters. They were both struck by the idea that all those other beings they had seen, who had walked around them to the waters, were *them*: Siel and Far Gaze, their souls embodied in many past and future selves. In that infinitely beautiful light they were filled with peace; thirsts they'd not been aware of were quenched. The waters assured them with the breathing sound of wind over sea that they'd known long lifetimes of far greater pain than this one, pain all healed or forgotten. What harm would carrying this brief lifetime's burden truly do them? They were eternal.

Gently their bodies floated, their heads above the water. Far

Gaze let his mind go altogether, forgetting everything, remembering everything. In that place, it became true that no pain had ever really hurt him.

Siel dived down, seeing how far she could follow the shafts of crystal light. Huge things moved down there: souls who had come to bathe here and decided to stay, shaping themselves as they liked, dreaming up new lives with the delight of children at play. Would she do the same? She was welcome to stay. The water's depth was infinite. It would gladly share infinity and abundance with her, if she wished.

Not yet, she thought, joyful now to know she was *not* trapped in life. Her life was no longer a prison sentence: it had become a choice. Not yet! But I will return here. And perhaps the next time I come, I will stay . . .

34

GODS OF THE SOUTH

They had little memory of walking away from that shore and climbing the steps back to their guide. For a long while they sat there, not resting, needing no speech or thought. Their haiyen guide waited, then spoke into their minds in a silent whisper: 'The waters give all who come the choice to remain. You have chosen to return. It is time now to remember again. Remember who you are, why you are here, why you have come. Be at ease with your burdens. This place soon shall become a faded memory in your minds. But deep within you, ever shall you know the divine freedom which waits for you.'

They travelled as if they moved from dream to dream. Their guide took them to where the ground had been pounded and rent by something huge. Craters sunk deep into the ground, the ground which was made not of rock, sand or soil: rather of rubbery skin which shone like glass. Great hammer blows had gouged crevasses and cracked fissures in it.

'We are close again to World's End,' said their guide. 'What you call Tormentors resulted from these cracks. Before the Wall was built, the air's magic was thick in our skies too. It came from your realm and we learned never to use it, for dragons could influence things if we did. We trapped the magic and stored it deep in the ground as buried garbage. When the great stone beast came . . .'

'The stoneflesh giant?' said Siel. 'The first to cross the boundary?'

'Yes. Many more have since crossed. When the first crossed over, it attacked all it saw. It was what sent up the foul clouds of trapped power, long gone stale, power which had developed its own poisonous consciousness. It had filled itself with curses of hate. This created what you call Tormentors.'

'The stoneflesh giant – have you dealt with it now?'

'We did not. But it is dead. Come.' Their guide took them for a short walk till they found a large shape of dark stone, half buried among green growing things, vines which seemed to slither and tighten about it even as they watched. Long winding pieces of stone had detached from the main mass – a stone-flesh giant's fingers. This was one's hand, overcome by what seemed the birth of a small jungle. 'The most benign of our gods slew it here,' said their guide. 'The one we name That With Affinity for Growing Things. It is also called the Teacher of Many Arts. If the Pendulum should swing high enough for gods to cross World's End, we have ensured this benign Spirit will be the first to cross into your world. It will do you no harm.'

'Will you show us this Spirit?' said Far Gaze.

Their guide opened a tunnel of light and wind and took them to a place where a crowd of men in castle colours – who had fled across World's End from the broken siege force at Tanton – stood at the edge of a ravine, staring ahead with awed faces. The cliff they stood upon was level with a stoneflesh giant's chest. They stood closer to it than men had dared to come to the great creatures before, but it did not notice them. It made a noise of distress. Its huge arm moved so turgidly it looked like something unseen impeded it.

At its feet and all through the gorge lay strewn pieces broken from the many cliff faces up and down the sheer valley. The giant had been pounding the valley to dust before the god found it. Now the giant's long winding fingers had twisted into impossible knots. Green growing things had sprouted from its eyes and from the great cave of its mouth (moaning still in pain, or fear). The basalt grey slab of its torso was slick and wet, just as if it had been lashed by rains.

As they watched, great splits in its torso opened, pushed outwards by green and wooden growths. One part broke free and fell into the valley with the other stone litter – the ground shivered when the piece smashed down. The great creature cried out a final time before the crack stretched from its mouth corners around its entire head, which then slid free and bounced on the slabs of stone beneath, bounced and rolled with tremendous noise. The giant's arms ceased all their motion. The men cheered and began to seek a way down. There was treasure in the head, they told one another. Gold and charms of great power. Already they argued about dividing the spoils they'd find.

'I didn't know men from our realm had crossed the border,' said Far Gaze. 'Is there danger in them coming here?'

'The Pendulum has swung too high now for the passage of humans and haiyens to matter,' said their guide. 'These men are in danger. There are things here that will find and prey upon them. I cannot help them. We are no longer in the practice of guiding souls to safety. When the lost haiyens parted ways with us, our work became our own survival.'

They watched the men climb down into the valley. One fell to his death, his brief cry echoing off the cliff faces. The others paused to watch, performed gestures with their hands, then they resumed their descent until they'd reached the stoneflesh giant's head. From up high they seemed like insects crawling over a large stone. They did not look up to see the Teacher of Many Arts shimmer into visibility for no more than a few seconds before fading out again. It was not as tall as the stoneflesh giant had been, but still it towered over them.

Far Gaze tried to catch that fleeting sight and hold it close: he saw two long antlers, not unlike a deer's except they moved and reached through the air. Two large black eyes seemed somehow kind and wise despite their strangeness. A gap for its mouth was partly covered by a blunt beak. Five long twisting legs like vines propped it up, one of which bent and coiled upon itself like a tail. It seemed made of long growing things all twisted together, arms very like tree limbs, with hundreds of branching fingers.

Filling the air for a second or two as the god faded from sight was a trilling note of peculiar song. It sent shivers down their backs, and reminded Siel of the sounds the haiyens had made which had healed her wounds and brought her back from death.

The men below all scurried out from the stoneflesh head, peering around to find what had made the sound. There was nothing for them to see, and no treasure for them in the giant's head.

Their guide said, 'There are other gods to see. They may disturb you more than this one. But the lords of your land should know their names and faces, lest they cross over to the North.'

Were it not for their healing in the waters, neither Far Gaze nor Siel would likely have been able to cope with the underground places their guide next took them, places where hideous beings of flat and pulsating form clung to the sides of cave walls and whispered with harsh voices like nails scratching stone. There were ropy clumps of pink glistening flesh, hung down from rock ceilings miles above those lightless places, with skeletons of many shapes now and then stuck to them, and remains beneath them – haiyen cities of underground refuge long ago ruined. Some of the beautiful and strange buildings were still intact though their occupants had all been consumed. Through such lost places, their guide led them in search of a hidden god, one not seen by any haiyen alive today.

And there it was at last, in an opening space unfathomably deep below, huge upon a pool of liquid darkness: That of the Realms Beneath, dozens of huge half-open eyes at the tips of each ropy winding limb, all twisted about its crescent-shaped torso. One of the many eyes turned their way, gazed at them. A sound of sighing breath filled the dank air – in response, a million curious others began to whisper, seeping up from beneath the black surface with thin trails of smoke.

In haste their guide drew them away, his fear so intense they felt it long after they were away from there. It was the first time their guide had been so afraid in their presence. They did not understand why, and when they asked what they'd just escaped, he would not tell them what had been about to happen.

Instead he showed them safer things for a while, such as a group of hooded haiyens making a long trek across hidden plains to where their nests were built: conical wooden-looking things with intricate designs etched on them. The things were reminiscent of the totem pillars the dark-skinned tribes left scattered on the edge of the Unclaimed Lands. A group of five haiyens solemnly poured a part of themselves into holes upon one such nest, energy flowing almost invisibly from their hands into the vessel.

'Here I show you how we are born,' said their guide. 'In infancy, we have a small amount of life. The life force within us slowly grows, until we cannot house more of it, just as a cup slowly overflows. When one's life force reaches fullness, it is shared with these nests, and others become born from it. In this way we too can be reborn, if we choose. He who pours all his life force into the vessel loses his body, is remade young and without memory. With songs and other arts, the group he travels with – what you would call his family – will remind him who he was, what work he performed in life. His memories slowly return. With time, fewer choose to be reborn in this place, going instead to other lives and forms. This world may be owned soon by the lost ones. And they may do to your world what they have done to ours.'

Siel and Far Gaze did not know the times before and directly after they encountered the god whose haiyen name meant That of Energies and Other Places. They later had no memory of how they came to the enormous temple built for it. The god was a clutch of shapes so disparate and strange that for a long while after, Far Gaze doubted his eyes could be trusted with *anything* any more. He supposed that among its writhing thrashing shapes was a head, a torso and limbs, but it seemed more a machine, spinning beyond control.

He and Siel saw only a portion of that entity, whatever it truly was. All surrounding memory was lost. There was just incomprehensible strangeness imprinted on them like a streak of light behind eyes squeezed shut. 'You're trying to drive us mad,' Siel said as they staggered out of the huge temple housing it.

They felt their guide's grief and regret. He said, 'I will take you to where we can recover.' Again with no surrounding memory of the journey they were inside a house-sized shell of stone, with moss and soft soil for its floor. Gentle flute music played. Haiyens were whispering in their ears as they seemed to wake from sleep. They whispered of Siel's and Far Gaze's own lives, talking about their memories as if they'd been there watching all of it unfold. 'Why do you recount my life for me?' said Far Gaze sleepily. 'I lived it already and didn't much care for it the first time.'

'You must ground yourselves again,' said the haiyen nearest. 'Having seen what you have seen, there is danger of losing who you are. To behold one god is confronting enough. You have seen three. Keep your feet in the land's soil for a time. Reflect upon your familiar world and life. You will then be ready for all else you have been brought here to learn.'

'How to kill dragons,' murmured Far Gaze.

'Rest then, if *that* is what you have come for,' the haiyen said quietly.

'I need not know,' said Siel. 'I want to see no more. If Far Gaze is willing to go alone and leave me to rest here, let him. I want to go home.'

So it was that Far Gaze alone saw That Which Governs Cycles of Events, that same Spirit Eric had glimpsed stalking between the ruined buildings of his home city in the vision shown to him by Shilen in the dragons' prison. The tall, impossible shape moved insect-like through its barren home, one light and one dark orb held aloft in each of its long arms.

Far Gaze saw too the tall desert tower platforms of those haiyens to the deepest south, the cities of the lost ones, who'd sealed their world off from other worlds, and made it a prison like the North, trapping their kindred with themselves. He saw the vastness of their high valley, the ingenious homes they'd built far above the reach of the foul things they'd summoned to the lands beneath. His guide told him how they had learned to pool consciousness in a way that opened a gate to a terrible world, and what hungry things had come through that gate.

And there was one now: an enormous ball of matter, halfway between flesh and stone. It rolled mindlessly, smashing itself into cliff sides. Only when they went near to it could Far Gaze appreciate the vast thing's size and horror. It was as big as a mountain, rolling slowly above them like an ocean of sickly grey, formed of infinite whipping tendrils of flesh, seeking ever to pull more matter to itself, to grow and grow. Here and there among its vast bulk were eyes and limbs, formed on its surface in mocking parody of the life forms it had subsumed. Far Gaze stood stunned and numb with horror, so numb he did not even particularly wish to flee the thing. He could only stare at it.

'When these are first summoned here, they are small and formless,' said his haiyen guide. 'Can you believe, to look upon it now, that this being was once smaller than an insect? They search for dead things, for flesh to borrow. They add living matter to themselves like shreds of clay, warping and preserving it, growing ever larger. The lost ones helped it grow, fed it living things. They sent one like this to our cities. It had not grown so large as this, but we'd not seen its kind before. We had not learned then how to slay them. By the time we learned, it had destroyed our city, and this and two others had grown too large to kill. Three now are god-sized, and no known arts may destroy them. This one claimed this valley and a great area surrounding it. It does not live, it does not die – it just exists and roams its territory. The Teacher of Many Arts cannot slay it. Perhaps the other gods could, but they show no interest in it. This one has the flesh of dragons in its mass. Now you know how dragons are slain. And you know how the lost haiyens will offer to help you slay them.'

When they were safely away from that place, back in the place of healing and grounding of consciousness, his guide told him how all through Levaal South, the hungry presences had roamed in search of more matter to bring into themselves. And of how the haiyens had once had cities and civilisations the envy of many worlds. Those places were trampled to splinters, trampled along with most of their nests, condemning them to live and breed in hiding.

'The treks to our breeding places are ever more dangerous. The Teacher of Many Arts came, and taught us to build homes which remained hidden from the hungry things' awareness. The lost ones do not regret for an instant for what they have done. They wrongly believe the hungry presences do their bidding, when in truth the things trap them in their high cities and do not let them leave. The only power the lost haiyens have is to bring more of the entities here. And they do. We hunt the small ones down as they roam north into our safe country. We find them when they are wearing the flesh of just a few animals. If one grows larger, many of us must gather to deal with it. Much life has moved below ground, where the things cannot go. That too shall be your future, if your lords listen to the lost ones. Or if the Pendulum swings high enough – then those hungry presences may leave their territory and cross World's End.'

'They are worse for our world than the dragons shall be?'

'It is for you to say. A dragon has a mind. You may communicate with it, even if it wishes you great harm. These presences have no mind, not that we can discern. Yet somehow they control the lost haiyens, and compel them to summon more of their kind here.'

Far Gaze already knew how easily men like Tauk could be persuaded to protect and feed the hungry presences until they grew huge, thinking perhaps the things could be trained as guardians or beasts of war. 'I sense your mood,' said his guide. 'You have my sympathy. But you must return and tell your lords of what happened to us, so that perhaps it won't happen in your realm.'

'My lords won't listen.'

'They must at least be given the choice to listen. I guided you through the darkest places of this world at my peril; not only mine, also my people's peril.' He raised a finger to the indentation between his eyes. 'We are not many left, those who can travel as I have taken you. Rare are our births, and I shall not be reborn to this lost world again. I brought you to the waters where you were cleansed. If you have gratitude for that, tell your lords what you've seen here. One of your men even now rides a dragon to the very south, to visit the lost ones and make bargains with them.'

As their guide had said, there was no knowing how much time had passed when they were finally returned to Levaal North. They were in the same country they'd been taken from – near Gorb's old village, near the tower. Tauk and his men were not in sight, but Far Gaze could sense that Blain was not far away.

'Decide your course,' said their guide. 'I will take you where you wish.'

'I will stay here,' said Siel, examining the tracks about the village.

Far Gaze asked for an hour more, then went through the abandoned village homes in search of paper. To his surprise he found a whole bundle of good quality stuff in the room Gorb had kept his Engineer. Much was covered in scrawled formula but the reverse sides were blank. A pot of ink and some thin charcoal sticks sat on the bench. By candlelight he began making rough sketches.

Siel came in and peered over his shoulder. 'Are those the Southern Spirits you're drawing?'

He nodded. The images of them had been hard enough for his mind to hold when the entities were right before him; with each moment the sight of those beings slipped further through his memory, leaving only a vague approximation of each.

When he was done drawing he blew dry the ink, carefully folded the papers and tucked them into his small pack. As he turned to leave he paused, studying Siel. He did not perceive auras very well, but there was something peculiar in hers. Something fey. 'What do you intend to do here, Siel?'

'Perhaps a little hunting,' she said with a shrug. 'Where will you go?'

'To the castle. Our guide tells me the Arch no longer dwells there. I will advise whoever has claimed the place, as I promised our guide I'd do. Then I will find Tauk and his descendants. I will give them many things, but none of it advice.'

35

AT THE ASH SEA

Lalie jerked and bumped against the caravan walls. It reminded her of being under Mayor Izven's small pot-bellied body, throwing itself over her with unnatural violence the night before they'd set out. The exertion had left him red-faced and panting. But he'd donned his composure again as easily as he'd dressed himself, peered down at her with his usual mild look, offered her a drink. Nothing seemed to have happened at all.

The edge of the Ash Sea was hours away yet, but their wagons bumped and scraped on the long-neglected road. The air grew thick with dark flecks and soot. It scattered down on the roof and against the wagon's window and made the sky too dark to tell day from night. There had once been a city where the Ash Sea now sat. The other Spirits had brought Inferno down but they'd been too late to stop him eating that city and its people. The massive crater remained, filled with wind and ash like an angry living entity in its own right. The old roads leading there were discernible but by now barely usable. Few travellers came this far: it was dangerous country, rife with angry elementals and many perils hidden from sight, or so tales went.

Many of those riding in the rear of their caravan were Mayor Izven's friends, people whom Lalie had seen helping themselves to the pleasure slaves every other day. All were wealthy dark-magic hobbyists, the kind Lalie's old friends would have sneered at. The kind who dished out fortunes for certain potions or relics, not knowing you could accomplish just as much with sticks twisted into the right shapes and a simple campfire.

There were genuine mages and mystics among them now too, who had met them along the way. Silent brooding people, who had each inspected Lalie and the other girls and women in the same way farmers inspect livestock before trade. Those mystics carried themselves as authorities of the arts, but they had hurried away when Strategist Vashun came near. Lalie began to think that she and the mayor were the only ones unafraid of him. And she felt that the mayor was foolish to be unafraid.

Out the windows now elementals could be seen, orange flashes winding distantly through ash kicked up to look like sleet. The handfuls of it thrown against the wagon roof and walls began to hit with greater impact, as if rocks were among it. The horses started making distressed sounds – they would need, soon, to be soothed with spells or they'd ride no further.

Lalie kept her eyes on the window, even though there was not much to see. Strategist Vashun had some time back crept into her wagon, and now sat opposite her. He looked at her with a strange kind of lust she did not understand. It was not a sexual desire; nor was it the hungry gleam of rites-mad zealots eyeing their Offering. She could not fathom what he really wanted, or why he was really on this journey.

'Be well, child,' spoke his rasping voice. With long fingers he twisted the lid from a canteen crusted with red stones and poured her a goblet of cool water. She bared her teeth at him, but it did nothing to change his smile. The air *had* gone very dry. She took the water and sipped it, the chains about her wrist clinking. 'Mm, those restraints,' he sighed. 'A pretty decoration they make. But, hardly needed on *you*. You enjoy this journey. You are . . . excited?' He reached for the lock, caressed it for a while with a finger thin as bone. The chains fell loose. Lalie scratched several itches they had kept her from and felt in spite of herself a moment's gratitude.

Vashun leaned closer to her and lowered his rasp to something confidential: 'I am . . . like you, child. Ancient and young at once. The young often have a certain . . . wisdom, about them, which says they have lived before. I have known dying children whose . . . eyes, bespeak a very ancient wisdom. A *knowing*. Which one must respect. From where they came, they made a choice to be here, and chose to make their visit brief. One cannot but . . . respect this. Whether it is truly courage or cowardice, once the layers are stripped back, it remains: they *chose* to face the . . . intolerable.'

He leaned back, shifted his long, stiff body on the seat, sucked at the air as if for a long while he'd forgotten to breathe. He said, 'For me, in this life, time enough has passed. Pleasures may remain, but all of them . . . *known* to me. All tastes now familiar. My . . . curiosities are all sated. No more . . . ambition left within me, you might say. Others I know, old as I, would play the game forever. Not I, child. For me, the game draws to its end, with but one or two jests to leave upon the board for others.'

He turned to check the curtained door through which Izven had earlier departed, then lowered his voice. 'The mayor. He is . . . different from you and me. Much he likes life, and his practice of living. Of course! A zest, a hunger to taste it all. Ah! This journey is but one more flavour for him, all an adventure for one so spoiled, so bored, so dim. Mm. The same way such men as he ride close to an unfolding battle, to . . . spectate, to smell the dead. He wishes to be eye to eye with that most *notorious* Spirit, child. Perhaps he feels it shall not really rise. Perhaps he doubts my—' like an insect on its back his bone-thin fingers twisted for the word '— my expertise? *You* know what comes, child. I see it all about you, that age beyond your body, that wisdom within. You have lived and died before. Do you remember? Some do remember, you know.'

He leaned closer yet for his answer. She shifted away from him, gave a quick shake of the head. He nodded. 'The memory, it is close to you. Hidden behind a curtain of thought, mm? The winds may soon part it. You know, as do I. What comes is our last hour. It is approaching. We alone in this group, you and I, we understand. The others know not.'

A gust threw hot powder against the wagon's sides and roof. Vashun smiled as if he had done it. 'Close now, child,' he said, shoulders hunching in the convulsive motions of a laugh. She looked out the window again. There was not much to see.

The door's curtain parted and Izven burst in, taken aback for just an instant by the sight of the Strategist with her.

'Have you a wish to be alone with the girl?' said Vashun.

'No, thank you,' said Izven. He wiped blood from his nose; it was caused by his preferred drug. Vashun rose to depart anyway, and gave Lalie a knowing smile.

When the road ended and the horses could step no further into the soft ground they set out on foot. All had scarves wrapped about their faces with just a slit for their eyes. Through that slit almost nothing could be seen, and torches were not advised lest it attract flame elementals. Blindly they went forwards in a long human chain across the flat, led by two mystics who could see about them with their minds. Izven had four strong servants to carry him on a seat propped up on poles. Vashun walked with a hand on Lalie's shoulder. It sat there coldly. The other Offerings cried and begged for freedom, as Offerings usually did when they sensed the end near. Lalie scorned them now as much as she had when she'd been on the other side of the sacrificial knife.

Soon the ash on the wind grew almost too thick for them to move through. The crusty ground underfoot began to sink in with the weight of their steps.

'Where shall we do this?' said Izven, barely audible. He'd been complaining about the air and heat for a while now.

'The deeper we go, the more pleased shall the Spirit be,' answered one of the mystics, voice muffled by his scarf.

'Does our expert have an opinion?' said Vashun, fingers tightening on Lalie's shoulder.

'Light your fire here,' she said. 'It won't matter. If Inferno wants to speak, he will speak. We are in his home now. If we have trespassed he will kill all of us. If not now, within a week. It will seem like illness and accident.'

The Strategist smiled at her. He motioned to the two men who'd lagged at the group's rear, carrying a heavy wooden chest. They threw back its lid. Vashun rummaged around inside.

Over an hour he carefully set up thin rods in a wide circle, taking a long while to measure the distance and position of each to the utmost degree. At last he had fenced in a circular area big enough to fit within it a large house. Inside the ring the air grew slowly clearer, as if an invisible barrier had been set. Only a small pattering of ash made it within. They could hear each other speak again. The mystics and the mayor's people watched Vashun like eager pupils. He said, 'It is a . . .

defiance of the will of the other Spirits, that we are here at all.'

'Will they not sense that we have come here?' someone asked.

Vashun shook his head. 'Much else occupies them. Vous, they closely study. Valour, they fight to contain, to keep away from World's End. The dragons stir above. Deeds like this? Far from their thoughts. Or so we gamble.'

'What's next?' said the mayor. He drank water from the flask he'd brought.

'The field I have cast shall do much,' said Vashun. 'Those with mage eyes, note the airs, if you can see them. Odd patterns begin. It's something I wished to try on Vous, but Avridis feared it would kill him.' His shoulders hunched up in a silent laugh. 'With a Spirit already at rest? No harm. Ah, but here is something unknown.' He motioned to another of those who had come just to haul equipment. A metal canister was dragged with difficulty across the ground: one of those stolen from outside Vous's chamber. With little ceremony Vashun undid its lid and let its pure airs seep out.

For a long while they waited in meditative silence. They sat to eat a feast of fine meat, fruit and wine. Izven began to eye the world outside Vashun's invisible fence with impatience. The air outside was so thick with an ash blizzard there was no chance yet of returning to the caravan.

A sweep of Vashun's arm indicated the girls and women brought as Offerings. All of them bar Lalie were chained in a line with large nervous eyes. 'Mayor, to pass time, some . . . entertainment? It shall do no harm to the process.'

'Are you sure of that?' said Izven.

'Of benefit, if anything. To the energies. Certain emotions play well, contain power. A feast of emotions poured into the airs. I suggest you leave one untouched. A courtesy, for the Spirit.' Vashun stepped between Lalie and the others while the mayor and some of his party had their way with the Offerings. Lalie turned away, annoyed by their cries and pleas.

Vashun lowered his lips to her ear. 'Does this business not . . . please your tastes, child? I find a certain humour. You shall too, perhaps. A pig who smells the dishes and wine from afar may be excited by his invitation to the table. Do you know the rest of the joke? Mm. Ah, you are older than you know, and wise.' He cupped her head in his stiff cold palms, turned it gently to the scene of writhing bodies in the ash. He whispered, 'You have done such things as these men do now. You have tasted yourself what they taste. It is certain. All of us wear every garment of soul that's made, by the end. We all dance every dance. Many lifetimes we reside, my young ancient one. We experience all.'

'I have tasted it in this life,' she said. She shrugged away from his touch.

'Mm. Answer this. Do you consider these men, these women, worthy of what approaches? Worthy even of a look at your dear one?'

'They are pigs to me. But it is for Inferno to say.'

'Ahh! I will show you what I think, mm? I will show you the rest of the joke.' Vashun pulled back his robe sleeve. His thin white arm was barely covered by skin and flesh. Wrapped around it was a black line thin as string. He prised it loose and let it hang from his hand like a short whip. 'Have you seen these perform?' he whispered. She didn't answer. 'Sharp. It has spells about it. To raise energies. The finest sacrificial blade you've known, young ancient one, was not near as fine as this.'

The Strategist approached the nearest pair of writhing bodies, an Offering's shoulders held down by a hooded mystic. The mystic made sucking noises, sipping from her distress as another raped her. Vashun stood over them, grinning down. Suddenly his teeth were as big as a wolf's. He lashed the thin instrument around twice with the *whoosh* of cut air. Both men's heads lurched up, a grimace on their faces. A line of blood appeared in the middle of the naked one's back. It seemed slow, the way his body fell apart along that slit, along with the victim's beneath him. The other's head rolled slowly away, pouring itself like a spilled chalice into the ash.

Two mystics who stood nearby gaped then ran blindly into the dark ash storm. The warriors drew their swords, hesitant, unsure if this were a proper part of the ritual or not. Vashun cast off his coat. His Strategist robe flashed with deep red, the colour of his own lust awakened. His eyes grew and shone red. His rasping deathly scream rang impossibly loud and drawn out. It made even Lalie cower back. Only then did the others seem to notice him. The guards dropped their weapons, faces to their hands, blood gushing through their fingers.

Smoke poured from Vashun's eyes and between his grinning teeth. Through the group he stalked, lashing figure eights with his thin blade. Heads and limbs fell. The mayor and his victim were the last ones alive. Vashun cast something to freeze the mayor as he fumbled for his clothes. Slowly, so slowly Vashun dealt with him.

When it was finally over he took Lalie's hand and brought her to the middle of the circle. Gently he stroked her hair and whispered to her, speaking for many long hours of the things he'd seen, and the things he'd done. She tried not to listen, but she found his words cast pictures in her mind so it almost seemed she was there at his shoulder while he did those deeds.

She learned what he had meant when he said his curiosities were all sated. Her skin got icy chills where his fingers touched her. When she tried to squirm away his magic held her there.

The field he'd cast did its work. Now and then he stood to stroll among the slain, calling forth the god with chants Lalie had never heard. Elementals came near but did not cross the circle's boundary. Heat trickled up through from the depths. Something shifted in the Ash Sea, making the ground shiver. Long fingers of fire threaded up from beneath. One reached and caressed the flesh on Lalie's thigh. She screamed. As if she'd called them, more threads of fire came. 'There is one flame,' said Lalie, declaring herself the Spirit's friend. But it made no difference, the flames burned her just as hot.

Vashun watched her writhing in the fires. 'How is it now, girl? Is it what you wanted?' He delighted in her pain, then delighted in his own as the flames reached for him in turn. Cracks split the ground and ash sank through it like sand through fingers. In a rush the Spirit came. Lalie felt an instant's joy before a blast of heat unmade her. The Strategist too was swallowed, a grin on his face. Should Avridis, Blain and the others see him now, he'd have given a world for their thoughts. They would be entertained by the Spirit's mischief, at least . . . whether or not they knew who had brought him back to the surface world.

36

AWAKENED

Inferno emerged from dreams into the physical world with great surprise. The strange airs that had funnelled down to his place of rest had woken him by the pain they'd caused, but despite this he was glad.

He found he was a shapeless collection of energy; he could not remember what his body had previously been. So he experimented with forms for a while, settling at last on something not unlike those beings who had woken him. Inferno became vaguely human-looking, though much larger.

He forgot too why he had been sent to this place of rest. All he remembered was something about a frantic mood and a fierce hunger, of filling the hunger with things that tasted wonderful. No such hunger troubled him now – the memory of it was confusing.

He examined the dead human bodies about him, seeking patterns in their mess, but there was little to learn. Why had they come here? Surely to hurt him. So many times had humans intruded on his dreams, dancing about fires, saying things he did not understand, directing thought and feverish emotion towards him. Why did humans need to hunt him in the physical realm too? In the non-physical realms, they had far more power . . . but here, their physical blades and spells could never have hurt him much. Was it in revenge for the city he had eaten?

Nearby were elementals of fire and wind. They offered themselves to him. He took them, enjoyed their touch, incorporated them within himself. Quickly he snuffed out their personalities and imposed his own. Their energies and knowledge he kept.

Ah, now he remembered: it was the other Spirits who had cast him down and buried him in ash. Far across the world, he felt their distant movements. Tempest was making great winds to inhibit Valour's movements. Mountain pushed against the sky prisons with all his strength, ignoring other happenings. And there seemed to be a new one among them. Strange! They were busy, they were frightened. Frightened that Valour might go across World's End, for the Wall was gone. How much things had changed! Inferno's sleep must have been long.

As soon as he moved outside the human-cast power field, Nightmare became aware of him. Nightmare rushed through the skies, already on his way here. Nightmare was strong, unpredictable. It was not a good time for Inferno to fight him.

Inferno called energies to himself from the airs, but the Ash Sea had little power of the kind he needed, other than inside the little field the humans had put up. The other Spirits had made sure the airs here would be empty. Inferno ran from the Ash Sea and found his legs moved quickly.

The new Spirits were deathly afraid. Their fear bled through into the magic wherever he went. He stopped and scooped a handful of stones, melted them with heat, even though it would anger Mountain. He tossed the melted stuff on the ground before him, observed the patterns it made and divined information. Why are the Spirits afraid? he asked the melted stone.

The Pendulum will swing high if a Spirit crosses World's End, the pattern answered. The other gods had managed to halt the Pendulum swing, and meant now to keep it still where it was, for aeons if need be, while humans re-established their domains. The Spirits did not wish to go south. They did not wish to battle their strange and mighty counterparts there.

What of the dragons? Inferno asked, melting more stone and tossing it before him.

The dragons too wish it to swing no higher, he perceived in the patterns he'd flung. The dragons had changed their plans. They had meant for the gods – some, or perhaps all of them – to go across World's End, so that their prison's foundation would weaken, even if it meant confronting the foreign Spirits of Levaal South. But something had changed. The dragons could now break free of the skies and descend without that desperate plan having to unfold. They no longer wanted any of the Spirits to cross the boundary. The dragons were uneasy about the foreign gods, as much as Inferno's kindred were.

Inferno contemplated all this. For now, the dragons and gods of the North were in agreement, on one matter at least. But Inferno had no friends among the dragons *or* the Spirits. He did not wish to be put to sleep again. He was awake but not yet strong, not nearly strong enough to battle the other great powers; any one of them could probably cast him down again. And although he had no friends in the southern realm, at least he had not made enemies there. No one there would hunt him, as Nightmare did this very moment, fast closing the distance between them . . .

So Inferno ran for World's End. He got there quickly. He paused before crossing, sensing the other gods recoil in distress, as they forgot their work with Valour and became aware of *him*, became aware of where he was, what he intended. But there was nowhere else for him. Inferno crossed the boundary. His footsteps scalded the southern land as he sought a place to hide. Perhaps Nightmare would follow him across. Valour surely would.

37

DRAGONS AND SPIRITS

Few human beings had ever truly understood the Spirits. When here or there some minds had hit upon the truth about them, seldom were those truths held distinct from the myths and fables.

Nor did humanity understand the dragons any better. With nearly all of human history lived apart from the creatures, few would ever have predicted things could change drastically within the span of one human life . . . let alone could any foresee that such a change could be weeks or even days away. Even as cracked lightstone pieces began to rain down, some suspected, but few truly knew what it meant.

So it was that life went quietly on for that brief subdued span of time, while the castle and its Aligned cities were cleared of the old regime's remnants. The biggest news in the northern parts was not the occasional shiver passing through the ground, the occasional lightstone rain; it was the new lord, the Otherworld lord named Shadow who had stepped from fables. For most, the new lord was sign enough the world had forever changed: Shadow was a peace-bringer, a purifier of evil. These Aligned lands for now were free from tyranny, free after all they had endured. There were no reasons now for war between men.

There was also talk that Vous had become a benign Spirit, a friend to humanity. Many had seen him. He'd appeared in a field where a refugee caravan headed north. Flower petals had rained down, the air had filled with beautiful scents and music, and fountains had risen from the soil. A kind of garden had erupted around the road, delighting the weary travellers. They had few other memories to recall than that: dancing gaily, feeling well fed when it was over. Some of them were cured of sickness and injury.

Strange times, these.

In the south, news went slow, with most travellers still fearing war and Tormentors roaming. It was slowly becoming known that something had slain most or all of the creatures – few guessed that Valour had done it. Still, taverns here and there had strange tales of *new people*. And the usual speculations followed: a war would come with them; they would ally with this or that city; they would take the world over, if not for Shadow's protection . . . so on, so on. And did you hear that a man was seen riding south upon a dragon? No, not upon a drake. Upon a *dragon* . . .

None but the gods knew that Inferno had awoken, and that he had crossed to the South. Not even Domudess, who had foreseen that future long years ago in the company of master seers. (Seen it among many alternate futures; he'd put stock in none of them.)

The wizard had set up his tower again, placing it quite close to where it had been before. For he enjoyed this sparsely populated country, now with airs much cleaner thanks to the haiyens and their work. He knew the mayor and his men could come for him again, but they were easily enough avoided, whether or not Valour had given them gifts and blessings.

He sat now on the uppermost floor, gazing out the high window, reflecting upon the night so long ago when the war mages first came screaming out the castle windows. How brief in the end was the reign which that night of violence and theft had signalled. That future too was one they'd foreseen, again one they'd not considered likely. They had made minor preparations on the off-chance it would come to pass, preparations completely insufficient when the attack began.

The encounter with Tauk had plunged Domudess's mood. When speaking with the haiyens, they had made it seem that there was really no valid reason humans could not be persuaded to walk a different path, that they would lay down weapons and grudges for just a moment and *listen*. He sat in deep meditation, trying to allay his sadness. Whatever now approached them could be so easily avoided . . . but then, had it not always been so?

Footsteps tapped up the tower's winding stairway. The haiyens could materialise here in this room without the need for doors and stairways, but they climbed the steps to alert him of their coming as a courtesy. He stood, surprised to be visited. When they parted, the haiyens had said it would be many days before they next spoke – they had much work to do to purify the airs throughout the realm. In thought, Domudess said: 'Welcome back.'

'A god went south,' said the haiyen named Luhan – he had adopted the name for the convenience of humans he dealt with. Domudess collapsed back on his chair.

'Which god?'

'The fire Spirit.'

'Inferno? That can't be . . .'

Sensing his panic, the haiyen came near, emanating a gentle calmness over him. Domudess gave Luhan a grateful look, and thought the matter through. Of course. The Strategists. If Blain had escaped, the others may have done too . . . men who knew the science of god-making. 'Be at peace,' said Luhan.

'What will happen now?'

'The Teacher of Many Arts is nearest the boundary. It will be first to come here, as we asked it to do. It will do nothing to provoke the Spirits here, nor the people, but the dragons may rage at its coming. That, as you know, is beyond anyone's control, and they would rage at whatever Spirit crossed from our realm. For our people, that Spirit is benign. Let us hope it is benign for the people of this land. We'd not have survived the changes to our realm, without that Spirit's teachings.'

'Do we know how our Spirits shall react to its presence here?' thought Domudess.

A burst of mirth came to him from the haiyen, so keen that Domudess could not help smiling in spite of how he felt. Now he saw how they had managed to convince him Tauk would see to reason; when they laughed, all the world around them briefly flickered as if set alight with joy and mirth. Luhan's answer was, 'Of course not!'

Like the people of her realm, Aziel gave hardly any thought to the gods.

She strolled now through the castle's higher floors, seeking out a throne room to better suit the army of administrators who constantly came and went. Indeed there were more administrators than members of any army she commanded . . . the administrators outnumbered the half-giants guarding her vulnerable reign.

Eric of course was not to be found. What he had done – 'Favouring' a room full of administrators and clerks – had at least yielded some benefits. They attacked their tasks with furious energy. They'd recruited workers from the cities, who'd cleared the castle lawns of all signs of Vous's massacre. Masses of people were being moved from the old cities into those new ones the Arch had had stoneshaper mages build near the castle. A new start for thousands of people. Eric would be pleased at all this charity . . . and even Aziel conceded there was some sense in it. She needed those people desperately, needed their loyalty. Being fed and housed and left in peace (for a while, at least) might be enough for her to gain it.

A voice at the window she strolled past startled her out of her skin, or just about. A tremulous voice said, 'Sorry, Aziel! O so terribly sorry we startled you.'

'Ghost!' she said, and she laughed. 'You're still here? I'd have thought you'd have gone when Father went.'

'No, Aziel. This place is home. But there are . . . strange things . . .' The faces battled fiercely for the chance to hold the window glass.

'Stop that: share the glass. I'll speak to you all. What strange things?'

All their voices spoke at once: 'We sometimes . . . stay in the outer panels of the windows. And watch *outwards*. Outwards, at the realm. We sometimes go forth and look around.'

'Of course you do, I remember. You visited me when I was captured. And? Out with it, have you seen something to bother you? Have the half-giants left their post?'

'No, Aziel. They make so much noise it disturbs the lower staff. But it's . . . Invia, Aziel.'

'What about them?'

'Lots have been flying around. Around and around. Lots! A cloud was thick with them. They descended. And . . . we thought there was with them . . . something . . . *bigger*.'

'Everything is so frightening to you. You probably saw a storm cloud.'

'It had wings, Aziel. It flew around, wheeling as a bird would, then went south with great haste! So terribly large.'

'A dragon?' she laughed. 'It couldn't have been a dragon. Shilen shall forewarn me when they are coming down. Unless it was her that you saw. Was the dragon white?'

But Ghost had departed from the window as if something had frightened it away. Something moved behind her in the window's reflection. She screamed, turned. Nothing was there. For a brief instant she'd have sworn her father stood behind her. Vous. She remembered so clearly now his blazing eyes full of hate, his bared teeth. But of course he wasn't there.

Something softly brushed her cheek. A pink-white flower petal fell at her feet. A small rain of them poured down, caressing her hair and upturned face with gentle touches. She looked for the source of them, but the little shower ceased as quickly as it began.

38

RIVAL LORDS

Eric had begun to think of himself as Shadow. Why not choose his own name? He was free. Had he really, truly mourned his nine-to-five life? His sitcom existence, making half-witted wisecracks as if expecting a laugh track to play in response? How much like slavery that life appeared, looking back on it from the skies aboard his drake. The lands and cities before him seemed a majestic sculpture, one he no longer had a desire to leave.

For now the wars had ended and a strange silent inertia replaced them. The roads seemed safe from brigandry, even though there were no roadblocks and patrols. People no longer moved about with secrecy – strangers on the road greeted each other, shared food with one another, and tales. Wherever Eric went people seemed to know him, and to love him. Hard men looked at him as if he were like them, as though he'd seen all the war they'd seen. He began to believe it too.

People asked him of Otherworld, along with many other questions. The sort of questions one might ask a god. He amused himself with creative answers for a time.

But soon the questions began to bother him, and he was unsure why. With time he discovered a kind of contempt for these people. Most of them were wiser than he, more virtuous, harder working, braver. Yet in a moment they handed their trust to him, and pinned their hopes on him, someone no better than a stranger. They read wisdom he'd not intended in every remark he made.

The sky now and then sent shivers down through its far-flung walls to shake the ground. It spat down lightstone pieces: little pebbles or fist-sized rocks. With more pressing concerns at hand – food in bellies, roofs overhead, rebuilding – no one paid much heed to it.

One day Eric thought that the country beneath him, of cliffs and natural pillars, looked familiar. He'd seen before that line of strange, rib-like mountains and that shimmering river threading through them. He knew where they were – these were the same skies the war mage had carried him through. Elvury City was not far, the last place in Levaal still infested with Tormentors. Or so tavern talk claimed.

He spoke into the drake's ear. Case wheeled to the south.

Below them now was the pass, littered with broken skeletons in armour and castle colours. Birds still picked through the mess, their calls echoing up the sheer cliff walls. Eric remembered watching this slaughter, filled with numbing horror.

Case came to rest atop the city's high gate. Here he'd shot the war mage so eager to serve him. There below, sure enough, stood a widely scattered group of Tormentors, no more than a dozen of them. Now and then the occasional sweep of their spiked arms shifted them to a new pose of their strange slow dance. Many buildings were half burned down, the ash scattered, but there were no fires burning in the city now. Distantly through the buildings one or two huge Tormentors could be seen standing motionless along the river.

Case sighed as if deeply saddened by all this. He rested his head on his forelegs and slept. His snores softly growled like an idling motor. Eric patted his neck then gazed down at the dead city. Why did I come here? he thought, and it was something he couldn't answer. He felt a pang of peculiar nostalgia for those times when this world was so new and horrifying to him. How he wanted to reach a reassuring hand back through time and say, *It will be all right. It will be better than you'd ever guess.*

Case needed rest, so Eric stayed awhile gazing out at the city which Shilen would have him believe he and Aziel now owned, or at least controlled. Silent tears filled his eyes. An hour or more passed, the day fading to evening, the stillness only broken by the shivering rumble of dragons in the skies pushing against their cage . . . a sound which could easily pass for distant thunder. Somewhere there would be a rain of broken lightstone; maybe great slabs of it were beginning to come down. But although pieces littered the city and valley, none fell here now.

Wheeling into Eric's line of sight across the eastern sky was a shape his eyes took at first to be a bird. But it was too large for a bird. A rider's silhouette could be made out against the grey-white sky behind.

Case stirred in his sleep. Eric knew then that what flew over Elvury was not another drake, but a dragon. Its tail fluttered like a streamer behind it; its wings were held still and at an angle. With suddenness Eric found alarming, the dragon swooped down to the city below, down and up again in a fast long arc. Many times it dived. Eric found his hand closing about Hauf's amulet.

Nearer the dragon swooped, till its rider's cries could be heard. And the voice was familiar. Why Eric should laugh to recognise

Kiown, he didn't know. But he *did* laugh, just as though he'd found an old friend.

Kiown and his mount were now close. They swept down to the area called the siege grounds, the dives so fast they were a blur. Each time the dragon came up from its arc, the falling pieces of a shattered Tormentor had not yet hit the pavement. Before long all those Tormentors visible below had been broken to pieces. All the while Kiown cried out and whooped in joy.

Eric called out to him. Shocked to hear a voice, Kiown stared around. When he recognised Eric, his laugh echoed and clattered through the city's emptiness. 'Lord Eric!' he cried. Dyan swept a circle in the air above him.

'My name is Shadow.'

'Lord Eric, inn-finder. World-stumbler-inner. Um . . . drake-rider? What else can we call you? What other feats of great renown have you to your name now?'

'Vous is a god now,' Eric called. 'The change has happened.'

That got Kiown's attention. He landed Dyan on the gate some distance away, spoke quiet words to the dragon. It peered at Eric with curiosity and amusement, then went still as a statue, eyes closed. Case woke up, bounded over to it and fawned before it. The dragon opened one eye to peer at him then shut it again.

Kiown marched over, twirling a chained piece of jewellery on his finger. 'Do you like my steed?' he said. 'Never in history has a dragon like this been a man's steed or servant. They've banished him. He serves whoever holds this amulet. Dyan doesn't care, he was sure the big ones were going to eat him. A supply of human women and he's content. You're looking well, Eric. Not lordly by any measure. Fed, at least. Met any dragons yourself?'

'I have. Just one, Shilen.'

'Ah, yes, I know her.'

Eric was taken aback. 'How? She said she was my advisor. Has she been going back and forth between us?'

'Sure has. I doubt she thought we'd meet up and speak like this. She knew we were opponents in the past. She also knows how men usually behave when thrones are at stake. Dragons are sometimes surprised, Eric, by how much a human can break out of what they consider typical behaviour. We are not as predictable as they think us to be.'

'So you're my rival lord of the south that she spoke about. The one who'll claim my throne, if he's more "worthy" of it. Have it, if you want. It's yours.'

'If you're giving it away I don't want it,' said Kiown. He leaned his forearms on the wall and gazed down at the steep cliffs fencing in the valley filled with skeletons and carrion birds. 'Since you're here, I've got to ask you something. Why did you spare me that day, on the tower top? You know, when you claimed Nightmare reached down to touch you.'

'I've asked myself that too. I still don't know.'

'Consider the favour returned here and now.'

Eric reached for his gun. 'Don't be so sure of that.'

Kiown laughed. Then he moved, fast. Eric found he was upside down, the blood rushing to his head, the pavement directly beneath him. Case growled, but with a look the dragon held him there. 'How about now? Am I sure yet?' said Kiown. 'You spared me, I've spared you. Do you agree?'

'Not yet.' Eric pressed the gun into his chest to keep it from falling, clutched tight to the charm in his other hand. Bits and pieces fell from his pockets.

'We, my friend, are now even. And since I have your attention, let's negotiate. Dyan and I shall clean up this city. We slay the Tormentors, even the big ones. Then I get to keep it. You and your squad of half-giants don't seem inclined to tromp over here to clean it up. So, Elvury's mine. It's my capital, my base of operations. Got it? In a few years I'll allow you to put agents here, but I say who comes and goes. No fighting over it. It's a trading centre. My house, my rules. Understood? The rest of the map we'll discuss another time.'

Eric could hardly think with the blood in his head. Kiown's grip on his shins was firm. 'Talk to Aziel.'

'Fuck Aziel. Assert yourself!'

'Fine, take it.'

'This city's not where I'll live, understand. The haiyens will build me a tower. They found a way to kill dragons. Even the big ones. Have you noticed the lightstone falling? The haiyens will help us with that minor problem. Say nothing to Shilen about it.'

'Kiown, let me up, would you?'

'Soon. You have something to say?'

'We have a chance to make a new world. At least until the big dragons come down and probably kill us all.'

Kiown hefted him back up, set him on his backside. Eric allowed a minute for his spinning head to ease, then said, 'Why do you want to play the part of villain, just because Shilen asked you to? They're using us both. We're doing a job for them.'

'Here's the beautiful part.' Kiown crouched down beside him, made his voice a whisper to hide it from Dyan. 'I *can't* do a job for them.' Kiown showed Eric his amulet. 'Giving this to me was a big mistake. I am loyal to Vous. Even now. Even though I *know* it's mind-control. All my life I never knew it was mind-control. Now I know, but it hasn't changed things. You saw him? Is what's said about him true? Does he dance and toss flowers?'

'Apparently. Loup said he may be the god of beauty.'

'Whatever you call him, he's Vous. He is a god. I therefore work for the gods, not the dragons. Eric, here is the gist of it: Shilen wants us – humanity – divided into two competing empires. I can play along. She told me the same thing she probably told you, that this power is mine to use as I like, freely. What if I want to use it to help rid the world of dragons? There's a way to do it. The haiyens of the far south said so.'

Eric looked at him, startled. 'I think we have the same idea. Shilen said I rule freely, but she told me to stop them from waking Inferno. I'm going to let them do it, if they haven't already. See how free we really are.'

Kiown winked. 'Send word to your queen or lady or whatever you call her. This city's mine. I mean it. No one comes here until I'm ready, not unless they want to fight Dyan and the army I'll soon bring here. War benefits neither of us right now. Don't tell Shilen we spoke.'

'Will Dyan keep your secrets to himself?'

'He won't tell her. He's got no friends now among the dragons; they hate him. He came here to do a job for them but frolicked instead. Humans are all he has left. We'll talk later about the other cities, who gets what. And remember, don't ever take all this too seriously. Whatever messages I send you in the future, even if it's a declaration of war, always remember this: we play the game as co-operating opponents, with agreed rules. *Never* as true enemies.' Kiown stood, yawned, stretched.

'I don't want any wars in the game,' Eric said. He pointed down at the valley full of skeletons. 'We're not creating that. I don't want that on my head for any reason.'

'So you just handed me your throne again.' Kiown sighed. 'Listen. Blain's right about some things. Power *is* a game. Life is too. Serious games. But there's no reason they can't be fun. Look at those skeletons down there. None of them were mind-controlled like I was. Every one of those men could have dropped his sword in the dirt, refused to fight. Had all of them done it: no war, no lords. A world instantly born without such things. This is what those dead men wanted. They marched into this valley because they wanted to, whether for money or loyalty to a lord or for their own glory. I can't promise you we won't ever war. If we do fight, it will be a show for Shilen's benefit, not mine or yours.

'But that might not matter. Keep an eye on the dragons. There may be something we can do about them. Sooner or later they're coming down here, Eric. And it could be sooner.' As if to demonstrate, there was again a thunderous rumble, a faint shiver which they felt in their feet. Pieces of lightstone – no more than a few handfuls – rained down into the valley and into the city, clattering on rooftops and cobblestones.

Kiown went back to Dyan and climbed aboard. 'Till next we meet, O Eric the Dangled. If ever. We never spoke today. We hate each other's guts, understood? You never quite know when *she's* watching either of us. She usually doesn't bother, but I think she checks in now and then. There are some advantages in being considered an insect and beneath notice. Am I right, Dyan?'

Dyan did not answer. His scales glittered. He leaped skywards then they dived so fast he was only a blur of colour.

39

CLAIMING THE CITY

It took another two days to find and slay the last of the smaller Tormentors. A few perhaps remained underground, though they seemed to prefer the extra stimulus of the surface world. There'd been no sign of people other than a small gang of treasure hunters who came through the south gate the previous day, perhaps former citizens of this place come to seek prized possessions, theirs and others'. The fight had been nothing special. They'd barely got their amazed gobs shut on sight of a dragon before Dyan had dealt with them. Their flesh would prove useful.

Dyan landed now on a luxury home's rooftop: the compound below was replete with gardens and fountains which still tossed trickles of water around. Someone important had lived here. They had a good view of the river and of the massive Tormentors standing motionless along its banks. Dyan wanted a rest before attempting combat with them. He sat with his neck arched back regally, long tail curled around him, gazing with narrowed eyes towards the river.

'What's the difficulty?' Kiown asked him.

'Their time play pulls at me,' the dragon replied. His voice held a hypnotic rumble. He'd lately fashioned it to sound like that of a cultured elderly man.

'You've only fought the small ones so far. Was it the same with them?'

'For them, it's easily overcome. The large ones will have more *pull*. It is unusual magic. More a mistake of reality than actual spell craft. You had better not fly with me for these battles. There is risk.' Dyan's scales bled through several colours as he eyed his prey, considering strategies.

Kiown sighed; the thrill of riding at those enormous spiked demon-things was something he'd long been anticipating. He said, 'Do be careful.' Dyan was a priceless gift, perhaps the greatest gift any human had ever owned. For a so-called Minor personality his magic was versatile and potent; and he flew faster than any of the other dragons. His speed was the main reason they'd sent him down to do their work, as the first free dragon. Kiown said, 'Do you dragons have a fondness for jokes?'

Dyan pondered his question at length. 'No.'

'What, never? You never laugh at one another?'

'I have heard no laughter among the Eight, not with the kind of humour familiar to you.'

'I just wondered. Because the dragons picked Eric to be my opponent in this system they're devising. It's a gift.'

'Why did you not slay your rival?'

Kiown laughed. 'You jest. Eric's a fool, an idiot. Sentimental for starters. Why would I kill a rival like that? May he live long and prosper. He *gave* me this city.'

'Are his words binding?'

'With a little help from us, they shall be.'

He twirled the precious amulet on its chain. Dyan enjoyed gazing at it as much as he did, conscious of its power over him but intrigued by it regardless. Most of the object's other powers Kiown was still discovering. Certain situations seemed to unlock them: conversing with the haiyens in their high tower, for instance, his knowledge at times had elevated well beyond its norm. He'd understood at a glance the nuances of their body language, had known the meanings of the symbols adorning their homes and garments.

It had been quite a sight for them to see Dyan wheeling through their skies. Long generations had passed with no sign or hint of dragonkind. But landing there in their home city with no forewarning had been a mistake. Delicately the haiyen assigned to speak with him had made the point: Kiown had come *exceedingly* close to a quiet, uneventful death. Every haiyen he'd seen in those high levels could have slain him with a thought while he was still in the sky.

They had been named 'the lost ones' by their kin. They had names for *them* in turn: the savage ones, the wild ones. The savage ones had befriended a god who did not belong in their reality at all. It was no more than the lost haiyens had done.

It was a long stroll from tower to tower, across miles-long thin bridges stretched so high that the land below would not have been visible with normal sight. Lesser towers, a multitude of them, were like spear tips to either side: a city of the lost ones. They had thrived, his guide told him in what seemed a completely impartial observation. They had adapted. The dragons would not have allowed this prosperity. It was true they could no longer live and build homes down on the surface . . . but with all they'd learned, there was no need.

Eventually their walk reached an end point, a kind of outpost. There they'd waited for a length of time Kiown had not been able to gauge. Time was so strange there it seemed his visit had been both recent and very long ago.

The rumbling sound carried to them on the bridge well before he saw the thing, gazing down with eyes the charm had enhanced. A huge bloated mountainous rolling thing, bigger than anything living he'd ever seen. Its flesh was grey and brown, at times like molten rock, at times gelatinous. It left a residue behind. A peculiar swishing windy sound emanated from it. As they watched, it came to rest and spread its heaving mass across the ground. 'They are not unintelligent, as the savage ones claim,' said the haiyen. 'I shall not tell you this one's name. The sound you hear is its speech. Much meaning can be discerned by those sufficiently trained. Its wisdom is infinite. Listen for a short while and one's thoughts are not the same afterwards.'

'Why is it they slay the dragons, but not Spirits?'

'Spirits do not attack them. The dragons did. If this being came to your realm, it would probably be the same. It would leave your Spirits alone, perhaps become great friends to them.'

Kiown understood that these haiyens felt about the summoned ones similarly to the way he felt for Vous. He had understood completely.

'That great one you saw has claimed this land,' said his guide as they strolled back towards the tower where Dyan waited. 'No others of its kind come here. Each claims a large area. We summon them only when conditions allow it in their native reality. Their young venture away to claim new lands. If they stayed here the greater ones would incorporate them. Some of the new ones succeed in growing large, but most are hunted by the savage ones when they are small. We hunt the savage ones in turn. The war is old and slow. We capture their places of breeding one by one, while ours are safe here in these high towers. The savage ones will ask your lords for permission to build more breeding nests in your lands. You must not allow it.'

'I'll help you, if you help me.'

'We shall give you a presence. One at first, until you show you will nurture it. Grow it large. That is all you need – you do not need us. *They* will help you. Learn to understand their speech and song. Name them. Devote yourself to them. They know their benefactors. What we have learned from them enhances all our arts, enhances everything we do.'

Returning through their towers he saw this was so. Their artwork, their creations, their devices – nothing in the North compared to it, nothing but Vous himself.

Kiown's fingers drummed the glass case they'd given him. Within it was the real reason he wanted this city for his own, and it was nothing to do with the reasons he'd given Eric. The 'presence' inside the case could not even be seen. It was no more than a tiny ball of invisible purpose. They had summoned it right there in the tower, over a thousand silent haiyens gathered to pool their minds. All that effort and power to open a gap between their world and wherever this had come from. They'd told him to guard the thing fiercely as it grew. When it had found enough matter to form its own shape, it was vulnerable and could be slain.

As far as the world knew, Elvury was still filled with Tormentors. Here, the presence would not likely be pestered.

Kiown hunted around in the rooftop's overgrown garden, found a cricket, squashed it between his fingers, then carefully slid it under the glass case's lid. For a minute or two nothing happened. Then something pulled at the dead insect. A leg separated from the body. Kiown laughed, delighted.

The air whooshed as Dyan took off and soared towards the river. The huge Tormentor he flew at slowly moved one arm upwards as if in greeting. Dyan became a white light painful to look at. The light vanished. A splitting crack rang out, echoing through Elvury's dead streets. Slowly half the Tormentor's huge face slid free and fell.

Dyan reappeared in the sky some distance away. He landed back in the same spot he'd taken off from, taking deep breaths, heat wafting from his body.

'Is it dead or just hurt?' said Kiown. While they watched the huge Tormentor leaned backwards, then fell with a great splash into the river. The others all turned, facing where it had stood. Their bodies erupted into motion: dancing, it seemed. The skeletons of slain men shook from their spikes and fell to the ground, into the river.

Dyan lay flat, head on his paws. 'I rest, before slaying another. They are now roused and know me for a threat.'

'They're not as smart as we assume. But fine, rest.' Kiown drummed his fingers again on the glass case lid. The dead insect was now a little mashed-up grey-green ball. One crooked leg still protruded, twitching. Kiown found more insects, stomped them to paste, fed them into the glass case. He told Dyan to fetch him a bird or a dog – one or two dogs had barked when they first arrived. Dyan left, soon to return with the requested dead animals in his mouth.

What need for ceremony was there? Kiown left the case's lid open. The little ball of matter seemed reluctant to leave. Kiown dragged over the bodies of those men Dyan had killed a day before. 'Enjoy your meal,' he said to the presence. He stood, stretched. 'Ready for a long flight?'

'If it is your wish, I must be.'

'Fine, we'll rest awhile. But it's time to check on Tauk. See if he's willing to be a general or not. I have a feeling he won't be easily handled. May have to see if Blain can impersonate him.'

'And those?' Dyan nodded to the distant huge Tormentors, still dancing on the riverbank.

'Leave them for now. It's enough to know we *can* kill them. The presence won't be big enough for them to notice it, not for a while yet. The haiyens said it can use bones and Tormentor flesh. There's no shortage of either all over the place down there. It won't go hungry.'

40

A LITTLE HUNTING

From the voices which carried through the abandoned village it was clear to Siel that in the mayor's group someone was arguing. She listened at the window in Gorb's abandoned home. Through the parted curtains she could just make out their camp-fire. There'd been a little preserved bread and meat in Gorb's cupboard, somehow missed by whoever had taken the rest of his store. Despite the preservation it had begun to go stale, but she ate it gladly.

She remembered Eric saying that his people in Otherworld knew none of those simple arts which kept bread and meat preserved; they had devices to do that, devices to do everything. She thought of that strange world, the brief sight she'd had of it with Kiown and the others. The strange dark sky alive with points of light, 'stars'. Incomprehensible strangeness. Perhaps more strange than anything she'd seen in the world to the south.

How joyous and free she had been in the light of that huge suspended crystal. Ever her mind returned to it. She felt again the slow press of this weighty world coming down upon her. After coming out of those waves she'd been refreshed, cleansed of things which had caused her pain before. Memories of her parents and their murder did not bother her any more. Yet now she was *here*. While things and places infinitely better waited elsewhere, she was still *here* . . .

The argument grew heated. Tauk's voice was loudest among them. Looking out the window she saw a silhouette marching away from a campfire. A short figure – perhaps Blain – hobbled after him, arms out, beseeching.

Siel let the curtain fall back. She smelled a kind of ending coming, as surely as animals could sniff out a storm. Her own life ending perhaps, or maybe the end of this world. Spending the last days hidden away like this would not do. Why walk meekly into the healing waters, when one could run and dive with flourish?

She had no bow, but there were blades left lying around, in this house and in others. Maybe she'd need no more than the murderously sharp short-sword she'd recovered from the litter of a caravan, not far from here. She laid the blades out over her bed, weighed each with care, strapped one to her ankle, the short-sword at her waist. She crept out the place's back doorway, crawled like a cat through the overgrown grass, the wind shielding her rustling movements till she was near enough to their fire to hear them.

Evelle's cackle was drunken. Siel knew little of the Hunter Evelle, but suddenly understood: Evelle was enlightened. In whatever she did, good or evil, she found divine purpose. There was great wisdom in that; Siel wished her own life had been similar.

A little away from the fire Tauk was snarling at Blain: '. . . or *your* schemes either. You're a treacherous wizard like the others, and I'm no one's general.'

Blain said, 'Just play along for a while! We can slay him! If you or I possessed that amulet it would all change.'

'No! No more scheming. I return to my city and my people. We have Otherworld weapons the half-giant brought us. *We* are the new rising force, not him, not you. At Tanton we shall not suffer anyone else's rule, man or beast, wizard or dragon.'

'Dragons care not for flung rocks!' Blain cried. 'Listen to your-self. I've had that little shit as my underling for these past weeks; I know his true nature. A wretched imprisoned thing, kicked and despised. His like should never rise to power! Not *him* as lord and master, anyone but *him*. Talk to Evelle! Defy him and you are stewed guts. You and your city. He'll never let you return there. Pledge allegiance, pucker up, bow and scrape. Then slay him, take his place! Take the amulet!'

'*You want the amulet yourself!*' Tauk roared at him. Angrily he marched away.

'Shh!'

'He has a *dragon* with him!' cried a third voice, one of Tauk's men who'd wandered over. 'How do you suppose . . . ?' Their talk drifted away as Blain scurried after the mayor.

Siel crept closer in the long grass. Stranger – a forlorn bundle – slept not far from the fire. Evelle swigged from a bottle enough liquor to put the hardest of warriors to shame. Siel could smell the bottle's contents from where she lay. Evelle swayed a little as she watched the men argue. Her smile was gleeful. Tauk's other man held a hand out for the bottle, which she passed to him.

Siel waited. She watched them all for a long while with deadly patience. Tauk's man by the fire – now as drunk as Evelle – lurched up, wiped his mouth with his sleeve, and staggered past where Siel lay, seeking a tree to piss against. Silently Siel went nearer to him. Wind through the grass covered what little sound she made as she rose from her walking crouch, pulled his head back by the hair. The man's last surprised breaths were liquid gargles. He fell and twitched for a while but died with little more fuss than that. Evelle's cackling laughter boomed out from the campfire.

Siel crept back to the hut to clean off the blood. She felt calm, even pleased. Perhaps what she'd just done had been murder, since the kill had not been in open combat. If so, it was the first time she'd murdered. Once, such a deed would have bothered her. But the man was in a happier place now, washing free his soul just as she washed his blood from her arms.

Something occurred to Siel for the first time as she dried herself: of all the creatures and life forms she'd seen marching to bathe in the crystal's waters, she had seen no dragons. Not one.

She went back to watch the others, maybe to catch them on their own too. Hunting game for food had never been this gratifying, nor had it made her feel this alive. None of the prey seemed to have noticed yet that a man was missing. The arguments went on: Blain persuading Tauk of some plan, or attempting to; Tauk's speech growing angrier and more violent. 'I've seen you off in the woods,' said the mayor. 'Just what in the fire god's *flames* are you doing there?'

'Shh!' Blain pleaded. 'Because of *him*. The bastard sapling means to rule us. That's why I go. I never know when he's coming back here, he and that dragon of his. I must keep my powers sharp for when he returns. Try it yourself, there's *power* to be had. But keep it quiet from the rest of them.'

With a nod Tauk sent his man back to the fire. 'What power?' he demanded. 'Try what?'

'Come! I'll take you, you'll see.'

Blain hobbled as fast as his short legs would take him. Tauk followed, a hand on his sword hilt. Siel followed them both, risking a dash out of the grass into the open, skirting around to the path leading into the woods. No one saw her. Soon they were in the same woods the dragon had drawn her to, down from the tower. The waters had cleaned away any shame or anger from that memory.

Blain and Tauk crouched now in a small clearing, murmuring quietly. Blain was digging something up, and there was nothing frail about his movements now. It was an opportunity to dash in, cut their throats, but she held off when an *arm* flopped out of the ground. Pale and slender. Blain washed the dirt off it with a canister of water. 'Should it . . . should it not be cooked?' Tauk said.

'No need. Blood's better, if it's fresh. O, it's worth a pretty sum too, the risk one takes to harvest it. Flesh will do us. Still potent magic in it, though not as sharp, nor lasting.'

'How long has it been here? Why hasn't it rotted?'

'They're not like people, these Invia. Their flesh lasts longer. This is not an attempt to poison you, Mayor. Watch. I'll eat first, if you like.'

'No. I shall.'

Siel turned away as Tauk leaned forwards. There was the sound of chewing, then gagging.

'Needs salt, eh?' said Blain. He chuckled.

'I feel something,' Tauk whispered. He stood, exhaled deeply, laughed. 'I feel it! I could pull these trees out with my hands.'

'Good! Now you know why I come to these woods every few hours.'

'And every time you return with dirt on your hands,' Tauk laughed. 'Now I see why.'

'I've had many lifetimes' worth of years in this rusting old body. It's not going to culminate in being that little bastard's slave. When the little shit returns, we get him away from his dragon, Tauk. Then we have him. Some story. We'll concoct it together, you and I. Don't tell your men! They'll follow your lead when the battle starts. Don't tell the women either. Evelle, she's mind-controlled like he is. They'll be of the same purpose when the swords come out. Don't be fooled by the tits! She's deadly. Keep her drunk. No more beating your chest, Mayor. No shouting. Even drunk, even sleeping, she *listens*. When we get back there, we argue as before, or else she'll know we've a plan to act on.'

Tauk murmured something Siel didn't hear.

'Every few hours,' Blain replied. 'We come back here, eat some more. Understood? We need allies. I've bared myself to you. This dead Invia's my last good card to play until we get his amulet. I'd rather you wore it than me or any other among us. You are all I have left. Return my trust, Tauk!'

They covered the Invia with soil and leaves, not troubling too much to make the ground look undisturbed, then headed back to the village. When they were gone Siel dug up the corpse. She had no idea how long it had been buried, but the flesh indeed seemed well preserved, without even a smell to it. In death its scales were more pronounced, so much it hardly looked human at all. They'd taken their bites from its upper arms.

The flesh was hard to cut. When finally she got an arm separated at the elbow she did not bother burying the body again. She carved a rune in the ground which actually meant nothing at all, so far as she knew – it was only to confuse them if they returned here. She took the arm to a place where she could watch the others from the cover of trees.

*

She watched them as day broke, as they began to search for the missing one. She watched them find the body, drag it to camp, inspect it. Watched Tauk's and his other man's tears, watched them strip from the body the armour and weapons. She watched Tauk point an accusing finger at Evelle while Blain stood between them, trying to calm things. Tauk's other man accused Stranger. Rushing to her feet, Evelle agreed it *had* been Stranger! She'd seen her lurking over there where the body was found! She'd seen her earlier with a blade in her hand!

Stranger, backing up, palms raised, pleading. It did no good. Tauk's man screamed as he cut her down.

With no sadness Siel watched the death of the woman who'd sold herself, and sold out her kind to the dragons. She felt no pleasure in Stranger's death, perceived no justice or crime, felt no guilt or pity. The waters awaited Stranger, awaited them all.

Many times Blain and Tauk went back to the woods to eat from the Invia corpse, in case Kiown should return. They'd noticed the missing arm, for they came back from that first trip nervous indeed. Frequently they went off to chat in private. Siel went as close as she dared to listen in.

Blain whispered, 'Nothing's hunting us. Maybe it *was* Stranger.'

'There were none of her prints near where he died.'

'With all that long grass? Of course not. It had to be Stranger. Someone greater than us would have battled us. Someone in fear of us wouldn't have bothered to kill him at all! A bandit would have robbed him, but no one took what was in his pockets. The sword's clearly priceless yet they left it with him. Yes, Evelle probably lied about seeing a knife, I agree with that. It doesn't mean there wasn't one! Stranger was insane – love-mad for a dragon who didn't love her back. You know how they get. He –

Fithlim, was his name? – gets drunk, forgets his honour, makes an offer, perhaps grabs at her. She grows angry. Hides it. Off into the grass she goes with him, eager for fun. Or so he thinks. Out comes the knife.'

Tauk digested all this. 'That symbol gouged in the ground . . .' he began.

'Never seen its like, I keep saying. No reason to think it's related to the death.'

'Who made the rune, wizard?'

'Could be a dragon cultist; they were never completely wiped out. Could be the new people. A mourning symbol! That may be it. They're sentimental beings, the new folk, not the type to murder. That's what happened: they come through, meaning to find the tower, not knowing Domudess had gone from here. They see us . . . but, fearing attack, pass us by. By some means they find the Invia's body, perhaps sensing the thing's trace of magic. They dig, find a body, grow sad, and make a mourning symbol.'

'Why did they take its arm?'

'I wasn't there!' cried Blain. 'I don't know their ways.'

'I begin to think *you* made the rune as a play against me.'

Blain emitted a growl of frustration. They both moved out of earshot.

Siel was enjoying herself. She went to her hiding spot, chewed a little of the Invia flesh. It was tough and had little taste to it, thankfully. But her whole body seemed to vibrate after she'd swallowed it, seemed to fill with strength and heat. She had to do something, anything, with this energy. She dashed down and carved more meaningless runes on a part of the path the men would surely see on their way back to the Invia's body when it grew light. One of the phoney runes looked like a human arm, cut off at the elbow. Back in her hiding place she kept her laughter silent.

Since the group put out their campfire Siel had been lightly sleeping in her hiding spot among the trees. She had been dreaming of the lake, its crystal light, and the multitude of beings around her as she'd walked with Far Gaze towards its shores.

Something rustled the undergrowth in her hiding place, waking her up. Day was close. A glimmering green light bathed her hiding spot. Something whispered to her words in a tongue she hadn't heard before, and yet found she understood. An image came to her mind: a man with a sword – Valour. Riding across World's End, the ground seeming to rattle with the hoofbeats pounding down. Across the boundary, blade raised high, his steed veering to run over haiyens who could not flee quickly enough, a thousand men or more from the city of Tanton riding behind him. Through the haiyens' stone-shell homes his horse stomped, crushing them to shards. Onwards Valour rode, the war cry from his throat an eerie, dreamy trumpet call, echoed by the men behind who followed and mimicked him so uniformly they were surely in his thrall.

Siel could not divine the presence about her that showed her these things. But it was benign – she knew it would not hurt her. Something spoke in a voice like rustling leaves, and placed another image in her mind: of Siel herself, at peace. The world falling to pieces around her, but none of it *mattering*. Would she like to be taught new things? she was asked.

'Yes,' she said. The little place she hid in came alive around her. Small glowing things dropped down from above, like stones made of light. Strange soft music played. Briefly she worried that all this would draw the attention of those by the campfire.

Whatever it was, the benign presence spoke a final time to her. It assured her she would be well, though many others would not; that she was honoured, the first in this place to be taught new arts, though she may not understand them yet. A cleansing was upon them all – the lands were young, but wise for their age. All things meant to be, would be.

She was responsible enough to hold power, the rustling leaves told her. She saw herself moving through the campfire group in naked daylight, fading and twisting like smoke in and out of sight. This was one of the new arts she would be taught. *You are a good hunter*, it said. *Eat the things I shall leave here for you. This will open powers within you.* There was more to learn, but the haiyens could teach the rest, if they wished to. *For now, I must depart. When the time comes, you will go to World's End, where Road meets Road, and wait there for the final Pendulum swing. Your role there is one of honour.*

All went quiet; the faint luminescence dimmed away. The small glowing lumps remained behind. Hesitantly she reached for one and ate it. It felt as if cold clear water flushed through her veins.

When morning light came in full, Kiown and his dragon returned.

41

NEW POSSESSION

Dyan had only just set down when Blain and Tauk took Kiown by an arm each and began to lead him away from the others, as though they had urgent tidings for him. Angrily Kiown shook them off, shoved Blain to the ground and viciously kicked him. The old man was briefly airborne. He got up, spat blood from where his face had scraped the ground, then bowed to show reverence. The rage flashing in his Strategist robe was so bright it bled faintly through the plain garments covering it.

Tauk bowed too in faux apology. He spoke with urgency, pointing off into the distance, his face grim. Kiown listened. Siel heard the mayor say, 'If this is true, I must ride there at once.'

'You'll stay here,' said Kiown. 'We have other things to discuss. Dyan will take care of it.'

Kiown spoke privately with the dragon. Dyan gave the mayor and Strategist a long look with his head cocked to one side, the way he looked when puzzling something out. But he took off as he was asked to and was quickly gone into the clouds.

Kiown watched him go, deep in thought. Before he turned around, Blain had split into a dozen copies of himself, all of them with eyes glowing red as they advanced. Tauk ran at Kiown with his sword angled, aimed a slash at his body. Kiown's spin was deft. The way he avoided the blade seemed impossible: as if he had dodged it *after* it should have cut through him. The eye claimed for a moment that he'd surely been cut. Tauk was stunned, off balance. With a blow from both palms Kiown sent the mayor flying backwards through the air. Violet light shone from the Hunter's eyes.

Evelle had looked to be sleeping off last evening's drink, but she leaped to her feet, knives in each hand. She sprang upon Tauk and stabbed the forearm holding his sword. He released it. She got him in a choke-hold with one knee bent around his neck and grinned down. Her look said killing him was a game she'd been dying to get back into.

Whether it was from Valour's armour or else where, Tauk found strength she'd not expected. He writhed, broke out of the choke-hold, kicked her off then scrambled for his blade.

Kiown had his own sword drawn. The violet light in his eyes made his whole face ghoulish and savage. In fear, the real Blain backed away behind the group of illusions he'd made, for Kiown ignored them and gazed only at *him*. Kiown dashed through the copies of Blain, slicing at each with almost an Invia's attack speed, his arm a dozen lashing whips. He paused to grin at Blain, enjoying the old man's fear. Like Evelle, Kiown was in no hurry to make the kill – after all, he had many slights and insults to make up for.

Meanwhile Evelle threw a knife at Tauk but Valour's armour deflected it. She threw her other and hissed in rage when it missed, for she *never* missed and her throw had been perfect. Tauk raised his sword, pounded his chest with the bleeding arm she'd stabbed, began to shout about his city, and his honour, and his ancestors. She got to her feet and into position for hand-to-hand fighting as she backed away from him.

Tauk's man Vade joined the fray. He left his mayor to handle Evelle and slashed at Kiown, who did not see him coming. There was a spray of blood. Kiown gave a hissing scream, clutched his side. He spun on Vade, leaped at him. Such was his rage he forgot his sword altogether and used his teeth instead, faster and more vicious than a dog. Blood poured from Vade's throat and his shout became a gargle.

Siel walked down through the fight with hardly a thought or plan in her mind. She had never felt calmer or more relaxed. It was the exact vision the Teacher had shown her of herself: walking seen one moment, unseen the next, purely as the moment required to preserve her from harm. There was no need for her to try and control this power, as long as she trusted it. As long as she didn't fear for her life, nor for anything else. Even if it looked as if her life were about to end, she must not fear.

So it was they didn't see her, none of them. She picked up Evelle's knife, the one Tauk's armour had deflected. Kiown, given completely to his rage, attacked the dying Vade with greater savagery, hissing and spitting, the violet light pouring from him. At last it occurred to Kiown to summon back his dragon. He stuck his head up and whistled.

At that moment Siel took a handful of his hair, pulled his head back. Her every move felt graceful, part of a dance. 'Think of me, in the waters,' she whispered in his ear. He froze, recognising her voice. There was comprehension in his eyes as he rolled on his back, hands to his chin where blood poured from the great gaping slit she'd opened up from jaw to sternum. His fist closed tight on the dragon-made amulet, even now refusing to release it. She cut off the hand that held it. Only then could she pry his fingers away.

Blain had begun hobbling back towards the woods, not expecting to make it there. They'd not supped of the Invia flesh recently enough – that, or the flesh had begun to lose its potency. Now he looked back, expecting to see Kiown bearing down on him. He let out a horrified rasping scream to see Siel take two reeling steps, the dragon-made amulet in her hand. In that moment Blain's own death would not have been half as horrible as seeing someone else seizing the precious charm he longed for. Blain prepared to cast a combat spell, but as he did Siel faded from his sight.

There was a *thud* as Evelle's head dropped in the grass. Tauk spat, wiped his face where many nicks and cuts had been made by the assassin's razor-sharp fingernails. Panting, Tauk beheld the scene around him. The sudden quiet and stillness seemed impossible. Quickly Tauk searched Kiown's body. 'Where's the dragon charm?' he said in a hoarse voice.

'Gone,' Blain whispered.

'You've kept it?' Tauk roared at him.

Blain groaned, made himself vanish. The mayor gave in to his rage, slashing his blade down at everything in sight, kicking the bodies, screaming.

'All of them will be cleansed,' said Siel. 'There's no need for grief or anger.' Tauk heard her. He looked frantically about but did not see her. He threw his sword aside and wandered away, face buried in his hands.

A flood seemed to have poured into Siel's mind when she closed her hand upon the charm, a flood of information she would later have to sift through bit by bit to properly understand. But she knew now that *she* was the rightful ruler of this land, and she knew the dragon quickly flying back towards them would not harm her.

Dyan too knew that he had a new master. He landed before her as gracefully as a cat. He took an uninterested look at the carnage about him then lowered his head to Siel. 'I am yours,' he said.

'What if I don't want to own you?' she said.

'Then you may order it so.'

'Your Great Beauty is dead. Stranger, as we called her. Do you care that she's dead?'

Dyan appeared to think about his answer carefully. 'In this I must answer truly. "Love" meant different things to her and to me. I found pleasure and delight in her, even when her moods were bad. I would rather that she was not dead. Yet I do not mourn her in the way it is human custom to mourn the dead, for I expect humans to have far shorter lives than I. My duty is now my one true interest. The spells upon the symbol you hold make this so. To that symbol I am now bound.'

'It doesn't anger you that I killed Kiown and took this charm from him?'

'I have no say in who possesses the symbol, New Beauty. Such is the sentence given to me, by those who crafted the symbol you hold.'

'I see. If I ordered you to tell me all you know of the dragons and their plans, would you?'

'No, New Beauty. For I am not privy to all their plans.'

'I see. Then take me to Eric. Find him, and take me to him.'

'He who rides a red drake?'

'Yes. You'll help me kill him.'

Dyan pressed himself to the ground for her to climb onto his back.

The dragon flew fast. It was not as fast as Shadow had moved when he'd brought her to Stranger's cavern from the wizard's tower; she did not think anything could move that fast in all Levaal, or all of Otherworld for that matter. Now and then she ordered Dyan to slow down, for his speed made her dizzy.

'You may sleep upon me while I fly, Beauty,' he said. 'I sense you are tired. I shall not drop you.'

'Don't call me that. Use my name.'

'I will call you Beauty. This lone freedom is mine. A prisoner may gaze outside his cell and admire what he sees.'

'How do I know you won't drop me?'

'I could not let you come to harm, Beauty.'

'You would not need to obey me, if I were dead. You could go and find someone you find more beautiful.'

'The symbol you own does not allow it. I obey the symbol, not you, Beauty. Its authority travels through you, not yours through it.'

Their flight went over Faifen. There, great ditches were dug alongside the city. The ditches were filled with dirt and ash. The great piles of clothes and other belongings spread on the ground nearby were the only clue of what the ditches were for. No living people could be seen inside the city walls, or outside them, though there was the odd curl of smoke from chimneys. She felt no sadness for those whose bones and ashes filled the ditches; since possessing the charm, her memory of the waters had been pushed to the back of her mind, but still she knew how lucky those dead people really were, to be free now.

Sitting on Dyan's back soon felt perfectly natural, like she'd grown into an extension of him (or perhaps he'd become part of her). While they flew, the charm unravelled its secrets in her mind. She need not strain to use its powers, she saw; as the need for its powers arose, they would come. She had but to experience the pleasures of ruling an empire, to taste the power . . .

Dyan perched on a mountain without her bidding him. He sniffed the air for many long minutes. His tail swished behind him, which it did when something troubled him.

'What is it?' she said, climbing down from him to stretch her legs.

'The fire god has awoken,' said Dyan. With his mouth permanently upturned in the corners it was not obvious that he was afraid, but she knew that he was – and for the first time that she'd seen.

'Woken? How?'

Dyan didn't know so he didn't answer, just took more great sniffs of the air. 'He came near here, but is here no longer.'

'No longer in this part of the country? Or no longer in the North world at all?'

Again, Dyan did not answer; she supposed he didn't know. She climbed to where the rocks reached higher. Ah, how the charm gave her arms and legs new strength. She climbed a sheer face with barely any handholds for her. How easy it was! She went out on a thin limb of stone stretched like a pointing finger, and crouched upon its tip. Without the charm it would surely have snapped and sent her to the ravine beneath. Down there, a dry riverbed wound through the stone valley. She clutched the stone point with her hands, swung around like a child on a tree branch, laughing at the abyss beneath her feet.

'Something else is here, Beauty,' Dyan called up to her. 'Be wary.'

'What else?' she called back, her voice echoing over the rock faces. She pulled herself back upon the stone finger.

'Another power. I do not know what it is.'

'It's surely not the fire god,' she replied. She held the charm up to the sky, admiring its beautiful stone. She had never felt this before, a jealous craving for something she already possessed . . .

The thin length of stone she crouched upon seemed to shift. A cascade of small rocks and dust slid down the cliff. Strangely, she thought she heard a voice speaking in the clattering noise it made. She gazed above at where the stone curved up like something's huge round shoulder. A wide clump of hanging white vines almost formed the effect of a beard. A crevice above the 'beard' was cut into the stone like a wide mouth. One corner was curved up. She searched higher for eyes but did not see any.

Not that it *was* a face, she knew . . . but turning her gaze to the stones beneath, she saw there were interesting formations there too. One jutting shelf seemed from above to be shaped like something's folded knee. 'Beauty, be careful,' Dyan called again. 'Something stirs in the stone.'

'Why? There is nothing here but us.'

'Something is conscious. And aware of us. Stay there. I will come to you and we will leave.'

Many stones broke with a loud burst of cracks and slid down the sheer cliffs. The whole mountain shivered. Siel yelped, fell, grabbed desperately at an oval slab jutting from the cliff side. Her grip on it was good but the slab seemed to shift around as if it were loose.

From below Dyan's cry of panic rent the air. She craned her neck to see him. A hand made of sandcoloured stone and bigger than the dragon had pinched his tail between its thumb and forefinger. Dyan thrashed around as wildly as an insect picked up. A rumbling noise seemed to shake the whole world. Boulders cascaded and thumped down, one flying past Siel so close she felt its wind. Whether it was the charm's protection or the work of something else, somehow a thick rain of stones missed her.

'Nightmare told me of you,' said the voice she'd heard, spoken with the crack and whomp of the falling stones.

Dyan screamed words in a language Siel didn't know. Whatever he said provoked rumbling laughter from the mountain all around them, echoing off the opposite wall of cliffs. After that Dyan kept quiet. A rain of dust scraping on a sheer face of stone said to Siel, 'Was it you who woke Inferno?'

'No!'

'It is a great crime,' said a spray of falling dust. 'One of your kind did it.'

'It wasn't me. No more than you are responsible for what Inferno does now.'

'Hm,' said the rustle of the beard-like vines above her.

'I'm falling; help me.'

'Stones live too,' said the wind blowing through the pass. 'You did not call for the rescue of those stones which fell to break.'

'I'm sorry we intruded on your home. Let us leave.'

'The dragon came here because I called him,' said a clatter of falling pebbles.

'Please, help me before I fall.'

'You have said rites to please Tempest,' said the spraying dust.

'I was a child. My parents needed rain. I'm sorry,' Siel gasped.

Despite the amulet's power her arms were weakening around the stone, for it kept shifting.

'The groundmen's work pleases me. They shape stone with care.'

'I set groundmen slaves free! I helped them – a group of them. They've named me a friend!'

'Your heart has forgotten that friendship, and cast it out for other things,' said the loud noise of breaking rocks. Hard things pressed into her ribs. They were roughly shaped pillars of stone: the fingers of a huge hand. It lifted her high into the air, higher than the mountain's highest part. Below, the faces of stoneflesh golems a hundred or more embedded in the mountainside twisted up to peer at her. On the cliff across the ravine, there were more: square faces, some small, some large, all roused from sleep in the stone to watch her.

'Dyan!' she called.

The stone hand held her level with a hollow cave dug near the mountain's peak, whose shape was not unlike an eye examining her. She knew of course this must be Mountain, who was said to be the first of the Spirits, if not their master then the closest thing they had to one. From this height, she could see the god's individual features spread about the mountain below: arms, hands, legs. Each limb and feature was apart from the others, as if Mountain had divided and distributed himself throughout the valley.

A third great stone hand extended until it was beside her in the air, this one smaller than the others. Its palm was out. 'That charm you hold,' said the falling rocks Mountain's movements had disturbed. 'Place it on my hand.'

'No!'

'I am patient. The most patient. Events now unfold with haste I dislike. So I will shake you if you do not do what I ask.'

'Shake me, I don't care. Kill me! But you aren't getting my charm.'

'It is not a thing for me to keep,' said a howl of wind. 'It is a thing to mend.' Good to his word, the hand which held her shivered, shaking her till her bones rattled. Something invisible pulled at the charm in her clenched fist. She clung with all her might till in one movement it sailed away from her. She screamed and slapped her hands against the stone holding her as Mountain's fingers closed about the charm. She swore she heard it breaking like glass as the fist clenched on it. The grinding-glass sound it made said, 'This thing was made by dragons, designed to change your nature. They should know that is a deed forbidden.' Dyan wailed and thrashed as Mountain shook him too. 'One forbidden deed makes another such deed allowed. So I shall change the charm with my own design. Now your nature shall turn back, and this thing will be a thing of use.'

'Don't kill Dyan. Please. He is an outcast among the dragons. I need him.'

'The dragon shall remain with you, and he shall obey you as before.' The stone fist slowly unclenched. Siel felt the altered charm's different effects even before taking it off his open palm. There was no stone in the charm any more and its metal had gone from silver to a brilliant clear crystal. It gleamed and flashed as she turned it in her hand with what seemed a small captured red flame twisted like a ribbon within.

Suddenly Siel knew that since slaying Kiown and taking the old charm she had forgotten the true beauty of the crystal lake and its waters. That memory rushed back to her now. She wept with gratitude and looped the altered charm around her neck. 'How can I thank you?' she said.

'Be,' said all the stones about her, their voice echoing off cliff faces all through the ravine, as if that one word had more meaning than any other. Indeed it must have, for Mountain said no more to her.

42

MEETING AGAIN

They flew again with greater haste. Dyan went higher than the clouds to evade notice: people were becoming a more common sight beneath them. Up there, Invia now and then dipped in and out of cloud blankets as playfully as children diving into water. Dyan grew restless on sight of them, but he seemed more comfortable to be spotted by them than by the humans below.

A group of Invia darted over with a chorus of whistled song. They stared with open mouths, apparently shocked to find a human riding a dragon. Siel stared back, for something was different about these Invia. Something was wrong with their skin. It had gone a strange colour, and even looked in parts to be peeling away. 'Are you sick?' Siel asked them. They didn't answer her – their whistling voices seemed to be directed at Dyan.

Dyan growled at them, or perhaps spoke harsh words that sounded like a growl to Siel's ears. 'What's the matter?' she asked him.

'They ask if they can take you,' he replied in his more human voice.

'Take me where?'

Dyan didn't answer her. The Invia flew alongside them for a

while longer but were unable to keep up with Dyan's bursts of speed.

Every so often Dyan landed in some high place, sniffed the air. 'The drake has been here,' he said once, then dived back into the sky.

It was a day or two more of flight before they found Eric in the plains not far from Elvury City, swimming naked in the River Misery while his lazy drake slept some way back from the banks. All across the horizon no other living thing was in sight, human or animal. Nothing but stalks of grass and curls of thorny scrub. The blue mountains loomed over, not filled now as they'd always been before with the city's spies. This land had been empty of people since the Tormentors came.

'Shall you slay him now, Beauty?' said Dyan as they wheeled into their descent.

'Slay who?'

'Eric, as you said you would. Once you slay him, what plans have you for the drake?'

'*What?* I never said that.'

Dyan was quiet for a moment. 'Then you have corrected a false perception I somehow acquired. I am grateful, Beauty.'

Dyan set down in the grass. Case woke up at once and bounded over. Dyan arched his neck in an attitude of royalty and went still as a statue while the drake fawned and pawed the ground before him.

Out in the water Eric hadn't seen them yet. He was in rather deep, amusing himself with dives that kept the soles of his feet poking above the water. Siel stripped off her clothes and stood naked, not caring if the dragon saw her. Eric tilted his head to get water out of his ears, turned and froze upon seeing her. For some reason he looked frantically around upon seeing Dyan. It took her a moment to understand he was checking to see if Kiown were here – he must have known Dyan was recently Kiown's steed. 'He's gone,' she told him. She picked up a knife from her belongings and showed it to him. 'This set him free.'

He laughed as if she'd made a joke, but she had meant those words quite sincerely: *Set him free.* Eric swam to the bank, then stood there dripping and smiling. She pressed her lips into his with too much force, so they toppled back into the mud of the riverbank, laughing, then rolled into the cool clean water. She wrapped her legs around his lower back.

'I want to take you to the hilltop,' he said. 'The place we first met.'

'Fine,' she said.

'Do you know the way there?'

'Yes, but it's a long flight. Your drake is slow. He won't keep up with us.'

'No hurry,' he said, slipping himself inside her and laying her back on the soft muddy bank. Eric's charm was looped by its chain over his neck. When it clinked against hers, both of them saw sparks flash behind their eyes.

Both of them climbed aboard Dyan to give the drake a rest from carrying people around. Dyan flew slowly so Case could keep up and, after many stops along the way, they found the hilltop where Siel had shown him the stoneshaper mages raising pillars of rock, back when Eric was new to this world. The stoneflesh mages had by now completed their work. Not only that, people lived in the new city.

At the other edge of the platform was the place an Invia had torn through a group of castle soldiers, where Kiown and Sharfy had lusted like pirates after Eric's black scale. Here was where he'd met Anfen, where he'd first laid eyes on the castle in the distance. He stood now upon the same stone – there it was again. His home now, if he chose it to be.

He and Siel spoke for a long time, lying beside each other, naked but for their dragon-made charms. He ran his fingers through her hair when she set it loose from her braids. They had both changed a lot in so little time, just as the world around them had quickly changed. They talked about all they'd seen since he flew away from her at the wizard's tower. She did not have the words to describe the sights of the South, especially the crystal's waters which had cured her of any fear of death.

'Aziel will have me killed if I go back to the castle,' he said, which somehow struck him as funny. But it was quite true, he was sure.

At that moment a rumbling came from the sky, though the weather was clear without any hint of a storm. Lightstone hail fell about them on the rocky platform. Something struck Siel on the hand. It just nicked her, but it was enough to make her cry out. They ran to crouch by one of the stone shelves. But the stones kept falling, and it was not protection enough. 'Where're Dyan and Case?' he said.

'I told them to fly away for a while. They shouldn't be far.'

They ran for shelter in the same cave Anfen had hidden in when the Invia had attacked him – the place Sharfy and Kiown had carried Eric through when he'd collapsed after the claustrophobic nightmare march through groundman tunnels. Outside the cave, pearl-white stones kept raining down on the platform. They faintly glowed.

The lightstone kept falling in scattered bursts between intervals of quiet. Now and then larger pieces dropped with lethal force. Siel, still naked, drew close to him for warmth. He rubbed her goose-pimpled arms.

Night began to fall. They watched the lightstone about the platform dimming its light in synch with the dimming sky. In the last minutes of daylight a voice cried out in distress, the sound carrying up to them from the stoneshapers' new city. There was a commotion as if a fight had broken out. Eric and Siel went back down the path, tripping over the lightstone pebbles and larger stones now littering the platforms. When the voice cried out again it seemed to come from the sky. Sure enough, an Invia flew off with someone in its arms.

A second Invia flew after it carrying a man bigger than herself, his legs kicking like an insect picked up. Down in the new city, two other Invia flew away from a gathered mob of people. The crowd threw stones after them but the Invia were quickly away from their reach. Each of them carried a crying child in her arms.

By the time Case and Dyan returned, it was too late to pursue the Invia. Dyan answered no questions about why Invia would be carrying people away. He looked at them with big jewel eyes as if he were saddened, but he kept silent, no matter what threats or pleas they made.

They slept in the cave's mouth, not troubled by the whispering sounds which seemed to waft from the depths now and then (each time so faint they could not be sure they heard anything at all). Eric half woke in the night and reached to put an arm around Siel, but she wasn't beside him. He sat up, rubbed his eyes. The lightstone pieces spread thickly over the rocky plat-form outside were just faintly glowing, enough to cast a full moon's light just outside the cave.

He rubbed his eyes again: Siel was out there, naked, and not alone. A group of four haiyens stood around her. One pair of eyes luminous as a cat's peered Eric's way.

He went out there, somehow sure they were not a danger. Neither Case nor Dyan stirred; the dragon rarely slept, but Siel had explained that when people slept he went into a deeply meditative state in which he'd cast his thoughts to faraway places, still aware of what went on around him, but less so. Dyan was in such a state now, his eyes closed and faint light gleaming through their slits.

Lightstone pebbles skipped and skidded away from Eric's footsteps. 'One must love them,' he heard one of the haiyens whisper. 'One must hold no fear. Whatever happens, whatever they do. Teach your people. It is the only true way.'

'My people won't listen to that advice,' said Siel.

They looked at her sadly, only their faces didn't change – sadness seemed to issue from them in a way Eric could feel, like cold curls of mist.

All four turned to him, seeming to expect him to speak. 'I am Shadow,' he said. 'The new lord of these lands. That doesn't mean I have any control over the people of these lands. I welcome you, but advise you to use caution when dealing with the people here. Does our dragon know you are here?'

'He does not know we are here. He does not see us,' said one of the haiyens. And they melted from Eric's sight too, gone in a few seconds as if they'd never been there at all.

In the morning, Eric asked Siel what the haiyens had spoken with her about. She said she had no memory of them coming, other than in a dream she'd had.

43

THE DESCENT

On the day the dragons descended, Sharfy had gone to the city of Athlent, where Vous was said to have been born. Lining the roads to the city were smashed statues with Vous's likeness. Once, such deeds were seen as an act of war. Entire families had been butchered for treachery for as little as a joke at Vous's expense, or a joke about the Strategists or any other castle authority. It had been the same in all Aligned cities.

There was a high place looking down on Athlent, crested with a pleasant wood the city's ruling strongmen had used in recent years for hunting and other pleasures, which explained why it was still so preserved and full of game: starving citizens had been kept out by fences now destroyed, and by guards with pikes. There was no sign of those guards now. Sharfy would have felt safe to bet that one or two fragments of wood lying about the edge of the woods were pieces of those same pikes.

When Sharfy entered those woods, his scars and the weapons he carried frightened the group of young people who'd already gathered there, presumably to play around with magic or each other's body parts. They moved deeper into the woods to get away from him. Fine by him. He set his back against a tree, unearthed a flask of liquor from his pockets and took a pull.

He gazed at the city beneath as the people went about the new business of freedom. It was not yet a scene of celebration. It looked like hard work. They were cleaning the streets, repairing buildings. It was hard to see who was in charge – everyone acted in spontaneous cohesion, giving the impression the city was a big organic body healing itself through these people, its instruments. The air was filled with the *thock, thock, thock* of hammers or axes at work.

Fields beyond the city walls had been deliberately ruined so the castle could control the food supply. People were out on those scorched bare fields now, laying new dirt across them and picking out the pieces of fallen lightstone. Great stacks of the stuff were piled off to the side. The sight of all that lightstone still got Sharfy's heart beating, though surely lightstone was all but worthless these days.

Something about watching all this while his legs rested gave Sharfy a sense of peace, even contentment. A sense that all the wars and fighting had somehow been worth it. He understood it now: the war no one ever thought would end was now in fact over. A new war would start in time, sure enough. But that was someone else's story. His own had ended and that ending was peaceful. He could die right here and be glad about it. Maybe he would, right at this spot. No hurry.

A food train arrived from the castle as Sharfy watched. The people lined up before it, patient and orderly. That alone was a sight to behold. Once in this city, and in many others, the sight of a food train would have caused a riot. Sharfy swigged from the flask of burning liquor. It was strong, brought tears to his eyes, but he knew that some of the tears were of happiness at what he witnessed below.

He sensed that he was not alone. He didn't need to turn

around to know it was Shadow come to pester him some more. There was no getting rid of this ghost. At least he'd listen to a battle tale and keep his mouth shut with no sarcastic remarks. 'The traps are pulling at me stronger,' said Shadow.

'Go away.' Sharfy glanced over to the group of young people. As he'd suspected, they sat in a circle, which meant they were trying to cast something. Wouldn't work, no magic right near cities. 'If those kids see you they'll be a lot more scared of you than they are of me.'

'Where should I go?' said Shadow.

'Anywhere.'

'Anywhere could mean here. Couldn't it?'

'Clever, eh? All right. Then go find out if Loup's still following me. Go look for Loup. Go on. Do that and I'll teach you some more stuff.' To his surprise, Shadow went. Sharfy grunted in satisfaction. So, that was how to deal with him: send him on stupid errands.

He drank some more from the flask and had dozed off when the huge splitting sound woke him. It was like the cracking of a whip bigger than all the world, the sound somehow far away and near all at once. A ripple went through the ground; Sharfy felt it pass beneath his own rump. He'd not have been able to say what it was that made him look up at that moment . . . but he did look up, just as the great slab of grey skystone dropped through the lower layers of cloud.

The slab fell upon the city. It could not have been better aimed had someone above intended to destroy Athlent. The noise of it was terrible, more terrible than anything he'd ever heard. The ground heaved more than it had heaved at World's End when the stoneflesh giants began walking around. An enormous cloud of smoke, bricks, wood and people flew high into the air. Wood and bricks rained down near where Sharfy sat and all through the fields outside the city walls. Sharfy crouched low, covering his head with his hands.

A second piece of skystone fell some distance from the city. Not quite so large as the first, perhaps; but again the ground quivered and rolled as if for a brief time it had turned partly liquid. Another great dust cloud rose up. The distant booming sounds he thought at first were echoes from the two falling slabs, until he realised more pieces of skystone were falling elsewhere.

The ground's shaking eased. The distant thunderous rumbling eased off too and the screams and cries of people could be heard instead. That sound was just as terrible, maybe worse. The skystone block was completely intact, though only a corner of it protruded now from the crater it had pushed for itself into the city. Sharfy stared at the slab – in fact he could hardly look away from it. The impact of its fall was not enough to break it . . . and yet something *up there* had hit it hard enough to split it from the rest of the sky.

Shadow searched for Loup among the large groups of people moving north from the old cities, to be closer to the castle. The people thought they'd be safest there. They'd begun to move when the lightstone started raining down. The dragons were coming, and some of these people knew it. The pull of the traps on Shadow had grown strong. Two of the three charms were now nearby – the third may have been too, but he could not perceive it. It seemed the traps called him more urgently at different times, as if whoever made them had a specific place and time for him to be kept. If it weren't for Sharfy, and what Shadow had come to regard as their friendship, Shadow would have gone to the far south, perhaps even across World's End to be away from their pull. One of the traps was in the castle, of course, in the charm Aziel wore. He remembered that prison, the spinning room of chains, the way they'd soothed him for a time, but burned him in the end.

Being within Eric's charm-trap had been different from Aziel's; in a way it had been beautiful. There was a temple of white stone, with water through a stream cut in the middle of its floor. He'd dived into that water at one time, floated far, but the temple moved along with him, no matter how far or fast he went along the water. There'd been no days and nights in that place, no way to count time, but it had seemed a long while that he stayed there, learning nothing. No one to know, no one to speak with, not even anyone to fight. In that place he'd been *solid*, unable to do these things he did in freedom, like cut across the face of a world in just moments.

The loneliness of that place had worn him down, perhaps more painfully than Aziel's chains had burned. He'd thrown himself at the walls – hurled himself into them till he'd known nothing but pain and bruising. So gradually had the cracks begun to appear in the stone he'd never thought it'd break completely. When it finally did, when the will keeping it together had just for a moment weakened, or turned its attention elsewhere, he'd flown through the gap and found freedom again.

Ah, here at last was Loup, very near the castle. Why did Sharfy want him? His magic was not at all strong. Another mage was showing Loup drawings and trying to convince him of something. Errand complete: Loup had been located. Shadow sped back towards Sharfy.

He was halfway there when a voice said, 'Shadow,' with enough authority to jag him from his sprint. A woman stood before him. He knew her! It was the one who'd tried to kill Sharfy with the silver scale. She was alone. He made his face terrible, made it so it would have frightened off anything that wanted to live. But she showed no fear, in fact gave no reaction at all. 'Speak with me awhile,' she said.

He tried to shadow her but she became a million or more tiny pieces of herself, and he couldn't separate one piece from the others. 'How did you do that?' he said.

'I am not truly here,' said Shilen. 'You cannot exercise your power over an illusion.'

'Where are you?'

'Far away. Don't fear me. And don't fight me. I am here to help you. I have answers you need. Have you questions for me, Shadow?'

He had many, but would he know the difference between truth and lie, if it came from her?

'Ask me what you need to know, Shadow,' she said.

'What am I here for? I am not like anyone else.'

The illusion of Shilen smiled. 'It is a good thing, to be like no one else in this world. None of the others have any worthwhile purpose. You do. You are a weapon, Shadow. You were created to help the dragons.' She paused. 'Why does my answer seem to confuse you?'

'Vous is my father. Eric is my mother. Not dragons.'

'Who told you those things? It's true that Vous made you. But we dragons made Vous. Rather, we controlled the men who made Vous. Controlled them from a distance, very subtly, and for a long time, by mortal – human – measure. They never knew it. A push in the right direction now and then, that was all we needed to do. We cared nothing for how they conducted their wars. Nor did we cause them to enslave and murder their own kind – that was their own doing. Shadow, it was no accident that they found the rites, spells, tools and power sources which made Vous's ascension possible. In the process, Vous made *you* possible. You owe your existence to us, Shadow. To the dragons. Do you believe me?'

'No.'

'It doesn't matter whether you do or not. There is an ancient conflict, Shadow. It was ancient before the first humans came to this world. Now it approaches its end with remarkable swiftness. One part of that conflict is a battle between the dragons and the Spirits. We dragons want no war with the Spirits, but they shall attack us. To them, we do not belong free in these lands. To be a weapon in that battle is your purpose, Shadow. You are made to help us fight the gods.'

Shadow grappled with understanding. 'A man with a sword cut me and hurt me. A woman can hurt me just with words. I am only sometimes strong.'

'The man who cut you had a sword given to him by a god, Shadow, by Valour. And you mirrored that man, so you were his equal, or near enough. Do you see? That's why it was possible for him to hurt you. Had a dragon been there with you, and had you mirrored that dragon, you would have slain the man with ease. Did you know I slew that man for you? It is another reason you are in the dragons' debt. He will never hurt you again. No dragon, no human mage and no haiyen has ever known the power you have, Shadow. It may be that you can mirror *anything*. Anything at all. No such being has existed in this world before.'

'Mirror means copy. But I don't copy things. I . . . become *like* something, not the same as it.'

'A likeness is enough. You are able to use your power on the lesser dragons, as you have shown. Do you recall mirroring Dyan? He is a dragon, like I am. Do you remember?'

'Yes. I did not know what a dragon was, back then.'

'Can you mirror the greater dragons? Those of the Eight?'

'I don't know.'

'You must find out. You must attempt to do it. But you must never attempt to shadow a god. That is important.'

'Why?'

'Because the dragons forbid it. That is reason enough. We created you and we have dominion over you. We have many ways to hurt you, if you defy us. It is the dragons who designed the shadowtrap charms. Do you like being imprisoned within them?'

A hot flush of rage went through him, though he didn't understand why a question should so enrage him. He sped around her so fast the ground caught fire. Patiently she waited within the burning ring for an answer. 'No, I don't like it,' he said when his rage was vented.

'Only the dragons can make it so you are free of those prisons forever. We can destroy all the shadowtraps, and those who wield them. We shall, only if you help us. Will you help us, Shadow?'

'You use lies.'

'Only with foolish men. Not with you. You are more important than all the men and women in the world. The time for a test has come. A dragon – one of the Eight – shall descend on this day. He will come to the place your friend Sharfy waits for you. I steered your friend to that place, in order that you would be there when the mighty dragon descends. His name is Tzi-Shu. But he does not know of you beyond a rumour, for the others share no thoughts with him, and Tzi-Shu does not care for the myths and stories of humankind.

'Mirror him, Shadow. Prove that you are useful to us in battling the Spirits. If you battle the Spirits with us, we shall remove from the world all that torments you. We shall give you the learning you seek. We shall give you a place of honour. Do you believe me, Shadow? You have no choice. If you refuse to help us, I will slay your friend. We will make more shadowtraps, until the land is filled with them, and you will never be free for more than an instant. Never free, not even free to destroy yourself. Do this task for us. Go now.'

He screamed at her, swiped one arm like a sword at her, but it passed through the illusion as it would through smoke. She was gone.

There was a rumbling noise, and something made the ground shiver.

44

TZI-SHU

It had turned into a poor day to be drunk. There was no telling how much time had elapsed between the sound of the great stone falling and the descent from the skies of more Invia than Sharfy had believed existed in the world. All around the city they landed. At first he wondered if the drink in the flask had gone bad and was playing with his head.

As things progressed in the newly ruined city it looked as if the Invia were *helping* people. They were digging furiously through the rubble of collapsed buildings, tossing aside pieces it would have taken several men to lift. They moved through the wreckage as fast as they moved when in battle. They carried wounded people from under the debris and flew them out of the city: men, women, children, many of them unconscious in the Invias' arms, possibly dead. The Invia carried them over to the fields where there had been stacked piles of lightstone (now scattered everywhere). They placed the people gently down. Some Invia stayed there among the wounded, while others flew back into the city to fetch more. Scores, dozens, hundreds of people were soon brought clear of the ruins, where fires had begun to burn.

The group of young people had come to the woods's edge to

look down upon the scene. Sharfy didn't notice them until one or two began crying. Their houses were probably under that great skystone slab, maybe their families too.

Sharfy ducked deeper into the woods to piss, half expecting a great chunk of skystone to land on him before he'd finished. He thought he heard the *whoosh* of beating wings. One of the kids cried out in alarm. Sharfy got his sword out and ran back. He had indeed heard wings; there was an Invia flying away from the woods, back towards the city. 'What happened?' he asked the kids.

'They took my sister,' said one of them.

'Why? She hurt? Must've been hurt. They're helping people. I been watching them down there. Getting hurt people out of the city.'

'You need to look closer, old man. They're tying people up down there.'

'What? No they ain't.' He peered down. Maybe his eyes weren't what they used to be (and the liquor had made everything a touch blurry) but he'd seen nothing like that. 'Why'd they pull people from fallen-down houses only to tie em up? Bah. You don't know nothing. Too young to know nothing.' Sharfy lost sight of the Invia in question among all the others swooping in all directions. 'Invia don't bother you if you leave em alone,' he insisted. 'What'd your sister do first?'

'I . . . I don't think it was an Invia,' said a skinny young boy. Tears were starting in his eyes.

Stupid kids! 'Course it was. Got wings, looks like a woman? Invia. You never saw one before is all.'

'It didn't look like they're meant to look.' The others nodded agreement, eyes wide in fear. 'Its *face*. It was *ugly*.'

'It's coming back,' said another of them. 'What do we do?'

Sharfy entertained the possibility that something peculiar was going on after all. The Invia *were* coming back – this time there were four that he could see. They flew languidly, but they were coming. 'Climb up in the trees,' he said. 'Up there quick. The ones with thick leaves. Can't fight Invia. Even if you kill em you're Marked. Better hide.'

He followed his own advice, scrambling up the nearest tree and shielding himself behind thick fans of green. He peeked through a gap in the leaves and saw the kids still just stood there gawking, like first-timers in battle. Then the Invia were upon them: wings beat the air loudly. *Now* the kids ran, for all the good it would do them. Sharfy risked leaning out a little to get a look, just as one of the Invia flew right past his tree. He had only a glimpse, but it was enough to know something was indeed very wrong: what should have been a beautiful woman's face was hardly even a woman's. Its mouth was wide, almost ear to ear. Its skin was tinged with green, its hair like damp coils of white rope. And its teeth . . . lots of teeth . . .

I've seen war mages prettier than that, he thought with a shudder. Maybe the creature was ill. The teenagers' voices erupted in a short-lived panicky chorus before they were all seized and carried down.

Sharfy swigged from the liquor flask again, deeply. Screams carried from the field below. Sharfy dropped to the ground, forgetting his years again – the jolt shot through his whole body, his knees and ankles flaring in pain. The people down there just kept screaming and screaming . . .

He hobbled to the woods' edge for a better view and soon saw why: something else was descending from the sky with slow majesty. Something big. The dragon's colour was a deep gold on its belly and legs, shining like metal. It ran to rich deep brown up the middle of its body, with black points along its wing tips and tail. Spikes fanned down the long length of its back, all down its tail. It was huge, far larger than the dragon Far Gaze had battled with.

As it descended it moved in a controlled shift from side to side the way a leaf falls, wings fanned wide. It was surreal to see the vast thing set down with just a few strides to halt itself in the same field the Invia had brought the rescued people. A hush fell.

Set into a sharp-featured skull atop a long curved neck, the great dragon's eyes were dark and set deep in wide slits. Slowly it drew back its wings and folded them, arching its head back, unmistakeably the pose of a king among its kind.

Sharfy's throat went dry; his knees trembled. He put a hand on the nearest tree stump to keep from falling. Renewed screams rang out among the people all over the field before it. Only a few managed to run away. Those ones the Invia quickly rounded up and brought back.

The great dragon's head slowly turned, surveying the scene before it. Sharfy was struck by a sense of malevolent intelligence like nothing he'd seen or imagined in all his years. It wasn't anything he could have spoken aloud . . . but watching the great creature, it almost seemed to him that it was *within its rights* to destroy a city of these lesser beings, to do what it would to these wailing, crying helpless ones.

'That's the one she meant,' said a voice right beside Sharfy. He jumped and screamed. Shadow was back. 'I'm not going to do what she wanted me to. She said she'd kill you if I didn't do it, but she lies. She lies to everyone.'

'Shut up! Don't want to hear your shit. Not now. Look at that.' Sharfy kicked the tree in frustration. He knew there would be no running away now that Shadow had returned. He couldn't run away, not with someone here to witness it. If he did, the last tale of Sharfy would be about a fleeing coward.

Maybe those kids would tell such a tale anyway, if they lived long enough. He'd scrambled up a tree, after all, and let the Invia take them down there. That had been a missed opportunity to die with the glory of a true warrior's death.

He undid the flask lid and tipped every burning drop down his throat. He said, 'Remember I told you, never back down? I'll show you how.' He drew his sword and marched towards the incline.

'Where are you going?' said Shadow behind him.

'Make that big bastard thing swallow this,' he said, shaking his blade. He was surprised to find he meant it, surprised to find he was so furious. 'Wrecked the city. They were just trying to clean up. Doesn't even care. Sits there looking at it all. It could help, if it wanted. Just *sits* there.'

There was a flurry of motion as several Invia approached the dragon with bundles in their arms. Sharfy was close enough now to see the bundles were children. What happened next made him stop cold. The dragon lowered its head, opened its mouth. The Invia placed two of those bundles on its lower jaw. They may have been already unconscious, for neither of them moved. The dragon closed its mouth, eyes shutting in pleasure. Its jaw worked as it slowly chewed then swallowed.

Those gathered suddenly understood why they'd been gathered and what awaited them. They screamed. Sharfy ran down the incline, now almost blind with anger, thinking he'd scramble up the huge thing's back, run up along its neck maybe, go for the eyes since its scales were probably harder than plate armour. But he tripped and slid the rest of the way down the incline, falling so awkwardly he was lucky not to break his neck. 'Stop it,' he yelled, his voice lost in the horrified screams, as two more bundles were put in the dragon's open mouth. These ones writhed and kicked, needing to be held by the Invia. A riot broke out among the more able-bodied people in the crowd. But they were unarmed, and there were far too many Invia for them to have a chance. Invia darted through the crowd with a blur of their wings' white. People fell.

The dragon reacted to none of this. Its servants had things under control. At its leisure it ate the morsels placed in its mouth, savouring them. It was in no hurry.

Sharfy got painfully to his feet – how old and useless he felt. Somehow it seemed to him that his younger self would never have let any of this happen. Tears blurred his vision. His sword arm shook. He'd staggered only a few more steps when, to his shock, a *second* dragon appeared beside the huge one. This new dragon looked small at first – only a little bigger than Dyan in size. But it grew, till in just a few seconds it was the same size and shape as the big one. It had no colour – it was black and featureless as a shadow.

As a shadow . . .

Sharfy dropped his sword as understanding hit him. 'Kill it!' he screamed. '*Kill it!*'

The big dragon whipped its head around, suddenly aware of the new presence behind it. There was a flash of light, like lightning but coloured with the orange of fire. A scream rang out unlike any scream Sharfy had heard before. Another flash of light. This time it was longer-lasting, temporarily blinding all who had their eyes open. There was the fast, heavy *thump* of the huge dragon running; and there was a flurry of whistling shrieks as all the Invia took to the sky at once.

When the light flash faded out and people's sight returned, the dragon and the Invia were gone. The ground where it had been was badly ripped and torn. Shreds of gold and brown skin were scattered around. Sharfy collapsed onto his backside and did nothing for a while.

He could not tell how long later it was that Shadow appeared beside him again, blinking in and out of visibility, talking. 'I hurt it but I couldn't kill it,' he said. 'It went away . . . but it fought hard. It hurt me a lot to shadow it.'

Sharfy supposed that after what Shadow had just done, he owed the ghost the dignity of an answer. 'You sound sick. You dying?'

Shadow's voice was indeed faint. 'Too much thought came into me, when I shadowed it. I knew too much. Its thought was like . . . worlds of water and lightning, all running through me, fast. I didn't understand it. I didn't have control any more, not till it flew away. Then I came back. I think I must have fought it.'

'Speak sense,' Sharfy said weakly. But the magnitude of what Shadow had done was slowly occurring to him: Shadow had actually done it. Somehow, he'd actually made the huge beast go away.

'Well done,' said a familiar voice behind them. In human form, Shilen walked down the incline, smiling at Shadow like a proud parent. Sharfy was too drained to care that she'd come. He didn't bother reaching for the sword, which had fallen from his hand.

Shilen said, 'Fear not. Tzi-Shu will think it was a god who attacked him. Besides, soon you will be in Vyin's protection and shall need to fear no one. You did very well, Shadow. Are you hurt?'

'Take away the traps,' said Shadow, his eyes growing as they turned upon Shilen in a way Sharfy found unsettling. For if Shadow could scare away a huge dragon like that, he was a friend worth having; and an enemy Sharfy, for one, didn't want.

'Soon we shall change the traps, so you may leave whenever you wish to, and go to them only for healing,' Shilen answered him. 'Remember, the traps have been designed to replenish you when you are weak. First, you must continue to practise mirroring great powers. It will grow easier and safer for you each time. Do as we ask and we will show you how to break free of the traps whenever you wish to.'

Shilen gazed at the ruined city, and at the field now vacant of all living people. The group who'd been brought there to be a dragon's meal had already headed for the road, carrying the wounded with them. A few returned to pick through the city's rubble.

'This what you wanted?' Sharfy said to her. 'Glad with what you see?'

'Dragons are not all the same,' said Shilen. 'Tzi-Shu hates humanity and did this for his own pleasure – it does not mean all other dragons would do the same. Not all of us wish harm upon humans. But you need us to protect you from those dragons who do, for you are not capable of stopping them. So be more careful with your words.'

'You didn't do much protecting today,' said Sharfy.

'I would have stopped Tzi-Shu, had I the power to stop him. I do not. Those dragons who may have stopped him have not yet descended from the skies. Do not hate the Invia – they must obey, if any of the Eight give them instruction. Shadow, rest now. Recover. There will be another test soon. If you survive it, you will be assigned to Vyin, to be his weapon. You will shadow him if he is attacked by either dragon or Spirit. None of the gods could withstand a battle against *two* of him, nor could any of the dragons.'

Shadow lashed at her but again she had come as just an illusory copy of herself. Although he didn't succeed in hurting her, for some reason she looked surprised and worried. It was as if she'd expected him to be pleased with her words. She said, 'Think, Shadow. Vyin is a friend of humanity. For the good of your own kind, you must help him.'

Shadow knew he had no kind. He took Sharfy in his arms and took him away from there, going only half as fast as he might have – he felt weak and sick. Shadowing the huge dragon had made a blank page in his memory. There was just a haze of ache and light, and the pain of having lifted an enormous burden.

Inside the traps he would be healed, however hard it was to finally break free again. The dragon woman could not reach him inside the traps with her lies. Shadow felt the pull of Siel's trap – though he did not know who wore it – and went towards it. There she was, sitting about on a flat stone place, talking with Eric.

Shadow set Sharfy gently down. Not expecting to be moved, let alone so far and so quickly, Sharfy was dizzy and sick, with little idea of what had just happened. Siel didn't have time to see Shadow before he'd dived into the prison she wore about her neck.

45

THINGS HAVE CHANGED

They gave Sharfy what time he needed to recover before asking him how he'd apparently materialised out of thin air. 'How'd I get here?' he said between dizzy heaves. He looked around in disbelief. 'I was at Athlent.'

'Shadow must have brought you,' said Siel. The charm about her neck had grown hot when it had sucked Shadow inside itself. Now and then it vibrated as if something small was fluttering around inside it.

Recovering his wits, Sharfy got up and grabbed Eric by the collar of his shirt. 'Get all the people to the castle. Now! Everyone. They'll be safe, at the castle. Dragons can't go there. Now!'

'Easy, slow down. What happened?'

'Dragons are eating people.' Sharfy noticed Dyan for the first time. He spat, drew his sword. 'Admit it,' he yelled. 'Tell them. Dragons are eating people. Invia don't look the same any more. They're helping. She knows about it too.'

'Who does?'

'Dragon woman. Dragon, hides in a woman's body. Killed Anfen. *Her.* She knows all about it.' Sharfy looked for all the world like he was going to lunge at Dyan with his sword. The dragon leaped gracefully into the air and flew till he was well out of reach and out of their sight.

Eric put a hand on Sharfy's shoulder. 'Dyan's our servant. Siel's, I should say. Siel killed Kiown and stole a charm, and Dyan has to obey whoever owns it. He's not a threat to us, but you'd better not attack him.'

'Killed Kiown? Good.' Sharfy did a double take. 'Siel – alive? Shadow said he killed you.'

'He tried to.'

'Where's Shadow now? They're using him, the dragons. They think he's their weapon. I heard her say it. Using him to fight the gods.'

They calmed him down enough to hear his story. Anger burned in Sharfy's eyes and his hands shook now and then as he spoke. Eric remembered Sharfy's embellished tales and he didn't think this was one of them.

'There are old tales of Invia carrying away lost children,' said Siel when he was finished. 'But they are only tales.'

Sharfy spat. 'I *saw* that huge thing chew and swallow them. Two at a time. Invia helped out: put em in its mouth. You're lord now? Do something.'

Eric said, 'What can I do? Tell me and I'll do it.'

'*You're* lord,' Sharfy said, grabbing him by the collar again. '*You* decide. That's what lords do.'

At that moment the ground shook and a great splitting noise echoed all around them. They were knocked off their feet. The ensuing *boom* was like an entire city falling from the sky. A wave rippled through the ground, opening a split in the smooth rock platform, the crack almost perfectly straight. A second *boom* followed, then a third, the last one fainter and further away. 'That's more skystone falling,' said Sharfy. 'They're coming, more of em. Hear it?'

'What do you think, Sharfy, did I hear it?'

'Joke all you want. Know what it means? More dragons just got free. Big ones. You're lord now? Get people to the castle. Dragons can't go there. Everyone! Right now.'

'Sure, well let me just snap my fucking fingers . . .' Eric snapped his fingers, and for a second or two thought the dragon-made charm had indeed given him powers of a kind he'd not imagined; for in that same instant four haiyens appeared in their midst. One of them spoke to Siel: 'Be prepared. She is coming.'

This was the first time Sharfy had seen haiyens and, given his mood, the timing was not good. He raised his blade to strike the one nearest. A blink later and his blade skidded across the stone. He threw himself at them instead and wound up sliding feetfirst after his sword. There was no indication of how the haiyens had done this – it did not appear they had even looked at him.

One among them spoke to Siel, its voice a rustling breath. 'Be prepared. All things approach their end now, with great haste. In moments, Shilen will be here. It is time to see if you can apply our lesson. If you can, it means other humans can, and there is hope for our peoples to live here, together. It is as we told you. Love her. Hold no fear, no anger, no matter what the dragon does or says.'

Siel nodded and closed her eyes. The haiyens began to fade, their bodies little more than smoke being blown by the wind. As quickly as they'd come, they vanished.

'Do you remember now?' Eric asked Siel. 'They came last night too. We spoke with them. You told me it was just a dream, but it wasn't.' She didn't seem to hear him – her eyes remained closed. 'Siel, snap out of it and answer me. Did I hear them properly? Did they just say Shilen was coming here? If so, why?'

She didn't answer, but he saw for himself the white dragon flying towards them, almost invisible against the sky's whiteness and its grey cloud. Her wings seemed to move slowly, but they carried her fast. She wheeled above their platform twice, surveying to see that they were alone, then she descended on the far part of it hidden by the incline, over by where they'd looked down upon the city.

Shilen was in human form by the time she strode up the path to them, the wind throwing her hair around. Case had perked up the moment Shilen came near them. Now he bounded down the path, clumsy with joy. Shilen said one harsh guttural word; Case halted and took to the sky, flying languidly away. 'Greetings, man-lord,' she said to Eric.

'What right do you have to order my drake away?' he said.

She ignored this and gazed around the platform with suspicion. 'Dyan has been here, and he is still close. Why?'

'Ask Dyan, not me.'

'Dyan is not your servant. Where is the man you name Kiown?'

'Do you know Kiown, Shilen? But that's a stupid question. You couldn't possibly know him, because that would mean you had been double dealing with us the whole time. Maybe setting up a fake rivalry so you could use one of us against the other, when it suited you. Keep the humans busy fighting each other, paying no thought to what the dragons might do when they get free.'

'That arrangement won't be needed now. Things have changed.' Still Shilen's eyes roamed the platform, lingering on

Sharfy, who'd not risen since the haiyens sent him sliding over the ground. She called to him, 'You. Where is Shadow?'

'Leave Sharfy alone and speak with me,' said Eric. 'Shadow is trapped.' He took a tight grip on the charm in his pocket. 'There's no more need to call me "man-lord". You can find another person to play my role, if you like. It was never real in the first place. But I'm finished pretending to be any kind of lord.'

'That no longer matters. Is it your charm in which Shadow is trapped? Or is Kiown hiding here too?' Siel still hadn't moved, nor opened her eyes from what looked like peaceful meditation. Shilen's eyes swept past Siel as if she didn't see her at all.

Eric said, 'Are the dragons eating people, like Sharfy says?'

Shilen scoffed. 'Of course not. The Eight have power to create their own foods and pleasures. Why would they stoop to eating human beings?'

'Then why is it the Invia are carrying people away?'

'I have not seen nor heard of this.'

'Why do the Invia look so different now, Shilen?'

'Effort is needed, to disguise them in a way pleasing to human eyes. There is no longer a need for disguise. They have always been as you now see them, beneath a thin illusory veil. You did not fear them before. There's no need to fear them now.'

'Things have changed all right. It's true, isn't it, Shilen? All along the dragons meant to come down and kill us.'

She laughed. 'How important you like to think yourselves, as though dragons have no grander purpose than killing you. Yes, some humans shall die, but only those who are in the way.'

'And if you decide we are all in the way?'

'Some are Favoured. They will be perfectly safe. That promise shall be kept. Three among the Eight insist it shall be kept. I told you to choose Favoured ones with care. Did you? Or did you treat it as a game?'

Eric felt sick. He crouched down, dizzy. Another great noise rolled over the ground from far away: another great piece of skystone falling. Eric looked to Siel, who still had her eyes closed. Shilen followed his gaze and confirmed his suspicions. 'What do you keep looking at, man-lord?'

'You don't see her, do you?'

'There is no one there to see. Answer me. Why was Dyan here?'

At the edge of his vision he saw that Sharfy had quietly got back to his feet and taken his sword again. It occurred to Eric to signal *stop, stay put*, but he knew it would be pointless. Now Sharfy ran at Shilen – tried to, rather. It was more of a fast hobble. He got close enough to strike when, with one quick movement, she plucked the sword from his hand, snapped it across her knee then threw him to the ground, not troubling even to look at him. She said to Eric, 'Hand your charm to me for a moment, so that I can be sure Shadow is trapped inside it.'

Eric saw clearly then that Shilen had not come here to talk at all . . . and that the charm's protection was the only reason she hadn't killed him where he stood. She'd do it, he knew, the instant he parted from it, for Shadow was her interest now, not this business of establishing faux human kingdoms with phoney lords. In fact she would probably kill him soon regardless, whether or not he handed the charm over to make the task easy for her. Would Hauf help him, if it meant Hauf must attack another dragon?

Eric turned from Shilen, held the charm in his cupped palms and whispered, 'Hauf, I need you. Come quickly.'

He had not really expected anything to happen, but at once the stone floor began to shake. A thin, flat section of stone near to him folded upon itself like a sheet of paper, bunched up as if kneaded by invisible hands which lengthened it into the shape of a torso. Wings formed on its top side and slid into their place. A jaw distended with jagged stone shards for teeth down its length.

It took only a few seconds before Hauf had appeared in full, this time his skin the same light grey as the platform's stone. He crouched now by Eric's side, growling at Shilen with a voice of grinding rock.

Shilen's mouth hung open, aghast. 'You may not fight me,' she said; it was unclear whether she was addressing Eric or Hauf. There was a flash of light about her. When it faded, Shilen had resumed her true form. Her wings spread and she jumped, but Hauf leaped and struck her like a wrecking ball, knocking her off the rocky platform's edge. With a *thud* the two dragons slammed into the road below.

Eric ran to the platform's edge. Down below, Hauf had Shilen pinned with one of her wings gripped tight in his jaws. He wrenched back his head with the noise of meat being split from bone. One wing was partly ripped free. Shilen's scream was like a sadly sung note. It seemed her cry also cast a spell, for blinding light erupted around the two dragons. A gust of wind pushed Eric back from where he stood watching. He didn't see it but he heard the noise of Hauf being thrown at the cliff face with enough force to embed him in it. Webs cracked in the stone around him.

Shilen attempted flight but one of her wings was now useless. She ran instead through the high pass.

With much effort Hauf finally wrenched himself free from

the cliff face, causing a small avalanche to tumble around him. He turned his head up to Eric. 'The threat is gone,' he growled. 'You may summon me once more. Then I am free.'

'Wait, we need to speak,' Eric called down, but Hauf collapsed to a pile of smooth round stones. The stones in turn quickly crumbled to dust.

Eric ran to check Sharfy's injuries, for Sharfy hadn't got up since Shilen had thrown him to the ground. He was bruised, scraped and pissed off but had suffered no worse.

'She couldn't see me,' said Siel, finally opening her eyes again. She laughed. 'It works! Eric, you have to listen to the haiyens. We can all be safe from the dragons, all of us. They cast no spells on me, just now. There was no magic to it at all. And she couldn't see me.'

'Will Dyan be able to see you when he gets back?'

'If I allow him to see me, yes.'

'How does it work, if there's no magic to it?' Sharfy demanded.

'To escape the dragons' awareness I raise my consciousness higher than normal. It is like climbing steps to a higher room they aren't even aware of. If I want them to see me again it is easy enough to climb back down. Eric, yes I remember now. Last night, the haiyens told me Shilen would come. It had slipped my mind – perhaps they intended it to. They told me she would come, that she'd seek the one who had killed Kiown. She knows full well that Kiown is dead. She may also be seeking to gather the shadowtrap charms.' She held aloft the amulet Kiown had possessed. 'The dragons don't yet know that Mountain altered the way this one works.'

'How did the haiyens know Shilen would come here? Can they see into the future?'

She shrugged. 'A short way perhaps; I really don't know.

There's not much they're willing to share with us yet. If you'd seen how Tauk and the others behaved, you'd understand. There's nothing the haiyens could have done or said to make Tauk trust them. Now they're learning that a lot of men are just like that. They're going to speak with you and Aziel about the dragons and what we can do. Help them if you can. Convincing other people is going to be harder than fighting the dragons could ever be.'

They helped Sharfy bandage his various abrasions and to clean off the blood caking his skin and clothes. Eric said, 'Sharfy, I believe you about the dragons eating people. But Dyan is on our side. It doesn't matter that he's forced to be . . . we still need him. He may be the only dragon we can trust. Don't attack him when he gets back here. And if you ever attack the haiyens again I'm going to let them kill you.'

'Some friend, that dragon,' said Sharfy. 'Fight's on, where is he? When you see what I seen at Athlent, then we'll see. See how much you trust dragons then. Any dragons.'

With a swoosh of air, Dyan landed in their midst. Case thumped down beside him a little later with much less grace. 'Beauty, what has happened to you?' said Dyan. 'You look to have faded. I see through you as if you were made of stained glass.'

'I am still here, Dyan,' said Siel. 'But since you keep secrets from us, I will now keep one from you. I won't tell you why I look this way to you.'

Dyan lowered his head in supplication. 'As you say, Beauty.' He sniffed the air. 'There has been battle here.'

Sharfy scoffed and spat.

'Where were you, pray tell?' said Eric. 'We could have used your help.'

'When the ugly human attacked me it seemed best to leave for a while,' said Dyan. 'I have not been idle. Other dragons passed nearby. When I sensed them, I went to watch and gauge their intentions. They are just exploring, still in a mood of celebration to be free again. Many more dragons are free now, Beauty. The sky prisons soon shall be empty.'

'How many came near us?' said Eric.

'None of the Eight. Several lesser dragons came within two miles of here. I call them lesser dragons, but you would call them mighty, compared with humans. They were not here seeking you.'

'If they come here, can you protect us from them, Dyan?'

'I will be unable to slay them, especially if they travel in groups. With magic I can hide you. Not all of them know magic as I do. Some know magic better than I. We must be careful. There are those among them hostile to your kind. Beware of Invia too. They serve whatever dragons instruct them. Those your lords named Favoured shall be safest.'

'He's not *my* lord,' said Sharfy, jerking a thumb at Eric. 'No one's lord. Lords're supposed to decide things.'

'You're right,' said Eric, stung by the truth in it. 'I'm not a lord. They only wanted me to pretend to be one for a while. I think that time has finished.' He told Dyan of the fight with Shilen, of Hauf coming to help them. 'Do you think it means Shilen is going to attack us the next time she sees us?'

'Only if her masters instruct it,' said Dyan. 'It would please her to kill you, I am sure. She has no love for humanity. Her hatred for me is greater, if that soothes you.'

'Is Vyin her master?'

'Her master is whichever of the Eight she finds herself before. She has taken more instruction from Vyin than from the others.

Vyin holds no hostile intent towards you. That may be said of two others among the Eight.'

'So five of them want to wipe us out,' said Sharfy. 'Good news, eh? Your move, Pilgrim. "Lord".' Again he spat.

'There are things of more interest to all of the Eight than the matter of human existence,' said Dyan in the tone of someone not wishing to offend.

Case went and lurked by their gear packs, something he did when he was thirsty. Siel told him, 'If it's water you want, find a puddle and leave our skins alone. We need cleaner water than you do, plus you drank the last of the wine already.' Case looked crestfallen.

Dyan said, 'I could summon wine for him, but I shan't. He does not fly quickly, yet insists on following me. It is becoming a hindrance. There is also something I sense your drake wishes me to tell you. He is a man, not a true drake.'

Eric laughed.

'It is true,' said Dyan. 'Vyin changed him from a man into his current form.'

All three of them looked doubtfully at Case. 'Was he someone we knew?' Eric said.

Dyan gave the dragon equivalent of a shrug, a quick sideways flick of his head. 'He has no speech, and understands your speech in only limited ways.'

Eric looked closely at Case. The drake met his eye with a look that seemed imploring, but in his features there seemed nothing reminiscent of anyone they'd known.

46

THE CASTLE LAWNS

On the castle lawns, Loup and Far Gaze sat upon the same patch of grass where old man Case had slept after his first night in Levaal. Before the castle's nearest entrance a group of half-giants stood in quiet conversation with one another, ignoring the people milling about in growing numbers, demanding to be let in.

Not many would be willing to take up arms against the half-giants, not yet. But the people knew there was food in the castle stores and soon enough they'd be hungry. Earlier today two half-giants had been killed in a fight with a dragon, a couple of miles south of the castle. It had been quite small as dragons went, a Minor personality none had managed to name or find word of in any known lore. It had been stalking some of the roads which fed into the Great Dividing Road, biting people in apparent playfulness, yet inflicting terrible injuries. The half-giants had done nothing about it until a delivery of goods bound for the castle had been left abandoned on the road. Its traumatised crew had arrived at the castle covered in blood and with arms missing. A gang of ten half-giants marched out at once, and killed the dragon with their bare hands. They'd dragged its body back before a cheering crowd, which evidently mistook the half-giants' deed as a defence of humankind, rather than the defence of castle property.

Those fleeing from the south arrived with far grimmer tales of dragons, especially people coming from Athlent, Kopyn and other nearby cities. So far, Aziel was allowing no one inside and would hear no tales about dragons eating people.

'She'll have one angry mob to deal with out here, if she keeps blocking em from going up to tell her what's gone on,' said Loup, as he and Far Gaze watched the crowd numbers swell. 'She won't have you up there to see her neither, don't matter how long you wait down here. She don't want *me* here, truth be told. It'd help a bunch if Eric got here and kept an eye on her like he's meant to.'

'Eric having been chosen for any role of importance is a fitting tribute to Vous's insanity,' Far Gaze muttered.

'This is just for your ears, but rumour holds Aziel wants him dead. Just on the quiet. Some of those clerk boys talked about it; I heard em. Soon's he gets back here. He's made her job hard, insulted her by his mucking around, and so on. She wants a half-giant to do the job, but none of em will. They know how people scheme and play around, they want no part of it. Heard talk among *them* that their hiding places out in unclaimed lands all look a lot better to live in than these parts now that the dragons are here.' He looked pointedly over to where a never-ending group of spectators lined up for a look at the dead dragon. 'I don't think we'd fare half as well as that without their help, against even the Minors. That's a little un. Wait till the great big ones get bold enough to come closer to the castle. Even half-giants won't be much help then. We'll need the gods.'

'The dragons won't come here,' said Far Gaze.

And everyone seemed to know it, for those able to make it

to the castle were coming in droves. Not just city dwellers, either – the villages and rural lands had begun to empty. Surely that included the farm lands. The castle warehouses were mostly full of spell-preserved food, but with no more deliveries coming, the stock would drain quickly enough.

Aziel's administrators emerged throughout the day with orders for people to go to the newly built cities nearby. Cities the Arch had built, so new they did not yet have names. But very few people complied – tales had reached them of Invia carrying people away from those places to be dragon food. There was no army to move them along, for the half-giants' control extended only as far as keeping people out of the castle.

More arrived, and then more. The roads in and out were soon blocked. Fresh tales of horror arrived with each new group, tales of dragons doing all manner of terrible things. The people began to ask for Shadow to come forth and speak with them. They'd murmured it among themselves at first, but they had begun to shout it at the half-giant guards.

'You!' someone called through the growing noise. It took a moment for Loup to understand he was the one being addressed. It was one of Aziel's advisors, judging by the gown he wore. The harried-looking man stood between two particularly large half-giants at the foot of some narrow steps leading up inside.

'I got a name,' Loup said peevishly as he walked over, Far Gaze with him. Seeing them as mages, the crowd was eager to clear a path for them.

'Mage of the Realm,' said the advisor with an apologetic bow. 'I called to you by your title earlier, Mage of the Realm, but you did not seem to hear me.'

'They call me Mage of the Realm instead of the new Arch

Mage,' Loup explained to Far Gaze. 'Whole thing was Eric's stupid idea.'

'Our lady must speak with you, Mage of the Realm.'

'Rare honour, that is. What's it about?'

Aziel's advisor looked around at the swarm of people. 'I would say it is about *this*, Mage of the Realm.' The advisor lowered his voice. 'The lady is . . . in a panic, sir.'

47

GO TO WORLD'S END

It wasn't long before the haiyens returned to Eric and Siel. This time the wizard Domudess was with them. He peered around with an air of serenity very reminiscent of the way Siel's face had looked when she was hiding in plain sight from Shilen.

Among the four haiyens was one with a small indentation in its forehead. Siel recognised him at once. 'Our guide,' she said. She moved to embrace him. Unsure of that concept, the haiyen instead took her hands in his. A pulse of warmth ebbed out of him, directed at Siel but touching Eric too, like a brush of warm breeze. It filled him with a moment or two of serene happiness. Dyan evidently felt it too, for he shuddered and moved away, peering back in confusion as his master Siel spoke to beings he could not see or hear.

'I have taken a human name for your convenience,' the haiyen said. 'Call me Luhan. We return to you in great urgency. We find we have misjudged in our plans. Perhaps we have failed altogether. Time as it functions in this world is very strange to us. Events cause other events like stones tumbling down mountainsides, unpredictably dislodging other stones. In our world, we can often separate the stones and judge precisely where each will fall. It is not so, in this place. We must now hurry.'

Domudess said, 'My friends have built for me instruments which allow one to observe distant events. I have seen dramatic things. The dragons as we speak are destroying humankind. To them it is play, but it may as well be called war. All across the land this occurs. No city is safe. People flock to the castle in large numbers, but larger numbers will never make it there. Of those who do, it is *you* who they think will help them, Eric. They call you by the name of Shadow, as you have sometimes called yourself. It is best you return to the castle, if I may presume to advise you. Just the sight of you upon the balcony may well calm those gathered there. A slimmer hope – but one we must hold – is that those people will allow the haiyens to teach them the arts Siel is quickly learning. If the people believe you are a myth come to life, that you are Shadow . . . we dare to hope they will listen to you, when they would likely listen to no other.'

'You can presume to advise me whenever you like,' Eric said. 'What do you think I should tell the crowds, when I'm up on that balcony?'

'Tell them there is a way humanity can live and thrive, even in a world where dragons also dwell. All who are willing to learn will be taken inside the castle, and the haiyens will teach them the arts. You must make Aziel allow this. Siel, you too have a duty. You must go to World's End, and you must have Shadow with you.'

'Why?'

Dyan peered from Eric to Siel and back, his head swaying like a serpent's. 'Who do you speak with, Beauty?' he called.

'Hush, Dyan.'

Domudess paced for a little while, considering his words. 'There is a chance the dragons will set the Pendulum swinging again. At present, the haiyens have halted it. They ensured the god who came to our world would be the Teacher of Many Arts. It is not a warlike god – it will do no harm here. It will not cause the Spirits of our world to go south in response, to fight as would soldiers at war for this reality. As things stand, no more gods of either side will cross the boundary. In other words, the Pendulum has gone still. As things stand now, the dragons' Parent shall not awaken.

'The Eight great dragons are the only ones with the power to change this. You must be at World's End, Siel, in case they do so. I cannot tell you your task there, should the dragons indeed cross to the South. Tell me, is Shadow still imprisoned within your charm? Does he struggle for freedom?'

'He is here. But I can feel nothing to suggest he wants to break free.'

Eric said, 'When Aziel had Shadow in her charm, she complained about it being hard to hold him. Every now and then I felt something similar, back when I had him trapped. It's not like that for you?'

'No,' she said. 'It seemed to me that he returned to us on purpose, and became trapped on purpose. Probably he hides from Shilen, and the other dragons.'

'Indeed the dragons seek him eagerly.' Domudess clutched her arm, stooping down to look into her eyes. 'You *must* keep him within your charm's prison, if that is something you have influence over. He must not break free. You must keep him at World's End. Do you understand?'

'I'll understand better if you tell me why.'

The wizard shut his eyes, pained. 'This becomes difficult for us both. I can tell you where you must go. But at this time I may not tell you why. You must now trust me more than you have trusted anyone in your life. And we must trust that you shall do as we ask you, without our having to force you. Ride your dragon to World's End, as fast as he will carry you. You must stay near the Great Dividing Road. Within a mile of it, if not within sight of it. If the guardians of the two worlds rise from slumber, that is the place they will meet for battle. Whatever happens, *you must stay there.* And you must keep Shadow with you. Should any of the Eight come near World's End, seeking you, practise the arts we have shown you, and hide from them.

'Haiyen warriors will be near you, in hiding. They use arts of the mind more powerful than any swordcraft. They shall protect you as they can, from human beings and from whatever else may see you. Hide there, and wait. With your eyes ever on the Great Dividing Road, at the boundary of World's End. Leave now, Siel. It is not known how long we have.'

'How long until *what*? Why can't you tell me my part in this?'

'If Shadow should become free of his prison, he could access your knowledge and learn what we have told you. He must not! Shadow is the key, Siel. If the time comes, if the Dragon-god awakens, you will learn what you must do.'

The haiyen named Luhan stepped forwards and said, 'These worlds are small parts in the vastness, though it does not seem so now. Our lives are smaller yet, and are only borrowed things. Be brave. Know the waters wait to cleanse you again. Linger in them, if it pleases you. Your soul shall remember. All of this is fleeting. We are forever, and these trials are but lessons.'

Siel hesitated, then embraced Eric and held him long. Eric whispered in her ear so that the others wouldn't hear: 'Whatever it is they have in mind, unless I'm mistaken the haiyen just suggested you won't survive. Are you sure you want to go? You can refuse them.'

She laughed quietly. 'Do you truly believe they'd allow me to refuse?'

'Give the charm to them, let them do it.'

'It doesn't matter anyway,' she said. Suddenly her smile was radiant. 'We live on, Eric. Part of us goes on forever. I have seen the truth in that. Be well, be safe. We will not be parted for long, whatever happens. You will see.'

'You *must* leave, Siel,' said Domudess. He said it gently but with deadly earnestness. 'The flight is long. There is no more time.'

'Dyan flies quicker than you might think. But I'll do as you ask.' She took her pack, climbed aboard the very confused dragon, who'd never before seen humans conversing so seriously with non-existent things. With one last look at Eric, she took to the sky.

Eric did not know how he was so certain, but deep within himself he knew the image of her sitting poised between Dyan's tilted wings was the last sight of her he'd have. He did not know what she knew . . . he had not seen the crystal's waters which had so drastically changed her, although she had tried at times to describe them to him. He longed to believe what she'd said – that their lives would go on eternally. But he could not share her certainty. He wiped tears from his face and tried not to hate the haiyens and the wizard who'd sent her away.

48

DEAD DRAGONS

'I may transport you two men to the castle,' said Luhan the haiyen traveller, 'but I cannot bring your drake. He is too large.'

'I'm not leaving Case on his own,' said Eric. 'I'll fly him to the castle.' Having just watched Siel part from him at the haiyens' and wizard's orders, he was in little mood to be in their company.

Domudess quietly took Eric aside. 'Do you believe Aziel will speak with me?' he said.

'I have no idea. The half-giants might not even let you and the haiyens inside: you might have to find a way past them.'

'That is no difficulty. But I shall be alone. The haiyens will not enter the castle, not yet. They must first go home and heal. You would not know it, but being this far inside our world makes them very sick.'

'Because of the magic in the air?'

'Because of this world's time. Time varies from world to world in ways difficult for us to fathom. This world's time is something created and imposed by the Dragon-god. Our haiyen friends say that Otherworld is affected by the same design of time. Your home world, Eric, is a prison world as much as this one. And it has the same gaoler. The Dragon-god guards the doorstep of your world, so that a more free reality may not enter.'

'Call me Shadow, not Eric.'

'You're not Shadow,' said Sharfy, as one would speak to an imbecile. 'Shadow's not you. Shadow's your ghost. How come your ghost and you are alive at the same time?'

'People accept me because they think I'm the same "Shadow" of their tales and myths. They've heard for years that Shadow will come from Otherworld to bring an age of peace and abundance. They'll listen to me only if I am known as Shadow. That's what you'll call me, especially in front of Aziel. Got it?'

'That is wise. We shall next meet within the castle,' said Domudess, addressing both of them with a low bow.

So Sharfy and Eric flew north aboard Case, meaning to go straight to the castle's high towers. Eric had not counted on the swelling masses of people gathered on the roads as they got near. Sharfy grabbed his shoulder and pointed. 'Look, dead dragons. Take us down. Let's see em. We need to know who killed em.'

Teams of men hauled thick ropes looped around three large corpses, dragging them along the road. From the sky it was plain to see they wouldn't get much further before the road was completely blocked by the crowds ahead.

Going down there was very nearly a mistake. When the people saw a winged creature descend on them, weapons came quickly to hand. It was lucky none beneath had bows or slings. 'It's Shadow!' someone said. 'That there's a drake, not a dragon.'

The group spoke the greetings Eric was accustomed to receive when he stopped at villages and cities. They backed away from the dragon corpses to let Eric and Sharfy see them. All three were larger than Dyan, although two of them were not larger by much. The third was at least double Dyan's size. 'None of these are from the Eight?' said Eric, and felt immediately foolish for the laughter his stupid question brought. He heard Sharfy groan behind him. He'd never felt like less of a lord than he did then.

A burly man held aloft one of the dragon's severed heads by the horns, although the head looked too big to be lifted by one man. He strode forwards and dropped it at Eric's feet. Its eyes still looked very bright and alive. 'We've had trouble, as you see,' the man grunted, wiping sweat away with a huge meaty arm. 'I am Huldeel, chieftain of our village.'

'What village?' Sharfy said.

'In the lowlands of River City. The name of the village does not matter, for it no longer exists. We began to rebuild it when River City was liberated, after your very visit, Shadow my lord. Do you recall? When you flew in with news that Vous had left the castle.'

'I remember.'

'We hung the last of our overseers high on the walls that same day, Tempest toss their ashes. Our rebuilding work went well. We'd just got a taste for peace when the sky began to fall and these very dragons beat our village to splinters. They had help from another, a smaller dark-coloured beast which we didn't see again, but whose face we'll not forget. It is well you've come, Shadow my lord, although you must take care with your drake. Your people are at war. Yet again, at war. Our enemy's no man nor mage this time, and by now we all know it. You know it too, or so we hope, Shadow my lord. The sight of your drake did us ill.'

'They been eating you?' said Sharfy.

'More than that besides,' said the man, steel in his eyes. 'Slaying us for sport. Carrying off our women and children for we know not what cause. Biting our men in half, good men of honour.

They seemed to make games of the killing which I'll not speak of. We'd not have made it here but for the aid of a god.'

'Where you going to take em?' Sharfy nodded to the dead dragons. 'Invia see em, might be trouble.'

'We have "trouble" already. We'll take these bodies to the castle. We have heard that people from all the cities gather there, with grudges forgotten. We shall form a new army and go to war. Join us. All who hear our story will surely join us. We've no fear. We're not alone in this war. The gods fight the beasts with us! These bodies we will show to all fighting men, so they know that the beasts *can* be slain.'

'The Minors, maybe,' said Sharfy. 'You seen the one I seen? At Athlent? Huge. No one'll kill that. Not even gods.'

'There was one of the Eight at River City,' said someone in the crowd. 'I saw it. People got away. Some said it was guarding the place from other dragons. I'll not credit that, but it slew no one.'

'I saw that very dragon. It did not guard our village from these,' said Huldeel, striking the dragon's head with his boot. 'Nor did it stop the Invia stealing away with our people.'

'Tell me what happened,' said Eric.

'A great flood of people began the trek from our city and from its surrounding lands, as soon as the skystone began to fall upon us. The rain of heavy stones killed some of them. As the good man says, the great dragon who came to our city did no harm, not by itself. But it was huge and terrible to behold, even from the distance at which I saw it. All in the city who saw it fled. As they fled, Invia came in great numbers, carrying people off west. We know not what became of them. They fought, and slew some Invia at great cost. These dragons you see then came to our village and ruined it. We let them have the place and fled but they followed us.

'We went underground as long as we could, for we'd had commerce with groundmen near there. But their passages grew too small to pass so we had to surface. The children alone kept on underground. We've no idea if they made it to the castle or not. When we surfaced, the same dragons came at us again. They watched us for miles, taking one or two of us at their leisure. We heard screams but did not see what they did. We could not fight them. One of them knew magic and it did things I'll not speak of.'

'How'd you kill em in the end?' said Sharfy.

'Something helped us. We know not what.'

'It was Vous,' said someone from the crowd.

'I'll not credit that,' said Huldeel. 'But it was surely one of the Spirits. I'd guess Wisdom. It used such magic as kept the dragons spellbound. Illusions of the dragons appeared on each side of the road. Each illusion was just the same as the dragon it copied, but larger. Far more beautiful too, it must be said. We ourselves were spellbound awhile. The dragons, more so. They could not look away from these visions of themselves. We could see them battling to try and pull away. I have never seen such beauty; there, I'll say it. And I've naught but hate for the foul things and all to do with them.'

'They sang,' said another from the crowd.

'Aye, they did. I've never heard its like. Stillness fell on us – we were all taken in it. Only Uon was not so taken, for he's deaf as wood. He cut one of their heads off while it stared at its likeness. Even then the others did not stir. They went into a kind of dance, I swear it. Slow and swaying. But I stirred.' The look in his eyes said clearly it was he who'd cut off at least one of the dragons' heads himself. 'So that's our tale. Tell the people we're all one now, Shadow. No difference of the past is worth a pit devil's turd. If the Arch still lives, *he's* a chance for penance now, if he'll but slay one of those beasts. If he dies in the trying I'll tip a drink to him, whatever the past.'

'He is gone,' Eric said.

'Fine. But tell the people of your realm: all who can are trekking here to join our fight. Tell them a war's upon them. Road talk says all cities are lost and unsafe to go to. They took Esk; they took Athlent as your man here says. They'll take all the realm. We've only each other now, all of us are brothers and sisters.' The village chieftain grabbed Eric by the shoulder. 'The people will hear you. If you've weapons in that castle, pass them out. Tell the people to fight!'

'I won't,' Eric said. 'Maybe you haven't seen the dragon called Shâ. I saw it slay a thousand war mages all by itself. *Easily.* They didn't even hurt it. I'm not going to send anyone off to fight it, nor the other Major dragons. This will be hard for you to hear, but this is not a fight for us. Get to safety and stay there. Get inside the castle. There is room there for many people. No dragons dare come there.'

'Word travels back that the giants let no one in,' said someone in the crowd.

'I'll see what I can do about that,' said Eric.

'Leave the dragon bodies here,' said Sharfy. 'Or take one to all major roads. A body at one, a head at another. Can cover six roads. Dragons will see it's a warning, come no closer.'

A murmur of chatter rippled through the crowd, some of it angry. 'And just who are you?' said Huldeel to Sharfy.

'Do what he says,' said Eric. 'The roads in are blocked. You won't get much closer to the castle than you are now. Don't fight any Invia you see, unless you absolutely have to. This will sound strange, but fighting the dragons is the worst thing you can do. There are other ways to handle them.'

The whole group of them seemed stunned to silence for a moment. 'Our children climb through dark tunnels below the ground. Many of these men about me watched their women carried off, could do naught about it. If you mean to preach surrender . . .' Huldeel bent and lifted the dragon's head again, grunting at the effort. 'And if those gathered at the castle have been through what we have, or anything like it, then my holding this head aloft shall have more sway with them than any crown, any throne and any title.'

A murmur of strong agreement swept through the crowd. Sharfy caught Eric's eye with a look that said: *It's time we left.*

Eric said, 'I feel the same way you do. And if it were possible to fight them I'd agree. But trust me on this: there's a better way.'

'What way is that, Shadow my lord? We are listening.'

Eric did not know how to explain it. He knew how the haiyens' advice would sound to these men. Had he not seen Siel employ the power of it, making herself invisible to Shilen, he'd have doubted it himself. 'All of us will be taught the way to hide ourselves from the dragons. The new people of Levaal South – the people known as haiyens – will teach us, if we will allow them to live here among us. We will build a new world, one where we live among the dragons, hidden from their sight. We will be invisible as the winds are to them. There will be no more wars between us. Our new cities shall be hidden from them too, built with arts the haiyens will teach us.'

The group looked at him like he was a madman, or worse.

'Tell me, good sir,' said the village chieftain, 'why is it you choose to ride a drake? A drake is kin to dragonkind. Is it not?'

'Not all dragons are—' Eric began, but Sharfy yanked his arm. Reflecting on what he'd been about to say, he was soon thankful for it. When they got aboard Case, he flew away from there much faster than he usually flew.

49

THE LORD AND LADY

It was hard to tell how many thousands made up the crowds milling about the castle. People had come from every city but the southernmost ones. Their angry rumble seemed to have morphed into one great voice with a common complaint. When Case flew over them some screamed, thinking a dragon had come to a place they'd believed they were safe. Case headed for Aziel's old bedroom window, ignoring Eric's instruction to take them down near the steps . . . he had wanted to tell the half-giants to allow people inside.

But before they reached the window something caused an eruption of angry cries beneath. Sharfy pointed out the Invia diving down from the clouds into the throng of people, diving just as birds would dive to catch fish. Some Invia came up from their dives and flew away with struggling people in their arms. Others did not make it back to the sky. The loud otherworldly shriek of their wails sounded four separate times.

'See?' said Sharfy, triumphant.

'I told you, goddammit, I believed what you said. Since you have all the answers, how the hell am I going to keep these people calm now?'

'Shouldn't be calm. It's war.'

Eric got off Case's back and climbed through the window. He saw no point arguing, but Sharfy was wrong – this wasn't 'war' at all. It wasn't even hunting. It was just farming . . . farming human beings like penned animals. Shilen had known this was what waited, once the dragons got free. Surely she'd known all along. Eric said, 'Serious question. If you were lord, Sharfy – and maybe you should be – how would you make those people out there believe what the haiyens have told us?'

Sharfy leaped from Case's back onto the window sill with no regard at all for the distance he'd fall if he slipped. 'Wouldn't try. I don't believe em.'

'Why not? You saw what happened when Shilen came. Shilen didn't see Siel at all. You saw that it worked.'

'That's just how she acted. Tricks. Just tricks. S'what dragons do. She tricked you too. Remember?'

A voice from across the room surprised them both. 'Our task is not going to be easy, Eric. Or Shadow, as you have rightly said I should call you.' Domudess stood with his head stooped to avoid the top of the door frame.

'Call me whatever name you want,' said Eric. 'It hardly matters now. We're being attacked by Invia. People aren't safe even here at the castle. There won't be time to teach them the haiyens' arts now. So what are we supposed to do?'

Domudess smiled at him sadly. 'It may be there's nothing we can do. You and I know that raising our consciousness is a way to avoid dragons, and to avoid Invia. To avoid all the pain and death these people are soon to march towards. It is a simple thing to practise, but impossible to teach those not willing to learn, especially in such a short time as we have. Your valiant companion has seen the effects and does not believe what his own eyes showed him. I am old, one of the

oldest men alive. You are young, Eric. To you, this helplessness is a new feeling. I have watched humanity all my life. I
am no longer surprised, no longer even disappointed. They are
what they are.

'If you go to that balcony and address the crowd, you may
tell them either truth or lies. Neither truth nor lies will change
things now. Or you may stay here, away from them, and leave
them to have what they insist upon. I do not know which course
is best. That is for you to decide. I am here for a similarly futile
cause, only because I promised our haiyen friends I would try.
They too are new to the futility of trying to change humanity.
Somehow, when speaking with them, I too forget that it is
futile.'

Eric said, 'I'll tell them the truth. The myth about Shadow
may be the only thing which gives them a chance to believe it.
I just don't know how to say it.'

'Say that the haiyens have taught us a way to stay hidden
from the dragons, a way to ascend out of their perception altogether. One must bring positive energy into one's mind, and
it's nothing to do with the magic in the air which mages use.
They may do it simply by thinking and feeling positive things,
by banishing all fear, even the fear of death. In the haiyens, this
does not translate into what we describe as love. In them, it
brings more a kind of peaceful awareness, a harmony with their
surrounds. In us it looks and sounds like love, and in fact that
may be what it is.

'But, to say to stirred men, many bearing wounds from dragons
and from Invia who serve dragons . . . to tell them they must
love the dragons? That they must bear in their hearts no hate
or fear, that they must hold no desire to hurt them, that they
must find admiration and understanding for that mighty and

advanced race . . . and cling only to that? I feel it is not possible for them to accept. They will react as did Tauk the Strong. As I knew he would react.'

Domudess planted his hands upon the doorway's frame and held on tight. It seemed he knew with three seconds' warning that the castle would shake itself, for that's what happened. For a minute or more the floor seemed like shuddering liquid. Sharfy fell face-first into the wall and was very lucky he wasn't tipped the other way – straight out the window. The drake leaped off the sill in panic, belching a gout of flame which singed Sharfy's hair.

'How peculiar,' Domudess said mildly when the shaking eased to a halt. 'The haiyens have told me they have ceased the Pendulum swing, and that the Dragon-god will not waken.'

'Is that what that shaking was?'

'I suspect so. The Dragon may wake regardless of the Pendulum effect; it may not wait for the influx of foreign gods. It may rise just to police its escaped brood, given how the brood are behaving. If it does, I do not know what will happen to us. Nonetheless, we must continue as if the future has a place for us. Come. We shall speak with Aziel, whether or not she listens. She can do no worse than pick up a sword and try to run us through.'

'Don't rule that out.'

To Eric's surprise, Far Gaze and Loup were already in Aziel's chamber. Eric had forgotten all about his 'Mage of the Realm'.

However busy Aziel had been with other things, she'd found time to decorate the large room with artworks, finery, tapestries and hangings of deep red and gold. They had heard her raised voice well before they entered the chamber and now she rounded on them, looking for all the world as though she'd gladly bite them. Faul stood like a dozing statue at the room's lone window, not bothering to turn about as they came in. She'd surely seen what went on outside with the Invia . . . Eric wondered, remembering the rage she'd flown into when one was killed on her land, whether she felt as much sympathy for the creatures now.

'And where have *you* been?' Aziel snarled at him. To Domudess she said, 'If you want to remain in this chamber, prove your worth. Why did the castle shake?'

'Because the dragons have descended, and their sleeping Parent may be aware of it,' said Domudess, striding towards her until his way was blocked by an armed bodyguard, surely little older than sixteen and looking scared to death. Domudess smiled at him kindly. He added, 'Such shaking may continue. The haiyens say the Dragon shall not wake, but I feel otherwise. Within the coming days, you would be wise to depart the castle. All of you. To those here with mage eyes, have you examined the airs? Do so now.'

Eric did. He had heard much of the power of the airs within the castle, and had seen for himself the wild twisting sheets of colour outside it, back before the dragons had taken him and Aziel up into the skies. But now . . . 'There's nothing,' he said.

'Indeed. Something has reclaimed all the airs' magic. Can you guess what force that is?'

'Well, it's probably not Loup,' Eric said.

'Mage of the Realm to you,' said Loup.

'It is the work of the Dragon-god, drawing all nearby magic to itself. It is awakening. It is a guess, but I believe it to be correct. No one alive today has lived through such an event except the dragons themselves, and they do not recall the last time fondly. What frightens them should most assuredly frighten us. None of us knows what shall happen, nor how long the process of awakening takes. At any moment? Or will it be years? Or am I wrong, and the Dragon-god merely turns about in restless sleep?'

'Why leave the castle?' Eric said. 'Is it going to erupt from the ground beneath us?'

'It may.'

'No!' said Aziel. 'I am not leaving.'

Far Gaze said, 'Eric. I have been trying to convince her lordship—'

'*Lady*ship!'

'—of a very different course of action, regarding which she is just as reluctant. That we allow people inside the castle. She feels the food stores will be ravaged, that she herself will be ravaged, and her mandate to rule will be ignored by a screaming mob.'

'The mandate the dragons themselves provided?' said Domudess mildly.

'I have told her that the mob will more likely befriend her if she extends her hand to them,' said Far Gaze. 'If they are kept out, they will get louder, hungrier and angrier.'

'He also claimed he'd been to the South and seen the gods there,' she said. 'Am I supposed to believe that?'

'He has been there,' said Domudess. Aziel laughed at him. 'May I ask why convincing Aziel of the best course is seen as necessary?' said Domudess.

'That's why,' said Aziel, pointing at Faul, who still hadn't turned away from the window.

'Aziel, a quiet word?' said Eric.

The pair of them walked away from the rest of the group. He

said, 'Listen. Shilen lied to us – do you know that yet? The dragons have been eating people out there. Whole cities full of people. Sharfy saw it, so did most of those people gathering down there. What's more, Shilen knew it would happen. Last time I spoke to her, she said the Favoured ones are still safe from the dragons. She's lied so much already, how do we know even *that* much is true? I never understood what she meant, Aziel. She hinted but didn't say it outright. She meant anyone *not* Favoured is fair game. Maybe we all are. You and me included. Maybe the Favoured just get eaten last.'

He paused for breath, surprised to find she actually seemed to be listening. He went on, 'We also have to be very careful of the Invia. They're snatching people right outside as we speak, taking them to the dragons. What's more, they're not afraid of coming here, inside the castle. They're not our friends, Aziel. Maybe one or two of the Eight are on our side, and maybe not. They sure aren't stopping the others from killing people. In fact you could call what's happening a war – those people outside are calling it that. If you and I are really running things here, we need to get a handle on all this *real* quickly. Those people down there, they're about to take up arms and march off to fight the dragons. I'll bet there are rousing speeches going on right now.'

'Let them march,' said Aziel.

He was briefly speechless. 'Do you know what you're saying? We have to listen to the haiyens. They know how we can make ourselves hidden from dragons. They're willing to teach us.'

She raised a palm to quiet him. It was the gesture of a wise and weary queen, not the girl Aziel had so recently been. 'I know what the tall wizard is going to say,' she said, 'about how we can survive the dragons. A summary of the idea was already presented to me. It's not going to work.'

'It works, Aziel. I've seen it work. Listen to me. Siel vanished from Shilen's sight.'

'It might work for you and me. Explain it to that crowd and it will sound like surrender. They will pull us limb from limb. We have not had time to put a structure in place to protect us from them.' She gave him another weary look. 'Actually, we *had* enough time. You insisted instead that the stupid mob out there was to be well fed, before all else. So, that is what our administrators have been doing, since you set a great number of them loose. Distributing food and other goods. We have no army. I have a few hundred volunteers on the lower levels, whose loyalty to us we cannot gauge. They are not mind-controlled. *You* wouldn't allow such a thing. Assuming they fight for us to their very deaths against the mob outside, they would be trampled in a minute or two. We are probably finished. The half-giants are all we have. Even though they are each worth several men apiece, they are now far outnumbered. They do my bidding – some of it I should say, and only if my instructions suit them – because I have made them an offer. One which anyone else in this room can match. Although few can better it, since the half-giants have received everything they asked for.

'Shilen's and the dragons' endorsement is the only claim to this throne I have. You heard what the wizard said, just now. He has already begun to take it away from me.' She smiled helplessly. 'So. If the mob outside insists upon fighting the dragons, we cannot stop them, nor should we want to. If we stand in their way, be assured we are the first they'll trample. The best thing you could do is go out there and tell them now is the time to fight, then if they're lucky the gods might step in to help them. But I know you won't tell them that.'

Eric was surprised to find he'd underestimated her grasp of

things. He said, 'You know we can't trust Shilen from here on? She only put us in charge in the first place because she didn't know how long till the dragons would come down from the sky. She wanted all the humans to be well-managed and busy until they came. You and I were supposed to be so busy fighting Kiown that we'd never consider how we might deal with the dragons, if and when they came down.'

'That doesn't matter now. Do you see why I asked the half-giants to kill you, Eric? I tell you this here and now because it is certain to come out, sooner or later. They refused to do it. And there is no longer a point in killing you, since your damage is done, so you may relax. There will be no attempt on your life – not on my orders, at least.' He didn't want to betray that he was shocked to hear this, even though he'd suspected something of the kind . . . but he knew his shock showed. She saw it and laughed bitterly. 'You grew up in Otherworld as a peasant, working and playing games. So you played games here when you were put on the throne. I grew up watching lords. They were evil lords, I see that now – just look at the mess they left for us. But at the very least, *they* took power seriously.'

'So does every tyrant who ever lived. I just didn't want to be a tyrant, Aziel. I didn't come here to rule anything or anyone.' But he felt the pang of guilt she meant to inflict, and he did not at first understand why it was so powerful. He *had* been indulgent aboard his pet drake, treating the world as his own private amusement park. Taking none of it seriously, never seeking wise heads for advice. The whole thing was a farce. He'd seen that right away: the idea of his lording over human beings at the behest of a dragon. He'd be a puppet at best, perhaps even a traitor to his own kind. But he hadn't for one minute acted to make it otherwise, to move people out of the cities, to anticipate any of the things that had come to pass. While he'd played around, lives had indeed been at stake upon his decisions. And now, people were dead because of it.

It suddenly hit him: he had blood on his hands. The blood of many people. How many? A dozen, a hundred, or more? He thought of the way he'd spared Kiown's life at the tower top, and the fact he'd behaved as if that deed had been a permanent mark of his decency which nothing else could erase or mark over. How self-righteous that had made him feel. Now he felt sick.

Aziel was silent. She seemed to watch all this play through his mind, to read it on his face. She put a hand on his shoulder in consolation, though her expression showed no pity. 'Real rulers also look forwards when there is crisis,' she said. 'However futile it is, look forwards now. If I am to remain here, in charge, it will only be because you say so. You are "Shadow" to those people. I need you now more than you need me. But you owe me this throne, since your foolishness has all but removed it from us. So, from now on . . .'

She didn't finish, for at that moment the castle shook again. It went on much longer this time, and no one stayed on their feet except Faul, who clung to the window sill. 'EASY!' she bellowed, as if her voice could halt it. Aziel grabbed Eric by the arm and held on for dear life as they slid into the wall. When the shaking stopped he said, 'If that keeps up, Aziel, maybe we really can't stay here.'

'There's nowhere else to go,' she said flatly. 'Not for me.'

'What about . . . what about the high valley behind the castle? I was there when I first came. It's near what they call the Entry Point.'

Domudess evidently heard him. 'As it happens, I had that

very place in mind,' the wizard said, picking himself off the ground and striding over. 'The stairways are difficult to find, but I shall try. Before you leave this place, order your workers to empty the warehouses. There is no point letting the food rot there uneaten as the castle becomes too unstable to dwell in.'

'So, we will go and sit on the grass?' Aziel said with rising anger.

Domudess shook his head and slowly produced from his pocket a little leather bag. Aziel stared, not understanding. 'My tower is contained within this bag,' said Domudess. 'I shall reconstruct it, and watch events from there. You are both invited to join me. Although in that place, there are no lords and ladies, only guests. And in that place you are not to wear your dragon charm.' He looked at Eric. 'Nor are you.'

'I can't get rid of it,' Eric said. 'I throw it away and it comes back. Aziel's is stuck to her skin.'

'Then you may not join me in the tower.'

'SO THAT'S WHY IT'S SHAKING,' Faul's voice boomed from the window.

'Why, Faul?'

'IT'S THAT STUPID GOD OUT THERE. IT'S MAKING THE BIG SLEEPING DRAGON NERVOUS. WHICH GOD IS IT? TEMPEST? LOOKS LIKE A BUNCH OF TREES, ALL TIED TOGETHER.'

50

THE TEACHER OF MANY ARTS

They rushed to the windows either side of Faul. Far Gaze said, 'That's not Tempest. That god is from the South world. I saw it with my own eyes. Unless her ladyship would care to correct me?'

'Enough from you,' Aziel snarled at him. 'I will have you ejected and beaten till your bones are splinters.'

'EASY, YOU TWO,' said Faul. 'WHAT IS IT AND WHAT'S IT DOING?'

None could say. A hush had fallen outside. Indeed some calming influence seemed to exude from the god, powerful enough for them to feel it where they stood. The god – known by the haiyens as the Teacher of Many Arts, among other names – stood tall above the milling crowd. But after a couple of minutes it vanished, and the crowd's murmuring voice resumed.

It was not long before a messenger arrived from the lower floors with news. A thin young man of no more than eighteen stood panting from the long climb through the castle's levels. 'A new Spirit introduced itself,' he said when he'd caught his breath. 'Its name is . . . it's something I can't pronounce.'

'FAT LOT OF USE THAT IS,' said Faul, stomping towards him. 'YOU RAN ALL THE WAY HERE FOR THAT?'

'No, ma'am.' The young man backed away from her with wide eyes. 'It said it has things to teach. And a message for those of authority in the realm. That's . . . that's not exactly what it said, but that's the best way I could think to say it. The message . . . well it's more a feeling which I have to put into words *for* the Spirit.' He looked at them helplessly.

'Tell your message to me in private,' said Aziel.

'Are you sure, Lady? Everyone down there heard it. It wasn't just me. All those people know what it said.'

'Then you may as well tell us all,' said Domudess. 'Does the half-giant agree?'

'SHE DOES. SPEAK UP, BOY.'

'The Pendulum has stopped swinging, that part of the message was clear. I don't know what that means, with your pardon, Lady.'

'What else?' said Aziel.

The young man battled for words. 'I'm sorry, Lady, the way the Spirit spoke, it kind of seems like I'm trying to remember a dream for you. That was the main part: they stopped the Pendulum. Who I can't say, nor what it means. O, there was something about, the higher powers dare not cross now. Something else too, about Valour being killed. That part's sort of strange to me, Lady . . . something about cycles? Cycles, killing Valour. Along with an army who travelled with him.' Nervously, he added, 'I don't know what all this means. It can't mean Valour the god, Lady, for he's just myth, as I was taught. Maybe you know what to make of it . . . ?'

'Maybe we do,' said Domudess. 'Did the god of the South say no more?'

'Some things, sir, but I don't recall too well. Its voice sounded like bursts of wind going over all of us. When the Spirit faded out, it took a lot of people with it. It kind of seemed to ask a question to everyone at once, sir. About who would like to come and learn some things. Not many people did, most were afraid, I suppose. But those who vanished with it, they wanted to go. Maybe a hundred people or more.'

'What sort of things did it wish to teach?' said Domudess.

'Something about the dragons, sir. That's the other thing, there's fighting down there between people and the half-giants guarding the entry-ways. I should've mentioned it when I first came in.'

'If that's all, you may go,' snapped Aziel. She glared at Domudess when the messenger had gone. 'They deliver messages *from* the chamber too,' she said. 'Such as, peculiar wizards ask the questions and give the orders. Do you people never think about how we are perceived by the mobs out there? Such things matter!'

'They have other things to consider at present, Aziel, I would venture,' said Domudess. He began to say more but instead went quiet, staring at something out in the hall.

Following his gaze, Eric was astonished to see a large group of haiyens had gathered out there. There were more here than he'd ever seen in one place, including several of the taller 'travellers', and others dressed in garments more elaborate than the usual dull-coloured travelling robes. All of the haiyens stood silently gazing in. Their mood was almost palpable: sombre, sad.

Far Gaze, Eric and Domudess were the only ones who'd so far noticed the haiyens' arrival. Domudess caught Eric's eye and whispered: 'Keep the others busy, something is wrong,' then he quickly strode out there and shut the door behind him.

*

It was only a minute or two before the wizard returned. Through the door behind him Eric saw the haiyens were gone. Domudess was grim-faced. 'The haiyens are leaving us.'

'What? Why?' said Eric.

'We have betrayed them. They are abandoning us. They will wait now until we destroy ourselves, or until the dragons destroy us. Then they will come to dwell here, if the lands are liveable. They were going to teach us ways to build homes that the dragons would never see. Now they won't do it. At last they have come to my understanding, that trying to teach humanity is a futile task.'

'Who betrayed them?'

'Someone brought . . . a summoned presence here, to Levaal North. To Elvury City. And it has grown too large now for them to kill. It has . . . become near enough to the size and power of a god, that they would need a huge gathering of haiyens to slay it . . . and they cannot all come at this time, or there will be no one to protect their own lands from the lost haiyens.'

'How did this happen?' said Far Gaze.

Domudess looked around the room as if he could not really see it. 'The presence had dead organic matter all through Elvury City to collect for itself. Human bones, Tormentor bodies. The arts the haiyens have taught us to deal with dragons . . . are of no effect against *those* beings. Perhaps other presences have been brought here too. Someone has betrayed us. Someone has dealt with the lost haiyens. That is the one thing our haiyen friends could not easily forgive.'

'It was Kiown,' Eric said. 'He was at Elvury. I saw him there.' All eyes in the room turned silently to him. He quickly regretted speaking.

'You . . . *saw* this being brought here?' said Domudess, breaking the heavy silence.

'Well, no. I didn't know what Kiown was doing there. He said he wanted that city as a base. I said he could have it, since he would have killed me then and there if I hadn't.'

'You didn't feel a need to tell me of this?' said Aziel, shaking her head in disbelief.

'Why do the haiyens hold us responsible for what Kiown did?' Eric said to Domudess.

Far Gaze answered, 'The haiyens are a whole, a collective. You could almost say there are no individual haiyens, for each is only part of one large whole. It may be they see us the same way.'

'It is not just that,' said Domudess. 'It took only one of us to fly to the home of their lost ones. One man's decision. Now a great swathe of our realm is unsafe for them . . . and for us. When the summoned entities grow strong, they can connect good haiyens into the collective of lost ones. The haiyens may decide they can risk trusting us again, but it will take time. More time than we have. You have no idea how wonderful are the things they could have taught us.' Domudess wiped a tear from his eye. He went to the door, paused there. 'In grief, it slipped my mind. Eric, the haiyens bore a message for you too. They said it was their last word of advice to us, for the present. You must make of it what you will, for I have no light to shed upon it. Their message was: *Let them.*'

'That's it?'

'That is it.' Domudess said no more. The castle gave another faint shiver as he walked away. Eric ran after him, but when he rounded a corner the tall wizard was no longer in sight.

Eric looked back in the hallway to Aziel's chamber, where

the real leaders talked among themselves. He didn't belong there and he knew it.

He wandered away, lost, not knowing where he was headed until he arrived at Aziel's old bedroom. They'd left Case there to sleep with a bowl of water, a bucket of ale (now empty) and some thick bones to devour. The drake slowly opened one eye as Eric came in and sat on Aziel's unmade bed.

51

MESSAGE FROM SHILEN

Eric slept briefly, despite the odd shiver passing through the castle and the smell of neglected sheets. He woke when something moved onto the bed. 'Let me sleep, Case,' he mumbled. A murmur of voices ran through the room. Strange voices. When his eyes opened to find a pale green scaly face packed with teeth very close to his own, he screamed and scrambled backwards on the bed.

It was an Invia. The room was filled with them. 'Where's Case?' he said. He fumbled in his pocket for Hauf's amulet.

The Invia said, 'Walker. Are *you* the man-lord they want?'

'Back up, back off me. Who wants the man-lord?'

'The dragons,' said another, reaching to paw at his leg, as if the feel of it would determine whether Eric was the one they sought. The others nodded in agreement, thick ropes of hair swaying about their heads. 'All the dragons want to speak with the walker man-lord who rides a drake. You have a drake. But there is more than one drake. There is more than one walker. Are you the walker man-lord?'

'Your aura is like the man-lord's aura,' said another. 'We were told what the man-lord's aura looks like. Shilen told us. She manages the walkers.'

'*We* were the ones chosen to fetch him,' said another. Around the room their heads bobbed.

'What do the dragons want with the man-lord?' Eric said.

'*Man*-lord, they want,' one Invia said, speaking very slowly for his obviously dim brain. The others nodded.

'The walkers outside were angry when we came,' said another. 'They shot bows and threw stones, but we're not to fight with them here, even if they are Marked. We were told this.'

'Where's Case? The drake that was in here?'

'We are holding him. He tried to block the window to keep us out!' The whistling rustle of their laughter swept the room.

'Are the dragons angry with the man-lord? Tell me that, and I'll tell you where you might find him.'

'Do you know him?' said several of them. They peered at him eagerly. He could back no further away from them, but he tried. Rows of sharp teeth were all he could see. He shut his eyes. 'Yes, I know him. Are the dragons angry? Just tell me that.'

'*Very* angry,' they said. More nodding heads, swaying coils.

'Walkers are hiding what they want,' said another.

What they want? Eric tried to think. 'OK, listen. I know where the man-lord is, but I won't tell you. I'll tell Shilen directly, and only Shilen.'

'You must tell *us*.'

'No!' said another. 'He must tell the dragons. He must tell *all* the dragons. They are waiting.'

'They're all waiting in one place?' said Eric.

'Vyin is not there,' said one.

'Ksyn is there,' said another. They seemed to be competing to make the most important statement.

'Is Shilen there with them or not?' said Eric.

'*She* is just a Minor.'

'*She* is not important. It's why she manages the walkers. *They* are least important of all.'

'I'll talk to Shilen,' he repeated. 'And Shilen only.'

'You cannot say that!'

'We could kill you.' The heads all nodded, bouncing coils of white rope.

'Do that, and the dragons will be furious with you.' He had not thought a lie so simple would work on them, but the Invia gasped and drew back as if he'd brandished a deadly weapon. 'If you even harmed me, they would be furious.'

'We could harm you, that would be permitted. Your legs and arms, we could break or pull away. As long as you could still *speak*.'

'Thanks for that correction,' he said. 'How close can the dragons come to the castle?'

'Four miles away. They can go no nearer. Stupid! Didn't you know that?'

'Walkers *are* stupid.'

'You got that right,' said Eric, nodding his head with the rest of them. 'Tell Shilen to meet me there, four miles from the castle, at the Great Dividing Road. Tell her to come alone. I will tell her many things about the man-lord. He is just about the stupidest of the walkers, I guarantee it.'

'Why just Shilen?' said one amidst a wave of unsettled chatter. 'She's just a Minor.'

'Because she manages the walkers, and I am a walker. Who will be first to tell the dragons what I have told you? Surely they'll be pleased with whoever among you tells them first.'

Instantly – the very second he finished saying it – the furious beat of wings made the room a gale of feathery air. They poured out into the sky in a blur of movement, with many hard thumps as their bodies hit the window frame.

Case sat in the corner, looking at him serenely. He didn't seem to have minded being held down by a group of Invia at all; in fact it seemed he'd rather enjoyed himself. Maybe they looked better to him since they'd shed their human disguises and wore scales instead. 'Rather you than me, my friend,' Eric said. 'We've got to fly, I'm afraid.' Case's look at him seemed questioning. 'I'll go meet Shilen. I don't care any more, even if she kills me. I fucked it all up, Case. I could have summoned Hauf back at Elvury, and had him take Kiown out. Could have shot him at the tower too, like the real Case said I should have done. So I don't think I've really earned a long and happy life. Let's go.'

As they flew over the familiar castle lawns, the stream of people pouring into the castle was quiet and orderly. Whether the half-giants had acquiesced and allowed them in, or whether they'd been overwhelmed by sheer numbers, the matter had clearly been settled some time previously, for the roads leading to the castle were clearing up.

As they flew away from there, Eric thought of Domudess's message from the haiyens: *Let them.* Were the haiyens just reiterating what Aziel herself had said? Let those people march into the dragons' jaws, and to their deaths? If that was the message, were the haiyens really friends?

But Aziel was right on one count at the very least: if that was what the people wanted to do, they would not be stopped by any speeches or any promise that there was a better way.

The flight to the part of the Road where Shilen waited seemed very brief. She was gazing up at him in her dragon form, white, feminine and beautiful. But she was not what took his breath away, nor what made Case's panting breath send forth little excited bursts of flame. Back some way behind her, just at the edge of sight, four enormous dragons had gathered side by side. There was no doubt these four were of the Eight; their power was tangible enough to feel. It was like a pressing weight on him, pressure squeezing his temples. With his mage eyes he saw enormous spires of colour twisting and tumbling about them. He'd seen nothing of the like since the airs about the castle during Vous's great change. Here were only *half* of the great dragons. How could even the gods withstand them?

In the far distance was the more familiar shape of Nightmare, waiting in the sky like a storm not yet ready to blow over. The dragons surely sensed him there, but none so much as looked in his direction. Nor did he come closer.

With the huge dragons was a collection of lesser ones, a few of them airborne, suspended motionless while others languidly beat their wings. Those dragons did indeed seem small compared to the four mighty ones of the brood.

It took desperate coaxing to make Case descend to ground level. Shilen's head arched high over him and her eyes glittered. There was no way to tell by looking at her that she bore such hate for him and hate for humanity, as Dyan had said. She was beautiful and graceful to behold, a nobody among her own kind but a queen to him. He felt like an animal, an ape, as he dismounted Case and stood before her. One of her wings still hung loose, torn at the shoulder. 'I'm sorry about your wound,' he said, sensing it was a dangerous thing to mention at all.

Her head reared back further. 'There are other things for you to regret. Or shall be, soon.'

'Couldn't the great ones heal you?'

'Of course, if they wished to. They leave me injured as a mark of my failure, my shame. I accept it. They will injure me far worse, if you don't help me. I do not expect such a thing to matter to one who does not even care for the lives of his own kind.'

He took the charm she'd given him off his neck. 'You can have this back. I shouldn't have kept it at all.' He tossed it towards her. Her head snapped at it with alarming speed. She caught the charm in her mouth and clamped shut her jaws. The charm fell to the ground in pieces.

'Where is Shadow?'

That's what the Invia meant – Shadow is what the dragons want. 'You would know if I lied, wouldn't you? Of course you would. Then here's the truth: I don't know where he is. The haiyens told Siel to go somewhere. She had Shadow caught in her charm at the time.'

Shilen's head swayed side to side like a serpent's as she appraised him. The ground faintly shivered as one of the huge dragons behind her took a few steps into his range of sight. Its skin was a silver not unlike Valour's armour, with threads of red wound through it. Eric thought: It doesn't matter any more. This world is theirs again. Maybe there are other worlds than the ones I've known. Maybe death is the only way out of Levaal and Earth both, the only way into a better place. So be it.

Eric tried not to betray his amazement at what he saw next: a line of people walking towards the huge dragon which had stepped out of the group. The people provoked no reaction from it. They ran across the ground until they were close enough to touch it. To his further astonishment they began to climb up onto the beast's tail, up along its back. Their calls and laughter carried across the distance between Eric and the great dragon . . . but like the great dragon, Shilen did not react to the sound. He knew she did not even hear it at all.

He understood: these were the people the Spirit from Levaal South had taken away from the castle, just hours before. The Spirit had taught them to be unafraid, taught them to be filled with love for these enormous, deadly creatures, who only hated them in return. And it had worked. These people now laughed and whooped as they climbed aboard the enormous creature, unseen by it, unfelt and unheard. And untouched by its magic.

Shilen's head craned around to follow his gaze. 'You are right to be impressed,' she said. 'It is a privilege to see him. A privilege to die to him, as many of your people have now done. Listen, man-lord. You feel you are safe from us, in the castle. If so, it is the last safe place for you in this world. We will change that on this day, if you do not tell me where I may find Shadow.'

'How will you change it, Shilen? By sending Invia to the castle?'

Her laugh was rich, soft and musical. 'We shall wake our Parent. The four great ones you see behind me will do it today, if you do not tell me where I may find Shadow. We now know the haiyens worked with you to halt the Pendulum's swing, to keep our Parent sleeping. If these four great ones cross to the South, our Parent's rival in the South shall rise for war. Our Parent shall rise in turn. Humankind will know no sanctuary. These four behind me – plus one other – are agreed to perform this action. Vyin has not the power to stop them.'

Suddenly it hit him: the haiyens' message. *Let them.* He fought to keep his thoughts blank, lest Shilen's glittering eyes could somehow read them. He said, 'You lied to us, Shilen. You knew the dragons would devour us when they were free.'

Again she laughed. 'Suppose I knew it. How would you have relayed that information, in my stead?'

'Why do they do it? You lied to me, but this part was true enough: you are grand enough beings to create your own pleasures. Why bother with us? Aren't we beneath your notice altogether? I just don't understand.'

'Do you explain reasons to the cattle you butcher, or the game you hunt? If you did, what reason would you give? Those creatures are beneath you; it is your right. The dragons' reasons are the same. Where is Shadow?'

He knew Siel would be hidden from these dragons, even if he told Shilen where she lay in wait. The haiyens' message repeated loud in his mind: *Let them.* What harm was there in telling? 'Siel is at World's End. Where the Great Dividing Road meets the road from the South. Shadow is with her.'

Shilen let a silence draw out. 'You have spoken truly. But if we do not find Shadow with her, we shall wake our Parent, and those of your kind gathered at the castle will die in an instant.'

Let them. 'Won't your Parent kill the dragons too, Shilen?'

She hissed in anger. 'Do you think dragons alone are subject to our Parent's laws? The Southern gods are not of Levaal. They are not even of Levaal South. They are from other realms altogether, and they are forbidden to come here. Our Parent decrees it. And yet at least one of them has come! It has interacted with humankind, and given aid to the gods of this realm. *This* is a greater violation of our Parent's laws than the dragons gaining freedom. You will be destroyed if our Parent comes forth, not the dragons.'

'You seem so sure of what will happen, Shilen.'

'We have seen it happen before, man-lord. Our Parent will battle its rival for a time, and then both will retire to change their realms as they see fit. Should our Parent defeat its rival, the dragons will claim the southern realm too. And we shall reshape it to our liking. There will be no place in either realm for humankind.'

Behind her, the huge dragon stared directly at him. He wanted to meet its eyes but he couldn't. It saw him in totality: everything he was, everything he wasn't. And yet the enlightened people climbed over it unseen, easily as children at play.

In the distance the tall foreign god – the Teacher of Many Arts – appeared on the horizon for just a second or two, its antlers twisting against the grey-white sky. The people climbed down the great dragon's back then ran across the fields towards where its image had briefly been. Eric felt hope wash over him like a faint breeze from that direction.

Shilen had been speaking while all this transpired, but he'd barely heard her. Now she said, 'None of the endless kings and conquerors among you ever felt my kind steering them. Only the Spirits ever challenged our influence. Your world has always been ours, man-lord.'

'You forget, this isn't my world. You never steered *my* world. You never had any influence there.'

Her eyes glittered, and he could practically see her human form before him, smiling. 'How little you know of us,' she said. She turned and walked back to the other dragons. She gave no sign of seeing the group of people who now skipped and sang as they ran from the Great Dividing Road.

The ground shivered with the huge dragons' steps as they turned around, ran, then flew. A great gust of wind went up. They flew to the south, surely to find Siel. It seemed a stifling weight had been lifted from him, lifted from the very air he breathed . . . a weight those other happy people had not even felt.

He did not know who to pray to for Siel's safety. So he addressed the prayer to no one and hoped it would find whoever might act upon it.

52

PENDULUM SWING

The world as they flew south seemed to Siel's eyes like a table ruined after a ravishing feast. Even mountains seemed to lie in tumbled messes, destroyed by quakes from falling skystone if not smashed by direct hits. Lightstone pieces large and small glowed, scattered over vast miles. Dark grey skystone slabs had smashed deep holes down into the honeycombed groundman tunnels below the surface.

Those few people they saw on the ground would invariably run for cover upon sight of Dyan above them. All along the Great Dividing Road, where inns and small townships had stood, there was ruin and wreckage as if marauding armies had been through. Siel felt no anger or pain that the dragons had brought this ruin. After what the haiyens had taught her, there was nothing the dragons could do to make her hate or fear them ever again. Now that she knew human life was immortal, it could be said that nothing bad truly ever happened at all. This life was a fleeting borrowed thing, a short time to collect the experiences of suffering through a prison world; that was all. Each person born into it would one day escape it, as surely as they would die a mortal death. How absurd it was that people held such fear of death! The ultimate blessing perceived as the ultimate curse.

Great as the dragons were in this little sphere of existence, the dragons did not have that part of them: soul. That was why she'd seen none of them marching towards the crystal lake's waters to refresh and cleanse themselves. They would ever be here, or in realms like this. This really *was* their world; what had looked like a man-made hell of war and slavery had all been orchestrated by the dragons from their place of hiding, through their corruption of a few key rulers, just as they'd begun to corrupt Eric and Aziel. The dragons had created the preciousness of human suffering. And that was why Siel had learned to love them not as some trick of the mind, but with all sincerity.

And because she now loved them, *truly* loved them, they could not see her. She even faded at times from Dyan's perception, despite the link between him and the charm which commanded him. He would turn his head back, saying, 'Are you there, Beauty? I sense the symbol you hold, but I lose sense of you.'

'I'm here,' she would assure him, and will herself to be more clear to him.

'Was it true, Beauty, when you said you loved me?'

She laughed. 'It was true, and is still true. But love means different things to me from what it does to you. And to all your kind.'

Now and then Invia came to examine Dyan, flying briefly beside him and peering with faces seeming more and more grotesque and inhuman. But they did not ever see Siel, nor could they keep up with Dyan's speed for long. 'You spoke to them?' said Siel after one such visit.

'I gave them instruction, but they ignored it. Higher powers than I already have them at work.'

'Doing what?'

'Finding me, Beauty. For they know I am in service to the symbol you hold. And they are seeking it.'

'They won't find me.'

'Perhaps not, Beauty. And yet I may not hide from them forever.'

'What will they do to you when they find you?'

'I know not, Beauty.'

Shadow did not stir in the charm about her neck . . . or if he did, she could not feel it. When they stopped for rest she dreamed of him. He asked her questions in that dream, simple things a child might ask, and she explained as would a patient mother. Why am I here? he had asked her.

In the dream she'd known the answer, and she'd told it to him. But upon waking for another morning's flight, the answer had slipped from her memory.

She reached World's End a little over a day before the dragons came. From the ruins of an old wagon she made a lean-to among thickets bunched on harsh rocky turf, tying thorns and weeds over it for camouflage. A groundman hole nearby was just big enough for her to hide in, should the need arise. On sight of it she wondered with a start what had become of Tii. Perhaps the groundman knew where she'd gone, and was on his way here.

Dyan waited without speaking, his eyes ever on the northern sky, never to the south. He kept his body pressed low to the ground, his scales coloured to blend in with the surrounds. He seemed far more nervous about being at World's End than she was.

That force along the Great Dividing Road – which Anfen had

called the 'push' – had done much to speed their flight. Now the push had grown so strong it made standing by the Road impossible. Even where she'd set up her camp, two hundred paces away, she could feel the edge of that invisible force. It made the trees and shrubs lean south, and made the stones, sticks and gravel slide slowly across the ground.

A similar force had to be at work in the South, for their clouds too were pushed along their own Great Dividing Road, whatever name the haiyens gave it. Above that point where both Roads met, clouds rushed together with equal speed, creating a huge winding coil of white, grey and black.

If the haiyens supposedly protecting her were there, they were too well-hidden to see. The wind and the soft heavy growl of Dyan's breathing were the only sounds. 'I can provide you physical pleasures if you should need them to pass the time, Beauty,' he said. 'I have not lost those talents.'

She laughed. 'Not necessary.'

'If you change your answer—'

'I won't, Dyan. Drop it.'

'You have faded from me again, Beauty. Your body seems transparent as clear water. Will you tell me yet what magic is at play?'

'I can't tell you, Dyan. I don't think you would understand.'

'Are you hungry, Beauty? Shall I hunt game for you?'

'Please do.'

A ripple went over his scales as the colour went out of them and he became almost invisible. He flew off, only to return within a few minutes with nothing for her to eat. She could tell something had disturbed him. 'What is it?'

'Dragons come,' he said. His neck was arched back, and ears were flat to his head as he gazed north. 'Many of them.'

'How far are they?'

'An hour's flight, by their measure. They fly not as fast as I do.'

'Can you sense them if they are so far away?'

'There are some among the Eight. *They* can be felt from a long way away. They could keep their presence hidden, but for now they do not trouble to.'

'The Eight?' She sat up. 'How many?'

'I sense four, Beauty.'

'*Four?*'

'There are gods too, surely watching their passage. Beauty, you must not stay here. It will not be safe for you.'

She laughed. 'They won't see me. What do they want, Dyan?'

Dyan's voice went urgent and his scales turned off-white. She'd not seen that colour in him before, but she knew it meant he was genuinely terrified. 'Beauty, listen. If it is true that you may hide from Shilen and me whenever you wish, you must know she and I are not of the same stature as those who now approach. They perceive much more than do Shilen and I. Whatever human magic keeps you hidden will not work on them.'

'They won't see me, Dyan. Trust me on that.'

'They will know *I* am here, regardless.'

'If you want to go, go. Until they're gone. Then you must return to me.'

She had hardly said the words before he'd bolted off for the South, a blur across the sky crossing World's End in seconds.

Siel turned her eyes north, watching where the Road met the horizon. For what seemed a long time there was nothing but the wind, blowing in steadily harder gusts. She began to wonder if Dyan had misled her, for more than an hour passed with no sign of approaching dragons. Then the skies darkened with a rushing shape, with what seemed a cape of black cloud blending out to form long stretched arms and an enormous face like a tribal mask of pale bone. It was Nightmare . . . but she had never seen his eyes glowing with this blazing red, nor seen lightning flicker this way from his outstretched hands. The Spirit hovered off in the north-eastern sky.

The temperature quickly dropped; the wind picked up. There came a massive continent of cloud from the west with – just vaguely – a face imprinted in it. Perhaps this was Tempest. Siel had never seen that god in person before, but what she now saw reminded her of many depictions.

On the horizon beyond Tempest's clouds, a huge bulky mass of stone had come up where it had not stood minutes before. It had peaks like a crown at its head and a vast mossy stretch of vines hung across stone features just vaguely resembling a face. Mountain did not simply *stand* – it prowled forwards with steps which shook the ground, only to blink out of sight in seconds, its rumbling silenced, the shaking ground still again.

If this place was to be a battleground between the Spirits and dragons, Siel knew she had made a mistake in remaining here. She'd not be able to run far enough now to get to safe ground from the kinds of magic likely to be wielded. It did not greatly matter if she perished now, but she had to wonder why the haiyens had sent her here. What part could she possibly play in a battle such as this?

And at last the dragons lumbered into view. The four great ones flew side by side, all at the same slow pace, their huge wings moving up and down with a motion slow and mechanical, the tips of their clawed feet seeming to scrape the ground. She felt the incredible ancient power emanate from them, felt the stirring of old familiar fear pulling at her. She closed her eyes and brought herself to a state of love which was reasoned thought as much as it was a feeling; one spark of the flame feeding the other until both burned warm. She bore nothing but gratitude for what these incredible creatures had done for her – they were the hammer and anvil sharpening the blade of her soul, sharpening of all humanity's collective soul, giving humanity wisdom unattainable any other way than by this suffering. She beheld the savage wise beauty in them . . . she *understood* them, or at least an aspect of them, perhaps better than they understood themselves. And suddenly within her – so suddenly Dyan may well have been right after all to call it magic – there was no fear. Why not go out onto the Road to wait for them?

So she went as close as she could, and though she stood some way from the Road, the push drove her back, her boots sliding on the rocky turf. The wind threw her hair around so that it whipped her face with little stings. For the first time she felt Shadow stirring in his prison. 'It's all right,' she whispered, cupping the charm in her hands. She had no idea whether or not he could hear her.

Behind the great dragons were a score or more lesser ones, the largest among them about a quarter the size of the greats. Their heads swept the land. They were seeking her, she knew . . . and seeking Shadow. They wouldn't find her; they wouldn't see her. One of the great ones turned its head and bellowed a warning to the Spirits who watched. Siel laughed in amazement as the power of its voice went through her and shook her bones.

They were upon her. The one who had called out flew right past her, right over her. Its claws dragging on the ground dug ridges. Siel dropped to her knees, hardly containing her awe and love. Its scales seemed like dull silver at a distance; up close she saw a thousand glittering points of colour all over it. Its claws scraped the ground to either side of her. There were many varieties of its fellows behind it, shapes and colours of other-worldly beauty, power beyond human measure. Their eyes too swept to either side of the Road, swept right over her. She no longer existed in their world. As animals hear sounds beyond human hearing, she was a sight beyond their seeing.

At the same steady pace they went to where the Wall had stood. The gods did nothing. Nightmare howled in helpless rage as the dragons crossed to the South, and at the same steady pace flew beyond the foreign world's horizon.

53

SHADOW

When Eric returned to Aziel's chamber, Far Gaze sat outside the door with a smile on his face. 'Banished,' he said with clear pleasure.

'If she's still lady of this place, I'm still its lord. I hereby un-banish you.'

'She's about to lose any semblance of authority. You too, most likely, but I doubt you'll grieve for that. Loup and I spoke quietly with Faul. It took ten minutes. The half-giants are equal part-ners now in our new coalition. The people have overtaken the lower levels anyway. We are just aligning with them as Aziel should have as soon as they began arriving. They're going through the food stores and the armouries as we speak. Faul's people let them in.'

'None of that matters now. I just spoke with Shilen. I think they're going to wake the Dragon.'

'Who is?'

He told Far Gaze of his encounter with the dragons. The moment he'd finished it seemed enormous hands lifted the entire castle and wrenched it side to side. Eric fell into the wall, then away, then back into it. It took a long time for the quake to cease. Even then, a faint background shiver remained.

'Time we departed,' said Far Gaze, rubbing away blood with his sleeve from where his head had struck the doorway. He nodded to where cracks had appeared in the walls, roof and floor. It was as if there'd only been a shell covering them. Parts of that shell now began to peel and fall away. Frowning, Far Gaze went to one such jutting piece about the size of his own torso. He pulled it free. The wall beneath it glittered with many colours, like gems with light run across them. They were large scales, scales the size of those which people crushed up and consumed for visions. The scales mined from the ground at World's End.

Eric tapped them with his knuckle. Colour splashed with the impact. Loup's voice played in his memory: *This little scale, all crushed up, is made of the great god-beast's very stuff . . .*

The walls' and roof's cracks spread further. Far Gaze went to the other wall and wrenched away some more of the white shell, thick as a finger length. There were scales beneath that too. 'I see,' he murmured.

'You see what?' said Eric.

'We are to leave this place, right now. We'll ride your drake.'

'You see *what*, Far Gaze?'

'We have been mistaken for a very long time. The Dragon is not *below* the castle. It *is* the castle.'

'But how . . . ?'

'I am not the world's only shape-shifter. It's changing form, right now. It is awakening. Take us to the drake. Now!'

'Aren't you going to tell the others?'

Far Gaze rolled his eyes but followed Eric to the doorway. Within Aziel's chamber, as outside it, the walls were breaking and peeling, revealing colourful scales beneath. 'Get out,' yelled Far Gaze to those still in the room. To Eric he said, 'Satisfied? A daring rescue.'

With no more delay the two of them ran through the shaking castle to find Case. Once mounted, they flew up to the high shelf of turf behind the castle, where a green valley sat between two sheer walls. The grass had been littered with corpses when he'd first seen it; now lightstone and skystone rocks were scattered over it, in parts ankle-thick.

Domudess was there already, standing at the top of a set of ancient stairs cut into the sheer cliff face. The wizard's bald head bobbed in polite greeting as Case set down in the lightstone litter nearby, then he gazed serenely as before at the vastness below. Their high vantage point seemed miraculously stable compared with the shivering castle, which made the world shiver along with it. It seemed to happen in bursts, but in the lulls it only ever calmed; the shaking never ceased completely. Now and then the ground rippled with waves they could see, as though it became for brief moments a heaving sea.

'It could take days to fully awaken,' said Domudess. 'Or longer.'

'Or three more minutes,' said Far Gaze.

Unconcerned for all this, Case lay down and went to sleep.

Domudess walked a good way back from where they stood watching and opened his leather pouch. He tipped out the handful of sand therein and spread it across the ground. In a few minutes his tower materialised from the ground up, as if poured from the sky above by invisible hands. The moat's water burbled up through the grass. Domudess went inside; his silhouette was soon visible from the top window.

Eric and Far Gaze stayed at the edge of the world and watched. It was an hour or two before cracks could be seen on the castle's great round domes and towers, spreading all across it in webs. Small pieces of the shell broke away, before great sheets of the wall's outer coating began to slip free and crash to the ground, revealing a scaled hide beneath. A tower leaned slowly away, then fell in pieces to the ground.

'I don't understand why the dragons did it,' Eric said.

Far Gaze smiled. 'Do you think Shilen was liable to tell you the true reason for their waking their Parent? The dragons fear the gods of the South. With good reason. I have seen those gods and they are terrible. If the Pendulum were to swing back and forth to its conclusion, before their Parent woke, they would have to confront That Which Governs Cycles of Events. And the other gods, all of them terrible beyond my power to describe to you, Eric. They surely fear their Parent as much as those gods. No, from their view, it is better to risk their Parent, which they would have to face anyway, and bypass the encounter with those Southern gods. Shilen would not speak to a human of the dragons' fear. *That* is why they have chosen to cross the boundary and wake their Parent early.'

'It's all about to end, isn't it?'

Far Gaze sighed wearily. 'It is all about to change. Knowing this world as I do, that cannot be a bad thing.'

'This world is a small part in the vastness,' Eric murmured, not sure where he'd heard those words before. They seemed right to him, wherever they had come from.

In Levaal South, the world shook just as hard as in the North, for the same doom was upon it.

Blain had said in the tower that there was a Dragon-god in the other world; he was wrong about that, at least in part. An entity of that stature did indeed exist there and, at the same time as the North realm's Dragon-god awoke, the South realm's governing power too was rising from its slumber.

The conflict between these two great forces had never truly

ended. Rather, it had gone to the realms and arenas of thought while their bodies slumbered. Their worlds' creatures, people and events were as immaterial to them as a man's thoughts seem to him. Neither entity controlled all actions and deeds within its world; each had laid out laws of existence which its inhabitants were bound to follow. But although neither entity had complete control of the small parts of their realities, both entities had the ability to sweep from existence all things within the limits of their realm, just as easily as a person sweeps objects from a table to set it with new things, with little care for what may break, and what may survive the change.

Eric, Far Gaze and Domudess were too close to the Dragon when it rose. All those human beings, half-giants, Invia, and others who were also too close, effectively ceased being themselves for a short while. They ceased existing altogether, as if deleted from a story's pages.

There was no measuring the time the Dragon-god's awakening took; for it governed time, it was not governed *by* time. When Eric, Domudess and the others returned to existence and returned to themselves, it may have been centuries, or aeons, or just moments that had passed.

When Eric was aware of himself again, the world's surface seemed completely liquid, coated by no more than a thin layer of colour: mountains and forests bending as wildly as shadows on a disturbed pond. Something moved through it all, something so enormous that it seemed to move slowly. Each step thrust great ripples in all directions. Lightning seemed to flicker from one instant to the next, dark-light-dark-light . . . great enormous bunches of forked flashing light spearing and flickering to mark each passing second.

The sight of the beast was too much to understand: those watching had nothing in their consciousness to compare it to. They could not even be in awe of it . . . for now, it was all they knew; it was nature, time, life, death, it was *them* or may as well have been. What were they, but minuscule aspects of it, observing its own motion? It passed now through this realm, whose reality imposed itself through its own incomprehensible dreams. It fed upon the energy of all things here, though none – not even the brood or the gods – knew they were fed from. It was and always had been a nightmare realm, a hell realm for those other observation points who called themselves human, or half-giants, or groundmen, or other names.

It understood the brood a little better. They too were but observation points, albeit from higher places. They knew there *was* no 'why' to anything, when thought reached past the grappling reasoning of those insects. There was only existence, being, 'is'.

Ah, but there was also that *opposite*, that rivalry, that dark a light banishes, that light the dark snuffs out . . .

Light, dark – which of the two entities was which? It didn't matter. Soon, one or the other would be extinguished, for something had been born in one of the worlds to bring about a final change . . . in *this* sphere of existence, at least. Whichever was the Light and whichever was the Dark, they now moved towards one another at equal pace.

Siel felt them coming long before she saw them. There was light, dark, light, dark, from one moment to the next. The light when it came was so complete that nothing could be seen within it. The dark was so total that it seemed nothing existed where it fell. Her hand squeezed hard as it could upon the charm where Shadow was trapped.

A desperate voice said, 'Beauty,' and then something grabbed her and lifted her. Away from the heaving, rolling ground, she could think again. '*Where do I take you, Beauty?*' said a voice speaking into her mind.

'*Where is safe?*' she said.

'*Nowhere. They are awake again. Soon they will collide and things will change. All shall be changed when it is over.*'

'*Take me to the waters,*' she said. '*To the South.*' She knew that whatever changed, *that* place was eternal, and would remain.

Dyan began to fly that way, but then she saw it: the Dragon of the South was not a dragon. It was huge, as huge as the castle . . . but a golden light burned all around it. Its enormous eyes were fierce but of such beauty she would never have feared them. Huge wings were upon its back but it was not covered in scales. Its enormous face was feline.

Dyan shrieked in fear and turned to the north, but then there was the *other*, the Parent of the Eight, coming towards them with lightning flickering from its gnashing mouth, its eyes alight with savage erupting red fire. The two powers rushed to their collision, faster now that they'd seen one another. A force seemed to draw all things towards the point at World's End where the two would meet. Dyan tried to fly east but he could go nowhere except directly up.

Siel looked down as the two entities met. She was the first human being ever to see this moment. Such energy blasted from that contact where they met that she was blind. She was deaf. She did not know that only the golden glowing love of the feline god kept her and Dyan from being destroyed. She did not hear

Dyan say, 'Are you alive, Beauty?' From the impact, scales by the million rained over the ground.

She felt Shadow lashing and writhing in the prison she still clenched tight in her hand. She felt rather than saw the two entities – one feline, one dragon – pushing against each other at World's End, where the Great Dividing Road met its twin, where the Wall had stood. Two worlds, two realities ground and pushed against one another.

And Siel understood now. She whispered into her cupped hand, though she could not hear her own voice: 'Shadow. Come. It's your choice now.'

She threw the amulet away, not knowing which way it flew. It sailed down gracefully, far too small to be noticed by either of the grappling powers, even as it landed on the back of the feline and bounced to the ground behind it.

Neither power knew of Shadow, any more than they knew the names and powers of other minuscule aspects of their respective realities. And Shadow in an instant grasped at last his purpose, the answer to the question no one had ever truly understood. The feline's golden light poured love upon him even as it fought savagely for its own existence against the Dragon-god, for it poured love upon everything it touched. The lightning of the Dragon poured something else, a feeling he was too familiar with: an *unknowing* sense of nothingness, hiddenness, devoid of love and light, just as his life had been.

Shadow made his choice.

The Dragon screamed, not understanding how it could have *two* rivals now. An instant was all it took. Shadow destroyed himself in the same instant he shadowed the Feline-god of the South. But in that fleeting time, the Dragon turned in confusion to face this second rival, which it had not in all its time-